The Ghastly Year

Diana Mathur

These are works of fiction.
The characters, their actions and dialogue
are products of the author's imagination
or are used fictitiously.

The Ghastly Year
© 2018 Diana Sowell Mathur
ISBN-13: 978-1718801554
ISBN-10: 1718801556

www.TheLindenTree.info

"And how we burned in the camps later, thinking: What would things have been like if every Security operative, when he went out at night to make an arrest, had been uncertain whether he would return alive and had to say good-bye to his family? Or if, during periods of mass arrests, as for example in Leningrad, when they arrested a quarter of the entire city, people had not simply sat there in their lairs, paling with terror at every bang of the downstairs door and at every step on the staircase, but had understood they had nothing left to lose and had boldly set up in the downstairs hall an ambush of half a dozen people with axes, hammers, pokers, or whatever else was at hand?... The Organs would very quickly have suffered a shortage of officers and transport and, notwithstanding all of Stalin's thirst, the cursed machine would have ground to a halt! If...if...We didn't love freedom enough. And even more – we had no awareness of the real situation.... We purely and simply deserved everything that happened afterward."

— Aleksandr Solzhenitsyn
The Gulag Archipelago

For Kārlis

Kārlis Smiltens

War Artist & Latvian Legionnaire

October 24, 1921 – February 10, 2017

For Cornelia

For Biruta

Article 58

1940 Latvia, perilously positioned between two
maniacal, totalitarian dictatorships.

PROLOGUE

THE SUMMERHOUSE, LATVIA
MIDSUMMER'S EVE, 1992

"I AM KĀRLIS PĒRKONS," KĀRLIS called, peering down into the root cellar. "This is my house."

The man in the suit was squatting on the cellar floor, examining a shovel at the body's head. He looked up at Kārlis, and ordered, "Don't go anywhere, old man."

Kārlis straightened up stiffly and looked around. Root cellar access was just outside the kitchen door. The dozen assorted police officials tromping through the house and property disturbed him, the green, tangled overgrowth of spring at odds with a corpse. He breathed deeply, calmed by the verdant earth, especially Latvian soil. All had gone as planned until now, he reassured himself. This too would be handled in the proper order.

Kārlis moved aside for men in blue jumpsuits carrying a stretcher. They paused at the cellar entrance, a wooden rectangular frame that jutted up from the ground at an angle, and started to descend the steep, narrow steps. The cellar door lay where it had been flung in the surrounding tall grass, rotted right off the hinges.

"Don't trust those stairs," Kārlis told them. "They're decrepit."

Kārlis walked to where the police cars and ambulance were parked, and waited. Emergency lights pulsed red over the summerhouse's crumbling plaster and stone edging. Minutes later, the man in the suit, a detective, emerged from the cellar and approached Kārlis, flipping his notepad.

"Hmph. Private property," the detective said. He had a Russian accent, dripping with sarcasm. "And you, the owner."

It was more a jeer than a question, so Kārlis didn't answer. He was an obvious westerner, the only one in town dressed in pastels and running shoes.

"You waited a long time to get your hands on the place," the detective said. "Most people in your position have given up."

"I always kept the paperwork in order," Kārlis replied.

A police officer with tall black boots and handcuffs dangling from his belt strode over to where they stood and addressed the detective. "The victim, name: Igor Volkov, lived here. Retired KGB."

"That's Volkov?" Kārlis said, pointing at the root cellar. "Ak tu kungs."

"Oh, my lord," the detective mimicked. "Yah. That is Volkov. Murdered in your private root cellar. Did you and the victim argue?"

Kārlis said nothing. He wouldn't call a lifelong vendetta an argument. During his silence, birds screamed, reveling in the extended hunting of the prolonged dusk, kids yelled playfully, a distant firecracker popped.

"All right, Pērkons," the detective said. "We'll talk at the station."

Kārlis nodded. "I'll get my jacket," he said, heading toward the kitchen door.

Kārlis would not get in a police car if he could help it, nor go to the station. It was an aversion learned young. But his knees were sixty-eight years old now and still unfolding from the long flight. He must slip over to the Bier Schtube, somehow, to the nearest telephone, and call his lawyer. But how?

A curse bellowed from the root cellar. Kārlis glanced up in time to see a blue jumpsuit, climbing the stairs backwards with the stretcher, suddenly drop from view. Amid a splintering crash of wood, Kārlis heard the man scream. The stairs had collapsed.

The detective rushed to the root cellar and dropped to his knees beside the gaping hole. He waved an arm trying to clear rising dust. A ring of uniformed personnel pressed around him, peering down and shouting to one another.

Kārlis stared at their backs, heart drumming. This was his chance. This would be his only opportunity to get to a phone. Guts roiling, he strolled past the unmanned police cruiser. The radio squawked. The ambulance driver nodded to him. The linden tree, tired leafy sentry, leaned against the old house in a sloppy profusion of yellow flowers.

He'd made it around the side of the house, stepping through overgrown shrubs and tangled vines, without being stopped. Now headed into the forest, he walked faster. The Midsummer sky was bright as silver, illuminating an unused path Kārlis had once known like the back of his hand. After hiking for several minutes, he paused, turning his good ear toward the house. Blood pumped noisily in his head, drowning all sound. He pushed on, not hearing the running footsteps as much as otherwise sensing them. His heart nearly popped knowing that someone was overtaking him. Living in America, he'd forgotten how it felt to be afraid. There'd been a time here when he'd known the whole gamut of fear, ranging from constant dread to abject terror. It was all coming back.

I

DECEMBER 21, 1940
BASTION HILL PARK
RIGA, LATVIA

KĀRLIS PĒRKONS DIDN'T TRUST ANYONE else to be the look-out. He had more to lose than the others, now that he'd been accepted to the Art Academy. He had more reason to avoid the secret police until at least graduation in June, besides the obvious fact that Stalin's henchmen, the NKVD, were vicious thugs. The problem was the fog. He parted the twigs of a frozen lilac bush and scouted below. A cloud pressed over the park like cotton packing the top of a pill bottle. Kārlis couldn't see, but he could hear his friends, buffooning around with the sled as if their lives depended on having some fun.

"It's just as dangerous to stay at home, you know."

"*Ak tu kungs!*" Kārlis nearly bit his tongue. Peters was right at his elbow. "Don't sneak up on me like that."

"Safer in the open," Peters contended, sweeping his arm across the hilltop view of the snow-clad park, its descending drifts and slopes, dim outlines of bare trees in the mist, and the suggestion of the distant

Freedom Monument. "At home they know right where to find you. A bang at the door and *whammo* you're trapped." Peters flapped his arms like he was warming up for an Olympic event. "They come to my house, badgering my parents. I say stay on the move. Keep them guessing."

Kārlis removed his eyeglasses, steamed up by anxious breathing, and wiped the lenses with his wool glove. "But this could be an illegal assembly."

"What! Sledding?" Peters said.

"Well then where is everybody?" Kārlis said. "A year ago the whole senior class would've been horsing around in the snow."

The park was empty except for Eriks and Hugo dragging the sled up the hill, their every noise a deafening echo.

"*I threw flowers in the Gauja,*" belted out Eriks Gailis. He emerged from the white haze looking like a cross between a Viking raider and a trained bear. "*To send greetings to my girl.*"

"*Shhhh,*" Kārlis hissed. "I heard the folk songs are illegal."

"If his singing's been outlawed then there's a silver lining to this occupation," Peters said.

Eriks pushed the oak racer. It glided over hard packed snow to where Peters stopped it with a boot.

Peters and Eriks were about the same height, tall, and both loved besting the other. But Peters was the picture of fitness, the epitome of sportsmanship, whereas Eriks delighted in cheating. You never knew what he'd lummox into next.

"I was just telling Hugo here, the Communists are now organizing striptease performances," Eriks said, relishing the boys' attention. "All the party faithful went to the opening night at this cabaret in Riga, but after seeing the first show nobody went back. It was a huge flop and they had no idea why." With a mock-Russian accent, he said, "It vas superbly organized and all the strippers had solid Party records. They vere Bolsheviks from 1905!"

Peters chuckled and Hugo unleashed a silly, spasmodic laugh. No one cared whether the joke was even funny. They were starved for a good time, no matter how forced it felt.

"The bags were ancient," Hugo explained to Kārlis, mistaking his worried expression for idiocy. He cupped his hands under his breasts. "Shriveled elf shoes... in their fifties!"

"I get it," Kārlis said.

Hugo shrugged.

"Some of them even knew Lenin personally," Eriks added, wiping a tear from his eye.

"Ditch that bulky coat, Kārlis," Peters said, ever the competitor. "Mitigate degrees of wind resistance critical to peak sledding speed." He straddled the sled and maneuvered it to the hilltop's tipping point. "Let's show these turtles how it's done."

Kārlis played along. He made a show of removing his jacket and hanging it on a branch. He did it so he wouldn't lose his wallet in the snow. It held the card admitting him to the Art Academy, his ticket to the future.

Climbing on behind Peters, Kārlis crouched, bracing his feet against the runners, folding his knees like a cricket.

"Here lemme help," Eriks heckled. "I hope you like to eat snow!"

Kārlis felt the rascal push against his back, until the ground dropped away and the sled nosed downhill, chasing gravity to the bottom.

Freezing grits of snow nipped his cheeks.

"Yah ha!" Kārlis hooted, letting his guard down.

Then a runner caught, Peters yanked the steering bar and the sled jerked out of control, spraying a rooster tail of snow and spilling the boys over in a wipeout. Kārlis lay laughing so hard his guts shook.

Finally catching his breath, he adjusted his spectacles and rose on an elbow. He came nose-to-toe with a black boot.

A black, Russian boot.

Kārlis stopped laughing.

Wiping his face, he looked up.

The knee-high boot gave way to olive-green woolen breeches, which disappeared beneath a service coat cinched at the waist with a leather belt. The coat was buttoned to the neck, from where pointy collar tips aimed down at Kārlis. The man looming over him was old enough to be his father, but looked far sterner. He had big ears protruding beneath an officer's visor cap. The cap badge looked like a head wound, between the eyes, red under a gold hammer-and-sickle, the emblem of the NKVD.

His stomach churned. He was at the feet of the Communist secret police, the Cheka.

The big-eared officer said something in Russian that Kārlis didn't catch. The aggressive consonant clusters jackhammered his brain.

"I said, why aren't you in school?" the officer repeated, this time in Latvian.

Kārlis's throat clenched so he could barely breathe, let alone answer. Then he grasped that the officer wasn't addressing him, but Peters, who had rolled to a seated position in a nearby snow bank. Peters always attracted the attention of grownups, probably due to his athletically winning looks, strong jaw and assertive air. The coaches had always called Peters Leadership Material. Right now, Kārlis was glad to be the Poindexter-type that no one usually noticed.

"My classes are over for today," Peters said, rising slowly, brushing snow from his coat. "Comrade."

The officer clutched a handful of Peters's yellow hair and yanked him over.

"You go to high school, right?" he said, releasing Peters's head with a shove. "You're required to learn Russian."

"Yah, Comrade," Peters said. *"Я учусь на русском, товарищ."*

The language was alien, bewildering, and evil to Kārlis.

While Peters was trying to convince the officer that he *was* learning Russian, a dark-haired agent with sloping shoulders and swinging ape-arms was yelling and clomping up the hill. There was also a third man, standing behind the officer, younger, with a smooth, expressionless face, and a rifle butted against his shoulder pointed at the hilltop.

A *troika*; Kārlis had heard they worked in gangs of three. His stomach cramped at what else he'd heard.

"Come down with your hands up or I will shoot!" shouted the rifleman.

Kārlis was surprised, judging by his speech, the rifleman was a local, not one of the Russian occupiers. The rifle was pointed at a slender figure at the top of the hill, whom Kārlis knew was Hugo, peering down to see what was happening.

Kārlis held his breath, sensing Hugo's indecision. Would his friend obey the authorities, or listen to the unseen Eriks on his other side, who was no doubt urging him to run. More likely Eriks had already fled the scene. Did Hugo even know, in this fog, that someone was aiming a gun at him?

Click.

Cocking the trigger cut the air sharply, commanded absolutely. Clear in any language.

Hugo obeyed. "Yah, okay," he said, picking a path down the slippery slope. "I'm coming."

Kārlis exhaled, relieved Hugo hadn't been shot, but at the same time wishing he'd gotten away.

"You have identification?" demanded the big-eared officer.

Peters reached into his coat. His hand was trembling when he took out his wallet and his school ID.

"Peters Kalnins," said the officer, squinting at the card. "I see you're *captain of the hockey team.*" His voice dripped with sarcasm. "You're a regular sport."

Peters's eyes flashed between the officer and the ID card, looking bewildered. Kārlis couldn't understand the mockery either. Adults usually praised Peters for being the best at everything.

"Who's your girlfriend?" the officer said, nodding toward Kārlis. "Let's see some ID."

Kārlis knew he could go to jail for not carrying ID at all times. He was just about to explain he'd left it on a tree when Hugo saved him by reaching over and presenting *his* student card.

The officer took it with a scowl, and compared Hugo to his photograph. Same willowy frame, silver-white hair, and ghostly-white skin, but the blue eyes were twice as big right now and brimming with tears.

"Hugo here is on the honor roll!" said the officer with contempt. "What's your father do, boy?"

"He's a police officer. Was a police officer."

Kārlis held his breath, sensing that fact might get them in trouble. The Latvian police had been discharged from duty six months ago when the Soviets annexed the country.

"Uh-huh," said the big-eared officer. Then with a nod to his cohorts, he said, "That's enough. You maggots are coming with us."

Kārlis cursed silently. *Ak tu kungs!* They were screwed.

"We haven't done anything," Peters said.

"I doubt that," said the officer, sizing up the boys. "Student fraternity, church-going family, subversive reading material…you're guilty of something and I promise you'll confess it. Let's go."

The officer withdrew a club from his belt and gestured for them to move.

Something collapsed within Kārlis as huge hands grabbed him and shoved him down the trail out of the park. His heart pounded while details around him leapt into focus: fountains edged with icicles, statues of Latvian heroes, benches and shrubberies making odd, vague shapes under a thick blanket of snow. Crossing a bridge over the frozen canal that had once been the city's moat, they marched away from the stately Opera House, away from the spires and gabled rooftops of medieval Old Riga, toward the city's business district. The sled was left behind.

Kārlis felt he was on display as the NKVD paraded him down the slushy sidewalks of Freedom Boulevard, past the line-up of tall stone buildings. He prayed some adult would step up to help them, but shopkeepers and others disappeared into doorways and scurried elsewhere. He sensed the hidden audience watching him from behind shuttered windows and through the cracks of curtains.

"We didn't do anything," Peters said again, in a casual tone like he was trying to befriend the uniformed gorilla.

After a half dozen blocks, it became clear they were headed to the Corner House. The knowledge made Kārlis break out in sweat despite the freezing temperature. The NKVD headquarters was rumored to be a place of interrogation so ghastly no one spoke of it by its proper name. Instead they called it the Corner House, referring to its location at the intersection of Freedom and Stabu. *You go into the*

Corner House, you leave a corpse. Peters knew it too, because when Kārlis met his eyes they were electric with terror.

Suddenly Peters stopped. He twisted around to face the agents surrounding him. "We'll answer your questions right here," he blurted. "Right now. What do you want to know?"

The tide sucking them toward the Corner House let up for a moment as the agents paused, staring curiously at Peters. Their red hammer-and-sickle cap badges glowed in the late afternoon light like monstrous, bloodshot eyes.

"Shut up," the rifleman said, resuming the march.

"Officer, you're Latvian," Peters said, appealing to the rifleman. "Please, just let us go home. I promise you'll never see us again."

This seemed to infuriate the man, the suggestion that he, as a Latvian, might be sentimental toward one of his own. To prove that he could be as nasty as any Russian, he pounced on Peters, poking him in the chest and neck with the barrel of his gun and backing him up the concrete steps leading to the door of the Corner House.

Turning abruptly, Peters charged sideways into the ape-man, knocking him off balance. But the man recovered quickly, catching Peters and twisting his arm behind his back while Peters thrashed like a hooked bonefish.

The Cheka cursed furiously, manhandling Peters up the remaining stairs and pushing him toward the door.

At the last moment Peters kicked his legs forward with a scream. He braced one foot against each side of the doorjamb, refusing to cross the threshold and yelling, "We didn't do anything!"

Kārlis stood horrified. People were executed for resisting arrest, and that's what Peters was doing, two men could barely subdue him. It suddenly dawned on Kārlis, that only the old officer with the club was left to watch both Hugo and him.

Hugo must've had the same thought, because when Kārlis turned his head to look, Hugo was gone.

The old officer snapped his head around in time to see Hugo's back at the bottom of the concrete steps. He lunged after him with a vicious swing of his club, slipping and falling to the sidewalk.

Kārlis vaulted over the officer's splayed limbs, sliding and bumping hard down the stairs, impervious to pain. Using gloved hands like another set of feet, he righted himself and ran in the opposite direction as Hugo.

A whistle blew.

Kārlis didn't look back.

2

KĀRLIS RAN THROUGH A MAZE of city blocks until a stitch in his side nearly paralyzed him. He ducked into a recessed doorway, clutching his ribs. Trying not to gasp conspicuously, he studied the boulevard. Daylight had ebbed away. Yellow rectangles of light were appearing in tall arrays on the buildings above. Commuters with nervous, pinched faces were venturing out with the shadows, hurrying to the rails, probably trying to be tucked in somewhere safe before curfew. An approaching trolley clanged, and an automobile nosed its way down one side of the street. Contrary to what he'd assumed, no one appeared to be chasing him, nobody seemed aware of his crime or cared that he had abandoned his friend at the NKVD torture chamber. He wished someone did care. He felt like yelling,

Hey everybody! They took my friend to the Corner House! A good boy! He didn't do anything.

Suddenly he was freezing. Since no one appeared to be following him, he cut directly to the alley behind Freedom Boulevard, and hurried home. It was an easy walk. Most of the alley had been cleared of snow and the back doors of the shops were as familiar to Kārlis as the storefronts. His father's leather workshop was on the next block. Papu would know what to do.

Slowing his pace, Kārlis approached warily. Some large-scale activity was underway in the alley, just outside Papu's loading dock. A sledge was parked there; harnessed to a mammoth Percheron blowing streams of white vapor from its nostrils and stamping giant hooves in the slush. At its head stood a man wearing a dusky blue fedora, fawn-colored gloves and a knee-length fur coat. The man held the animal's bridle near the bit, steadying the beast with strokes along its muscular neck.

This was probably someone picking up a shipment of leather goods, Kārlis surmised. Private commercial transactions were illegal as far as he knew, but Papu still engaged in the practice. Coming closer, Kārlis recognized the man as one of his father's associates.

"*Sveiks*, Mr. Zales," Kārlis said.

Zales and the horse both jerked as if Kārlis had run up flinging acid.

"Oh, it's only you, young Pērkons, er, Kārlis. I didn't see you coming," Zales said. He exhaled audibly, pressing his body against the horse's neck until the beast relaxed. "You mustn't call me Zales anymore, young man. I'm going by *Hill* now." He looked around furtively from under his fedora. "Everyone with the name Zales has been lined up and—" he dropped his voice, "well, executed. On account of there being parks and streets with the name."

"I'm sorry," was all Kārlis could think to say, wanting to cover his ears. He couldn't take in a grown man's problems right now, couldn't even absorb his own harrowing escape. "I had no idea, Mr. Zales."

"*Hill*, my boy, Hill. Distant cousins. Can't say I really knew them. Nevertheless, can't be too careful. Don't underestimate Communist brutality."

Kārlis nodded at the warning, immediately applying it to what must be happening to Peters at the Corner House.

"I recommend you change your name as well," Zales said.

"Kārlis!" This was a high-pitched voice coming from the sledge. Kārlis was astonished to discover his little sister sitting up there, on the high-backed passenger bench amid a pile of furs.

"Biruta, what are you doing out after dark?" Kārlis said. "And in the alley to boot?"

"Did you know Papu is milking a cash cow?" Biruta said. Blonde braids tumbled from the hood of her cloak. On her lap she clutched a cardboard box poked with holes. "I want to know where he keeps the cow."

"What's going on here?" Kārlis said, perplexed to find his sister and her cat with Mr. Zales.

"I am escorting you to your summer house this evening," Zales said. "I owe your father a personal favor, you see. Great business instincts, your father has. Excellent sense of timing. If I hadn't listened to him, I'd be destitute, like everyone else in this city. Wake up one morning and *Poof*. Bank accounts drained. Everything over a thousand *lats* sucked away by the Politburo. Don't go up there," Zales said, seeing Kārlis about to enter the building. He dropped his voice, "There are Russians inside."

Kārlis froze mid-step. Russians. Here. *Ak tu kungs*. Had they come for him?

"Spies," Zales said in a loud whisper.

Kārlis processed the news, trying to reconcile it with the bumping and scraping he heard coming from the workshop. A moment later Kārlis's father emerged, dragging a trunk.

Janis Pērkons wore his usual fitted suit, vest and bowtie, spies and draft horses notwithstanding. He saw Kārlis and dropped the trunk.

"Ah! You made it!" his father said.

The next moment Kārlis was lifted off the ground in a bear hug, and held airborne. Suddenly, his eyes stung, his throat felt tight. He wiped his nose on his sleeve.

"Just in time," his father said, setting Kārlis back down.

"In time for what?"

"We're moving tonight," Janis said in a low voice. He nodded toward the upstairs family apartment. "Unexpected guests. A Soviet officer is here, wants to quarter a so-called apprentice with us. Someone to watch me at work. Probably my replacement." His father balled a fist, and looked like he wanted to throw it through the brick wall. "He's planning to sleep in the hallway outside my bedroom."

"You should abandon this operation now," Zales interjected, still holding the horse. "Before they drop the ax."

"Moving?" Kārlis said, suddenly grasping the meaning of the loaded sledge. "When are we coming back?"

Instead of answering, his father hoisted the trunk onto the sledge, lodging it firmly between other crates. Pushing off his fur-lined cap, steam rose from the top of his shaved head.

"So they haven't come for me?" Kārlis said.

"Why would they come for *you*?" his father asked, turning sharp blue eyes to him. His father's moustache and goatee were always precisely trimmed, exuding the comforting notion that Janis Pērkons was working a plan.

"Because they caught me sledding and took me to the Corner House," Kārlis said, the words pouring out in a panic.

His father listened to the details with a cold stare, giving vent to an oath.

"I barely got away," Kārlis concluded. "But they took Peters in there and we've got to get him out."

Janis exchanged a look with Zales, and by the time he faced Kārlis again, a hardness had set around his eyes. "Son, I know you want to hear me say that I can fix this," he said. "That I know someone or some way."

That was exactly what Kārlis wanted to hear. Everyone knew Janis Pērkons was a problem solver, a big-thinker, a man with connections.

"But I don't!" His father pulled out his cigarettes and Mr. Zales stepped forward to light him up. "I have your mother and sister to think about, too."

Kārlis said nothing while Janis blew smoke toward heaven, still certain his father had a brilliant solution up his sleeve.

"You know what they do to people there," Kārlis finally said, his voice cracking. "That could be me dragged in there."

Janis looked like Kārlis had slapped him.

Mr. Zales ran his arm over the horse's neck.

An impatient *meow* came through the holes in Biruta's box.

Finally, his father said, "Son, do you understand the principle of triage?"

No, and Kārlis wasn't in the mood for a French lesson.

His father took the tone of a sympathetic philosopher. "On a battlefield, medics separate the wounded into three groups. Those who are not seriously injured; those who are seriously injured but may be saved; and those who are too far gone—"

"That's garbage," Kārlis blurted, eyes bulging. "I'm not listening to that. If it was me in the Corner House right now, would I be *too far gone?*"

"Thank God it's not you," his father said with a steely edge. "Because there still would not be a goddam thing I could do, but so help me I would put up everything trying to save you."

Kārlis didn't know where to look or how to stand, his world suddenly foreign.

"The fact is, you escaped, for now," Janis said, taking a last drag and throwing his cigarette down. "God help me for rejoicing in that." He looked Kārlis in the eye and clapped his shoulders. "Look, son. I didn't expect to be moving tonight, but a Soviet squatter is here to watch us. I won't have him making himself at home with your mother and Biruta. And you should stay as far away from this so-called apprentice as possible. He's trouble. That's why I'm taking the family to the country right away. I wish you'd go with them."

The box *meowed* again.

Kārlis felt hopelessly flat. He'd been clutching at the string of his father's balloon, only to find that without the lift of Papu's will, he was left holding a damp, heavy heap of nothing. His father was not going to step up and make things right. Kārlis didn't want to cry in front of the men, so he shifted to the offensive. "Why aren't *you* going with them?"

"I have a business to run," Janis said, returning to the job of packing the sledge. "I'll commute on the train as often as possible."

"Well, I have to go to school," Kārlis said, his voice husky. "I have to pass classes to graduate. I have to graduate to attend the Art Academy." *His ticket to the future.*

"I understand how important that is to you," Janis said. He was securing the load with a leather strap, tugging with unnecessary force. "But if the NKVD has your name, they can easily pick you up at school. Or arrest you here at the Leather Works. Might be better for you to come out to the country for now. Maybe when the situation's less volatile you can go back to studying art."

Kārlis didn't like the sound of that, but he didn't know what to do. He'd thought he'd escaped the NKVD running through the streets, not knowing they were already in his home, moving in while his family was moving out. If they wanted to, they could track him down. There was no getting away from them. But that didn't mean he should just hide in the country with his mother.

"I think I should keep going to classes," Kārlis said. "The Cheka didn't even get my name."

"Son, they will get your name from Peters," Janis said darkly. "If they want it."

Kārlis's stomach curdled. People kept saying things that sent him down the dark corridors of the Corner House to where the Cheka did unspeakable things to Peters. He stared at the sledge.

"They're not that systematic, thank God," Mr. Zales said, weighing in with his two centimes. "But what they lack in organization, they make up for with an unfathomable cruel streak."

The tap of footsteps made them look toward the workshop, from where Kārlis's mother emerged, slipping on the hood of her travelling cloak. She hadn't taken time to tidy her hair, a brown strand seemed plastered to a wet cheek. Her eyes and nose were red. Seeing his mother upset always made Kārlis feel terrible, even when it wasn't his fault.

At a glance, she said, "Have you lost your coat?"

Kārlis folded his arms over his thermal undershirt. Now that she mentioned it, he was freezing.

His father helped his mother up the running board to her seat on the sledge.

"Climb up here before you freeze," she said to Kārlis. "Come on, get under the rugs."

Kārlis's thinking felt numb and slow, but he knew he didn't feel right warming up under the furs with his mother and sister. "I'm not ready to leave yet, Mother," he said. "I just—I have school and some things to straighten out. You know, about being accepted to the Art Academy. But I'll come as soon as I can."

"But I've packed your things," Mother said. "Janis, what's wrong with him? Make him come."

"He knows how to find his way home, Anna. He's nearly eighteen," Janis said. "Let him find his sea legs. That way is safer in the long run."

His mother looked unconvinced but before she could argue, Janis said, "Son, if you insist on staying in Riga, vary your routine. Don't be predictable."

"Changing addresses has become the national hobby," Zales said.

"I have places to stay," Kārlis said.

"Don't trust anybody," Janis said.

"Let's get cracking," Zales said. "Curfew sneaks up quick."

"Here, put this blanket around you," his mother said, handing down a velvety-thing with long, silky gold fringe.

Janis held the horse's head while Zales climbed up on the driver's bench. "I just realized tomorrow's the solstice," Zales said, organizing the reins and hunkering into his fur coat. "The darkest day of the year."

Janis released the harness and walked to the horse's rump. Looking up at Zales, he said quietly, "Rudolfs, if anything happens to me, promise you'll help Anna and the children."

Kārlis felt he shouldn't have heard that and wanted to cover his ears.

"Of course I will," Zales said. "But dammit Janis, stop taking unnecessary risks. These black market deals are foolhardy. They've noticed you." Zales tipped his head upward, presumably to where the Russians sat around Mother's dining table having tea.

"I have no choice," Janis said. "Surviving this will require reserves. The deeper the better. They'll eventually get around to taking the Leather Works. And then it's going to be dry for a long time."

Janis stepped on the running board and leaned over boxes and duffels to kiss the passengers, saying "Goodbye, Cookie. Take good care of Katkis. Anna, I'll see you soon."

"*Sveiks*, Papu," Biruta said.

The horse moved out energetically, as if also eager to beat curfew. Starting with a lurch, the sledge then glided smoothly. Biruta flipped around in her seat. Rising to her knees, she poked her head over the seat back and held up a small hand.

Kārlis waved back, following the sledge down the alley for a few steps, the reality of their leaving sinking in with an empty chill.

Turning back to the Leather Works, Kārlis sucked in his breath and froze. Someone had crept up and was lurking in the doorway directly behind his father, silhouetted by the light of the workshop. Whoever he was, he also watched the sledge depart, with a vacuous expression that made Kārlis's skin crawl.

His father was holding his pocket watch up to the dim window light. "They should be there by nine," he said, snapping the cover closed and sliding the watch into his vest pocket. He must have read the alarm in Kārlis's eyes, because when he turned to go inside he didn't act surprised to see the guy standing there.

"Igor Volkov, my worthy apprentice," Janis said, smoothly.

Igor Volkov didn't return the greeting. He was looking around the workshop and at the departing sledge, as if he'd caught Kārlis and his father pilfering supplies. Kārlis immediately resented the Russian, who was around his own age, for acting like he had some sort of authority over them in their own family business.

Volkov had a heart-shaped face with vigorous red circles on high cheekbones. A wave of brown hair dipped over his forehead. His lips were perfectly symmetrical. Kārlis would've called it a pretty-boy face, were it not for the haughty eyes of stone and the muscled upper body that made Kārlis feel like a bespectacled idiot wrapped in his mother's blanket.

Janis spoke like everything was business as usual. "It's time to give the immersion drums a final rotation and close shop for the day," he said. "Give me a hand with these doors, Igor, will you?" Janis grasped one side of the steel door and began dragging it, screeching, on its rollers.

The apprentice ignored Janis, staring acidly at Kārlis.

His father hadn't introduced him as his son or even acknowledged Kārlis's presence. Janis Pērkons held a reputation for gallantry, so Kārlis understood the slight was deliberate, probably an attempt to shield him from this nasty Russian infiltrator. Still Kārlis felt somewhat disinherited.

"Grab the door," Janis repeated, pointing to the handle near Igor Volkov.

"Comrade. I came out because I need a key to this place," Igor said, declining to help.

"Yah, of course," Janis said. He made a show of patting his pockets before turning to Kārlis and saying, "Do you happen to have a key on you?" Then he went to close the other side of the door himself.

Kārlis was stupefied. On top of everything else, his father now intended to give this interloper his key?

Kārlis extracted his keys, which were on a fob of leather and amber he'd crafted in this very workshop. He pried the key off wondering what next? This *kāpost galva* freeloader would be bunking in his room among his clipper ship models and books and sketches?

Janis had, by now, closed the workshop doors by all but a few inches, through which Kārlis passed the key. Janis took it and tossed it to Volkov, giving Kārlis a nod. It was a portentous nod, a compendium of fatherly advice and concern.

Volkov snatched the key midair. Through the narrow crack between doors, Kārlis saw Igor Volkov smile and was reminded of a wolf baring its teeth.

Then his father shut the doors with a clang, and Kārlis was standing alone in the freezing alley.

3

THERE WAS NO QUESTION WHERE to go next. Kārlis flew down the alley like a homing pigeon. After fifteen minutes he'd reached the Leopolds family bakery at 24 Freedom Boulevard, where he'd find Jekabs Leopolds, one of his best friends. Checking both directions to be sure no one was watching, he barged through the back door to the kitchen.

Mixing bowls clattered as the baker turned sharply. "Oy! Kārlis!"

"Sorry to frighten you, Mr. Leopolds."

Mr. Leopolds exhaled heavily and crossed the room. "Been a little jumpy lately, that's all. Get over here, boychik," he said, pulling Kārlis close and thumping his back, which was a minor beating because the baker was very muscular from pummeling dough all day. "You made it." Apparently he'd heard about the Corner House. "Thank the Lord."

"Yah," Kārlis said, "I made it." *Peters didn't make it. I was supposed to be the look-out.* Kārlis kept his face in a frozen mask, but eventually the tingle of a thaw crept over him. Not only had he escaped the

NKVD today but, for the first time in his life, he'd taken a course independent from his parents. He felt vaguely uneasy as he warmed up in the brightly lit kitchen, suddenly wishing his family were with him. This haven, with its soothing aroma of fresh bread, contrasted miserably with the memory of his mother and sister leaving home, and his father shutting him out in a dark alley with the parting advice, *don't trust anybody.*

"Look who's here, Hugo," Mr. Leopolds said to a slumped figure sitting near the ovens. "One more buddy you can stop worrying about."

Kārlis nodded at Hugo, relieved to see he'd also gotten away.

Against the blackened brick, Hugo's face and hair were shock-white. He met Kārlis with red, swollen eyes. Then he returned his gaze to the embers, watching them with a dazed expression, until his face was jerked by some hiccupping twitch.

"Did you tell anyone you were coming here?" Mr. Leopolds asked Kārlis, cracking the back door and surveilling the alley.

"No," Kārlis said, disgruntled that Mr. Leopolds even had to ask.

The baker closed the door, grabbed a log off the firewood stack and stoked one of the ovens, fanning with the bellows until flames erupted. Dusting off his hands, he went back to the mixing bowls, kneading a large blob of dough with the fervor of one man strangling another. Stopping suddenly, Mr. Leopolds straightened his yarmulke with the back of his fist, and said. "Any news about Peters?"

"No," Kārlis said, feeling shame heat his cheeks.

"A terrible thing," Mr. Leopolds said, shaking his head. "God forbid! It shouldn't happen. You look beat. Want a roll? Cup of coffee?"

"No, thank you, Mr. Leopolds. I'm not hungry."

"Well, my nephew's back there, with the usuals," Mr. Leopolds said, pointing toward the pantry. "Tell them to keep it down, would you? Juveniles need a place to blow off a little steam, make some sense of things. That I know," he said, wiping his brow, "but six of you in one place—whew! We're in trouble if we're caught." He worked the dough with a grim set to his jaw. "Still, you can't just cave," he muttered. "A miserable year."

"I'll tell them to keep it down," Kārlis said, proceeding to the pantry. Hugo got up and followed him.

The pantry was a large, windowless room lit by a bare bulb hanging from the ceiling. Exclusive as a clubhouse and chummy as a locker room, it was stacked with 50-kilo bags of flour that had been positioned like furniture. Turning the doorknob triggered a subtle change in the room's pulse, as if the cronies inside had all shifted slightly to form some desired tableau. They were hiding something, Kārlis thought, maybe just the fact that they'd been crying.

Jekabs reclined in the corner, a cigarette between his lips, nose in a textbook.

Standing over him was Sniedze, who jerked his head up, saucer-eyed.

Vilz appeared to be reorganizing pans on a shelf.

Eriks sat slumped in the chair, which he'd lowered from its tipped position.

After Kārlis walked in and Hugo closed the door behind them, there was a nearly imperceptible, collective exhale.

"It's just Kārlis," Jekabs said, by way of greeting.

With a moan, Vilz shoved the nest of pans aside revealing, to Kārlis's dismay, the hiding place of her portable typewriter.

Eriks lifted a flask from behind his tree-trunk of a thigh, tipped the chair again and took a swig.

Jekabs sat up, fanned the pages of the textbook he was supposedly reading, to where he'd slipped a scrap of paper. "Where were we?" he asked, standing to look over Vilz's shoulder.

Vilz read from the sheet in the typewriter, "Among them were Lukins Nikolajs, police officer; Guntis Kesteris, clergyman..."

"Right," Jekabs said, referring to his scrap. "So, what? We just add Peters's name to the bottom of the list?" He wiped his nose on his sleeve.

"Yah," Vilz said, clacking at the steel keys, "Peters Kalnins, student."

"What's that?" Kārlis asked.

Vilz held her hand out and Jekabs passed her the cigarette.

"List of people arrested for counterrevolutionary activity yesterday and today," Vilz said. She blew a stream of smoke at the light bulb. "I happened to be writing it up for *Free Latvia.*" She nodded at the typewritten sheet. "Thought it'd be just another list of names and crimes. Then Eriks careened in, told us what happened at the park. Suddenly it's personal. We got Peters on that list now." Vilz pushed her lips together grimly, making dimples appear in her cheeks.

"Counterrevolutionary activity?" Kārlis said. "We were sledding."

Kārlis looked up to Vilz Zarins, who, at eighteen, was the oldest of the friends. Vilz brought a worldly air to the pantry since she regularly attended "secret meetings". She wore her dark hair in a short wave barely covering a creamy neck, and parted decisively down the middle, framing agate-blue eyes. Curves shifted under her long-sleeved thermal when she positioned the Adler toward the light to read what she had typed.

"Offenses include being a wealthy farmer, a capitalist businessman, member of a student organization, decorated with the

Oak Leaf military order, criticizing the Communist Party, hiding in the forest, not singing at a labor rally, and, oh, the one you boys know so well," Vilz added pointedly, "illegal assembly and singing a folk song."

Kārlis squirmed.

Eriks tipped the flask up, a grim twist to his mouth. "Kārlis was supposed to be the *kāpost galva* look-out."

"It was your idea to go in the first place," Kārlis said. "And your singing like a buffoon that brought the Cheka down. Then you get away without even being seen."

"The entire episode was disgraceful and demoralizing." Hugo interjected, sounding like one of their teachers.

Clack, clack, clack, clack. Vilz was back to typing.

"Is it true you two left Peters to fight NKVD agents alone?" Eriks said.

"What's the point in casting blame?" Vilz said loudly from behind her typewriter.

"You were not even there," Kārlis told Eriks. "So just shut up." Then something caught his eye. "What in hell is that? Are you actually wearing a boutonniere? What, are you going dancing tonight?"

"Now my button hole bothers you?"

"What bothers me is that at some point during the last hour while I was running for my life, you were pinning a sprig of holly to your lapel."

"When we argue among ourselves, it works out great for the Commies," Vilz said.

Kārlis took a deep breath and closed his mouth, deciding to drop it. Shaking his head, he took off his gloves one by one and pelted them at the corner.

"Can't change what happened," Vilz said, without looking up from the typewriter. "Can only do it different going forward."

"What do you think they're doing to Peters right now?" Hugo said in a croaky voice.

The burning question hung there, sucking air from the room.

Kārlis dropped his eyes to the baseboard. He tried not to think about the slow ripping of fingernails, temple screws and things that shouldn't even be done to animals. "We ought to be talking about getting him out of there," he said. "Hugo, can't your father do something? Doesn't he know someone from his police force days?"

"My dad's in no position to stick his neck out," Hugo said. "We don't even have a place to live anymore."

"What about the League of Nations?" Kārlis persisted. "Latvia's a member, doesn't that count for anything?"

"No. Nobody cares," Vilz said. *Clack, clack, clack.* "The world only cares that Nazis have overrun Paris. Nobody's going to help us, but us." She tugged the paper off the roller with a zip, faced the others, and said quietly, "In the next edition of *Free Latvia* I'm going to inform people about what happened." She gave the article to Kārlis. "As my tribute to Peters. Everybody will know what those red *kāpost galvas* have done."

"You don't have to talk about Peters like he's dead," Kārlis said, swallowing dryly. Something told him he should leave now. Anything concerning *Free Latvia* was dangerous. But there was no place else to go. So, adjusting his glasses, he scanned the draft newsletter of the resistance.

Seeing Peters named with those who'd been rounded up by the NKVD made Kārlis feel like he was in someone else's body. He wiped his nose on his sleeve. Then he read the next line, and his eyes blasted out of his head.

"All arrested received the *death penalty* and were *executed* according to authority granted under Article 58 of the Russian Criminal Code!"

The room turned upside down.

"What is this?" Kārlis said. "You've already decided among yourselves that Peters has— what? Been executed?"

"Or will have been by the time this goes to press," Vilz said, latching the cover to her typewriter and returning it to its hiding place.

"I don't buy it," Kārlis said, looking around at the others. "We were just with him."

He looked to Hugo for backup but only saw a look of doom carved in the salt-white face.

"*You go into the Corner House, you come out a corpse,*" Sniedze parroted.

"No," Kārlis said, thinly. "That's just something people say."

Eriks lowered the chair to the floor and got up. He handed Kārlis the flask like it was an olive branch. "Sorry I jumped all over you," he said. "It wasn't your fault."

Somehow Eriks's humility made Kārlis feel even worse, but he took the flask.

"I brought your coat," Eriks said, tugging the fringy blanket.

Kārlis had forgotten it was draped around his shoulders. Maybe Eriks wasn't such a selfish clod after all, he thought, as a belt of vodka burned nastily down his throat. He went to the coat hook and checked his pockets. His wallet was still there, including the card admitting him to the Art Academy. Seeing his name engraved there made his heart flutter with relief. Maybe his entire future hadn't been flushed down the NKVD toilet today after all.

"I'm sorry to break it to you like this, Kārlis," Vilz said. "I know how you like to hide your head in the sand."

Kārlis ignored that. Vilz criticized anyone who didn't go to her secret meetings. "I just...I don't agree to admitting Peters is dead," Kārlis said.

"Pray to God he is," Vilz said.

These oblique nods to torture were getting under Kārlis's skin.

Sniedze Krasts pushed his way to the center of the pantry, blurting, "At least if he's dead, he won't be able to give our names to the Cheka." Sniedze Krasts, dwarfed by the oversized newsboy cap he always wore, was the runt of the gang, and a dimwit as far as Kārlis was concerned. His freckles looked weirdly prominent against a sickly complexion. "But if he's *not* dead, we should change our names, just in case, so the Ivans can't find us. You can disguise being Latvian by dropping the *-s* or *-is* off your name. You'd just be Karl," Sniedze said to Kārlis.

"Why would I want to Germanize my name?" Kārlis said, hoping he sounded aloof and scornful. His heart raced at the notion the Cheka might hunt him down.

"To disguise it so you don't match the name on the list," Sniedze said.

"What list?" Jekabs said.

"I'm keeping my name," said Vilz who, even when Kārlis first met her in nursery school, had always insisted on being called a variation of her father's name, refusing her given, pink ruffle of a name, Virma.

"What list?" Jekabs repeated.

"They put your name on a list before they come get you," Sniedze said. "My neighbor, Mr. Ozols, told me."

"There you go! See what I'm saying?" Jekabs said, smacking Sniedze upside the head. Jekabs could do that without being mean. There was something steadying about his no-nonsense practicality. "You talk like some eavesdropping, name-dropping schlub!"

"You are never to even utter my name," Kārlis told Sniedze. "Don't even let on that you know me."

"Seriously, stop it with the blabbing, Sniedze," Eriks said.

"Get some discretion," Hugo said.

"We ought to make aliases so we don't match the names on the list is all I'm saying," Sniedze continued, spitting defensively. "And maybe disguises, too. Stalin changed *his* name. From Ioseb Besarionis to Man of Steel. Guess what he did when his doctor told him he was clinically paranoid? Killed him! Then he killed a hundred thousand other doctors so no one could ever call him a madman again. *A hundred thousand. God*, I can't even picture that many medical professionals. Rubbing the six of us out would be nothing to him. Oh, what if Peters gives them our names?"

"Just stop talking gibberish for a minute, would you?" Jekabs said.

"Yah, let's get organized," Vilz said, using the calm, confiding tone that had lured a number of students to her underground meetings. "This is what we do."

Kārlis had to admit, it was comforting to let Vilz take charge.

"First off, we'll publish this," Vilz said, holding up her freshly typewritten page. "Along with the article about the legs poking out of the ground in the forest."

Kārlis nodded. So far it didn't sound too hard.

"I type the articles. Kārlis gives me some illustrations. Eriks, I need a brute like you to keep watch while Jekabs and me work the printing press. When the printing's done, everybody will distribute the flyers. Get them in the hands of readers *without getting caught*."

Jekabs nodded, fists on hips.

"Distribute the flyers without getting caught," Eriks repeated, eyebrows raised. It sounded more dangerous when Eriks said it.

"Yah. Don't be obvious about it," Vilz said. "Don't look like you're hiding anything either. Just *nonchalantly* drop copies here and there, under doors, in market baskets. Leave a couple around school and in the park and wherever you go."

"Nonchalantly drop copies here and there," Eriks repeated.

A nest of metal hit the floor with a clang that made everybody jump. Sniedze had somehow fallen, knocking pans off the shelf with a fumbling that would've been comic if it hadn't given Kārlis a heart attack.

"Like that for example," Eriks said, dryly. "Nonchalant like Sniedze." Everyone cracked up watching the nitwit try and fail to regain his balance, wobbling amongst the ringing bowls. It felt good to laugh, releasing the panic that had been tamped down and corked up all day.

Jekabs balanced a round pan on an upraised finger and set it twirling above beefy, flour-dusted forearms. "This is the way a Nonchalant does it," he said. He used the word *Nonchalant* like it was a title of respect, a moniker for specially inducted members to an elite society. "Notice the poise, the finesse."

"Right," said Vilz, going along with the play, "and a Nonchalant delivering flyers is a stealthy *kāpost galva*."

"A Nonchalant wears a sharp crease in his fedora," Kārlis said. "That's the look we want."

"Yah, and those black-faced watches you guys have. That's a sign of a Nonchalant."

"And English newspapers."

Everyone seemed pleased at the name. Each tenet of a Nonchalant was voted in with the tip and pass of the flask. The camaraderie made Kārlis feel braver, even somewhat invincible. By God, together they would do something about Peters and their doomed futures. Nobody else would. He'd acclimated already to the danger of the plan.

"A Nonchalant will never be bullied into hiding his Latvian name," someone quipped.

"Never abandon another Nonchalant."

"Never divulge Nonchalant secrets to an outsider."

Kārlis felt competitive and a little tipsy. No one wanted to be the next dolt in line who couldn't add to the code.

"A Nonchalant will never lie to another Nonchalant," one said.

"Or steal his girl."

"Or give up the names of our members, no matter what they do to you."

"We will valiantly defend a fellow Nonchalant."

Vilz was buoyant at the show of solidarity. "This is an auspicious beginning," she said. "Knowing we can trust each other."

Don't trust anyone. Papu's advice echoed unpleasantly in the chambers of Kārlis's memory. He ignored it, driving the Nonchalant vows like a stake into his heart.

"So, everybody's in," Vilz said, looking around the circle. "We are six intrepid Nonchalants!"

"Seven," Hugo said thickly, jutting out his jaw. "Peters. He went down fighting, I'm so proud of him."

"Yah. Peters is one of us."

"He's the chief Nonchalant."

"The epitome of how a Nonchalant should be, Peters."

"Eriks? You look doubtful," Vilz said. "You're in, right?"

Eriks seemed to be staring at something on the other side of the wall, as if the thought he wished to express lurked over there. Finally he said, "Seems to me anyone caught with a copy of your rag is dead meat. If I'm going to risk my neck, I'd rather do it for something that counted, not passing notes."

"I'm listening," Vilz said.

Eriks was breathing loudly.

"Let's torch the goddam Corner House. That hellhole of Commie sadism has got to be put down."

The silly one-liners dried up at once. Kārlis swallowed hard, realizing he'd graduated to swimming in the deep end. He was aware of his own breathing, of the thinness of the pantry walls, and of too much booze buzzing past his ears. He noticed the others had also been jolted by this thunderclap proposition. They seemed to proceed with carefully chosen words.

"And just how would you go about doing that?" asked Jekabs.

"With explosives," Eriks said. "Dynamite. A bomb."

"Not going to be able to get our hands on one of those," Jekabs said.

"At a minimum, we'd need some kind of accelerant," Hugo said. He seemed to be embracing the logistical challenges of arson as a welcome escape from the day's unfathomable emotional crisis. This might be a problem he could actually solve.

"Blow that torture pit to smithereens," Eriks said darkly.

"More likely we could interrupt its operations for an interval," Hugo said.

Vilz's eyes lit up. "Have you heard of a Molotov?"

"Russian Secretary of State," Hugo replied.

"Not the politician," Vilz said. "There's a very cheap, but potent little firebomb named after him. Easy to make. Finns put it to good use last year."

"Something we could concoct ourselves?"

"We just need bottles, rags and some petrol. I think high-proof Vodka would work," Vilz said. "Then we just *nonchalantly* drop a few of those babies in the basement window of the Corner House."

"I like it," Eriks said.

"Lob a few upstairs."

"Yah. All Nonchalant-like."

"That would start something burning. Be hell to put out. Incinerate those devils in their own cage."

"How's that gonna help Peters?" Kārlis said. "What if he's trapped there?"

"Too late to help Peters," Vilz said. "But we can help the next fellow, in Peters's name."

It seemed disloyal to point out any flaws in the proposal. It was now a matter of Nonchalant pride to execute the plan. Otherwise the code of behavior they'd just touted would be exposed as empty words, Peters's tribute mere lip service.

Kārlis felt the sharp horns of dilemma goring him in every direction: dangerous to go down this path, unsafe not to. He drained the flask when it came around. The scheme *could* work. With Eriks's nerve, Hugo's brains, Vilz's connections, Jekabs's practical good sense, and Sniedze staying the hell away, they might get away with such mischief.

"We got the rags," Eriks said, lifting Kārlis's fringed blanket. "Bet we can swipe a case of empty bottles from the alley."

"Where we gonna get that much vodka?"

The ensuing silence was worrisome, threatening to slow their momentum.

"Would denatured alcohol work?" Kārlis asked.

"Yah," said Hugo.

"Well," Kārlis said, "We could *nonchalantly* pick some up at my father's workshop."

Sniedze giggled.

"How soon could we get that?" Vilz asked.

Shrugging, Kārlis said, "No time like the present."

"I'll roll with your idea, because I'm glad you're finally doing something," Vilz said, "not because I think it's better than publishing the truth." She held up her typed page. "One newspaper is worth a thousand firebombs."

Vilz proceeded to lay out the plan. Tonight, Kārlis, Eriks and Sniedze would procure the necessary materials. Vilz, Jekabs and Hugo would print the newsletters, any risk in that having been upstaged by the sabotage plot. They would all meet the next day to assemble what Vilz called Molotov Cocktails. Then they'd roast NKVD for dinner.

The pantry door shot open like a cattle prod to Kārlis's ribs and Mr. Leopolds walked in. Kārlis caught his breath and tried to look natural. Mr. Leopolds was about to grab a can of shortening when he stopped. He plucked the empty flask off the shelf and sniffed the pour spout. Putting his hand on his hip, his eyes took in the circle of them.

"Oy, this makes me very nervous," Mr. Leopolds said, wagging the flask. "You kids, I understand how difficult it is to work through what's happening." He shook his head. "When I was your age I was, well, idealistic. It's a shock to learn that the world is not just." He looked at the flask, seeming frustrated that he couldn't find the words he wanted.

Kārlis liked Mr. Leopolds. He felt bad for plotting revolution on his premises and deceiving him about it. There would be consequences if they were caught. Mr. Leopolds was not a schnook, a word Kārlis had learned from the baker.

"But you have got to understand you cannot be caught drinking, you cannot put one toe out of line!" Mr. Leopolds said. "As it is, this is an illegal assembly. You can't even give the impression you're in some club or fraternity. You'll never understand how a Russian thinks. For that matter, you can't trust anybody."

"Don't worry, Uncle Eli," Jekabs said. "We won't."

"I just think you boys – and Vilz -- all of us -- should get a good night's sleep. Things will look better in the morning."

Kārlis looked at the ground. He heard Eriks say, "We were just going, Mr. Leopolds."

"Don't be seen leaving here all at once," Mr. Leopolds said, as everybody gathered their coats and filed out. "This is a bad situation, that I know. If you kids are having trouble handling this, come back in the morning. Let's have a cup of coffee and talk about it. But until then, well," Mr. Leopolds tapped the flask reproachfully, "promise me you won't do anything reckless."

Night Crawlers. K. Smiltens 1945.

4

ELBOW TO ELBOW WITH ERIKS and Sniedze, Kārlis marched along
Freedom Boulevard, the wind sinking its teeth into his throat. Already
less euphoric about stealing alcohol from his father's leather
workshop, he regretted leaving the toasty cocoon of the bakery. He was
thinking longingly of coffee and bread when Eriks nudged him in the
ribs. A trio of men had come around the corner up ahead across the
street. Without needing to see more, Kārlis felt an overpowering urge
to turn tail and run. That strategy had already saved him from the
clutches of the Corner House. But he stayed in lockstep with Eriks and
Sniedze. If he ran, they would all have to run. He pulled his fedora
lower and clutched his collar, hoping the men would go about their
business and let them pass.

As they drew closer, Kārlis could see the uniforms were not
NKVD green. The men had no insidious red cap badges or weapons.
They looked like city maintenance workers. In fact, they were painters.
One dragged a ladder, another carried buckets, and the third man

dripped paint from a long handled roller. Their monotonous painter chatter faded as the boys reached the corner and turned in unison, with the tight precision of three minnows trying to give the impression they were a bigger fish.

Just when Kārlis remembered to breathe, believing he'd gotten away, Eriks nudged him again. Without taking his hand from his coat pocket, Eriks pointed up to the cloisonné street sign embedded in the building's masonry. Freedom had been changed to Lenin. Grey paint dripped down the stones, the white letters were still shiny wet.

"Whew! That was a close one," Sniedze said, in a thin voice. "But they're just changing the name. Just paint."

Kārlis balled up his fists. "Shut up," he muttered. It was more than just paint.

They ducked into the alley and ran the rest of the way to Pērkons Leather Works. The premises were in pitch black. Kārlis had given up his key, so he intended to enter through the second floor window that his mother always left open a crack. As he studied the target window, snow slid off the nearby eaves landing in the alley with a plop. Jamming his toes in the grout cracks, Kārlis grasped the easy handholds of the rough masonry and scaled the building like a cat. At the second floor, he grabbed the concrete curls of a stone face and balanced his knee on the sill. The window slid open smoothly and he climbed inside, straightening up at one end of a hallway that stretched the length of the apartment.

Down in the alley, Eriks and Sniedze were watching him with craned necks. Kārlis gave them a nod and slid the glass closed noiselessly. Turning to the dark apartment, he watched and listened for the Russian punk who'd been assigned to the Leather Works, supposedly as an apprentice. He passed his mother's tapestries and bookshelves, his sister's collection of folkloric dolls, sensing on them the stench of foreign occupation fondling. Loath to confront the apprentice-spy, he slinked over to the tight wooden stairway that went directly to the workshop and descended, expertly dodging the creaky boards.

It was eerie, being alone in the high-ceilinged workshop where a crew of tradesmen usually hustled to fill his father's orders. Dim light fell on the shop floor making towering stacks of hides cast a gathering of shaggy-monster shadows around the large central cutting surface. Workbenches with dyes and blades, innocently lined up in neat rows by day, now looked weirdly ominous. Kārlis swallowed, grounding himself in the familiar aromas of saddle soap and tobacco. He'd take the denatured alcohol from the cupboard across the room, where massive rotating immersion drums chugged rhythmically as though the workday hadn't ended. It would be a simple errand, he reminded himself.

Then a murmur reached Kārlis's ear making the hair on the back of his neck rise. He looked up to his father's loft-level office where light seeped through cracks in the shutters. Had his father forgotten to turn off the radio? No. Men were up there, behind the closed door speaking in low tones. Kārlis instantly changed his plan, needing to know Papu was okay. He crept along the wall where stairs rose to the loft. At the top he pressed against the office door, listening.

"What is your decision, Mr. Pērkons?"

One of the window slats had closed crookedly, allowing a narrow view to the interior.

Half expecting his father to be hosting an illicit card game, Kārlis gasped at what he saw instead. The desk lamp illuminated Janis Pērkons, still in his bowtie and vest with rolled-up shirtsleeves, bending over a glittering pile of treasure. Lengths of gold chain lay serpentine on the desk amid coins and chunks of molten gold, a yellow heap flecked with jewels. With a jeweler's loupe pressed to his eye, Janis held a tiara to the lamp, scrutinizing diamonds set in the filigree that scattered a brilliant spectral refraction around the tiny triangle of the room visible to Kārlis.

His father shifted behind the desk, suggesting he faced at least two unseen men, black market operators, Kārlis assumed, waiting his decision.

Kārlis held his breath. He wanted to back away unseen, but was suddenly too afraid to move in any direction.

His father, however, set down the tiara unhurriedly. He picked up a gold chain at least two meters long and stretched a section of it against the light, assessing and calculating with a practiced eye.

A set of vulture-like shoulders lurched into the frame, belonging to someone who fingered a brooch and said in an unctuous voice, "You've been wise to diminish your cash position, Mr. Pērkons. Most of my clients are wishing they'd had your foresight in acquiring assets more suitable for the long run. We'll soon be lighting our cigars with *lats.*"

Janis Pērkons took his time answering. "True, Mr. Lapsins. The Russians have imposed a ridiculous exchange rate, impoverishing most of us." Janis returned the loupe to its case and closed it with a methodical snap. Leaning back in his chair, he ran a hand over his goatee, looking thoughtful.

"Mr. Pērkons," Lapsins said. "In our many recent dealings, haven't my articles always proved genuine?"

"Genuinely overpriced," Janis said. He smiled as if he liked Lapsins, and smiled at another corner of the room as if someone else were there. "This is highway robbery!"

Kārlis, suddenly hot, tugged his collar loose. How could his father seem so at ease with these sharks?

Janis withdrew a gold cigarette case from his pocket. It popped open with spring-loaded action as he extended it toward the others, saying, "Personally, though, I'd rather be robbed by you than by the Communists."

"Come now. I like to think I'm providing a valuable service at great personal risk," Lapsins said, accepting a thin brown cigarette.

There was quiet laughter, the flick of a lighter and the ritual passing and puffing. Kārlis stopped watching when a floorboard above his head groaned. He stiffened, looking up. Someone was moving about in the upstairs living quarters. His antennae zeroed in on the stealthy footsteps while, inside the office, the men bantered about volume discounts, ruble versus lat, contraband-carrying surcharges and what the market would bear. They chatted casually, though Kārlis suspected every word was laced with cunning, and they seemed oblivious to the distressing footsteps Kārlis heard approaching.

"So, Mr. Pērkons, what have you decided?"

Kārlis didn't hear the answer. Panicked that an NKVD informant was coming, Kārlis fled down the steps to hide in the workshop. A parting glimpse into the office saw his father absorbed in counting out bills from a large roll of notes. Midway, Kārlis turned back—should he burst into, what appeared to be, a high stakes currency crime to warn his father the spy was coming? No, the marketeers would react rashly. So, he crept back down, determined to forestall whoever was coming, to create a diversion if necessary, giving Papu time to hide the goods.

Near the foot of the stairs, Kārlis crouched behind some pallets while the apartment stairwell creaked under someone's weight. He strained to see who was there, chest clenched so tight he couldn't breathe. When he saw the unmistakable sasquatch-and-elfin figures of Eriks and Sniedze enter the workshop he could've strangled them.

"Eriks. Over here," Kārlis hissed, slicing the air with angry gestures until the two had joined him behind the pallets, Sniedze kneeling beside him. "What're you doing traipsing through the apartment! I told you about the spy. You're supposed to wait in the alley until I let you in."

Eriks who, much to Kārlis's annoyance, remained standing, said, "Yah, yah. We waited. What took so long? We figured something must've happened."

"Quiet. There are people up there with my father right now," Kārlis said, pointing to the loft.

The office door opened with a paralyzing click. A barrel-chested man in a pinstriped suit came out and, hands on hips, surveyed the workshop.

Next out was a clean-shaven fellow in a natty overcoat, the man called Lapsins. He descended the stairs with the spring of someone in expensive shoes. The office lamp went dark and Janis Pērkons exited, pausing to lock the door. He trotted downstairs after Lapsins and the corpulent bodyguard brought up the rear. Business must've concluded to their mutual satisfaction, Kārlis noted, somewhat awed by his father. The entrepreneurs were moving on now, shrewd and discreet as the velvet-feathered flight of owls at night.

Lapsins murmured to Janis as they passed where the boys hid, "They've bagged all the big game-- factories, farms, the press. Then they took over the mid-sized companies and now, they're scraping the barrel, seizing the livelihood of even the small entrepreneur." His voice trailed as they went through the swinging doors that lead to the retail shop and the storefront. "Time to close up shop, Mr. Pērkons. Lay low or get out of town—and by that I mean the country. The situation is far worse than we ever imagined."

Kārlis heard a muffled jingle, the bell on the shop door.

"Whew," Sniedze said after a moment's silence. "Where they going?"

"How should I know," Kārlis said. "*Ak tu kungs*. He might be back at any minute."

"Let's get the juice and get out of here," Eriks said.

Kārlis changed mental gears; he'd digest the transfer of treasure he'd just witnessed later. Carefully passing the cutting table in the dark, he took a key from its nail on the workbench. Eriks and Sniedze followed him back toward the immersion drums where he unlocked a cupboard and began scanning labels on the stocked shelves. "Chromium, ammonium sulphate, lime, ... Here." Denatured alcohol was stored on the lower shelf. He distributed two apiece.

"These are tiny," Eriks said, frowning at the liter-sized, brown bottles.

"What were you expecting? Barrels?"

"As long as I'm sticking my neck out, I might as well go down for a barrel as for a thimble-full."

"No one's going down—" Kārlis said, exasperated. How like Eriks to argue at the most inopportune— "That's the point. And this is considerably more than a thimbleful!"

"We're talking about torching the *kāpost galva* Corner House, not hosting a wiener roast," Eriks said. "We're gonna need more."

"How would we carry—"

"Like this," Eriks said, reaching past Kārlis and clanking several bottles together in each huge paw. He thrust them onto Sniedze, and turned for another grab.

"No. That's too obvious—" Kārlis said, crashing elbows with Eriks as he took them back from the witless Sniedze.

"Who goes there," came a voice.

Kārlis's head spun.

Light flickered across the workshop in a blinding flood. "Halt!" Igor Volkov, the Russian apprentice-spy, was staring at him, chest thrust out, at the cutting table.

Stung at first, to be yelled at on his own turf, Kārlis recovered, blinking. He stepped forward, hoping to screen Eriks and Sniedze, both hunched over clanking bottles behind his back.

"I said Halt," Volkov said. "Don't move." His hands were in plain view and, to Kārlis's relief, weaponless. His brown forelock looked disheveled and his shirt was untucked, like he'd been disturbed from a nap.

What a phony, Kārlis thought, a bitter taste rising in his throat. He was after all, only as old as Kārlis, but wielding the authority of the skull-crushing Soviet regime.

"Halt yourself," Kārlis wanted to say, but didn't. He plucked an awl off the workbench and faced Igor Volkov quietly from the opposite end of the cutting table. The two were similar in height, but the Russian had more muscle.

"So it's you," Volkov said. "What are you doing in cupboard."

"I live here, remember?" Kārlis said. "This is *Pērkons* Leather Works."

"I am superior here, not you," Volkov said. "You are trespasser and thief. Put your hands up."

"I'm the trespasser?" Kārlis said, amazed by the gall. "I'm supposed to be here. My duties require my attention at all hours. Somebody has to check those drums."

"You steal from state," Volkov said, pointing at Kārlis. "You back there," he called from behind the safety of the cutting table. "Step away from storage. What are you hiding?"

Kārlis didn't turn to see, but the clinking of glass added to his growing sense of calamity.

"I said Step Away." As Volkov advanced, a faint, familiar *thwop* came from his feet. Kārlis looked down.

"What in hell—," Kārlis began. Incredulous, he stepped back to see under the table. It took a moment to compute what he saw; it was so unexpected and disgusting. "You're wearing my slippers," Kārlis said, pointing the awl at the spy's feet. He stared at Volkov's eyes, daring him to deny it. "Who are you calling Thief."

A ripple of embarrassment crossed the Russian's face, seeming to knock him off balance for a moment.

"I know your scheme is to colonize the country," Kārlis said, hoping Eriks and Sniedze would pull themselves together while he blathered. "Get rid of us and move into our homes and livelihoods. But even into our shoes!"

"No need to colonize what already belongs to us," Volkov said, arrogance restored.

"That's such a lie," Kārlis said, vaguely concerned he was crossing a line. "You re-writing history?"

"No need to. Look around. Reality is outside of door. Statue of Mother Russia sits in middle of Lenin Boulevard. Is fact."

"The Freedom Monument?" Kārlis said, puffing with heat. "What a pervert you are."

"That's Mother of *Latvia*," Sniedze piped up, from behind Kārlis's elbow with a bulging, clinking rucksack slung over his shoulder.

"Mother *Russia*," Volkov said coolly. "Holding three stars, the Baltics, *in her hands*."

"A lie." Kārlis couldn't stop himself. "You try to look legitimate with rigged elections and changing the names of things in the middle of the night. You're a nation of liars led by a psychopath. And you don't know a *kāpost galva* thing about running a leather works."

Volkov smiled. He had a way of turning up the corners of his mouth while looking deadly.

"I have plenty experience," Igor Volkov said, idly picking up a strap of leather cut for a belt. He doubled it over and jerked the ends, making it snap. "You know Kalnins Bridge & Iron, I think?"

Kārlis's mouth went dry. Peters Kalnins's family business.

"Thought you might," Volkov said, eyes narrow. "Overfed fascists. Believe me, they were not what they appeared to be. I report them. The Cheka is pleased. Sends me here."

Kārlis started to feel shaky. Was this ratfink somehow responsible for Peters's arrest? And next he'd report Papu? He leaned against the cutting table to shore up his nerves.

Volkov stood there stretching and curling his fingers on the leather strap, looking titillated by Kārlis's sick reaction.

With a couple of deep breaths Kārlis was no longer shaking. Hatred was making him calm and murderous. He ignored the tugging on his sleeve.

"Let's go," Sniedze said, smelling of urine. "He must've did something to Peters. Come on."

"You in the big coat," Volkov shouted, looking toward Eriks. "Come out here with your hands up."

Eriks complied, emerging from the storage area, straightening to his full height.

Seeing Eriks's mass, Volkov took a step back, his pupils shrinking to pinpricks. "Stop right there," he ordered. "Show me your pockets."

Eriks looked strangely complacent as he opened the edges of his overcoat. "It's camel," he said, pivoting from side to side like a coat model. "The color is called camel. It's an alpaca blend, herringbone weave, double breasted wool number from Stockholm."

"His family owns the finest store in Riga," Sniedze blurted stupidly.

"Is that so?" Volkov said. "Well, it's mine now. Put it on the table."

Kārlis expected a mouthy retort. Instead, he saw Eriks's eyes go dark, a flex in his oversized frame.

Volkov noticed it too. "All I have to do is whistle," he said tightly." The Cheka will hunt you down. At your finest store in Riga."

Eriks walked to Volkov's end of the table. About to remove his coat, he seemed to change his mind. "But what if you can't whistle?" he said. "What if your jaw is pulverized to slop so you can't tattle on Peters or anybody else ever again?"

"You can't be so stupid you'd threaten me," Volkov said, eyes flitting sideways.

With a couple of giant strides, Eriks was behind the Russian, blocking his escape with arms spread like gaping jaws.

Kārlis tightened his grip on the awl and also closed in, determined Volkov not pass him without first getting stabbed in the throat. He felt like he wasn't in his head, but was witnessing the scene from the rafters, watching himself and Eriks cut out a cancerous tumor.

Volkov's eyes looked like white plates, seeing too late he was surrounded.

Do it. Be rid of him. A chemical in Kārlis's blood urged killing him now, fast and final. The opportunity wouldn't come again.

A muffled jingle came from the storefront, dully tugging Kārlis back within the boundaries of his usual self. Killer Kārlis kept screaming to slay or be slain.

Eriks also seemed in suspended animation, a bombshell in midair.

Kārlis's father pushed through the swinging doors, taking in the lit up workshop and the cornered apprentice-spy.

"*Sveikee.* Everybody," Janis Pērkons boomed, breaking up the testosterone vortex with a cheery greeting.

Seeing his father instantly reminded Kārlis of who he was.

No one moved for a second. Chests heaved.

Kārlis lowered his awl. He was not a murderer.

Janis acted like nothing was amiss. "It's good of you boys to help out in the shop this evening," he said, taking center stage, thumbs in his vest pockets. "I like that initiative." He nodded at each of them. "It's an extremely busy time. Seems everybody wants to buy a suitcase." To Volkov he said, "I see you've met my son."

Janis grabbed Kārlis in a rowdy bear hug. Rubbing his knuckles over his head, a gesture Kārlis hated, Janis whispered, "What's wrong with you! Don't antagonize him." Kārlis was released, a moment later, to find Eriks and Volkov still locked in icy stares.

Janis said, "Boys, Igor has recently moved here from—er, Russia. You're practically the same age! Probably have much in common." Janis stood between them all, sizing up the situation as if deciding which bill of goods to sell.

"He said the Freedom Monument represents Mother Russia," chirped Sniedze, pointing at Igor.

Janis raised his eyebrows. "You boys are worked up about a *statue*? That's funny," he said, shaking his head. "When I was seventeen we got a bang out of horseracing."

"It's mother of Latvia," Sniedze said, piously.

"Oh, who's to say," Janis said, a gruff edge to his voice. "Let's drop it."

Igor Volkov lifted his eyes, as if he alone could see something funny in the roof beams. "Your son is stealing inventory," he said.

Kārlis met his father's gaze, sobered by the concern he saw there, when his head exploded, hit so hard his skull lifted off his neck.

He dropped the awl, gasped, saw sparks of light, fumbled, clutching the cutting table.

"He has smart mouth," Volkov said, cradling the knuckles of his right hand. Then his fist hooked deep and hard into Kārlis's belly.

Suddenly Kārlis's face was on the cutting table, viewing the wood grain from the other end of a slick, throbbing nose. Shocked, hunched over, he couldn't pull air into his lungs.

Volkov was talking.

Noisy protests, his father, friends.

Words didn't register. He was going to puke as soon as breath returned.

The belt lashed his face like a fist of fire.

Kārlis tried to defend his face but arms held guts. He couldn't see. Eyes blurred, hot, stinging.

"Next time I tell you to do something, Citizen, hop to it."

Kārlis tried. Waved his hands feebly in front of himself.

The backs of his knees buckled. His body dropped to the floor, humiliation passing fast under a kick to the kidney and the lash, this time ripping his ear, burning. Slash at shoulder dulled by coat. Kick to head jarred brain, teeth clattered. Curl up.

Volkov whipped Kārlis's head in a furious onslaught.

Kārlis curled tighter. Was that him screaming? Blows pelted his back. Acute, throbbing deep inside, horribly wrong.

"No, Eriks!" His father's voice. "Don't touch him or we're all dead!"

Something about slippers.

"I said Are These Your Slippers?" Volkov cried. Another kick. "What?"

Torrent in head blurred sounds.

Sniedze was shrill, "Stop him, he'll kill him."

His father, shouting, "—some misunderstanding, I apologize—"

"What?" yelled Volkov.

Kārlis braced, but the whip split his face. He sobbed.

"No," Kārlis said.

"What?"

"No," Kārlis said. "Yours. Your slippers." He was crying.

Pray the beating would stop.

Answered by a kick in the guts.

Lolling head, light through blood-bleary slits. "Your slippers," Kārlis moaned.

"That's what I thought," Volkov said, standing over his head.

Ceiling swirl. Father watching, holding back Eriks.

Volkov folded the strap. "Get them out of here," he told Janis, snapping the leather.

"You gonna be all right, Mr. Pērkons?" Sniedze's high-pitched voice. "You're awful white."

"I'm—" his father said, "Just get Kārlis to a doctor."

Kārlis heard feet moving through the cement under his ear. He didn't want to move. Hands grabbed his armpits. He screamed going up, limp and soaked. Heart drumming in ears, muffled the jangle of keys, the door scraping open to the alley.

He was ushered into the freezing night air on the unevenly matched shoulders of Eriks and Sniedze. He felt he was flying, then slamming back into his body with the throb of each cell and nerve.

"I could've stopped him, Mr. Pērkons," Eriks said. "You should've let me."

"That—that boy is a representative of the Soviet regime." His father's low voice was trembling. "If anything happens to him, the Cheka will kill us."

Kārlis felt his father's hand on his shoulder.

"Now that that's out of his system," Janis said, "it's possible he won't harm us further. He doesn't matter."

Kārlis couldn't lift his head or return his father's goodbye. It hurt to raise his feet over the icy sludge of the alley. Every step was an ordeal, a marathon. Eriks supported his slow progress while Sniedze strove not to get in the way. Finally they turned out of the alley, where the sidewalks of Lenin Boulevard were smoother. Eriks decided it would be faster to carry Kārlis on his back, his hands under Kārlis's knees. Kārlis grasped his friend's neck and braced himself for the jarring pain of Eriks's stride.

"Someone's there. Up ahead," Sniedze said, stopping cold.

"It's just the painters again, see?" Eriks said. "There's the guy dragging the ladder."

"Yah," Sniedze said. "There's a sign—" Sniedze stopped with a sharp intake of breath. "They're not painters. Look. Oh God. Oh, God," Sniedze whimpered.

"Quiet," Eriks said.

"I'm not going past that," Sniedze said with a tinge of hysteria.

Eriks shrank against the side of the building. "No. We'll backtrack," he whispered, "and go another way."

The night was so quiet, even the wind had died to a light breeze. Kārlis couldn't imagine why Eriks was spooked. He opened his eyes the best he could and strained to see. From the glow of a streetlamp, a white rectangle shone from across the street, under some trees in the park. It looked like a sign, swaying. Trying to read it, the dark setting came into focus. The sign was posted on a man hanging by the neck.

"What's it say," Sniedze said.

Eriks whispered, "Capitalist."

Alone in the workshop, Igor Volkov stood shaking, titillated, breathing hard, and feeling magnificent.

Pērkons returned from the alley. Shoulders slumped under the fancy suit, he rolled the workshop door shut and locked it. Turning rigidly, he cast a searing glare at Igor.

Igor met the hateful stare. How dare Pērkons judge him? The capitalist Pērkons, if anybody, should understand opportunities had to be made from whatever at hand, no half measures. In Pērkons's echelon, you must be the one kicking, not the fool cringing on the ground. Igor was herculean, increased in power daily. But Latvians were a weak, spoiled species. He vowed to punish them.

Finally Pērkons broke eye contact and went to a cupboard.

"Weakness is a plague," Igor told Pērkons's back. "Weak people don't deserve rights. They must be checked in order to prevent future generations from falling into degeneracy."

To Igor's astonishment, the wealthy man dropped to his knees and wiped blood off the floor.

Igor turned to climb the stairs, unhurried, to the sleeping quarters, unafraid of reprisals. Scuffing in Kārlis Pērkons's deerskin and boiled wool slippers, Igor's toes throbbed after jamming Kārlis's ribs and soft belly, pleasantly, a sensation lost when wearing boots. But next time there would be boots. New, heavy duty, Latvian-stomping boots.

Igor quartered in the son's room, at the end of the hall hung with weavings. Next assignment he would require the master's bedroom. Pērkons had a king's bed, furs on the floor, and a door to a private running-water bathtub. But Igor was drawn to the son's room with sick fascination. Same age as the spoiled "artist", he and Kārlis Pērkons occupied separate realities. Snooping through the rotten little prick's belongings had given Igor an outrageous new view of the bourgeoisie that proved the true extent of the cruel injustice he'd suffered.

Igor closed the bedroom door and stood before the dresser mirror. Symmetrical facial features, cheeks blazing, lips full, he averted eyes from the handsome reflection of a superior being inexplicably and unjustly outcast from human community. "When I get the army uniform, all will see my true magnificence," he told himself. His talent was wasted in the Komsomol, the Communist youth helpers. Anger for not yet being selected by the military, darkened his mood.

His gaze riveted to a photograph stuck under the mirror frame. The stiff paper emitted a whiff of chemical fixative as Igor examined it. God Almighty. Did Pērkons have another house? That must be where the wife and girl were sent. Stalwart stone building blocks, it was an enormous, country manor on an expanse of grass and flowers. Over the balcony leaned a gang of feisty-looking young men, Igor's age, lined up from tallest to shortest. He'd never seen an image so shiny, sharp, stylish, modern.

Igor was gripped and incensed that Pērkons owned such a camera. The value must be astronomical. Since Pērkons, the blatant profligate, was not a photographer by trade, the camera must be a toy or hobby, used to flaunt his lavish excess and goad rivals to jealousy. Igor had been examining the photograph earlier that night, seething resentment, when he'd heard creaking from downstairs and policed the premises. He'd not only caught Kārlis Pērkons stealing, he'd recognized his cohort thieves from this picture. He'd thought of the picture while kicking Kārlis Pērkons senseless. Perhaps the photograph was why he'd kept kicking.

He recognized one face mugging for the camera. Knowing the guy made Riga feel like a small village Igor had already mastered. The tall one was Peters Kalnins. Igor knew this because the Komsomol had assigned him to Kalnins Bridge & Iron, and he'd reported captain-of-the-hockey-team Peters to the NKVD as a Harmful Element. Next to him was the dangerous oaf he'd just seen downstairs. Only instead of the coveted coat he wore a leafy Latvian holiday hat. Igor was determined to know that one's name. He could demand Pērkons tell him the name, or track the boy through the family-owned luxury store touted in the foolish boast. Next in the line of enemies were two with dark hair, arms around each other in horseplay. One muscled, one effeminate. Hmm. They were unknown to Igor. He scorned the next, the white-haired boy who stared down the lens with a cerebral conceit. Then stood Kārlis Pērkons, whose head Igor had just used as a football. Igor smirked at the wry insolent expression seen through the camera. Pērkons's bloody face was not so cocky now. Last was the runt of the pack. He'd also been downstairs tonight, screaming like a little girl.

The photograph had a profound effect on Igor, underscoring his understanding of how the world worked in hierarchies. Some people were better than others, more admirable than everyone else, having a better time and, like these young men, probably enjoying pleasurable sex lives with beautiful blond Latvian girls. Igor permitted a desperate fantasy. He imagined himself on that balcony, standing at the prestigious end, the tallest one of all.

His mouth soured at reality. He could steal Kārlis Pērkons's shoes, hang a smart army uniform in another man's closet, but he would never be admitted to that balcony, never wear the casual expression that bespoke the confidence of belonging, the look he could see even on the runt's freckled face. Igor wanted to rip that photograph into a million shreds, but stayed his hand. He would do better. He would destroy those pictured. He could do it. He would crush those boys like the gravel on his path to eminence. He imagined the balcony after what it deserved, a blood bath. His hand trembled as he shoved the picture back under the mirror frame. He wanted to do horrible things, wanted to inflict pain on all gentry... wanted to kill them all slowly, wanted to strip the skins off their flesh.

5

December 22, 1940

It was still dark the next morning when Janis Pērkons rolled the workshop doors open. Cold air stung the freshly shaved skin around his goatee as he looked into the alley. His two employees were already out there shoveling. Edgars, his devoted master craftsman, and Guntis, the dapper retail clerk, spread snow over the bald and slushy spots to prepare a uniform surface for the arrival of the sledge.

Edgars exhaled sharply. "Oh it's you, Mr. Pērkons," he said. "I thought you were, you know, the *apprentice*."

"He's still asleep," Janis said. "Big night." Last night he'd allowed a Soviet hoodlum to lash his son's face and kick him senseless. The memory was agonizing.

Janis grabbed a shovel, as if manual labor might work the remorse from his spirit. He reviewed the event incessantly and still didn't see what he could've done differently. Bodily injuries could heal. But if that Russian punk had a scratch or a bruise or even a bad taste in his mouth when he reported to his NKVD superiors... Were the rumors of summary execution overblown? Janis didn't want to find out.

"This is good," Edgars said, gathering the shovels and heading inside. "Don't worry, Mr. Pērkons. We'll load those pallets so fast it'll be like they were never here."

Janis nodded approval, looking up and down the alley. There was no sign of the buyer. He checked his pocket watch. Chest bound with worry, Janis lit a cigarette and paced, turning his mind from his son to easier calculations. What cash might be squeezed from the remaining inventory? Could he get away with selling the tools and the drums? Could he find a trustworthy buyer? The state would be watching closely, as leather production was essential to transportation, to soldiering, to war. On the other hand, divesting the capital equipment would stop the revenue stream. He didn't want to do that prematurely, just because of nerves. Hold the course. Maybe he had more time.

An indistinct groan and the beat of horse hooves made him look down the alley where a dark shape grew larger, the buyer's sledge. Janis threw down his cigarette and adjusted wire-rimmed spectacles.

"Let's make a deal," Janis said.

Edgars rolled the workshop doors open slowly, avoiding the screech.

The sledge was suddenly there; two horses pulling a triangular rig on wide iron runners. Janis recognized the driver, a longstanding customer, and directed him to the loading bay. Edgars and Guntis hustled out pallets of leather goods and secured the cargo. In the sensory rush that peaks during the commission of a capital offense, Janis stepped on the runner and said to the driver. "Your next order will be ready in a fortnight."

One of the horses whinnied loudly and stamped.

"No," the driver said, looking up and down the alley, forehead glistening with sweat. "No, we can't do this again."

Janis hid his disappointment.

"Boots. Holsters. Harnesses. Saddle bags. It's all there," Edgars said, thumping the stacked pallets. "We've thrown in assorted straps and hides."

The driver held out a thick envelope.

Adrenaline pumped as Janis took it, briefly thumbing the contents. He nodded at the driver and they parted with claps on the back.

Edgars helped turn the horses into the alley. Forceful white streams of condensation billowed from the animals' nostrils as they pulled away. Then he rolled the doors together.

Janis watched the sledge grow smaller as possibly his last customer faded into the half-light of a morning that held dim prospects for brightening. He checked the other direction. No one was there. Stepping inside the workshop, Janis rubbed his hands vigorously. Edgars closed the door behind him, snapping the lock. It appeared they hadn't been caught. Breathing deeply, the fragrances of leather and Neatsfoot oil soothed Janis's tight chest. Composed, he peeled a slab of bills from the payment envelope and gave it to Edgars.

The old man's hands trembled as he pocketed the money.

Guntis then reached for his cut, but froze midway, his eyes glued to something over Janis's shoulder.

Janis turned. The informant, Igor Volkov, was leaning against the wall watching, eyelids at half-mast. Janis hadn't heard him come down the stairs. He could've seen the whole deal.

Pushing the pad of cash into Guntis's hand, Janis demonstrated that they were to act like they had nothing to hide.

Volkov ambled over, eyes widening with interest.

Pivoting abruptly, Guntis fled through the swinging doors to the retail shop. Edgars was suddenly absorbed with a half-finished suitcase splayed over the cutting table.

"What's going on here?" Volkov said.

Janis cleared his throat. "People can't get enough of Edgars's luggage," he said, thinking fast how to placate the informant, to stop his going to his superiors. "In the old days we'd say Business is Booming."

Janis cut another stack of bills from the envelope with the same measured movements he'd done for Edgars and Guntis, and handed it to Volkov. "From each according to his ability, to each according to his need," Janis said, bandying a Communist motto.

Volkov was inscrutable. Janis found it impossible to comprehend the Russian mind, but if it was the glint of greed enlivening those black eyes, then Janis could speak his language.

Finally, to Janis's relief, Volkov grabbed the cash. When he did, Janis saw his hand was red and swollen from beating Kārlis.

Volkov folded the bills and slid the wad into his trouser pocket.

Edgars struck a rivet and it rang like a bell.

Disguising his loathing, Janis extracted tobacco from his vest and offered Volkov a smoke.

Volkov took a cigarette, eyes lingering on the gold cigarette case.

Janis scraped a wooden match across the cutting table and held the flame out to Volkov before he lit his own.

"Igor," Janis said, "like you, I started as an apprentice."

Volkov was still staring at the gold case.

"The satisfaction of creating something with your hands is at the core of this business," Janis said, spinning the cigarette case on the cutting table. The whirling gold seemed to mesmerize the young Communist, who watched it silently. "I suggest you get comfortable in the workshop today," Janis said. "Make a belt and a few simple items for yourself." Janis felt ill at the memory of the belt lashing Kārlis's face, but he kept on buttering. "With a bit of practice you can even make yourself some slippers." Janis bit his tongue. He recalled slippers had somehow been a point of contention in last night's brawl. He knew that the past decade in Russia had seen an acute shortage of leather, which led to a government ban on the private production of shoes. Russians could only purchase poor quality state-made shoes, which fell apart quickly. Had his son hit some footwear raw nerve that had nearly cost him his life?

"Anyway," Janis said, exhaling a stream of smoke, "Learn from the master. Edgars here can make anything out of leather."

"Is that so!" Volkov was at the workbench in a blink, nearly knocking Edgars off balance. "Can you make stew from a belt?" He fingered the laid out leather and bore into the old craftsman with his black eyes. "It's culinary specialty where I come from."

Edgars shrank back, bewildered, his craggy face creased in shock.

Volkov poked Edgars in the chest with a forefinger. "Since you can make anything, I demand you prepare belt stew, old man. And it better be tender because you are going to eat it."

"No need to be repulsive," Janis shouted, outraged by the abuse. He and Edgars exchanged looks. They were dealing with a fiend.

"As for you, cobbler," Volkov spat, rounding on Janis, "I require a pair of boots, strong, shiny, superior boots. As tribute to dear Comrade Stalin, the workmanship must be the best anyone has ever seen."

Janis nodded his head. Not so much agreeing to the boots, but in understanding that he was not submitting merely to state police, as if the NKVD weren't bad enough. This individual was sick in the head. He pulled a deep drag of smoke. There was no percentage in being furious with a lunatic, and no way to predict his moves.

"And don't bother tutoring me about your skins, Citizen," Volkov rebuked. "This foul, ragged shoe shop is just a temporary assignment until I can join the army. That's a career for men. Not making things people wear under their feet."

"You're right, of course," Janis said, impressed by the civility of his own voice. "Comrade." With a parting nod he turned to go to his office.

He left the gold case on the cutting-table altar, hopefully sufficient sacrifice to cover the morning's free-enterprising sins.

Climbing the stairs to the loft felt like scaling a mountain. Janis closed the door behind him and leaned against it, wrestling his collar loose. He calmed himself by looking at the photograph of his family. *Anna, Kārlis and Biruta*. The reasons for everything he did. Breath flowed again.

Suddenly Janis was struck by the memory of last night's meeting with the gem dealer. He hadn't thought about it once since walking into a shit storm between the kids and that junior representative of the NKVD. Unlocking the desk drawer, he was relieved to see the velvet bag of treasure where he'd left it.

Plopping in the desk chair, he unlaced his right boot. Edgars had crafted these boots according to Janis's specifications with secret compartments in the heel, accessed from the inside. He filled the heel compartment with jewels, pushed it closed, and replaced the inner sole. The knee-high fleece lining concealed long, slender pouches. He filled them with half the gold chains, adjusted the fleece lining and re-laced the boot tightly. Nothing was visible. He stashed the remainder of the gold and the cash from the morning sale in the other boot.

Minutes later he emerged from his office wearing his fur hat and overcoat, and locked the door.

The workshop was empty when he came down. The cutting table bare, the offering accepted. Maybe that bought more time.

Janis passed through the swinging doors to find Edgars standing in the showroom looking funereal.

"He left a minute ago," Edgars said. "The apprentice. Wish I knew where he was going."

Janis shook his head, not knowing if having the spy hanging around the premises was more or less worrisome than not knowing his whereabouts.

Guntis was refreshing the merchandise in the window with the same pride he'd always taken in the task. The display of boots, suitcases and equestrian tack looked, to Janis, like a friend on his deathbed. Pērkons Leather Works, decades of sweat and sacrifice, for what? Janis moved leadenly, a heaviness that had nothing to do with the gold in his boots.

"Good day, Mr. Pērkons," Edgars said as he left, ever his supporter.

Bells jingled as Janis closed the wood-framed glass door behind him.

He'd barely gone ten steps before thin trembling fingers grabbed his arm. "Mr. Pērkons!" said a scarecrow of a man, bony and ragged, with straw-colored hair.

Catching his breath, Janis saw the scarecrow push something in his face. His eyes focused on a gold band, probably a wedding ring.

Scarecrow whispered hoarsely, "Someone said you'd give me a fair price for this."

Someone said. Janis recoiled at the words, pushing the stranger's arm away.

Someone said rang in his head like a fire alarm.

"Must be a mistake," Janis said, looking around to see who was watching.

"Please sir," the scarecrow persisted.

"You'd do better keeping the gold," Janis whispered, chest pumping.

"I've got to buy potatoes." Desperate eyes flashed at Janis. "They want cash. We've got to eat. Take it. Take it," the man said, pushing the ring on Janis. It fell in his pocket.

The seconds required to pull off a number of bills while keeping his roll out of sight, seemed like interminable exposure in the public square. Janis looked around furtively as he paid the man.

Stalking away, Janis's chest was bound up with anger at himself for being caught off guard. Some fool had endangered his painstakingly wrought plans, exploiting a tendency he had to help others. Everyone was out for himself, Janis saw, bristling, every man a threat. Janis steeled up, trying to forget the desperation in the man's eyes.

Sympathy was unaffordable.

He couldn't help everyone. Janis saw with sadness that his foresight rent a chasm between himself and the ill prepared, separating him from most of his countrymen.

Kāpost galva Russians. *Kāpost galva* wedding rings, filthy lifeblood of the black market. The band weighed in his pocket like the headstone of a mass grave.

The sidewalk was filling as the bleak light of morning took hold of the neighborhood. A line of people stood outside the grocery store though it wasn't open yet. In the cafe, men sipped little cups of strong coffee while standing at tall counters. The tailor waved at Janis through the lighted window of his shop, his mouth full of pins, reworking a jacket on a dress form. The bookseller wore a glazed, vacant expression as he leaned against the doorframe of his near-empty store that had recently been purged of all inappropriate titles.

Janis did a double take at the corner. The street name had changed overnight, from Freedom to Lenin. How fitting. He barely recognized his neighborhood. More and more storefronts were vacant, abandoned. Janis imagined each darkened door meant an arrest, a deportation or, if rumors were true, an execution. It was only a matter of time before Pērkons Leather Works would get a visit from the Cheka. He continued down the block, stony as the gargoyles perched above him.

"Announcement! Announcement!" came an amplified voice from a tinny sounding public address system.

Janis stopped mid-step. He didn't move, except to turn in the direction of the voice.

A military-type stepped on a small, impromptu platform on the sidewalk so everyone else was eye level to his tall black boots as they gathered around him. It was becoming a regular choreography on Freed– Lenin Boulevard.

Janis and other passersby waited obediently, listening.

"Citizens are required to attend all scheduled labor rallies," the speaker said, scanning the crowd. "There we proclaim the equality and brotherhood of nations." He slapped a black riding crop into the open palm of his glove. "We will show the world how, since the Latvian nation expressed the ardent wish to join the USSR's fraternal family of nations and the Supreme Soviet unanimously agreed to accept that request, the Soviet and Latvian flags now fly side by side."

The crowd was silent. A couple of people clapped.

"Side by side," Janis thought. "Everybody's happy."

"Citizens are required to attend all rallies in support of the fight for a better future, a fight for the ideals of Marx, Engels, Lenin and Stalin." He slapped the whip, watching the reaction of the audience like a hawk sizing up rodents.

Clearly the purpose of the speech was to identify dissenters, the next candidates for purging. So Janis hid his disgust, trying to look mindless and blend in with the anonymous mass.

"I appeal to the working people of Riga to be helpful in the detection of hostile elements," the speaker concluded with a final smack of the riding crop against his boots.

The crowd was dismissed and shuffled off.

"You there! You!" The speaker descended the platform with alacrity. "I want to see your identity papers!" He stalked past Janis to detain a portly, older man wearing a fur lapel and a black band on his fedora. The gentleman looked flustered, obediently accessing pockets to produce his papers.

Janis moved away in terror-relief, struck by the capricious, bullying regime that stopped one man for a spot search and let another go. He slouched and slowed his usual brisk pace to blend in with the crowd. Head down, he boarded a streetcar and found a seat by the window.

Janis wanted to patronize an underground coin dealer twenty blocks away, irked that last night the gem trafficker had got the better of him. Passing the Freedom Monument en route, he twisted in his seat to admire Mother of Latvia, who'd been threatened with the wrecking ball. She towered above the surrounding treetops in her green gown of oxidized copper, the troublemaker. Guards patrolled her travertine pedestal, forbidding newlyweds to lay flowers there. She persisted in reminding everybody that Latvia was a sovereign nation. But her stoic eyes accused Janis of betraying his son for the sake of keeping the doors to business open.

Turrets and spires overshadowed the twisty cobblestone streets leading to the coin dealer, who operated from an antique shop in the medieval heart of Old Riga. The stone faces and statuary carved into the tall, narrow buildings didn't impart their usual wisdom-of-the-centuries to Janis as he lingered, beleaguered, at a nearby cafe. For nearly two hours he'd observed the antique shop and its visitors. Finally he got up the nerve to go in with his illegal proposition. The dealer swiftly sold him ten United States Golden Eagles, each with a face value of twenty dollars. He pocketed the gold with his loose change and exited the antique shop, his chest hard as stone.

It was around two in the afternoon and the sun would soon be setting.

He rode the streetcar back to his usual stop and walked the remaining blocks toward the Leather Works. Every street sign he passed now bore the name Lenin. Was it just yesterday the street was Freedom? He was exhausted.

"Mr. Pērkons!" Snip Cepurnieks, the tailor, was calling from the door of his shop. "Come back and have a cup of coffee with me."

"That would be excellent," Janis said.

He followed Cepurnieks into his shop and behind the counter. They passed bolts of fabric, a sewing machine, and a large mirror as they walked to the rear of the shop. Overstuffed armchairs surrounded a coffee percolator bubbling on a dainty woodstove. Wool gabardine, pinned in the shape of a suit jacket, hung on a tailor's mannequin. One section of wall was covered with layers of newspaper, making a pinboard in which pins, needles, and scissors were stuck.

The tailor chatted about the frigid weather while Janis hung up his overcoat.

Janis accepted a hot cup of coffee and a light for his cigarette and sat back in the armchair.

"Many of my customers seem to be missing," Cepurnieks said, extracting a pin from the pinboard and inserting it deftly into the jacket, repeating the motion over and over. "The city officials have been dismissed and replaced by, well, jailbirds. People with little regard for the decorum of public office, no sense of style." He sighed.

"Latvia may never again see the exquisite couture of my former clientele, and that's a damn shame."

Janis was uneasy with the conversation. It was illegal to criticize Communist officials, even their fashion sense. "I haven't given it much thought," he said.

Cepurnieks swooshed his creation off the mannequin with a flourish, and strode to the sewing machine where he positioned the jacket under the needle.

Janis sipped coffee and watched cigarette smoke swirl around the headless dummy. The yellowed news articles from the pinboard caught his eye. There was a photo of Adolf Hitler, triumphant after his blitzkrieg invasion of Poland, old news; and one of Josef Stalin in full military regalia. The two dictators reminded Janis of giant chess players manipulating smaller countries over Europe's checkerboard, millions of destroyed lives incidental to the game.

Cepurnieks raised his voice over the drone of the sewing machine. "The only people who can afford a good suit now want to wear military uniforms. But I tell you, a well-tailored uniform in itself advances a man through the ranks. Look how the raspberry piping on the collar and cuffs here adds zip to this olive green wool."

The coffee was bracing. Seeing that Cepurnieks was thoroughly engrossed at the sewing machine, Janis loosened the laces of his boots and added the newly acquired gold.

Cepurnieks chattered on, "I'll pull through this. The Communists don't want my shop. Factories, farms, publishers, yah, of course. But I'm an owner-operator, a one-man show. They'll leave me alone. Hold the course, that's my recommendation. This mess will blow over."

Raising an eyebrow at Janis, Cepurnieks said, "Tell me, Mr. Pērkons, how did you know to sell your holdings while prices were high?"

It had been obvious to Janis. Last year sixty thousand ethnic Germans had sold their properties and left the country. Something was up. He'd followed suit. Then, Boom. The Soviets had come in like it had all been pre-arranged. Janis shrugged. "Lucky, I guess."

"It's businessmen like you, Mr. Pērkons, who have outside employees and the means of production that the Communists want," the tailor said, "Or don't want, however you look at it. They say you are exploiting the working class. That you're an Enemy of the People." Cepurnieks spoke around a mouthful of pins. Clanging bells alerted the tailor to someone at the front door. Excusing himself, he went to the counter.

Janis blew smoke, perturbed to be considered an Enemy of the People when all he did was take risks on behalf of others and work his tail off. Of course, he knew it applied to anyone who doubted the rightness of the Party Line. He sipped his coffee, until loud unruly voices arrested the cup halfway to his lips.

The men who'd entered the shop had breached the front counter and were approaching where he sat. Janis jettisoned his cigarette in his coffee cup and hid at the side of the room behind a large mirror. Peering through bolts of fabric he saw three NKVD agents pushing a whimpering, disheveled woman out of view of the public, toward where Janis had been sitting.

Cepurnieks acknowledged the tear-streaked, shaking woman was a customer, admitting he'd finished a remnant dress for her the previous day.

Janis's eyes were drawn to the guns. Each Chekist wore one within a quick grab. That's what made him feel like a bug about to be squished.

"Citizen Cepurnieks," said the NKVD, "this person informs us that you have willfully mutilated the image of General Secretary Stalin."

"What? No, Comrade! Never! I swear!" Cepurnieks said, aghast. "Madam, what is this?"

"Rebellion against the People," cut in the NKVD, "in person or in effigy, is against the law. Hostile elements are not tolerated." He twisted the woman's arm.

"It's there," she screamed, pointing to the newspapered pinboard.

Another agent strode over to inspect the board. There, amidst hundreds of pins, one had pierced the picture of General Secretary Josef Stalin, between the eyes. An ugly smile crossed the agent's face. "Citizen Cepurnieks, you did this?"

"I, well, I'm a tailor," Cepurnieks stammered. "It was nothing intentional. I don't even notice those articles. That's just where I keep my pins." He turned to the woman. "What did you tell them?"

"I saw you do it. I reported you." She was shrill. "I know how this works! You were testing me—testing my loyalty. You mutilate Stalin's picture in front of me and then you turn *me* in if I don't report it."

"Good God," Cepurnieks said, looking horrified. "Please, this is a mistake. I meant no harm. I beg you to give me another chance." His chest was heaving. "I can help you."

Janis's heart was pounding so hard he thought everyone in the shop would hear it.

"I'm loyal but I know people who aren't," the tailor said, wide-eyed and shiny with sweat. "I can give you names."

A scapegoat. The tailor would use him as a scapegoat, Janis saw, edging along the wall toward the back of the shop. He was afraid opening and closing the door to the alley would give away his presence, but the scraping noise seemed muffled by a shot, a scream and hysterical sobs.

Outside Janis stumbled into a snowdrift. He thought he'd vomit, but cold air quelled the urge. His steps toward the back entrance of Pērkons Leather Works were ragged, uneven. Holding his guts as he ran, he glimpsed over his shoulder. There was a figure in the alley, but nothing to do with him. Ducking into his workshop, he clutched the doorframe, gasping, teeth chattering. Only then did he ask himself why the door to the alley was open.

They had come. His heart dropped to his stomach like a chunk of ice. Time was up. His loft level office door was flung wide. Inside, a uniformed man was dumping the contents of drawers. Igor Volkov stood with him, erect and rapturous.

Guntis was below, wringing his hands. Janis might have run, but he followed the clerk's gaze to the cutting table where two men flanked Edgars. One held the old man's arms behind his back; a second held the photograph of Janis's family in front of Edgars' face, tapping the frame with a pistol.

Janis's knees went weak. Finally he found the strength to step forward.

"Comrade Officer," he said, "I'm the one you want. That man is a citizen and a worker."

Three sets of NKVD eyes burned into Janis as the Communists pushed Edgars away and rounded on him.

"You are Janis Pērkons, claiming to be the owner of Pērkons Leather Works?"

Janis's ears still were ringing from the gunshot fired at the tailor, the preview to his fate.

"Yah, Comrade. I am," he said. It was over now.

He tuned out the ranting of the NKVD agent. The thug held his family photograph. Focus on their faces, he thought. *Anna, Kārlis, and Biruta.* Janis's chest rose and fell more easily as he thought of them. He regretted not standing up for his son last night. He would rather that have been Kārlis's last memory of him.

The sentimental distraction ended when the agent threw the photograph down, speaking rapidly while glass shattered. "By the authority vested in me by the USSR and by General Secretary Stalin I hereby nationalize this establishment in the name of the People of the USSR. I order you to place the entire contents of your pockets on the counter."

The Communists puffed up, as if hoping Janis might resist.

"Empty your pockets," echoed one of them.

Janis didn't argue. He fished his keys and some loose change from his trousers, setting them on the counter with the deliberation a man would summon for his last mortal act. He pulled his watch from his vest pocket, the chain rustled as he tugged it loose and laid it down. There was a package of tobacco and a clip of folded bills in his inside coat pocket and—oh, the gold ring.

One guy knocked Janis off balance and pushed him against the cutting table to pat him down—humiliating.

"Now leave. Immediately," the officer said. "Any attempt by you to return here will rightfully be viewed as trespassing and burglary and will be prosecuted by the Riga NKVD as a criminal offense."

Janis was frozen to the spot. Had he heard correctly?

"Do you understand?"

He must have looked as dazed as he felt. The officer was yelling now.

"Leave the premises, Citizen Pērkons. Do not return unless you want to be arrested."

Without endangering his employees with a look of farewell, Janis Pērkons walked away.

6

KĀRLIS WOKE, FOR A MOMENT not remembering where he was. The crack under the door lit up stacked flour bags and a shelf of baking ingredients across from where he lay. Rolling over, ribs screamed! *Ak tu kungs!* Never move again. He pressed two fingers against his neck. Hard to tell if his pulse was weaker now than the last time he checked. Pulling the blanket under his chin, he nestled his head onto the salt bag pillow, listening to the murmur of voices outside the pantry and wallowing in his miserable failures.

The door opened making Kārlis wince at the light. It was Mr. Leopolds again. Squatting in front of the wide shelf where Kārlis bunked, the baker prodded and pressed at Kārlis's ribs and abdomen.

"That hurts," Kārlis moaned.

"He gave it to you in the kishka," Mr. Leopolds said. "The no-goodnik. He should lie in the earth."

"My pulse is weak, Mr. Leopolds," Kārlis said. "You can be straight with me."

Mr. Leopolds flipped a switch. "You're not as bad as all that," he said, parting Kārlis's eyelids with a thumb and forefinger. He shaded Kārlis's pupils with his hand. Then he bared them to the glare of the light bulb, nodding at the reaction. "Eyes look like rotten plums, but functional. The schnozz is not broken, so you'll still have your pretty face." He pressed a cold cloth against the lash welts on Kārlis's neck, saying, "And the girls are gonna love these tough-guy stripes."

The girls! Kārlis shrank with fresh horror and humiliation. Lileja Lipkis was bound to hear about his pathetic performance. He wanted to stay in this closet for the rest of his wretched life.

Mr. Leopolds turned off the light and went out to the kitchen, leaving the door open. Kārlis heard him say, "Oy-yoy-yoy. Kārlis ever been in a fight before?"

"I've hardly ever seen him without pen and paper in his hands," came the reply, sounding like Vilz.

"Me either," said someone else, probably Hugo.

Hmph. As if Hugo was such a bruiser, Kārlis fumed from his heap of mangled limbs. He could just picture Hugo and all the others standing around the kitchen, sharing knowing looks over cups of hot coffee about how they might have predicted Kārlis would be skunked.

"He'll be okay," Mr. Leopolds said. "But in the future, when I say don't do anything rash, this is exactly what I mean not to do. Need I be more specific? Don't pick fights with Russians. Don't go to secret meetings. Don't set off fireworks or otherwise attract attention to yourselves." He was speaking slowly, as if to idiots. "I thought these things were obvious."

"This would not have happened if it hadn't been for that spy the Pērkons have to quarter," Eriks said.

"We coulda handled him if Mr. Pērkons hadn't come in and stopped us," said a fast, high-pitched voice, Sniedze. "Mr. Pērkons wouldn't let us do nothing while that devil whipped the snot out of Kārlis. I mean he flogged Kārlis to a bloody pulp."

Kārlis moaned into his salt pillow.

"Thank God somebody with a brain came along," Mr. Leopolds said.

"But you shoulda heard Eriks stand up to the creep," Sniedze said. "Eriks said he better keep his mitts off his coat. That it was made of camel and herring and lots of other animals and he better keep his mitts off it."

"By the way, Sniedze," Eriks said, "in case I forget to mention it later, Shut Up. Why'd you tell that jerk my name?"

"What? I would never," Sniedze said. "On account of the Nonchalant code and all."

"The what?" Mr. Leopolds said. "What code?"

"You told him my family had the finest department store in Riga," Eriks interrupted. "That's the same as giving him my name."

"I doubt he could afford to shop there," Sniedze said, sounding bewildered.

"Something else, Mr. Leopolds," Eriks said. "This so-called apprentice, this Igor Volkov, he bragged about being at Kalnins Bridge & Iron before he came to Pērkons Leather. You think he had any connection to what happened to Peters?"

It was so quiet Kārlis thought he heard water dripping in the sink.

"I don't know," Mr. Leopolds said. "The forge was nationalized months ago. That didn't happen because of some punk spy. You're saying you think the NKVD was sent to pick up Peters? It wasn't just bad luck you ran into them sledding?"

"Yah. What if?" Eriks said. "What is it, Mr. Leopolds? What's that look mean?"

"Well, I went over to the Kalnins place this morning," Mr. Leopolds said, "I thought I ought to talk to Peters's parents on account of what happened yesterday. But the whole family is gone. According to a neighbor they were all taken somewhere."

"What? Yesterday?"

"Yah. And, well ... "

"What?"

"Apparently the NKVD gave Mrs. Kalnins quite a hard time."

Kārlis rolled up on an elbow, cocking his ear toward the kitchen. The gang was silent at this appalling news.

"Makes sense in a way," he heard Mr. Leopolds say. "They'd have to make it rough for a lady like that, to force her to say where her sons were."

Kārlis was chilled to the center of his soul.

"If that's what happened, maybe it wasn't a coincidence that Peters was picked up," Mr. Leopolds said. "Seems farfetched though. I don't think the NKVD is that organized. It's safe to say, though, that they have it in for all of us eventually."

"You think this Volkov turd informed on Peters's family," Eriks said, like he couldn't shake loose that idea.

"Maybe. We might never know what happened to the Kalninses. Personally, I didn't appreciate their politics, but God help them if the Cheka got a hold of them. A miserable year," Mr. Leopolds said. "Well, I'll be back shortly."

The back door to the alley shut and Kārlis heard the snap of locks.

The kitchen was silent. Kārlis sagged back, assuming everyone there, like him, was horrified by the image of mother-torture. Finally, it sounded like someone threw a log in the oven. A couple of dishes rattled.

"Kārlis is in no condition to do this." It was Hugo speaking. Kārlis recognized his debate-team-captain voice. "We should wait."

"Kārlis has already done his part," Vilz said. "We'll finish it without him."

"When?" Hugo said.

"Today," Vilz said.

"I don't think we're ready," Hugo said. "I mean, you did an ace job on the bottles, but we should practice with them. Let's go out to the summerhouse and light some in the woods. Besides, Kārlis's mother always has something to eat. We should take him there."

The thought of his mother's cooking made Kārlis's eyes moist.

"We only have four cocktails," Vilz said, walking into the pantry and flipping on the light again. Wearing her black bomber jacket and Greek sea captain's hat indoors made her look like she was ready to sabotage something that very moment. "If we light some in the woods then we won't have enough for the Corner House."

Hugo followed Vilz, saying, "If these things aren't handled with respect they'll blow your face off."

"Exactly. I say we blow off some Russian faces first," Vilz said. "Then we go out to Kārlis's and lay low."

Eriks filed in, followed by Jekabs. Kārlis felt oddly comforted to be surrounded by the gang, included in the conversation. His injuries couldn't be as minor as Mr. Leopolds suggested. He was due some honor.

Jekabs reached to the back of an upper shelf and lifted a small, wire-handled metal crate, positioning it gingerly on the center of the floor. "Ta da! They're bang-up professional, if I say so myself," he said flinging off a dishtowel covering.

Kārlis sensed a pressure change in the room. Rolling on his side, he put on his glasses and raised his head to see what everyone was looking at: four ominous milk bottles, the mouths stoppered tight with black electrical tape and wax, tidy fuses of ripped gold-fringed blanket hanging over their sides. The guys must've made and stashed them while he'd slept.

"Mixed in kerosene for added sticking power," Vilz explained, which explained the oily stink.

Kārlis drew away from the bottles, scrunching up on the shelf. These were lethal, the real deal.

"I think the Finns would approve," Vilz said. She closed the pantry door and took a deep breath. "Me and Eriks will take the upstairs windows. Jekabs and Hugo, chuck these in the ground floor or basement. Whatever seems most vulnerable. Then run like hell."

"Where to?"

"Not here," Jekabs said. "We can't lead the Cheka straight to Uncle Eli's door."

"Hugo, remember those elaborate escape routes you devised the time Eriks hoisted Ludvigs Circenis's bicycle up the flag pole?" Vilz said.

"You want to base our egress on that?" Hugo said.

"If egress means getaway, then, yah," Vilz said. "You studied traffic patterns and train schedules and you came up with those routes and alternates."

"Yah. Nothing's really changed," Hugo admitted. "Those would work."

"Well, we can't plan everything exactly," Vilz said. "But that gets us to the train station. Try to catch the last ride out to the Pērkons place. We'll call the mission a success when all of us have made it to Kārlis's."

Kārlis looked around the circle. They all seemed to be memorizing the looks of one another. Vilz's gaze rested on Sniedze. "Except for Sniedze," Vilz said. "His job will be to help Kārlis home right away."

"I don't need any help," Kārlis said.

"Yah, you do," Vilz said. "We all have a job, and that's Sniedze's."

Oh-ho! So that's your angle, Kārlis saw. Vilz was giving *him* a job, the crumby task of babysitting Sniedze during all the Corner House excitement. He tried to protest, but jolting rib pain shut his mouth. What the heck? If he went along with it, at least he would be lying on his mother's featherbeds instead of this hard shelf.

"That all right with you, Eriks?" Vilz said. "You still mad or something?"

"No. But I'm not going to meet you at Kārlis's," Eriks said. "If I'm going to lay low I want girls and a piano to be involved. Other than that, it's a good plan."

Vilz shrugged. "Suit yourself," she said.

Eriks reached down and lifted a Molotov cocktail from the crate, slipping it into his coat pocket like he handled them every day.

"You're taking that now?" said Hugo.

"Yah. But I can't firebomb anything on an empty stomach," Eriks said. "I'm going home to grab a bite. We have to wait 'til dark anyway. I'll see you in the park in an hour."

"Bring your lighter," Vilz said. "I only have matches."

"We're really going to do this," Hugo muttered.

"Bring me something to eat?" Sniedze said to Eriks.

"Sorry," Eriks said, raising the wide lapels of his overcoat and turning to go. "I'm not adding picnic-smuggling to the list of tonight's felonies."

"Be careful," Vilz said. "You really stand out in that light color, and as tall as you are. The NKVD'll grab you, you know, just for looking spiffy."

Eriks put on his gloves, saying, "If being tall and debonair brings down the Cheka then let's face it, fellas, I'm a goner." He turned at the doorway, saying, "Next time I see you citizens, better have your shoes laced tight, because we'll be moving fast.

Street Urchins. K. Smiltens, 1945.

7

ERIKS STRODE DOWN THE MIDDLE of the alley, kicking a hunk of ice, worries itching like scratchy wool underwear. The worst was the fear that he'd endangered his family, Sniedze's blunder that divulged Eriks's family's business. *Dammit.* Now the name Gailis dangled like a fat mouse before a sadistic Igor Volkov cat.

Something else was becoming clear. Volkov was the common factor to a string of stinking events smashing up his world. The *kāpost galva* had practically bragged about destroying the Kalnins family. Then he'd gotten away with beating up Kārlis. Something had to be done about that sick weasel before he turned his deadly stone eyes toward Eriks's family. Eriks wanted to warn his parents right away.

He quickened his step.

After burning down the Corner House, he'd finish business with Igor Volkov. He couldn't do anything about this goliath Soviet occupation screwing with every aspect of his life, but he could do something about one Russian punk. And there would be nothing *nonchalant* about the way he planned to step on Volkov's neck, so he wouldn't tell the others. This time no one would be around to make him compromise or play it safe.

He'd do it for Peters, he thought, eyes welling up. And for Kārlis.

Eriks gauged the heft of the Molotov cocktail in his pocket. Then, looking around, he picked up a hunk of ice and heaved it at the blasphemous new street sign. Bullseye. That felt good. That's how he'd nail the Corner House window.

Brushing snow from his gloves, he turned out of the alley and strode down what used to be his favorite district of the city. Until a few months ago, a parade of swanky stores and restaurants had lined the boulevard here. Now most were dark inside or boarded up. It was depressing. The sidewalks were crowded with people in dark clothes, hunched over and hurrying, as if they wanted to be invisible.

Looming ahead on the next block was his father's department store, seven stories of elegant, mid-century art nouveau architecture dominating every corner of the block. When the light changed, Eriks crossed to it, saddened by the shabby presentation of a window full of empty cartons, its backdrop curtain bunched up and flipped over the rod. Window after dark window stared at him like empty eye sockets. Everything was dead. What the hell did the Communists do with all the Christmas decorations? They meant to destroy him, body and spirit. He saw that.

Crossing the street again, he put the store behind him.

Ahead on the sidewalk, a couple of NKVD agents stumbled out of a pub noisy with Russians. One looked smashed and Eriks reckoned he could snatch the guy's hat and disappear into the crowd before the brute felt his ears get cold. But he let the agent stagger away with his hat, saving his energies for the Corner House.

He crossed the esplanade, passed the Freedom Monument—keeping his distance as it was strictly off limits these days—and skirted Bastion Hill Park where Peters liked to sled. Was Peters really dead?

By the time Eriks reached the townhouse tears were dripping off his chin. The top floor windows were lit and he could hardly wait to be up there, telling his parents about everything. Dinner would be ready and his father and mother would be finishing the ritual cocktail at the window, admiring the onset of city lights.

Eriks ran up stone steps flanked by two giant, marble lions dusted with snow. He pushed open the glass door himself, hoping the doorman wouldn't see his red eyes.

"I've got the elevator, old man," Eriks said, unnecessarily. Old Topper seemed to be avoiding him anyway, probably still sore about Eriks's latest booby-trap heaping snow on his head. No one had a sense of humor anymore. Eriks closed himself in the elevator with a tug of the accordion-style iron gate and pushed the brass lever. The motor churned, rising floor by floor to the fifth, where it clanked to a stop at a deserted, oak-paneled vestibule.

The door to his home was open. Eriks went in, locking it behind him.

"Mama, I'm home."

Not stopping to remove his coat, he flung his fedora like a discus and proceeded directly to the sitting room. The view through the picture window always grabbed him. Lights from the Opera House, the Hotel Riga and the Art Academy glistened over the snow, with spires of the city skyline and the harbor cranes silhouetted faintly behind. But his parents were not there admiring it. The fire had been left to burn itself out. Father's whiskey poured, but not drank. Eriks downed a swig, glad his parents weren't there to see he'd been crying.

Going to the washroom, he extracted the Molotov cocktail from his pocket and set it on the counter, splashed water on his face and tried taming his hair. Then he plucked a sprig of holly from the flower arrangement, replacing the stale boutonniere in his lapel. When tears inexplicably came again he slumped against the wall, holding a towel over his face. After a couple of breaths, he wiped his eyes and nose and tossed the towel on the counter. Then he saw it.

In the corner of the mirror, written in red lipstick were the words, *Run Er—*.

The lipstick was broken off, the gold tube lying on the counter. It was his mother's. Barely breathing, he stretched his hand to the mirror and carefully rubbed the writing with a finger. The letters smeared creamy and red under his touch. Still staring dumbly, he heard pounding on the front door.

He stood motionless, as if unable to comprehend the meaning of the word before him. *Run.* Did it mean...? He locked the bathroom door, flew to the window and threw up the sash. Freezing air hit him as he sat on the sill and swung his legs through the window. Looking down at the inner courtyard central to the building, he paused thinking, *This is insane.*

When the front door crashed open, slamming into the wall, Eriks took his mother's advice.

He ran.

With one arm hanging onto the window frame, he swung as far as he could to the side, grabbing the drainpipes. His feet scrambled against the bricks as Eriks let go of the safety of the sill and clung to the vertical pipes with both hands. Fingers burned against the freezing pipes, but he held tight and began his descent.

He didn't look down. Already passing the windows of the downstairs neighbors, he didn't consider whether he could scale a five-story building. A gunshot thundered from his house and his drop became unthinking, a loosely tethered fall, skin scraping, stinging, skidding between the pipes and the wall.

A hard whizzing flick nicked his wool coat, echoing in a metallic ricochet around the courtyard. Eriks let go, plunging past the first-story into a pile of snow. He rolled off, sprang up and ran. In seconds he was out of the courtyard and running down the sidewalk. He pushed between an older couple in his path, darted around a cluster of impossibly slow figures, and sharply turned a corner before slowing to a stride, panting.

Was everyone looking at him? He didn't want to stand out, wanted to blend in with everyone. He tried to look like every other citizen rushing to be home by curfew, but his lungs screamed with every breath, hammers banging in his head. He needed to hide.

A streetcar was passing. Eriks loped into the street and sprang onto the back platform. He met the driver's eyes in a mirror, but the fellow didn't say anything. Seats were full so he clung to a pole until he noticed he was smearing blood all over it and hid his hands in his pockets.

People got off at a stop and Eriks took a seat, mind racing. What was happening? Where were his parents? What had he done? Resisted the NKVD? They killed people for that, for much less than that. They'd kill him. They'd already tried to kill him. He'd crossed a line. He couldn't go home. He'd be in danger there. He'd be a danger to anyone who helped him.

The trolley was emptying its passengers at each stop, making Eriks more and more conspicuous. *Blend in,* he thought, wishing he were invisible among those hunched in their dark coats, but with his mammoth frame, wild hair and bloody hands he stood out like the Yeti among villagers. His mind went numb as he frantically figured what to do.

He was headed in the exact opposite direction as Vilz and the others who waited for him at the Corner House. The Molotov cocktail! He'd left it on the bathroom counter! What an idiot he was! Now, if his friends did succeed in executing *his* stupidly, brazen plan, he'd just provided a tidy link between his family and the bombing of NKVD headquarters. His stomach cramped. He'd worry about that later. Right now, the streets were clearing. If he didn't get inside soon, he would be noticed and arrested for curfew violation.

A building at the end of the block looked familiar. He had once walked home a girl who lived there. Mentally ravaging the pages of his little black book, Eriks came up with the name Zelma. Zelma Barons. She'd been easy to talk to and before he'd known it he'd walked her all the way home one day after school. Zelma hadn't been very adventurous though when he'd returned that night and tossed pebbles at her third story townhouse window. He'd eventually abandoned hope of shenanigans with Zelma for the company of a game folk dancer. But the doorman might recognize Eriks and let him in the building. He just needed to get inside.

It was a shaky plan, Eriks admitted trying to tame his hair with his fingers. But in its favor was the fact that his family and friends didn't know Zelma. No one would be able to provide her name,

even under torture.

Where did *that* horrid thought come from? He shook it off and entered the townhouse foyer, scouting for the doorman.

Instead, Eriks met the last people he wanted to see.

The lobby was filled with the NKVD, identical in their long, green woolen coats, knee-high black boots, and caps bearing the shiny, red hammer-and-sickle badges. In every chair sat an agent. They stood in groups of three or four, chatting it up, drinking coffee and eating sandwiches. Some had sub-machine guns dangling at their sides. Eriks walked unwittingly into their midst, seen by them all.

"It's past curfew, punk," said a Chekist near the door. "Who are you?"

Eriks tried to appear calm.

The Chekist pushed him, knocking Eriks into the back of another agent who turned, acting highly insulted. "We don't want *that* walking around," the Chekist said, looking Eriks up and down. "Look at the size of its feet."

More Russians circled Eriks, looking eager for some entertainment.

A gloved hand slapped Eriks's face. "I said what's your name?"

His lips trembled. Is this how it had started for Peters? Eriks thought of the girl from school who lived in the building. "Barons," he said, using her name. "Eriks Barons."

"I can't think of one reason why I shouldn't arrest you right now, Eriks Barons. Let's see some identification."

He couldn't reveal his name, couldn't take his bloody hands from his pockets to feign reaching for a wallet. It's over already, Eriks thought, out of moves, caught in the closing circle of agents, suffocating.

"Eriks!"

Eriks jerked his head toward a huge, fair man in civilian clothes who pushed forward, barking at him.

Eriks had never before seen the giant Latvian, who squeezed between the NKVD and, to Eriks's shock, slapped him on both sides of the face, hard.

"You know not to miss curfew!" the man said, grabbing Eriks by his coat. "I've been looking all over for you. Your mother is hysterical." He shoved Eriks toward the stairway. "Get up there, boy, and get my belt."

Eriks stumbled away, hands in pockets, jaw jarred by the heavy-handed slaps. Aware that the man had pulled out papers, identifying himself to the NKVD, Eriks kept climbing and didn't look back.

"Augusts Barons, Comrade Officer. Worker at the People's Mill. You have my word the boy will never again be seen after curfew."

When Eriks reached the third-floor landing, a crack of light widened to reveal a lady on the other side. She had grayish-brown hair and the same slender build as his school-mate, Zelma. Probably waiting for her husband, surprise and suspicion crossed her face when she saw Eriks. Her eyes went wide when he stumbled over the threshold, Mr. Barons right behind him, but she closed the door swiftly, without a word.

Once inside, Eriks breathed. It felt like the first breath in an hour.

Mr. Barons leaned against the door, looking drained, pushing his hand against his forehead.

"Augusts, what's going on?" the lady said with a turn of shoulder meant to exclude Eriks. "Please don't tell me you stuck your neck out. They're watching us."

Mr. Barons's eyes were closed. He shook his head, still leaning against the door as if he was melting into the wood.

Eriks wiped his boots on the doormat, guiltily realizing the risk Mr. Barons had taken for him. *Paldies. Mr. Barons, I—*"

"Forget it, son," Barons said quietly. "Got a nephew your age." The corners of his mouth turned down. "Been missing for two weeks. But we'll talk later. Right now, the Cheka."

Eriks watched curiously as Mr. Barons proceeded to remove his belt and wrap it around his hand. "They love violence," Barons said, "so let's give them plenty of pain."

Eriks nodded vaguely, without grasping Mr. Barons's meaning.

Suddenly Barons faced the door and shouted, "You're going to learn the importance of curfew tonight, boy. I'm going to beat the hell out of you."

Then Eriks realized it was for the benefit of any listening NKVD.

Drawing back his arm, Barons whipped the armchair with his belt.

It took Eriks a moment to realize he had a role to play in the charade.

He cried out as if he'd been lashed.

Again, Barons whipped the armchair.

"Aghh," Eriks cried, shook by the anger he saw in Mr. Barons's blows.

"That was nothing!" Barons bellowed toward the door. Then he said quietly to Eriks, "Who the hell are you?"

Whap!

Eriks screamed. Then he whispered, "Eriks Gailis. I go to school with your daughter. The Cheka came to my house tonight but I escaped out the window. It happened so fast. I don't know where to—"

Whap!

"Please, sir, that's enough," Eriks pleaded loudly, "I'll improve, I promise."

Mrs. Barons pressed her ear against the door. A moment later she turned to Mr. Barons, shaking her head.

"No, I don't think you've grasped the lesson yet," Barons called.

Whap!

The belt lashed the chair with a hide-splitting *smack*. A button popped off the upholstery.

"Please, sir, no more!"

Barons looked to his wife.

Holding up a finger to signal she was trying to listen, she whispered, "I think they went back downstairs."

Barons gestured for Eriks to have a seat. Mrs. Barons removed a stack of books from a doily-covered armchair.

Eriks sat down shakily, trying to calm his heartbeat while Barons uttered fatherly threats and threaded his belt through the loops around his waist. He looked around the small, simply furnished haven, remembering the night he'd tossed pebbles at Zelma's window. If he'd known then how Zelma's father handled a belt, he would never have risked it.

Mr. Barons peered down at Eriks, which knocked Eriks off balance as he was used to being the tallest person in a room. The man looked friendly, but insistent, like he expected an explanation. He was blue-eyed and, oddly for someone of his age, freckled.

Eriks squirmed, clutching his hair, which no doubt looked as out of control as he felt. Suddenly he panicked at what he'd done and didn't want to admit to Zelma's parents that he'd defied the NKVD. He didn't want to tell Zelma's parents someone had shot at him for fear they'd think him a criminal. Zelma's mother was looking at his hands, bloody from his escape. He stuffed them into his pockets.

"Our family store is Gailis & Sons," Eriks said. "You know it? The swanky department store?"

"I know it," Mrs. Barons said.

"That's our store. It was nationalized a while ago," Eriks said, suddenly confused. "My parents cooperated. I don't see why they came for us now."

As he spoke, Eriks's mind wandered, circling suspiciously around the ratfink, Igor Volkov. He hadn't snuffed the cancerous parasite, and see what happened. He'd nearly been treated to a first-hand tour of the Corner House. He reined his thoughts back to Zelma's parents who were looking dubiously at him, the liability they'd let in the door.

"You took a huge risk pretending to be my father, Mr. Barons," Eriks said, grateful.

Mrs. Barons turned sharply toward her husband. She wouldn't have endangered her family for a stranger, Eriks guessed.

"How will I be able to repay you?" Eriks said.

Mr. Barons walked to the window where he stood as if pondering the view, though the blinds were tightly shut. Finally, he turned back, telling Eriks, "You can't stay here."

Eriks was hugely disappointed to hear that. He couldn't even imagine where else he might go. And what about that lobby full of NKVD agents? Must he pass through that again?

"The building is crawling with informants," Barons said. "It's a favorite meeting place of the NKVD as you've discovered. So you can't stay here. You can't return home either. I do know of a place, however. Safest place I know, as a matter of fact. My own daughter is there. You'll have to come with me to the mill. I'm considered an *unreliable*, but I'm still the foreman. A train loaded with lumber will be leaving before dawn. You should be on it."

"What about my parents?" Eriks said.

"They've probably been picked up," Barons said gently.

"*Picked up?*"

"Taken to the Corner House or the Central Jail," Barons said.

Aghast, Eriks fell into the armchair feeling faint.

"Some are loaded on trains to Moscow or points beyond," Barons said, in consolation.

Eriks felt like a storm-battered bird, blown off course, flying over the wreckage of what had been his life, seeking the remains of anything familiar, any landmark, somewhere he might alight for a moment's rest. All was gone.

"Believe me when I say your father wants you to run to safety, Eriks, not to go looking for them," Barons said. "If you want to repay me for helping you, then leave the city. Thank me by getting out of here alive."

8

THE TRAIN FROM RIGA WAS like riding thirty minutes in an icebox. Kārlis slouched on a seat in the back, disgruntled to be stuck with Sniedze while the other boys executed the glorious and defiant strike against the Corner House. Taking a folded paper from his pocket, Kārlis smoothed it out to examine a recent drawing: a caricature of Stalin, moustaches bigger than his arms, brandishing a trident and skewering skulls. He was pleased with the sketch, imagining an art critic reviewing his work with words like *Chilling* and *Evocative*. Inspired by the spires and castle walls growing smaller outside his window, he quickly drew in the iconic Riga skyline.

"Sheesh. I'd love a signed copy of that," Sniedze said, looking over Kārlis's shoulder. "One day when you're a famous artist—"

"Sniedze, I will throttle you if you ever mention my name in connection with a drawing," Kārlis said. "In fact, never mention my name, period. For any reason. *Ak tu kungs.* Sometimes I wish I didn't even know you." Kārlis wished he hadn't said that last part out loud. It wasn't true. It was just that he felt so crumby, being beat up and sent home to Mother.

They spoke little for the remainder of the trip.

Medieval architecture gave way to warehouses, then to silos and farms and finally, to forests. Kārlis hid his injuries by wearing his fedora low and his muffler high, like the Invisible Man in the movie poster. But he was still scared when he got off at the village and had to walk right by an armed NKVD guard, whose raised rifle barrel dominated the platform.

He can't read my mind, Kārlis assured himself. He doesn't know I've collaborated to firebomb his headquarters, or that his supreme commander is the butt of my drawing. Intimidated, Kārlis abandoned a notion he'd entertained all day of poking his head in the Bier Schtube to say *sveiks* to Lileja Lipkis. *Ak tu kungs*, it had been awkward enough during peacetime to come up with some plausible excuse to visit her. But now with that NKVD agent lurking about no one in his right mind would go to a pub, much less drink beer with neighbors.

Kārlis looked at the tavern's curtained windows, imagining what Lileja was doing behind them. Maybe she was peeking out in hopes Kārlis walked by. Maybe Mr. Leopolds was right about girls finding his injuries really attractive. Kārlis raised a bandaged hand to his fat lip. Ow.

"Hey, I just thought of something," Sniedze said. "We could go by the Bier Schtube and say *sveiks* to Lileja."

Kārlis stumbled midstep, taken aback, dismayed that Sniedze's mind ran parallel to his, especially where Lileja was concerned. "That's an exceedingly stupid idea, Sniedze."

"Why? She might give us some more cake," Sniedze said.

"What do you mean?"

"Last time I went there with Hugo she gave us some cake. Want to go?"

Suddenly hot and prickly, Kārlis tore the muffler away from his neck. "*Hugo* has been calling on Lileja? That white-faced traitor! He might have had the guts to mention it."

Sniedze looked at him expectantly. Kārlis could practically see the slices of cake in his shining eyes.

"I'm going to visit Lileja later," Kārlis said. "But I don't think you should be with me, no offense."

There was a proper way to court a lady. It was not with Sniedze in tow. And it wasn't with bloodshot eyes swollen shut. He would wait until the bruises and swelling had gone down. Do things in the proper order. That was Kārlis's motto. There was no rush. He said, "I haven't even told her yet that I've been accepted to the Art Academy."

Sniedze shrugged. "I'm pretty sure Hugo told her about that."

Kārlis stopped walking, appalled. Hugo had stolen a moment from him.

"Hugo doesn't know the first thing about the Art Academy," Kārlis snapped, feeling hollow. His hand went to his wallet, the matriculation card. He could still wow Lileja with that.

Fifteen minutes of walking warmed Kārlis's limbs and brought him to the turn where a long driveway led to the Pērkons's summerhouse and the river beyond. Kārlis had expected to see the place lit up and Christmas cheery, to see the colored glass around the front door glowing like jewels. Instead, the big-stoned building receded into the twilight, windows dark, as if it were hiding behind its flanking linden trees. The driveway hadn't been shoveled and it occurred to Kārlis that might be deliberate.

"Hold it. Let's go around the back," Kārlis said. "No sense making a trail of footprints leading to the front door."

Sniedze followed him on a circuitous route through trees. Then they skirted the stone walls to reach the front door, which was locked.

Kārlis knocked while they banged snow off their boots.

The curtain parted, framing the round eyes, round face and straight braids of his little sister. "You look like ground beef," Biruta said, opening the door. "What does *compulsory service* mean?"

"Hello to you, too. Where's Mother?" Kārlis said, shedding his coat and detecting a tantalizing aroma.

From the other side of the dining room, Kārlis saw Tante Agata's gray head emerge from the kitchen, her hand at her throat. His banging at the door must have frightened the old bird. Seeing it was Kārlis she turned back to whatever she was doing that filled the house with such savory warmth.

"Wanna light matches?" Biruta asked Sniedze.

"Okay," he said, following her to the fireplace.

Kārlis went to the kitchen where his elderly aunt stood at the sink skinning potatoes. Zeita, the house cow, was nearby, her gentle brown head lowered in a bucket of grain.

"Something smells good," Kārlis said, groaning with relief at the warmth and promise of dinner. "I'm starving."

Tante Agata scanned Kārlis from head to toe with pursed lips as if she'd seen plenty of bloodied up boys before and he was nothing special. "I'm going to put some meat on your bones if it's the last thing I do," she said.

The trap door to the root cellar was open and Kārlis could hear someone rummaging around down there. "*Sveiks*, Mama," Kārlis said, bending over the opening.

"Kārlis! Oh, Karli, we just heard," came his mother's voice. "I'm so glad you've come. Are you okay?"

"Not bad, Mama. Bastard caught me off guard that's what happened." He answered Tante Agata's dubious gaze saying, "It was not a fair fight at all." The old lady seemed to be comparing his wounds to her pharmacy of dried herbs hanging from the rafter.

"I was caught off guard as well," called his mother amid the clanking of jars. "Frankly, I'm in shock."

"News travels fast," Kārlis said. Wait. How was it even possible? The fight, if he could call it that, just happened last night. There was no telephone here.

"We're cooking your favorite meal," she called up. "Roast pork and potatoes. Herring in cream."

"And black peas with pig snouts," said Tante Agata.

"Who told you about it?" Kārlis called down the cellar. He would've rather presented his own version of the confrontation with Volkov.

"Just—the telegram," his mother's voice grew louder as she trudged up the stairs. "Wasn't very informative though, was it?"

"What telegram?" Kārlis asked, thoughts jumping erratically to the Art Academy.

"It said you had to report right away for a medical exam," she said. "I'm so glad you came home first."

His mother's head and shoulders rose into the kitchen, the light brown hair, swirled and mounded on top of her head, the puffy, starched sleeves of her blouse. When she turned to face him, he saw she'd been crying, gray eyes ringed in pink. Not only that, she was clearly stunned by his battered condition. Eyebrows frozen in arches, she stared at his face aghast. "What happened to you?"

Kārlis leaned down to take the basket of potatoes from her hands.

"What telegram, Mama?"

She pointed at the table where a formal-looking missive leaned against the salt grinder. Kārlis took the notice, reading it quickly.

"You've been called up," his mother said, dabbing her nose with her handkerchief, "by the Red Army."

He read it again.

Then a wrecking ball let loose, demolishing his inner edifice. Closing his eyes, Kārlis saw the carefully planned future crash, the dust of confusion billowing thick.

A call-up notice. He couldn't breathe. They'd make him be a soldier in his enemy's army. His future lay in the hands of some old man with rows of medals who wanted to impress Stalin. He gasped. So many things he'd been worrying about didn't matter anymore.

When Kārlis opened his eyes, Zeita's big head was looming over him, her huge brown eyes suggesting she might treat him to a tongue-grooming.

"Raspberry leaves and Lady's Mantle," Tante Agata said, a bony finger in the air. "I'll make an infusion." Eyeing his stripes, she added, "and a tincture."

"Good idea," his mother said. "Kārlis, do you want to lie down?"

"No. Not really," Kārlis said, scratching Zeita behind the ears and settling into a kitchen chair. He felt weirdly energized and calm after reading the telegram. He just wanted to sit here. He wanted to watch his mother cook dinner. He wanted to notice every detail, because one thing was for sure. He'd be leaving here. He rested the side of his head on an outstretched arm, absently smoothing the red woven tablecloth to its edges.

His mother went to the window, pulled up a corner of the curtain and looked out. Snow was piled all the way up to the windowsill. Putting her face near the glass, she craned her neck looking in all directions. Daylight was fading fast. The glass was steamy and beaded with moisture from the cast iron teapot bubbling on the woodstove and the pork roasting in the coal-fed oven.

"Darkest day of the year," his mother murmured, tucking the thick curtain back around the glass.

"Solstice," said Tante Agata. She reached a bony old arm above her head, toward bundles of herbs she'd wildcrafted on Midsummer Day and procured in obscure stalls of the Central Market. "The dark triumphs, but only briefly," she said, snapping off a sprig.

Kārlis felt mesmerized and restful watching her rub the herb between her fingers, green flakes falling in a square of cheesecloth.

"The coming days gradually get brighter," Tante Agata said, shrewd blue eyes looking over a sparrow nose at Kārlis. "How many are we for dinner, Anna?"

"Sniedze's here," Kārlis said, suddenly remembering. "And the boys might come by." The Nonchalants's urgent scheme of one hour ago was now remote and irrelevant. How long did he have left before he was shipped somewhere, and approved by the medical examiner to be healthy Latvian cannon fodder?

"How nice," his mother said. "Good for you to be with your friends— Oh! I forgot to mention … " Her face sagged, revealing a weariness before she quickly disguised it with the flex of her smile, saying, "The Kruminses will be staying with us."

"Hugo's family?" Kārlis said.

"Yah. As is happening to everyone, they have been displaced. A Soviet officer moved into their apartment. So, until they get—well, for now, they are staying here."

"People must always welcome persons visiting their home on *Kekatas*," Tante Agata said, as if they were celebrating a solstice tradition, not struggling beneath a military occupation.

"So Hugo will be sharing your room," his mother said. "That's a spot of cheery news for you!"

"Oh joy," Kārlis said, dropping his forehead to the table. How convenient that would make it for Hugo to call on Kārlis's girl.

A hot cup of tea was set next to him. He drank it in gulps and more was poured. Dreams and nightmares swirled together and vanished with its vapors. The women's voices droned indistinctly. Elza will sleep on a cot … guest bedroom for Hugo's parents. It will be a squeeze. Will you spoon the cream over the filets? Janis won't be home in time for dinner, but that still makes ten.

Everything was blown out of order. And Kārlis was out of time. He'd better go see Lileja.

"I'll peel more potatoes," said Tante Agata.

9

THE INDOMITABLE SIX-STORY HOUSE ON the corner had been a lavish apartment building prior to housing NKVD headquarters. Its ornate facade presented rows of iron-edged balconies, jutting out under arched porticoes spiked with icicles and backlit by the yellow light of interior chambers. The balconies looked very much to Vilz like the centers of a target. A target she could hit, she decided, flexing her right arm and realizing she hadn't even played basketball since the occupation. Afraid of meeting the eye of a guard, Vilz returned her gaze to her feet traversing the sidewalk. The NKVD presence here was intense, a swarm of red hammer-and-sickle cap badges and tall black boots, gun barrels sticking out from the balconies at cockeyed angles, aiming at the moon or down at the scurrying citizens.

Jekabs leaned over, speaking out of the corner of his mouth. "Notice," he said, referring to someone ascending the steps to the Corner House. "All anyone has to do, if they don't like someone, is walk in that lobby and report them to *those who need to know*."

"My mother says that's the tallest building in Riga," Hugo said, his voice stilted, laboring to talk over chattering teeth. "Because you can see Siberia from there." He'd hidden his white hair beneath a dark wool cap under his fedora, so he wouldn't be recognized as yesterday's fugitive.

"Very funny. But I'm not walking by that fortress of doom again," Jekabs said. They'd passed the Corner House twice in forty-five minutes looking for Eriks. "Gives me the heebie-jeebies."

"It has chinks," Vilz said. "Small weaknesses. We just have to find one."

"I swear that third floor guard is watching me," Jekabs said.

"They're changing all the time," Vilz said. "I think most of them are just out there to smoke."

"This is stupid," Jekabs said, as they crossed the street a block away and lingered with the commuters at a bus stop. "He's not coming."

Hugo said, "The longer we wait for Eriks, the emptier the street gets and the more we stand out."

The initial excitement that had surged as Vilz and the boys marched up Lenin Boulevard, each with a bottle-bomb hidden in a pocket, had peaked when the despised Corner House first loomed into view. But the optimism rapidly ebbed as they walked disorganized laps up and down the block looking, to no avail, for Eriks. Vilz was afraid that by now the verve needed to execute the ploy had leaked away entirely.

"Yah, but it's quickly getting darker, too," Vilz said, hoping to bolster their resolve, "which is in our favor."

"We're going to miss the last train before curfew if we don't get going," Hugo said.

"Face it, he's not coming," Jekabs said. "And if we keep walking around looking for him one of those guards is going to notice us."

"Doesn't make sense," Vilz said. "This whole thing was his idea."

The three of them stood with their shoulders together, clustered within a larger crowd of folks waiting at the bus stop. Raising her head, Vilz looked around. Everyone seemed to be minding his own business.

"So, do it without Eriks?" Jekabs said, rubbing his hands together.

"Guess we'll have to," said Vilz, also stretching and flexing fingers, keeping her throwing hand warm.

"Nay," Hugo said. "This changes things. We ought to rethink it."

"Doesn't matter whether we fling three bottles or four," Vilz said. "But if we fling zero, then we've failed."

"Don't you think we ought to find out what happened to Eriks?" Hugo said.

"How we gonna do that? What if he decided to go dancing or—met a girl," Jekabs said. "I picture him somewhere—what was it he said? Laying low with girls and a piano, the bum."

"He wouldn't do that," Vilz said.

"If he did I'll pound the numbskull," Jekabs said. "Leaving us hanging like this."

"He wouldn't do that to us," Vilz said. "Maybe something made him late."

"What if it's something terrible?" Hugo said. "Shouldn't we see if he's at home? If he's all right?"

"Then we miss our chance here," Jekabs said. "We risked making these things and bringing them here for nothing."

"I agree," Vilz said. "Let's do what we came for. Then hunt Eriks down."

"But what if something did happen to him," said Hugo. "What if ... what if he's in there?" Hugo nodded at the Corner House.

Vilz didn't want to hear that. "That's a stretch. That would be an unlikely coincidence."

"Yah, but it's possible," Hugo said. "In fact, I'm starting to think that's exactly what happened. You said yourself, it makes no sense he's not here. What if he got picked up?"

"Hugo, there could be a million other explanations why he's not here."

"Like what?"

They looked at each other.

Vilz sighed with exasperation.

"We should find out what happened to Eriks before we do anything," Hugo said. "That's the thing to do."

"But if he was arrested," Vilz said. "If he is in there. Isn't this what he would want? One of our cocktails to come sailing through a window so he could escape in the blazing chaos."

"I don't know," Hugo said, looking sober. "You could be right about that. I don't know what goes on in there. If people are locked up they might be trapped."

Vilz straightened and scanned the line of bus riders. No one appeared to be listening, but she leaned over so only Hugo and Jekabs could hear her. "The only thing Russians understand is violence. If we don't make it painful for them to occupy this place they'll never go away. We can't worry about hurting people."

"I worry about it if it's Eriks," Hugo said.

Vilz looked up and down the street, trying to remember how the fellow at the meeting worded it. A few blocks up, the bus was coming. She said, "This is the moment when we each have to decide: Are you okay living like this? Military occupation, curfew, not trusting anyone, every day until you die, while the world looks the other way, as if your death was nothing?"

"What is that, some kind of rhetorical question?" Jekabs asked, planting his feet. His folded, beefy arms looked tight under his coat.

"We didn't even practice with these things," Hugo said. His beanie dwarfed the refined features of his pale face. "Now that we see how it is, we should come back another time when we're organized."

Vilz mentally regrouped, imagining the fellow at the meeting. "So? Are we just going to get used to it?" she asked. "Until after a while, it's the normal state of things. Or is the way we used to live worth fighting for?"

Hugo pulled his collar up. He shoved his hands in his pockets with a shiver.

"Another thing," Jekabs said, looking annoyed. "Eriks was supposed to bring the lighter. Without that we only have matches. Takes two people to light one using matches."

"They've taken everything, but we still have the power to refuse to cooperate," Vilz persisted. "But it's vital that we act, and not rely on hope alone." The spiel sounded canned, even to Vilz. She couldn't summon the right words, the ones that tapped into the horrendous vein of rage flowing under her skin. Surely they knew the feeling, too. Crushing anger. Hatred that burned up everything you once liked about yourself. Fear you'd forget you ever knew the heights of life because you're always squirming under Russian boots. Hands always tied and never able to speak. Vilz clenched her fists, lips tight, unable to say what she meant.

The Corner House gloated at her from across the boulevard.

"Words and articles are great but—hell." Vilz looked around. She felt cloistered in the stream of head-down sidewalk-pounders. "Light me up, Jekabs."

Jekabs's head shot up, eyes darting around.

"If you don't want to do it, I understand," Vilz said. "Just give me a light."

Vilz's hand shook badly lifting the bottle bomb from her pocket. Holding it low before her, she feared the glass would slip from her sweaty palms and blow off all their heads.

Hugo fidgeted backward, probably thinking the same.

Jekabs stepped to face her. Bending slightly to shield the bottle with his squared shoulders, he struck the match.

Flame at the fuse, Vilz's right arm ejected the bottle immediately, arcing forcefully toward the second story portico. The Molotov cocktail flew off her fingers so fast, she was afraid the fabric wick had not caught fire. But before her hand was back in her pocket, glass crashed against the wall behind the balcony. An instantaneous *whoosh* of combustion drowned a man's scream.

Jekabs launched his bottle hard and true. And ran.

Hugo had long since vanished.

Jekabs's bomb punched with a blazing flashover. Twenty-foot flames and a spewing column of black smoke engulfed the portico. Vilz knew running would attract attention, but she could not control the voltage in her legs.

Distance from the Corner House was swiftly attained. Muscles fleet, senses charged, the corners and passages of her city opened before Vilz in gratitude. The bombs blasted with more power than she'd dreamed. The collective gasp of the bus crowd, the scream and shouts of confusion, all echoed in her head like harmonizing voices in a hymn of praise. Some lightness better than oxygen lifted from her lungs, perhaps hope or dignity. *Good God, what had she done?* She had to do this again.

K. Smiltens, 1945.

IO

THE SUMMERHOUSE, LATVIA
MIDSUMMER'S EVE, 1992

MEMORIES CHASED KĀRLIS PĒRKONS down the forest path. Nike running shoes stepped quick, still pursued by Igor Volkov even though his nemesis lay in the root cellar, a shovel at his crushed skull.

A lifelong wish for justice granted, the Russian colonist was dead. Kārlis wouldn't be the only one glad about that. After 1940, every Nonchalant hated the heart-shaped face that made the Russian occupation personal. Most every Latvian became a fervent enemy of the Soviet regime that year. But today the police would not dig any deeper than Kārlis to collar their culprit. He needed his lawyer. He readied his sixty-eight year old legs to race to the Bier Schtube telephone before the running footfalls from behind caught up.

A tug came from low, on his sports jacket hem. Chest thumping, Kārlis turned, seeing at first nothing but slashes of tree trunks against silver dusk. Then dropping his eyes to the blond head of his grandnephew, he was flooded with relief. It was just the boy, tugging at his coat and speaking in a rush. He turned his good ear toward the round face.

"Uncle Kārlis, the police are looking for you," Johnny blurted. "About that body in the basement. I know I wasn't supposed to go down there. I'm sorry. I was digging for the treasure."

Kārlis nodded, again searching the woods before settling on Johnny's lively blue eyes. It was to be expected, he reckoned with a deep exhale. Bedtime tales of the family history had lodged in the boy's fertile imagination. Kārlis had planted them there himself. The boy had pestered him for a shovel ever since they'd arrived in Latvia, obsessed with plunder.

Bang! The sky cracked. Kārlis flinched. Just fireworks, Midsummer festivity, not bursting artillery like the last time he was in these woods. But it unnerved him.

"Johnny, let's not get hung up on the treasure."

"But the stories are true, you said so."

"Yah, of course. But it's also true that the Russians leave nothing, especially that one who is…" Kārlis raised an arm in the direction of the summerhouse, "…dead…in the cellar."

"Somebody killed that man." Johnny was spitting with excitement. "On purpose! Who would do it?"

Kārlis said nothing, imagining all who would line up behind him to dance on Volkov's grave. "Johnny you should go back—"

"No, I'm staying with you! There's a murderer on the loose," Johnny whispered fervently. The boy's imagination was kindled to a blaze, the widening blue eyes on a manhunt in the murky woods.

"There's no need to be afraid, muzais puisits," Kārlis said, though he also searched the trees for unwanted intruders, especially the police. "The world is safer with Volkov dead."

Kārlis felt at home in these woods, which Russians were reputedly afraid to enter. The boy would be in no danger if he stayed. "Come with me," Kārlis said, reaching out. Taking his grandnephew's smaller hand in his made a certain sense of the whole crazy imbroglio. And Johnny's presence inspired a side trip. "I want to show you something," Kārlis said. "It will only take a moment." Following his gut instinct felt as vital to Kārlis now as reaching his *lawyer had been a moment before. "There's a giant oak over here, the granddaddy of the forest. You'll never see another one like it in your life."*

Kārlis soon discovered that the path engraved on his memory no longer existed. He and Johnny were forced to tramp single file, unable to take even five steps in any direction without having to stop and swipe at an occupied spider web suspended at face level, or negotiate a fallen log, a knee-deep bog, and shoulder-high ferns. But the riverbank was right where he expected it to be, the high Midsummer sun glistening on its current.

"The tree should be up ahead. I remember we had a swing there in the spring."

"Uncle Kārlis?"

"Yah?" Kārlis turned his good ear toward the lad.

"Why bother to get the house back if the treasure's not even there?"

"For YOU, muzais puisits," Kārlis said, feeling indignant. "And for your grandchildren." He followed a deer trail that rose and dipped pleasantly through the rushes. "That's what my father intended."

"Maybe he hid it so good, the Russians didn't find the treasure."

Kārlis stopped. The boy's imagination was exceeded only by his optimism. "Johnny, if you could've seen this place when your great-grandfather owned it, you would know. All has been taken."

The slim shoulders fell under the little windbreaker.

Kārlis felt bad to dash the boy's hopes. "He was an optimist, too, my father," Kārlis said, in consolation. "You're his namesake, Johnny. And today is your Names Day. You and my father, your names come from Janus, the Roman god of the entrance and the exit, of looking ahead and looking behind. A very suitable name for my father. Everyone knew when Papu came into the room." Kārlis stumbled in time for a dizzying moment, picturing his towering father as a young man, much younger than Kārlis was now.

"Jānis Pērkons was a man of big ideas," Kārlis said, trying to stuff the past back in its grave and marshal his thoughts to the current problem of staying out of jail. "Everything in the proper order," he murmured, reassuring himself. But even his organizing mantra did not dispel the feeling that he was *on the wrong track, missing something, the big picture.*

"I'm sorry I went in the root cellar," Johnny said. "It's my fault the police are after you."

"Ak tu kungs, this is not your fault!" Kārlis said. He lowered himself to his haunches, to the level of the mushrooms on the boggy forest floor, to convince the child eye-to-eye of one sure truth. "These events were set in motion long ago, Johnny. I've waited a lifetime to set things right."

K. Smiltens, 1945.

Witch Hammer

II

LONDON 1959

LET IT GO. NOT THAT YOU'RE WRONG, but for your own sake, lest you go mad. Let it go. There's no point plotting revenge.

"I'm not plo—Mama! I just keep track—" He tipped the metal folding chair on its back legs, balancing against the small table.

Expecting justice is a waste of time.

His mother was a broken record. Predictably, her next topic would be...

Isn't there a girl? Someone—

"Yah. I have friends," Kārlis claimed, voice rising with spirit. "Remember when Stalin died? How we met at the pub and drank vodka and sang late into the night." Kārlis felt the corners of his mouth turn up and he crooned with chesty force, "I threw flowers in the Dauga to send greetings to my girl, ta da da da ..."

The ballad bounced off the walls and the small, dim room seemed to close in and suffocate the singing that waned to agitated foot tapping. "But it costs money to go out," Kārlis pointed out. "So I don't often see those knuckleheads from the displaced persons camp. Anyway, they are moving like a stagnant pond." He quaffed the contents of the shot glass and stared stoically at the wall *until the burn of his throat mellowed.* "Well, it's hard to get traction in a new country, Mama. Don't I know it."

They drink too much.

"Because it's hard. We got nothing. Who wants us?" *Kārlis slammed his fist down on the table, making the bottle and ashtray rattle.* "They call me Charlie here. Mama." *He poured another shot, feeling punchy.* "The name Kārlis is too foreign for them." *He relit a cigarette butt that had a few more drags.* "And I don't want to be an outsider. So I'm Charlie."

You drink too much.

"My three best friends are beer, vine and wod – I mean vodka. Yah, yah. Vodka. The English make the v-sound where we would say a w, and vice-verse. Wice-werse. Ha ha ha. We should speak English. Don't sound like a stateless squatter! Remember to switch Vs and Ws." *He was nearly shouting. Why was that? Oh, who cared?*

Find a nice girl and settle down, Kārlis.

"Charlie. I'm Charlie. Mama, and if you're going to be cliché," *Kārlis shifted his chair, breathed heavily and made a point to enunciate,* "then I would rather discuss worldly affairs with Papu."

His parents stared into the room, black-lined figures Kārlis had painted on the wall. Angry slashes of black next to his mother marked the botched attempt to recreate his sister's face.

"As you know, the Communists want to build a wall, Papu." *Kārlis blew a stream of smoke.* "To stop those poor fools fleeing East Berlin. A wall!" *He snorted with scorn.* "What is this, the middle ages? Throughout history walls keep invaders out. Never before has a regime built a wall to keep people in, to keep its own people from getting away." *Kārlis shook his head, stubbing out the butt.* "Border guards in three hundred watch towers will shoot you dead for trying. But I would do it. Wouldn't you, Papu?"

His father's effigy, sporting a spiffy goatee, a gold chain draped from his vest pocket, and a permanent jolly expression suggested he would make the daring run.

"I can't hear you," Kārlis shouted. "Talk louder. Into my good ear."

Someone pounded on the other side of the wall.

Kārlis nearly fell out of his chair in shock. Heart thumping, he stumbled toward the window, switching off the lamp and flattening himself against the wall, chilled with clammy fear.

Yelling on the other side of the wall, in English, cursed Kārlis.

He snickered, still cringing. It was the ignoramus next door! Not the "knock at night". Ak tu kungs. Kārlis laughed at his own melodrama. Pretty sure the peals were weirdly high-pitched. He could never trust his ears after that damned shrapnel. It's all right, Mama. I'm jittery as hell. That's all. Overly vigilant. Wigilance, vigilance, wigilance. It's normal. Shell shock can take a lifetime. The cure is meat! Eating meat is what broke through the darkness, Mama.

Outside the window, snow blanketed the bleak London outskirt where refugee farm laborers like Kārlis were housed. Mist dulled the black sky, hiding stars. Kārlis stared up anyway, knowing they still shone beyond his view, somewhere in space, where Sputnik circled, souring even the sanctity of the heavens.

"Do the NKVD watch us from space, Papu?"

They're the KGB now.

Kārlis watched the sky with eerie deaf-ear dullness before turning back to his parents.

"I will do what's necessary, Papu," he whispered. The promise sounded like a muffled buzz within his skull. "Don't worry. I'm patient like a spider. One day I'll settle accounts."

He leaned against the wall and whispered, "Killing doesn't count in a war, Mama. Not if you're a soldier. God help me, it doesn't count."

12

THE CORNER HOUSE
RIGA, LATVIA
22 DECEMBER, 1940

KKKGH. THE STEEL DOOR clanked again.

Peters Kalnins jerked his head up. He'd fallen asleep.

"Eyes!" shouted the guard with the gloved fist. "I want to see your eyes!"

Sweat dripped from his shoulder blades as Peters rolled onto his back and forced open leaden eyelids. The light bulb, stadium bright, pierced his aching head.

Looming above, the black halo of an NKVD visor hat, with the red hammer-and-sickle cap badge protruded from a set of bulging shoulders. The guard was making a visual sweep of the men laying on the cell floor, and the dozen or so lucky enough to be packed onto the cots hinged to the wall.

Peters stared at the ceiling, still as a slit herring lined up in the fish case, hoping not to meet the guard's gaze. Let it be someone else, Peters prayed. Someone else to sit on the wooden chair at the small desk with the ashtray full of, what were they—ripped fingernails, across from the interviewer with the clipboard, the one with the rubber truncheon lurking just out of view.

Prayer turned to panic. If it was him, what to say?

We just need some information. Then you can go home.

One name. Then they'd let him go.

Needed sleep. Think clear. To know. Who. Or not.

Jackboots stepped closer.

"Spit in their face," wheezed the man heaped in the corner. Without lifting his jaw from the floor, he gave the same advice to each prisoner taken to interrogation. "However small the act. Defy them. Russian scum."

Not such a sacrifice for an old fellow to be crippled for life, Peters thought, but he was seventeen and captain of the hockey team.

The boots stopped at Peters's head. "Name."

"Kalnins," Peters said, praying the guard sought another.

A boot nudged Peters's shoulder. "Get up."

Peters rose unsteadily, catching trousers that fell nearly to his knees. At registration they'd taken his watch and belt and, with a large kitchen knife, chopped off buttons, excised his zipper and sliced his coat lining prior to the cavity search. Clutching his pants in one hand, he followed the guard to the door. Neighbor inmates expanded into the vacated floor space.

The steel door banged again. This time Peters was on the other side, staring through bars down a hall of heavily padlocked doors. Noises from different sections of the compound resounded through the hardened tunnel. An engine revved, gates or chains clanked, shouts and moans mingled in hellish cacophony. He thought he heard a gunshot, but tuned it out, feverishly devising what he'd say as the guard shoved him along labyrinthine hallways.

Peters had survived the last interview only because of a miracle.

"Who at your school is printing leaflets?" the agent with the truncheon had asked, studying Peters's reaction.

Could they see his cheeks burning? Hear his guts liquefy? Peters knew the answer. Vilz Zarins was the culprit, Peters's friend since kinderhood. And Kārlis Pērkons, another buddy, illustrated the leaflets with cartoons ridiculing Stalin. The students met secretly at Jekabs Leopolds's family bakery. They had tried to persuade Peters to help them print the secret newsletter *Free Latvia,* along with Eriks Gailis, Hugo Krumins and Sniedze Krasts. Any one of the names could be his ticket out of the Corner House.

Peters shook his head, wishing it didn't hold the knowledge. The agent's eyes bored into him, trying to read his mind. What would an innocent person do? Peters shrugged in the universal gesture of ignorance. Resisting the urge to loosen his collar, he tried to breathe naturally. That's when he smelled smoke.

Instantly an alarm on the wall started hammering, loud and shrill, right next to the truncheon wielder's head. With a swing of his weapon, he took a giant step away from the clanging bell. It was deafening in the tight space. Peters could've shouted rebel names at the top of his lungs and not been heard.

"What in hell!" the agent with the clipboard appeared to shout. "Go find out what it is."

His partner opened the door. He let pass two uniformed men running down the hall before stepping out, closing the door behind him.

The remaining agent sat across the desk, glaring as if the ear-splitting racket were Peters's fault. Big ears protruded from under the officer's cap. He was one of the *troika* who'd arrested Peters in the park.

The Chekist scowled alternately at Peters, the vibrating bell, the clipboard, the door. *"Проклятье,"* he cursed and strode out.

Alone, Peters exhaled and pushed his palms against his ears, thankful for the clanging reprieve.

Time crawled.

He watched the door with dread, wondering if everyone had forgotten him. When it finally opened a different guard entered. With bureaucratic indifference, he tied Peters's hands behind his back, giving him just enough slack to hold up his pants as he shuffled beside the guard down to the cell. By the time Peters found floor space among the other prisoners, the bell had stopped ringing.

The miraculous timing of the fire alarm had saved him last night. What would save him now? He vowed to not give the Russian scum a single name. But how bad would the truncheon hurt? How many whacks before a vital organ split?

"Don't confess! Don't tell them anything!" A woman's voice came through the feeding slot of a dungeon door as he passed. "They won't let you out anyway." She echoed behind him. "All you can do now is protect those on the outside."

Peters nodded, his heart tight as a clenched fist. The guard prodded him up the curving wooden staircase. At the top, Peters's knees went weak as he followed the red, carpeted hallway to the interrogation room.

13

DECEMBER 22, 1940

THE SUMMERHOUSE, LATVIA

AFTER GETTING HIS ASS KICKED BY a nasty Russian, Kārlis Pērkons had limped home expecting to find solace, only to get hit with a call-up notice drafting him to the Red Army. There was no escaping the Communist occupation, Kārlis thought, head in hands at the kitchen table. Clearly, Stalin's henchmen had known right where to find him, delivering the military telegram directly to the small village, to the rustic manor set off the forest road, and into the trembling hands of his mother. Kārlis felt fully invaded. He removed his glasses and slumped over the red woven tablecloth. Deita, the house cow, plodded over and nuzzled his swollen, bruised face, no doubt hoping for a carrot.

His mother crossed to the window. "Any word on Peters Kalnins?" she asked, lifting a corner of the curtain and searching the darkness. She did that every few minutes.

"You ever heard of a boy coming home after being arrested?" Kārlis replied, hoping she had, and that the ghastly rumors about interrogation at the Corner House were overblown.

His mother's shoulders slumped.

Kārlis felt the corners of his mouth sag. He didn't expect to see his friend Peters again.

The linden tree outside the window creaked in the wind, heavy limbs waving barren, twig-fingered branches.

"She complains," Tante Agata said, interpreting for the tree. Kārlis's elderly aunt cocked her head toward the creaking boughs, her long gray braid slipping over her shoulder. "A linden stands for justice."

Kārlis's mother left her post at the window. She opened the woodstove, lit a long matchstick, and put it to an oil lamp, invoking the biting fragrance of flaxseed oil. There was no electricity at the summerhouse, part of the rustic charm. Moving to the next lamp, she glanced at the window again and hesitated, as if thinking better of drawing attention to the second home of a capitalist. "No sense lighting up the house like a Christmas tree," she said.

The comment fell heavily. Christmas was a few days away, and there was in fact no Christmas tree. Any of the usual hoopla would be grounds for arrest under Article 58 of the Russian Criminal Code.

"Darkest day of the year," Tante Agata said reverently, emerging from her cabinet of curiosities with a small blue jar. "Solstice. Take your shirt off."

"Ow!" Kārlis said, lifting his sweater over his head.

His mother's eyes widened at his gruesome bruises. "How did this happen?" she asked, pointing to a purple welt over his kidney.

"That Russian ratfink the state assigned to Papu's workshop," Kārlis said, twisting to get a look at his backside. "That Igor Volkov, a spy posing as an apprentice." Ribs were red and swollen where Volkov had kept kicking him.

"He's the reason we left Riga. You crossed him?" His mother slumped against the icebox, aghast. "What were you thinking?"

"Somebody had to stand up to the thug," Kārlis said, embellishing his bravery for Mama's sake. He skipped the fact that his purpose for being at his father's Leather Works in the first place had been to steal materials for Molotov cocktails.

Tante Agata looked through the glasses resting on her wizened beak as if she already knew the whole story. "Bruisewort," she said softly. She smoothed salve from the blue jar over the lacerations on his cheeks and neck, her bony fingers cool and soothing.

Kārlis almost whimpered out loud. "That's where he whipped me with a leather strap," he said, feeling pathetic.

When his elderly aunt pressed a point at the base of his skull, tightness melted from his shoulders. It felt pleasing, the way she methodically pushed a path down his spine, flatly chanting, "The servant attacks with saw and axe, the lumber, stack and cord."

"Aggh!" Kārlis cried at the word "axe", feeling like she'd stabbed him with a filet knife.

Tante Agata hesitated, uttering something incomprehensible. "Axial trauma," she declared.

Growing up under her care, Kārlis understood that Tante Agata's mumbles were a mnemonic ditty, part of a routine for examining bone and tissue and recalling remedies. It was how she remembered the forest lore.

She poked every bruise along his throbbing skeleton before exhaling decidedly. "I'll wrap the ribs." Minutes later she'd pulled a strip of linen around his chest and snugged his heart and wind back into place. "There," she said. "Now sit in my chair."

Kārlis dropped into the cushions of the Queen Anne's wingback by the woodstove, carefully raising his feet onto the small tufted stool. As the throbbing subsided, he retreated into a quiet ward of his mind, nursing his wounds and savoring the peaceful, homey comforts. How much longer before he had to leave?

"It says you're to report for a medical examination," his mother said, rereading the call-up notice by the lantern. The shock of the Red Army telegram still made her dab the corner of her eye with a handkerchief.

"Maybe they will see my injuries and say I'm unfit," Kārlis posited.

"You're not that bad," said Tante Agata, pushing a pouch of warmed linseed under his lower back. "Nothing broken."

Kārlis was disappointed to hear that. Besides wanting to evade the draft, he'd already been composing his version of the beating into a gripping tale that would enthrall Lileja Lipkis. Grave injury might inspire her sympathy. Mediocre injury just underscored the fact that he'd had the snot whipped out of him.

"The master's eye makes the horse fat," Tante Agata said, giving him a cup of tea. Whatever that meant, the infusion and the linseed poultice worked like a charm, sending Kārlis into a calm meadow where his worries didn't follow. The moment was idyllic: flames quietly crackling, the promising aroma of dinner, loving women orbiting him - speculating how many would be home for dinner, Deita contentedly munching grain, dim light gentle on his closed eyes. He wished he could slow down time and stay here forever.

The blissful moment faded as the click of high heels coming down the hall grew louder.

"Here she comes," Tante Agata said.

"Some friction is to be expected," Kārlis's mother replied, sighing. "Two families coping with upheaval under one roof."

Kārlis opened his eyes, suddenly recalling that the Krumins family was now sheltering with them, the Russian occupation having left them jobless and homeless.

"We've no choice but to open our door and do our best." Mama sounded like she was giving herself a pep talk.

The heel-clicking rose to a crescendo and Mrs. Krumins blew into the kitchen like a frigid wind. An ice blue dress matching the color of her eyes swished around her tall, willowy figure. Her white hair was pulled back in a severe bun.

"Can't we light some lamps in here?" she demanded. Evaluating the kitchen activity, she beheld Deita with scorn. "Now that's unsanitary," she said with a sniff. "A heifer in the kitchen. Can't you keep it in the barn?"

Kārlis's mother didn't deign to defend the lovingly raised, impeccably groomed, purebred Latvian Brown.

"I've heard tales," Mrs. Krumins said, "of peasants doting on their cows, but I never expected the wife of a prominent businessman to—"

"*Deita* has a pleasing personality," interrupted Tante Agata.

Mrs. Krumins nodded curtly. "Gracious, boy, you've been through a meat grinder," she said, looking Kārlis up and down. "If you're thumped even before boot camp, I shudder to think how you'll fare in the army."

Kārlis nodded ruefully. He knew from spending time after school at his friend Hugo's house that Mrs. Krumins was high-strung and had to be handled like a vial of nitroglycerine.

"So the Reds are conscripting our boys now," Mrs. Krumins said. She turned to Kārlis's mother. "Mrs. Pērkons, *Anna*, if I may, you cannot bear up under this dreadful turn of events. So I am here to take charge of dinner. Go fetch a bucket of water, Kārlis."

"Don't get up, Kārlis," his mother said. "That won't be necessary, Mrs. Krumins. Tante Agata has already prepared everything."

Mrs. Krumins winced. "I'll be frank," she said, waving a hand at Tante Agata, who stood by her mysterious cabinet behind a scrim of hanging, dried herbs. "In these troubled times, your old auntie should not act so obviously eccentric. Your little girl will go to school and repeat everything she sees in this house, including that twisty folk craft your aunt practices, putting us all in jeopardy."

Kārlis's mother stopped stirring the pot on the stove and turned to face the visitor. "You needn't concern yourself with my daughter," Anna said, cheek color rising. "*My* family is getting along fine."

"I'm concerned about weird crones coming here to compare notes on ancient nonsense," Mrs. Krumins said. "This vagary is what alarms the Communists. And will bring them down on all of us."

"I'll have you know, my aunt is widely respected for her knowledge of herbal medicine," Anna said.

Tante Agata stood listening, resolute as a steel pole, displaying her wrinkled skin like it was the family's proud banner, determined to defeat the enemy with decoction and broth.

Kārlis's mother pivoted back to a simmering pan of cabbage. "Thank you for offering to help, Mrs. Krumins, but dinner is well in hand."

"Look, I'm not a free-loader," Mrs. Krumins said. "We wouldn't be imposing on you at all if the Communists hadn't ousted my husband from the police force." She was looking at Kārlis, as if repeating her tale of woe for his benefit. "Then they evicted us from our apartment to accommodate a high-ranking Soviet officer. It's very humiliating. I am not accustomed to asking for charity."

Kārlis nodded uncomfortably and moved over to the butcher block to slice some black bread.

"Not another word about it, Mrs. Krumins," said his mother. "Of course you must stay here. Especially since Hugo and Kārlis are such close friends."

"Take some tea to calm your nerves," said Tante Agata, going for her infusion.

"Nothing wrong with my nerves! It's the circumstances that are haywire," Mrs. Krumins said, picking up the call-up notice. "I've come down to give you some advice, Anna." She turned her back to Tante Agata. "It's the least I can do in exchange for your hospitality. The storm has now hit your family like it hit ours." She flicked the Red Army's telegram with relish. "This is just the beginning, mark my words. We must prepare for worse. Small measures will make a big difference in the long run. I notice you already hide the sugar. Don't leave the butter out either."

She whisked the butter crock off the table just as Kārlis was about to dip his knife into it. "I will take responsibility for rationing foodstuffs," Mrs. Krumins went on. "It's the least I can do."

Anna abruptly stood. "Give that boy back his butter this instant," she said, pointing at the crock.

Kārlis's jaw dropped at the tightness of her voice. His mother, always composed and gracious, sounded hysterical. "It's okay, Mama, I don't need it."

"And I do not hide the sugar," Anna said with a stamp of her foot.

"Not from your family perhaps," Mrs. Krumins said. "It's only natural you would hoard luxury items from outsiders."

Deita mooed.

"Hoarding? That's how you think you've been treated here?" Anna said, nostrils flaring. "That's ridiculous." She flung open a cupboard. "Though frankly I am concerned with a bigger picture than the location of the sugar bowl—"

"You think you know better than me how to manage because I'm homeless," Mrs. Krumins said. "Mark my words hard times are ahead. I don't know why you think you'll be spared."

"You don't know what I think, Mrs. Krumins," Anna said, slamming compartments of the enameled stove in her search for the sugar.

Kārlis couldn't understand why the kitchen had suddenly blown up. One moment, all had seemed civil, two matriarchs fending for their families after losing homes to the Communists. Then they'd snapped, making a dogfight between a Messerschmitt and a Spitfire look courteous.

"Here is the sugar! Behind the canning equipment," his mother said, gathering her skirt. She stepped on a chair and hoisted herself up to the top of the broom closet. The sugar bowl was made of milk glass, with two handles and a tight lid. Holding the closet for balance, she descended, presenting it to Kārlis like a trophy. "Put some sugar in your tea, Karli. Go ahead, as much as you want," she insisted, in a syrupy voice that sharply contrasted the acid tone taken with Mrs. Krumins.

"*Paldies*, Mama," Kārlis said, angling for a heaping spoonful. Talk of rationing made him ravenous.

His mother said, "We have more in the cellar, dear."

Mrs. Krumins said, "You won't for long if—"

"If rationing sugar would keep my son out of the army, believe me, I'd count every grain," Anna cut in. "But it won't. So I'm going to make our days together at home as *pleasant* as possible." She spoke pointedly, eyes boring into Mrs. Krumins, who finally looked away. "Tante Agata, use the Rosenthal tonight, the best china. If we have anything good, let's enjoy it while we're *together*." Anna's voice caught on the word. The handkerchief was at her eye again.

"Sloppy," Mrs. Krumins said, plunking the butter crock on the table, "and sentimental. That's a mistake." She exited the kitchen with the staccato of clicking heels.

"Doesn't she know she's insufferable," said Tante Agata.

Anna sniffed. "That woman was a wreck during good times."

"What's this?" Kārlis said, looking in the sugar bowl. He lifted a glittering, chandelier-style earring. "Diamonds?"

The women glanced at his hand and at each other, as if it wasn't the first time precious stones had been found in the tea service. Anna sat down, crumpling her hankie and picking up the telegram in shaking fingers. "That would be your father," she said, composing herself with a deep breath. "Spending cash like tomorrow there'll be nothing left to buy."

Kārlis stared at the diamonds. Even in the dim room and encrusted with sugar, the stones danced with light. He knew his father traded for gold and jewels on the black market. Obviously Papu had to hide his sneakily purchased valuables somewhere. It gave Kārlis an idea. He downed his tea and went to his room.

K. Smiltens, 1973.

14

Walking confidently into the dark bedroom, matches in hand, Kārlis kicked something that felt like a steel hammer nailing his little toe. "Ow! *Pie joda*," he cursed, grabbing his foot and hopping, stumbling over something and landing on his tailbone. Merciless pain shot up his spine and thrummed his ribcage.

"What the *kāpost galva* hell?" Kārlis bellowed. He crawled to the lamp, struck matches at the wick and looked around his room, immediately crestfallen.

Someone had rearranged the furniture! His mattress had been dragged off the boxed-spring frame and flopped in the corner, making the room a double. The floor was stacked with boxes. Punctilious labeling suggested Hugo's neurotic mother had moved in her son to share Kārlis's room.

At that moment, Kārlis realized how he'd cherished an expectation for privacy. He'd looked forward to being inside these four tight walls, where he could grieve for his friend Peters, arrested and possibly tortured, and digest the shock of being attacked and conscripted, and await news of his friends, whether they'd successfully firebombed the Corner House, or if they'd been caught, and all the other dung flung at him lately that needed thinking about.

Ak tu kungs. He sunk against the wall wanting to cry. He wouldn't even finish high school now, and that meant no Art Academy either. The future was in ruins. What a joke to think his bedroom would remain untouched.

Kārlis stared at Hugo's boxed worldly possessions, drained of momentum for what he'd come to do. Finally he worked up the nerve to see if they'd molested his most personal belongings.

Pushing aside the clothes in his armoire, Kārlis felt around the back of the top shelf. When his hands touched the heavy glass jar, he exhaled in relief, lifting down his collection of silver coins. He held it up, giving the jar a little shake, appreciating the weight of his nest egg. He would bury it. Then if he made it back from the army alive, he would at least have a few ducats to his name. Every single move he made now felt significant, potentially his final act in this mortal theatre, and at the same time everything was utterly meaningless. Still, planning for the future was like having some control in the matter. Dinner was almost ready. He didn't have much time.

Donning a sweater, Kārlis wrapped a towel around the jar of silver and slipped out his window. Freezing air sliced at his cuts as he edged around the stone masonry at the corner of the house. He saw the shovel leaning at its usual post near the kitchen door. Grabbing it, he struck out for the woods, the crunch of snow under his boots.

Kārlis hadn't gone far when he saw an unearthly vision by the light of the moon, lurking mere feet away. He stopped dead in his tracks, crippled with chill, watching. Before him, some hunched, shaggy creature with pointed ears and an upright twig-body careened with eerie energy. He tensed warily, ready to defend himself with the shovel, when a thin, cracking voice, uttered,

> *As I was going to war*
> *I cut a cross in the oak,*
> *So that father and mother shouldn't weep,*
> *So that the crossed oak should weep*

"Tante Agata," Kārlis said, exhaling in relief. "Are you—"

Kārlis could barely discern his great-aunt under her furs in the moonlight. She was fruitlessly tugging a rope tied to a log. A few meters behind her wandered Deita.

"Are you trying to drag a yule log?" Kārlis asked.

"Kārlis, I need your help," Tante Agata said. "This is too heavy for me."

Still processing the bizarre sight, Kārlis made no move to help her.

"When combating the powers of darkness, use your strongest weapons," Tante Agata said at his hesitation. "Be a good boy and pull this log around the property. Then bring it inside and burn it. Though it won't be a proper bonfire. We must do what we can to end the scourge of the last year."

Kārlis grimly accepted the rope held out to him. He'd do anything to reverse the Communist annexation of six months ago.

"And you better wear this," she said, pulling something bulky from her apron pocket.

"Do I have to wear a mask?" Kārlis said.

"Next year's fortunes depend on it," replied Tante Agata, holding up a shroud of matted yellow yarn, not unlike a dust mop.

"Can't I wear your wolf mask?" Kārlis said, now that he could see the pointy ears of the fur cap tied under her chin.

"Too small for you. But your Uncle Visvaldis always wore this haystack disguise or went skyclad."

Banishing the vision of his late elderly uncle cavorting naked in the moonlight, Kārlis pulled the yellow yarn wad over his head. He thought Tante Agata, who looked simultaneously frail and wild, should probably get inside the house.

"It's important you are thorough," Tante Agata said. "Now go on. I'll fool the evil spirits," she said, meaning she would handle noisemaking and *daina* incantation. "And mind you," she added as an afterthought, "don't run from Death. If you dance with Death during winter solstice, you'll not die during the next year."

She'd put a finger on his greatest fear.

"Okay, I'll do it," he said, injuries complaining already. Trudging away with the log, he was suddenly overwhelmed by a clutch of concern for the old bird. "Auntie," he said, turning back to her. "Don't let the houseguests see you mumming, all right? You can't trust anyone, you know that?"

"Ha! You mean Mrs. Krumins?" Apples rose on Tante Agata's cheeks. "Don't worry about her. Or the Communists either, for that matter. The deep lore has survived many burning times. Some even worse than this."

The comment troubled Kārlis. Right now armed NKVD agents were posted a kilometer away at the rail platform. If one happened to see Tante Agata in her wolf mask he'd put her down like a mad dog. "But Auntie, Mrs. Krumins is right. The Russian criminal code is brutal. If you attract attention or are different—"

"This is nothing new, Kārlis," Tante Agata said. Her voice no longer sounded crackly, but like part of the wind. "Today it's Article 58. Yesterday it was *Malleus Maleficarum*."

"Mal—what?"

"*The Witch Hammer*. A hunting manual, from a different era but with the same premise, exterminating anyone daring to wear her own shoes. You're a good boy, Kārlis. In fact, you're a man now," Tante Agata said, turning to go in. "Do as you know."

Kārlis felt a tender tug as he watched the old lady forge a path back through the snow, and exhaled deeply, his heart held by her linen bindings. He hadn't planned on a solstice masquerade, but under the circumstances it seemed the right thing to do. His soul was in turmoil. Why question the remedies of the ancients? Besides, this was a perfect excuse to be outside to bury his treasure. If anyone asked where he'd been, he could honestly say he'd gone mumming.

Kārlis tromped into some trees, trailing the log behind. Finding it impossible to dig a hole in the frozen ground, he had to settle for pulling up some floorboards in his mother's garden gazebo. He buried the jar of silver shallowly, but it was well hidden after he replaced the boards.

Then, ribs throbbing, he honored his word to Tante Agata and dragged the yule log from one end of the property to the other, without cutting corners. He pulled the herb-entwined stump at the end of the rope past the well, through a naked birch grove all the way to the river. On the way back he overshot the house, circumvented the dark and forgotten carriage shed, and went nearly to the public road before stopping to rest. Paws scurried overhead, a pine marten perhaps, traipsing the bough's silhouette against the silver sky. Kārlis wanted to absorb every detail of his childscape. You never really saw a place until you knew you wouldn't see it again, he thought. By the time he'd pulled the log back to the kitchen door, he could no longer stand the pain of the rope against his bruised ribs, but it felt good to take back charge of his life.

Picking up the log was painful. Arms full, Kārlis pushed open the back door to the kitchen, sensing with gladness that the house was full of arrivals. His father was home. Still in his suit, Janis Pērkons leaned against the butcher block, the outline of his goatee, usually precise as a razor's edge, was smudged by a long day's stubble-shadow. Kārlis's mother and wide-eyed little sister clustered around Papu. They stopped talking when Kārlis came in, staring at him.

"You look funny," his sister said, gawking, no doubt, at his swollen, bruised eyes.

"Good evening to you, too," Kārlis said, stomping snow off his boots.

It felt awkward facing Papu. Kārlis hadn't seen him since the night before, when his father had stood by watching the Russian bounder, Igor Volkov, mop the floor with Kārlis's beaten carcass. His father had not intervened, afraid of the consequences of defying the Soviet machine. Now with his mother and sister present, Kārlis realized that his reckless actions had endangered the whole family. How would they get along if the NKVD arrested Papu?

"Sorry about that fracas last night," Kārlis told his father.

"Doesn't matter, son. The business is gone," Janis Pērkons said. "Nationalized."

There wasn't time to digest the grave news before his father caught him in a rowdy bear hug, crushing the log against Kārlis's ribs and lifting him off the floor. "I understand the army has inquired after your health," Janis said.

"Ow! Papu! My ribs," Kārlis cried, struggling to get free.

His father released him. "Did you tell them you're Bolshephobic and don't qualify?"

"Yah, yah." Kārlis didn't feel like joking about his doomed future. The heavy log gave him an excuse to move quickly through the kitchen, barely pausing to exchange knowing nods with Tante Agata.

Cutting through the dining room, Kārlis's progress was hindered by the houseguests, the entire Krumins family huddled in meeting. Kārlis nearly bumped into Mrs. Krumins, who, her back to Kārlis, was busy scolding her white-headed spawn. "Just because the Pērkonses go out in the forest at all hours, does not mean you are allowed to."

Hugo, a practiced expression of deference on his pale face, looked past his mother's shaking index finger to greet Kārlis.

Kārlis was relieved to see him. Hopefully that meant the rest of the firebomb detachment had also made it back.

"And wipe off that lipstick, young lady," Mrs. Krumins said, swiping at Elza with a napkin. "You do *not* want to stand out from the crowd."

Elza, her long hair in obedient braids, looked like she had a saucy retort on the tip of her tongue, but she saw Kārlis and clamped her mouth shut, staring like she'd never before seen a man carry wood.

Mr. Krumins had, for some reason Kārlis could not fathom, grown mutton-chop sideburns since his eviction from the police force. He was out of his league in the wife-daughter lipstick dispute and, watching Kārlis struggle under the log, he was oblivious that his portly figure blocked Kārlis's path.

"*Sveiks,*" Kārlis told the Kruminses.

The houseguests stared stupidly as Kārlis tried to squeeze past, like *he* was the one intruding on *them*.

No wonder everyone's gaping, Kārlis realized. He was big news, notorious. Been in a fist-fight with a Communist. Drafted. Future scuttled. Just thinking of it all was exhausting. He pushed by, carrying the log toward the fireplace in the front room.

Hugo followed in his wake, using Kārlis as a vehicle to get away from his mother.

"So did you do it?" Kārlis asked over his shoulder.

"Can't talk about it here," Hugo muttered, with the irritating superiority a little knowledge can give a fellow.

A nod of the head wouldn't be *talking* about it, Kārlis thought, disgruntled and feeling outside the club. He was, after all, an integral part of the Corner House scheme, even though he hadn't actually thrown a bottle bomb. Kārlis was a founding member of the Nonchalants, a seven-member secret society formed the previous day to thwart the Communist takeover. "If not for me, there wouldn't be any Molotov cocktails to throw," Kārlis grumbled. It was he, for St. Peter's sake, who'd stolen the combustibles, and got beaten up in the process, which was why he couldn't take part in the actual strike. *Ak tu kungs!* He was as vital to the campaign as Hugo, that smug prig.

"Nice haystack disguise," Hugo said.

Kārlis halted in his tracks. He'd forgotten he was wearing the stupid hat. Is *that* what people were staring at? He was a spectacle! A beaten, bloodshot idiot in a foolish wad of yellow yarn. He shifted the log to yank the mask off, otherwise ignoring Hugo.

At the mantel, Vilz Zarins slouched commandingly in her black leather bomber jacket, a jubilant glow on her cheeks. Her dark hair was parted sharply down the middle, waves etched by fresh, comb lines. She saw Kārlis coming with the log and stood aside.

"Whatcha wanna know, Karli," Vilz said. Her smile activated dimples that divulged what Kārlis wanted to know.

She'd done it.

Kārlis dropped the log at the back of the grate, inciting an eruption of sparks. He didn't mention that he was fighting the Communist scourge with Tante Agata's yule log, which would sound anemic compared to lobbing actual firebombs. He nodded at Vilz and Hugo, somewhat awed, somewhat jealous of the heroism that must intoxicate them after committing a bona fide act of rebellion.

"Did you do it?" blurted Sniedze Krasts, horning his way into the ring like a pushy elf. "Did—you know— the bottle things, did they work?"

Kārlis cringed. He'd forgotten for a moment that Sniedze, the youngest of the Nonchalants, was even there. Kārlis had been obliged to invite Sniedze home with him so the clumsy kid, who idolized the older boys but had a disastrous habit of saying whatever popped to mind, wouldn't ball up the operation.

"We sent a burning message to our Russian overlords," Vilz said quietly, her pupils large and shiny. She stood taller. "Seriously, the magnitude of the blast caught me off guard, wouldn't you say, Hugo? That's one lesson learned. Those little bottles go *ka wumph*."

"It's a miracle if we got away with it," Hugo whispered, his drawn white face looking furtively into the corners of the room. "You're lucky you weren't there, Kārlis. Lucky you're the pen-and-paper type."

Kārlis adjusted his spectacles, irked. *The pen-and-paper type indeed!* Look who's talking! Hugo was slated to be valedictorian of their high school class.

Vilz looked oddly at Hugo, too. "It'll be easier next time," Vilz told him, with chilling confidence.

Kārlis turned his gaze to the burning yule log, hoping to heaven there'd be no next time. This was death penalty-level mischief. The Bolshevik scheme to communize the world did not include taking flak from impetuous adolescents.

"So where's Jekabs? Wasn't he in on it?" Sniedze wanted to know, again talking too loudly. "And Eriks?"

Vilz and Hugo exchanged a look. A froisson of intuition rippled over Kārlis's skin, making the hair stand up.

"Jekabs went home," Vilz equivocated. "Doing business as usual at the family bakery." She looked around the room before saying, "Eriks didn't show."

Kārlis felt the pressing weight of a heavy premonition. For a moment it was hard to breathe. "But the whole crazy plot was Eriks's idea!" he whispered.

"Did he *disappear*?" Sniedze asked.

Ice formed in the pit of Kārlis's gut. *Disappearing* was a national epidemic.

"We don't know what his problem is," Vilz whispered, with markedly less swagger.

"Sheesh," Sniedze said, suddenly breathing noisily. "The Commies are picking us off quick. That's Peters, Kārlis and Eriks." He counted on fingers. "Yesterday we were seven intrepid Nonchalants. Now we're already down to four!" He looked around at faces as if trying to foresee the next vacancy.

"I'm still here," Kārlis said, pushing Sniedze's shoulder. "Can't you count?"

"Maybe Eriks chickened out," Hugo said, dourly. "Or met a girl. Yah, knowing Eriks, that's what happened."

"Yah," Vilz said, lowering her head. "Let's not jump to the worst imaginable conclusion.

15

RIGA

ERIKS GAILIS LAY ON THE SMALL BED, muscles twitching in angst. Wherever his mind turned he found something he'd screwed up. He'd talked his friends into throwing Molotov cocktails at the Corner House, and then stood them up. But only because the NKVD had come to his door and he'd had to run for his life. His escape had been a triumph of sorts, except for stupidly leaving the Molotov cocktail behind, in plain view, for the Cheka to find, conveniently giving them evidence that would condemn his parents to death. Inwardly cringing, Eriks clutched handfuls of hair and rocked silently, choking down an animal cry. Sleep was impossible. It would be better for everybody he cared about if he didn't even exist.

He swung his feet to the floor and sat up, reaching to turn on the lamp. Now look. The bandage on his scraped-up hand had come loose and he'd smeared blood all over Mrs. Barons's sheets. Great. She'd been unwilling to hide Eriks in the first place, only reluctantly going along with her husband's heroic impulses. Eriks tightened the gauze bandage and dabbed at the linens, just making it worse.

Eriks exhaled at the futility of it all, looking around at the flowered wallpaper. So this was Zelma Barons's bedroom. He really hadn't known her that well in school, she being one of few to resist his charms. The little mirror propped against her desk was sweetly modest compared to the crystal-laden vanity table where Eriks's mother preened. *Used to preen,* he reminded himself, bitterly. He helped himself to a comb and tugged it roughly through his unruly mane.

There was a quiet knock. The door opened and Zelma's father poked his head through the crack, the freckles on the massive blond ever unexpected. "Good, you're up," Mr. Barons said, in a low voice. "Nearly time to go."

Eriks glanced at the window. It was still dark outside.

"Here, you can wear these," Mr. Barons said, tossing Eriks a pair of gloves and a well-worn fedora.

Eriks dressed and joined the Baronses in their small kitchen where Mr. Barons was gulping the last of his coffee. A cup had been poured for Eriks, but he only pretended to sip it, already too jittery as he followed Mr. Barons from the safety of the apartment, hoping to exit the Cheka-infested building unnoticed. By way of good-bye, Mrs. Barons pushed a paper bag lunch into his hands.

In the stairwell, they fell in behind some other pre-dawn workers. Eriks raised his collar and lowered the fedora. He steeled himself before crossing the brightly lit foyer, where the NKVD stood around, one holding his rifle in a casual one-handed grip, others sprawled in lobby chairs watching the departing residents with jaded eyes. Eriks felt sure his shaking legs gave him away, announcing that he'd defied their fellow goons last night. But somehow he made it past Stalin's secret police and into the biting, dark morning air.

Outside, tall apartment buildings boxed in the avenue, towering above the overhead wires that powered the trolley system. Eriks, eager to get far away fast, was relieved to see the shaky headlight of the streetcar rumbling toward him. He boarded behind Mr. Barons, nudging between strangers, one hand clutching his lunch bag and the other grabbing the hat-level handrail as the trolley lurched. He felt keenly aware of moving in the wrong direction, further away from home. Blocks passed, buildings lost bourgeois art nouveau garnishes, looking utilitarian under sparsely spaced streetlights as Eriks rode an unfamiliar route toward a shadowy vanishing point. This was someone else's life, he thought, finally getting off in an industrial district, a section of Riga he'd never seen.

"Darkness in our favor," Mr. Barons muttered, leading Eriks into a lumberyard.

Eriks had never been so grateful for the winter solstice, for the cloaking gift of the year's darkest day. He followed Barons along an angular walkway smelling of sawdust and machine oil, past mammoth piles of timber, appreciating Mr. Barons's responsibility as foreman here, and thus the magnitude of the risk he was taking for Eriks's sake. They stopped behind the shed nearest the railroad tracks. Farther down the tracks, a light bobbed in the fog. Someone swinging a lantern? Other than that, Eriks saw no one.

"We're going for that one," Barons whispered, pointing to a rail car loaded with milled lumber. "There's a hiding place in that wood stack. A couple of boys are already stowed there. You'll ride about two hours and slip off near a large dairy at the edge of the forest. Caleb'll show you. At an immense stone barn." Mr. Barons turned to look Eriks in the eye. "They'll let you stay there, but you'll have to earn your keep."

Eriks nodded sheepishly. Mr. Barons had already pegged him as a useless lug.

"When you get there," Barons said, his tone softened, "give this to my daughter." He passed an envelope to Eriks.

Eriks folded the unmarked missive and slid it in his pocket.

"If you have resisted arrest as you said. And if your parents have indeed been picked up," Barons said, "well, then this is the best situation I can recommend for you."

Eriks nodded bleakly. *Picked up.*

"The only option really," Mr. Barons said. "Fare well, son."

"*Paldies*, Mr. Barons," Eriks said, sad at breaking the tether.

"Let's go." Barons strode across the exposed lumberyard to the tracks.

Ignoring his clamping guts, Eriks followed Mr. Barons out into the open. It was only about fifty meters to the train, but he'd broken a sweat by the time he reached it. Hoisting himself onto the flat-bedded railcar, just like Mr. Barons had done, he stayed low, while Barons knelt before what appeared to be a solid load of lumber and began shifting pieces.

Eriks kept his eye down the tracks, at the light bobbing in the fog, probably a watchman.

"In here," Barons whispered.

Eriks crawled under some planks, and through an opening. The loaded lumber had apparently been cut in various lengths and stacked to create a hollow in the center. In the pitch black, Eriks couldn't tell the dimensions of the hidey-hole. He maneuvered from crawling to sitting, folding his limbs and ducking his head, cramped and tight-chested, unsure where to put his legs so they wouldn't bump the bodies he sensed nearby in the dark.

The hole closed with a thud, making Eriks's heart pound. He breathed hard and to his relief found there was plenty of cold air coming in through cracks. But the timber could shift and crush him like a bug, he thought, lightheaded with anxiety.

"*Sveiks*, mate," whispered a fellow, calming Eriks immediately. The voice sounded completely unworried, belonging to someone about Eriks's age.

"*Sveiks*," Eriks said.

"I'm Caleb," said the voice. "That's Kristaps."

"How many Cheka out there?" the one called Kristaps demanded, in a higher, probably younger, whisper.

"I didn't see any," Eriks replied. "Just a watchman or someone with a lantern down—"

"Quiet," Kristaps snapped.

Eriks stopped talking. He couldn't hear anything but the shuffle of someone's shifting legs.

"You didn't see them, but they're there," whispered Kristaps. "They're everywhere."

Great, Eriks thought. Just when he'd thought the situation couldn't get worse, he was now boxed in with a bossy paranoid. He settled back, bumping his head against a beam. "Where you fellows from?" Eriks asked. He'd detected an accent in the older boy.

"Poland," said Caleb. "Got out a year ago when Nazis tried moving us to the ghetto. Met Kristaps here in Riga after his parents were deported."

Ghetto? thought Eriks. *Deported?*

"Got anything to eat?" Caleb asked.

Eriks pushed Mrs. Barons's lunch toward the voices. He wasn't hungry. Someone crackled the paper bag with alacrity, and then it went silent.

"Why were your parents deported?" Eriks asked the younger kid.

"Teachers," came the reply, sounding from a full mouth. A second later the kid said, "Now zip it 'til the train gets moving. They're out there."

Eriks shut up, leaving a tortuous silence. Teachers had been deported. His parents had been *picked up*. He felt sick: twisted guts, the chills. He'd heard rumors like these, but they'd always seemed so distant, other people's problems. He wasn't political. Now that he was the victim, he was outraged that no one did anything to help them. Where were the police, or God, or America? He'd been so stupid, actually ridiculing his friend Vilz for trying to organize resistance with a secret newsletter. While Vilz had been taking a stand, Eriks had been drinking shot glasses of Black Balsams and playing jazz with girls who shared his be-merry-for-tomorrow-we-die mentality. He was disgusted with himself.

He'd change.

Finally, the train began creaking down the tracks, jostling the stowaways against their hardwood hideout.

Caleb shifted his sitting position and quietly asked, "You got a gun, mate?"

"A what?" Eriks was shocked by the question, then embarrassed to be shocked.

"A gun. Do you pos-sess a fire-arm?" Caleb enunciated each syllable like he was speaking to a simpleton.

"No," Eriks said.

"Oh, well." Caleb sighed. "Me neither."

"Me neither," Kristaps echoed.

I should hope not, Eriks thought, grateful he was not journeying with an armed and unstable gradeschooler.

"Guess you'll be running errands with us then," Caleb said.

There was a movement. Eriks sensed Kristaps had kicked Caleb into silence.

"What're you talking about?" Eriks said.

"Hey, we're probably in the forest now," Caleb said, instead of answering. "Let's go up top and twist a weed."

A wiry figure snaked past Eriks in the dark, opening the woodpile to a rush of cold air.

"What errands?" Eriks persisted as Caleb also crawled toward the opening.

"Oh, you know," Caleb said, noncommitally, "delivering groceries and what not."

The sky seemed bright as Eriks's head emerged from the faux lumber-stack hideout. He grabbed at boards for balance, taking a moment to get his sea legs before climbing onto the wood, as the other boys had done. Ears blasted by a daunting *whoosh* of cold pine air, he thought he caught the tail of their conversation, Caleb saying, "— but Barons wouldn't have sent him if he wasn't all right."

Eriks climbed over to where Caleb and Kristaps sat, sheltering a match between their hunched shoulders. By its flame, he finally got a look at his traveling companions.

The swarthy, taller one was no doubt Caleb. He had a good start on a moustache and wore circular wire glasses. Uncut hair supported his claim of being on the run for a year. Under a battered fleece jacket, his flannel shirt was unbuttoned low, despite the freezing torrent of air. He returned Eriks's stare with a stream of smoke, offering him a lit, hand-rolled cigarette.

Eriks took a drag, sensing the other boys sizing him up. By his shiny shoes or his alpaca-blend, herringbone weave, double-breasted, imported overcoat, they might conclude he was some cotillion ninny. It was time to establish his credentials. Pointing to his shoulder, Eriks said, "Look here. That's where a bullet grazed me."

Caleb leaned over to look, but it was impossible to see the broken coat threads in the dark.

Eriks went on, "The Riga NKVD was shooting at me." It seemed these bumpkins ought to be impressed by the big-city secret police. "I barely escaped by climbing down the drainpipes of a five-story building. That's how close I came to dying last night." He passed the cig back to Caleb.

"Whew!" Kristaps whistled. "You truly caught some Cheka heat there." The kid's voice had a madcap, scoffing ring. "Bet your tailor was furious!"

Caleb laughed.

Eriks felt his color rise. He leaned over to give Kristaps, who was sitting on the other side of Caleb, a warning eye.

Kristaps looked to be ten or eleven. Brown hair poked from his pointy-knit cap. He was muffled up to the cigarette stuck between rosy, wind-whipped cheeks. "Here's where a Soviet mortar blasted my trousers," Kristaps said with a snort. "See the holes?" He poked cricket-knees up through torn pants.

Eriks was about to grab the flyweight by the collar and hold him over the tracks one-handed, when he noticed Kristaps's feet, perched on the wood, sandwiched between sheets of cardboard and wrapped with cloth. Abruptly ashamed, Eriks turned away. It took grit to joke around when you didn't have shoes. The scrapper punched way above his weight.

"Yah, but my tailor's a mean son-of-a-gun," Eriks said, leaning forward to give Kristaps a nod. "He's the real reason I'm leaving town."

Caleb chuckled.

Eriks silently watched the white trunks of a birch forest whip past while the eastern horizon turned gray. Freezing air blasted commonplace ideas from his head. Wheels underneath him oscillated over the tracks, shaking off any hope he had of returning to his warm, vacuous lifestyle.

"So, you trying to get back home?" Eriks said finally, shouting at Caleb to be heard. "Find your family?"

"Hell, no," Caleb said. "You know what Hitler does to Jews?"

Eriks did not want to admit that he did not know.

"I'm lucky to be here in the Baltics," Caleb said, redefining Eriks's understanding of luck. "To Stalin I'm just as undesirable as the next guy, no more no less. The Commies will take my property." He opened his coat to show he had nothing anyway. "Nazis want my head!"

Eriks was appalled. One of his best friends in Riga was a Jew. Did the Leopoldses know about this ghetto business? And Nazis wanting their heads? If Eriks knew one thing now, it was that he knew nothing. But he'd better be a fast learner.

"So where do we deliver the groceries," Eriks said.

Caleb glanced at Kristaps. Then he pointed into the woods, the tip of his index finger poking from a wool glove. "In there," Caleb said. "To some really angry men."

At the moment the train was traversing a stand of Scots pine. Dark, pointy-topped evergreens, stalwart and protective, interlaced the bony white birches.

"I know there's men hiding in the forests," Eriks said, lest his companions think he was a complete rube. "They must be freezing their stumps off. But if it comes down to getting arrested or hiding in the—" Eriks was struck by a sudden thought. "Say, maybe that's why Mr. Barons sent me here, to join up with those kind of fellows."

"Well, unless you got a gun, delivering chickens is as close as you'll ever get to Silent Forest," Kristaps said, and spat.

"Silent Forest," Eriks repeated, trying not to sound like it was the first time he'd heard the name. "How do you find them?"

"You don't," Kristaps said. "That's the point."

"But there must be a headquarters," Eriks said.

"Every renegade band I've met in the forest is acting on its own, as far as I know," Caleb said, returning some salvaged shreds of tobacco to a little tin box. "But all with the same purpose."

"To string up Ivans by the nuts," Kristaps said. Clutching the opening of his thin coat with one hand, he announced, "I'm going in."

A moment later Caleb also scooted back inside the hidey-hole.

Eriks stayed up top, as if the rushing air might blow off the dread that kept settling on him. He didn't know what to do. Growing up in a swanky, family-owned department store had not prepared him for life as a fugitive. But he had to do something, fast. Now that his head was out of the sand, he was going to pay attention.

Riding the rumbling woodpile, Eriks tried to digest everything he saw: where the tracks ran parallel and where they branched off, a water tower in the distance, a power transformer, a bridge, impassable bog, the morning moon over exposed farmland, dense forest, an isolated house. He saw a police station, guards at a roadblock, and a fire on a hill. He noted the names of villages. He desperately watched the passing landscape as if it held the key to his survival, tears freezing at the corners of his eyes.

He would need a gun.

The train slowed to a bare chug, cornering a tight bend. Caleb and Kristaps crawled back out and the three boys watched in awe, the entire length of the train forming an arc. A weak sunrise imbued the fog with a silver glow, dramatically backdropping the churning black smoke of the locomotives. It'd been about two hours since they'd left, or so it seemed to Eriks. He said, "Is our stop coming up?"

"Yah," Caleb said, stretching and looking diverted. He removed his glasses and tucked them in his coat. "But who said anything about a stop?" Caleb was studying the tracks and rocking his weight back and forth. "Pay attention," he said, waving a finger to Eriks. "I'm only gonna show you this once." Then he hurled himself off the railcar in a forward somersault, rolling down the snowy embankment and out of sight.

16

"Gentlemen." Kārlis's mother was coming at him and his friends with a tray of crystal and a certain look-what-I-have enthusiasm. She had a fresh coat of lipstick in a berry shade, a white chiffon apron, and her brown hair was mounded around her head in elegant swirls, like when she entertained his father's company.

Tante Agata hobbled a few paces behind, carrying a corked flagon made of brown crockery. *Rigas Black Balsams*, the cordial's ornate black-and-gold label had always appealed to Kārlis.

"Mmm, Black Balsams," Sniedze said. "What's the occasion, Mrs. Pērkons? Can't be Christmas since that's not allowed."

His mother's eyes flashed at Sniedze, and Kārlis expected her to scold him, saying that Christmas-talk could get them arrested and, almost as bad, upset Kārlis's little sister. But she smiled at Sniedze with barely a trace of annoyance and set the tray on the sideboard.

"No occasion, Sniedze," Mrs. Pērkons said. "I just think if a boy's old enough to be a soldier, he ought to be able to have a nip of spirits."

"I won't argue with that," Kārlis said, raising eyebrows at Vilz, who was shrugging off her bomber jacket, getting ready to nip.

Tante Agata set the flagon carefully on the tray and turned to face the fire, her gray braid over one shoulder, and long necklaces of chunky amber glowing in the firelight. Her birdlike eyes seemed as hot as the flames while she watched the yule log destruct.

"May I help you with that, Mrs. Pērkons?" Hugo said, stepping over to the tray. "I know how to mix it."

Kārlis's mother said, *"Paldies,* Hugo."

Hugo uncorked the Black Balsams and, with Fred Astaire-aplomb, lifted it high so the viscous black liqueur poured out in a long, thin stream precisely into the slim opening of a crystal carafe. He was stirring in the vodka when the fathers, having ferreted the scent, ambled over.

Mr. Krumins went to the radio, a VEF in a large cabinet standing in the corner, and fiddled at the dials. A tinny voice from far away entered the room.

Kārlis moved closer, trying to block out Hugo's chatter and understand the broadcast, which was in Russian. He couldn't catch the gist, but thought he would at least recognize any mention of the Corner House. Had the Corner House gone up in flames? Had his friends succeeded in burning NKVD headquarters to the ground, resulting in the escape of detainees like Peters? Had they at least inconvenienced the brutes?

Vilz was listening hard, ear toward the tuner. "I swear," she whispered, coming over to Kārlis, "flames were seven meters high."

Kārlis nodded. Vilz wanted to be a journalist. Accuracy meant something to her.

"I assume you've registered the radio," Mr. Krumins bellowed, "so it's legal."

"Of course," Kārlis 's father said, though Kārlis doubted that was true. "Those broadcasts are baloney, anyway. Put on some Strauss."

Hugo had poured his elixir into tiny glasses. Mrs. Pērkons passed them around.

Kārlis waited by Tante Agata until everyone was served.

"Be advised," Tante Agata told him, nodding at the glass. "The Balsams is an erudite distillation. Sometimes called Black Devil, for good reason."

"Thanks for the warning, but I already feel like something on the bottom of a shoe, Auntie," Kārlis said. "Don't think I can feel any worse." It even hurt to lift his toasting arm.

But when everyone else did, forming more-or-less a circle of raised glasses, Kārlis held his up toward his mother, then to the other boys and Vilz, who were all watching one another. It was a silent, grim toast, more of a salute to those *not* there, to a cancelled Art Academy, to a confiscated Leather Works, than a cheer to the remaining Nonchalants, unlike yesterday's reckless vows of rebellious solidarity.

When glasses were already tipped, and before anyone could stop her from being so brazen, Vilz quietly said, "Free Latvia."

Kārlis quaffed the potion in one slug. A fireball burned to the pit of his stomach and flared back up his throat in a toxic cloud. *"Ak tu kungs!"* he said, eyes watering. That hurt. But he sucked it up, refusing to be like Sniedze, who was huffing between a scream and a choke.

A noisy crackle filled the air as Mr. Krumins dropped the phonograph needle on a record. Trumpets heralded a symphony.

Kārlis realized that he'd been holding his shoulders crunched up tight. He released them with a loud exhale. Then he noticed the shadows, lurching up the walls and onto the high ceiling, lending a gothic quality to the ambiance. Naturally! Being the *summer*house, he'd mainly been here during summer's hours of endless light. But tonight, the winter solstice with its plethora of candles, made the refuge look like the kind of place favored by bats.

His head felt lighter, swaying in three-quarter time with a string section. "What is this?" he asked his father, who was ensconced in the couch, tapping his foot and looking thoughtful.

"Treasure Waltz," said Janis Pērkons.

How could Papu be so calm? Kārlis marveled. The man's life's work was just confiscated. Kārlis had always assumed that *he* would inherit his father's business, not some Russian interloper. That Kārlis never wanted to be a businessman was beside the point. The Leather Works was gone, lost to the likes of Igor Volkov, and here they were listening to Strauss. Strange.

Hugo sallied over with the carafe. "I always say, when life hands you an empty glass, find the person that life has handed the vodka to." He refreshed Kārlis's drink without being asked. "You look like you've been trampled by bulls."

"Never fight ugly people, Karli," Vilz said. "They got nothing to lose."

"I would never fight for my beliefs," Sniedze said, "because I might be wrong."

"Let's eat while it's hot," his mother said, and Kārlis joined the household, following her to the dining room like a polite pack of hungry wolves.

Biruta was already there, climbing over chairs to light candles.

Kārlis sat down near his friends at his mother's end of the table, from where she could hop to the kitchen or gaze at his father over ten place settings of white linen. She set a steaming tureen of pig's head stew before him, and Kārlis was counting his blessings when he heard the click of high heels on wooden stairs.

Mrs. Krumins entered the room, casting a willow tree shadow on the wall. She took in the gathering with inscrutable eyes, and said, "Where is Elza?"

Kārlis had not noticed Hugo's sister was absent.

"Stomped out with her lipstick," said Mr. Krumins. "She can't have gone far."

"Surely we're not starting without her," Mrs. Krumins said, directing the comment to Kārlis's mother. "Anything might happen. Hugo, go down to the river and find her."

Hugo started to rise.

"Sit down, Hugo," Mr. Krumins said, pushing a palm out. "We're starting without her." To his wife's eviscerating gaze, he said, "We should not hold up everyone's dinner just because Elza is not on time."

Kārlis's father pulled out the chair on his right for Mrs. Krumins.

She looked at it with doubt before woodenly sitting down. "That's another disadvantage of staying here," she muttered, as Kārlis's father pushed her in. "Practically next door to that Lileja Lipkis."

At the mention of Lileja, a shot of tingle zinged Kārlis's brain.

"She's a fast one," Mrs. Krumins said. "And it's no wonder, raised in a tavern by her father. A bad influence on my Elza." She turned a steely gaze toward Kārlis's mother.

"Bon appétit," his mother said. "Please begin."

"Lileja's not like that, Mama," Hugo said, dishing potatoes. "She's a nice girl. I wouldn't worry."

Kārlis froze, the serving fork midway from the pork platter to his plate. Hugo had just defended his girl. He felt a blast furnace ignite behind his eyes, but he kept cool. Mimicking the others, he dished and passed the purple cabbage, then the sour cucumbers.

"It's not like we're in the city," Hugo said. "Elza and Lileja probably met friends and the time got away."

"That's exactly what I *am* worried about," Mrs. Krumins said. "Hanky panky with her so-called friends in the forest."

"It's normal the youngsters want to get together," chimed Kārlis's father. "Blow off some steam."

"You can't keep her home forever," Hugo said.

"Nothing normal about any of this," Mrs. Krumins said, looking like she'd drank vinegar. "I'll keep her locked in a closet if I have to."

"Please pass the herring," Vilz said.

"And the bread," said Sniedze.

The room went silent, but for the occasional scrape of a chair on the floor, and the clink of silver against china muffled by linen. Kārlis swirled a forkful of pork and potato through the cream on his plate, leaving a pink trail of juice that he sopped up with bread, which he chased down with milk.

Optimism grew with every bite. That was the power of Mama's cooking. He'd miss her the most. He'd miss dinners like this. Looking around the table, he sensed the mood of the company improving, and felt a soft spot for everyone there, for everyone, that is, except Hugo.

Chatter bubbled in small pockets along the table.

Papu was telling a story about a farmer who'd traded him garden produce for leather goods. "So he shows up with a wagon full of plums! Nothing but plums," Janis boomed, refilling the wine glasses of all within reach. "We had plums coming out our ears. How many liters did you put up, Agata?"

"Every jar, glass, and flowerpot in the house!"

His father laughed like Tante Agata had said the funniest thing he'd ever heard. The faces at Papu's end of the table were relaxing, Kārlis noted with admiration. Papu had changed their orbits by sheer force of personality.

You don't appreciate a thing until you know you won't be having it again, Kārlis thought looking around the table, like chit-chat and jokes at dinner. Simple stuff, but really as nourishing as any food they ate. He wished he'd inherited his father's gift of gab. Conversation was like throwing a lifeline to someone. Folks talking over a matter at dinner were weaving a net of sanity, however temporary, saving everyone seated there.

"Anna, you're a marvel," his father said, waving his fork and smiling wolfishly.

His mother nodded.

"Indeed," Mr. Krumins added, "Especially with shortages being what they are."

His little sister was under the table, crawling through a forest of legs in pursuit of the cat.

"Pour me some milk," Kārlis said, pushing his glass toward Vilz.

"I've heard in the army they expect you to pour your own milk," Vilz said, complying.

"That could be a problem," Kārlis said. "Once poured, who will raise it to my lips?"

"Seriously, Kārlis. It's outrageous," Vilz said. "Your call-up notice absolutely violates international law. An occupying nation may *not* forcibly conscript citizens of said occupied country."

"Uh-huh," Kārlis said, head starting to hurt.

"I was about your age when I was drafted into the Czar's Imperial Army," Hugo's father said, over a mouthful of food. "Boys become men. Men become soldiers. Show some backbone."

"Weird that Kārlis is one of *them* now," Hugo said, philosophically. "Guess we better watch what we say, right?" Hugo chuckled like he was such a comedian.

Under the table, Kārlis squeezed a piece of bread in his fist. Hugo had given voice to a vague, lonely idea gnawing Kārlis's stomach lining. More than the physical deployment, the Army could pit him against his home folk, and them against him. He opened his hand to find a knuckle-shaped lump of dough.

Ting, Ting. Mrs. Krumins tapped her fork against a goblet. *Ting, ting, ting.* Every tap felt like a stab to Kārlis's eyeballs. She stood holding up her glass. Kārlis had spent enough time with the Krumins family to know someone was in for it.

"This may be the last meal we share together before Kārlis goes off to join the Red Army," Mrs. Krumins said. She saw that everyone was suitably sober before gazing into her upheld goblet like it was a crystal ball. "It's just a matter of time until my Hugo will be drafted too." Her speech was speeding up. "Probably tomorrow's mail…or the next day's. My only son. Adding his name to the tragic list with Peters Kalnins and Kārlis Pērkons… "

"Oh, for godssake," her husband said, dropping his fist on the table. "Get a grip, woman."

Mrs. Krumins put the goblet down. "How can you think of eating at a time like this?" She screeched her chair back. "Why don't we *do* something?" Mrs. Krumins threw her napkin on the table and turned her head like she couldn't stand the sight of them.

No one answered her question. Kārlis kept chewing as everyone's gaze followed her clicking heels out of the room and upstairs. Why was only the Crazy Woman talking sense?

"Kārlis, why don't you just run?" Sniedze said. "There's guys hiding in the forests and—"

"That is foolish talk," Mr. Krumins interrupted, planting his hands on either side of his plate. "The Red Army's known to execute whole families, sometimes a whole village related to a deserter." He stood, squared his shoulders and spoke in stentorian tones. "Our only hope lies with Germany." Leaning over the table like a preacher into the pulpit, he directed his advice first to Kārlis then to the rest of the table. "Pray for the forces of Adolf Hitler. Pray to God Hitler crosses our borders soon."

Kārlis interpreted the silence to mean that nobody else felt safe, or foolhardy, enough to tout a political opinion.

"Cross our borders?" Vilz said quietly. "You mean storm through Latvia like he has everywhere else? I'm praying for a sovereign Latvia. Not one overrun with Nazis."

The table was sitting up now, leaning forward. Kārlis wasn't surprised by Vilz's views, which he well knew, but he'd never heard Vilz contradict an elder. He glanced around half-expecting the etiquette patrol to pounce or for Mr. Krumins to grab Vilz by the throat.

Vilz sat, hands in her lap, blue eyes alert, black hair slicked back neatly. She didn't have one line on her face compared to haggard old Mr. Krumins, but she had a kind of authority, probably gained from attending secret meetings and throwing Molotov cocktails.

"In fact, I'd rather we stop praying and start fighting," Vilz said. "The Prime Minister should have issued a call to arms immediately when Russia strong-armed the election. He was wrong telling us not to resist. But it's not too late."

Mr. Krumins crossed his arms, eyes narrowed. "You're a little young to be questioning the prime minister."

"Old enough to remember what it was like to have choice," Vilz countered.

"Lady and gentleman, we're not having this discussion here," Kārlis's father said, standing. "The consequences of loose talk are brutal. I won't permit it in this house."

"The devil himself does not know where women sharpen their knives," shot in Tante Agata, who was circling the table and clearing plates.

Foreheads creased as the diners puzzled over her proverb. Tempers seemed to cool.

"So if it were up to you, you'd send our boys to certain defeat?" Krumins demanded of Vilz, getting in the last word.

Certain defeat. The phrase hardened in Kārlis's stomach like a cold stone.

Vilz said, "No one would die in vain who established for the record, for all time, that Latvia did not go willingly to the Soviet Union."

Die in vain. No, Kārlis would rather die for a good cause. But he didn't want to die at all. Dying is what old people did. He was seventeen and, instead of adulthood, death taunted him from every corner.

"We need some tangible marker, and that's the last I'll say, sir," Vilz said quietly, appealing to Kārlis's father. "Bones on a battlefield. Some major act of rebellion. Something future generations can point to that says this was not the will of a sovereign nation. And it better be something that will stand up against a deluge of brainwashing."

"Where are you getting these ideas?" Krumins said, red in the face. "You sound like some penny-ante statesman, not a high schooler. I already warned you against those meet—" He closed his mouth at the approach of high heels, clicking like the clock on a time bomb.

Mrs. Krumins was back in the room. Kārlis saw his father and the other men rise and grudgingly stood up as well.

"Krumins," said Mrs. Krumins. "Elza is without a chaperone. It's past curfew."

"I'll get her, Mother," Hugo said, looking eager to leave. "Coming Vilz?"

"I'll come too," Sniedze said. "We might see Lileja." His eyes lit up. "And she'll want to know the news from Riga."

Mention of Lileja Lipkis roused Kārlis's heartbeat. He wanted to get up and leave with his friends, but he caught sight of his mother's bright eyes watching him. He had to consider her feelings at the moment. She'd made his favorite meal, after all. His buddies didn't miss a beat though, he noticed, as they loaded into their coats and went out. He might as well be gone already.

Mr. Krumins, grumbling and placating, followed his wife upstairs, leaving just the Pērkonses at the table.

His mother went to the kitchen and came back minutes later, with a warm plate. "Apple cake with vanilla sauce," she murmured, setting the dish before Kārlis. "I saved this especially for you."

"*Ak tu kungs*," Kārlis said, acting enthusiastic. "My favorite!" He had no appetite, but moved the cake around, shoving some down his throat.

He wanted to satisfy his mother's desire to talk, but every topic on Kārlis's mind was either bad news or taboo, and his little sister was listening.

His hours were numbered. He wanted to see Lileja.

"*Paldies*, for the cake, Mama," Kārlis finally said, rising, feeling like a heel. These might be the last moments at home with his family, but he was too distracted to stay. "That was delicious."

Kārlis collected some dishes and took them to the kitchen. He found Tante Agata in the chair by the wood stove, pipe-hand in her lap, mouth open and snoring lightly.

"Leave it, Kārlis," his mother said, following him. "I'll wash up."

As Kārlis buttoned his coat his father came up to him. Janis's beard looked grayer than it had an hour before, if that were possible. "Kārlis," he said in a low voice, "I must warn you again not to discuss anything political with anyone." He seemed to be debating telling Kārlis something else. "Even Mr. Krumins, son. Though he's an old family friend, he has the instincts and training of a police officer and… who knows. It might one day turn out that he has more in common with the local militia than with us. I'm not saying that is the case, and certainly don't repeat it. I'm just saying—" His father sounded tongue-tied, talking with his hands as words eluded him. "Just don't talk to anyone."

"Don't worry, Papu. I trust no one."

As he left, Kārlis heard his father say, "It'll be all right, Anna. The boy knows to get out of the rain."

17

KĀRLIS COULD SEE BY TRACKS IN THE SNOW that his friends had taken the forest path, no doubt headed to the noble oak. Before crossing into the wall of trees, he looked back at the house. It was sparingly lit, but the stained glass around the front door cast some color on the surrounding carpet of white crystals. The flip of a curtain at the window gave away the presence of his mother, the vigilant lookout.

The forest was desolate, the trail muddy in some places, icy in others. No matter how well you knew a forest, it could be spooky in the dark. When Kārlis arrived at the river's edge, fog was rolling over the water like a convoy of ghost tanks. Ten minutes further, the path skirted a village road where the local Communist militia had erected barbed wire and the sign *Halt or You Will Be Shot!* Maybe the barbarians succeeded in scaring most folks away from the woods, Kārlis thought, but this forest was part of him on a cellular level, its contours indelibly etched in his mind and muscle memory. He rushed down an outcropping of boulders like they were stairs. Nobody knew these woodlands better than he did after sixteen summers of hide-and-seek. Except maybe Hugo. They'd been as close as branches of the same tree.

How could he have stood the loathsome carbuncle for so long? A bitter taste invaded his mouth and he spat it out. Packing a snowball, Kārlis heaved it at a tree-trunk, wishing the broad bark were Hugo's white face. That felt good. He scooped up more snow and began to pack another one. It felt good to have a face to hate.

He couldn't blame Hugo for everything that had gone wrong. Not for Peters's capture or the derailed Art Academy, not for that despicable Russian who had ambushed him with a whip and stolen Papu's workshop, or for being drafted. But Hugo better think twice before messing with Lileja. Kārlis was going to articulate an understanding with her tonight. Scooping up more snow, he packed the ball harder. Hugo didn't know the first thing about that girl.

Kārlis, on the other hand, had observed his Lileja intently. His muse, she was the constant subject of his drawings and paintings. He could catch her wood-nymph posture and hungry coquettish expression with the flick of a pencil. If you didn't get the essence of someone's face in the first strokes, you might as well give up. No amount of erasing or redrawing could improve it. It was an organic thing, to capture the face. In the process of mastering Lileja's expressions, he'd learned a surprising contradiction about the barkeep's daughter. She could knock a man down with the bat of her eyelashes, but also she was as delicate as a porcelain dish about to fall off the shelf.

The result of Kārlis's studies was his masterpiece, a portrait of Lileja at the beach last summer. He'd given her the portrait during their last visit and in his view that cemented the indefinable something between them. All had been going according to plan until Hugo waltzed in, throwing a wrench in the courtship machinery.

Kārlis heard the voices before he saw them, comfortable low murmurs coming from the noble oak. The tree had a girth of seventeen folk dancers holding hands, and a glorious, spreading crown. The lowest branch supported a wooden swing, a community monument to rites of spring, and a hot spot for youth even when the ropes were frosted with crystals.

"Oh Hugo, your hands are fuh-reezing!" It was Lileja. Hot poison shot through Kārlis's veins. The varmint's hands were on her! He squeezed the snowball to the hardness of a diamond.

Lileja and Hugo were laughing.

"Here, finish it," Hugo said. "Warm us both up."

Eyes accustomed to the dark, Kārlis easily observed the clearing. Moonlight illuminated Lileja sitting on a wooden swing hanging from an oak bough. In front of her, glowed Hugo's silver-white head. The swing had been pushed high and was held there braced against Hugo's waist. Hugo was nestled into Lileja's furs; her long legs, covered in soft wooly stockings and dainty leather snow boots dangled above the ground. The air was foggy around their heads. A low, encroaching cloud veiled the edges of the clearing with intimacy. Lileja tipped her chin up, drinking from the flask.

"This is so dangerous," she said, giggling. "You really have a Moddletoff cocktail?"

"Mm-hmm," Hugo crooned.

Plying her with alcohol! Divulging Nonchalant secrets! Kārlis was disgusted.

"Thissis what we're drinking?" Lileja said.

"No, no," Hugo said. "We're drinking a mixture of very good quality vodka and Black Balsams."

From his mother's kitchen! The snake thief. Kārlis was livid.

"You see," Hugo explained. "Molotov was dropping bombs on the Finns and calling them bread baskets. So the Finns, like they're playing along with it, invented the cocktail. To go with the Molotov bread basket."

The back-story was lost on Lileja. "Issit in your pockets?" she asked in a gooey voice. "Hmmm?" She leaned into Hugo, sliding her hands around in his coat and pockets.

"Careful," Hugo chided, holding up a milk bottle with a gold fringe fuse. "And no smoking! This could take our heads off." Hugo moved around the trunk of the tree for a moment, like he was stashing the incendiary weapon. Then he came back and held Lileja, or perhaps steadied her, so she wouldn't fall off the swing.

Kārlis approached them rigidly, an angry outsider, aware his disapproval was not stylish. He stood on the opposite side of the raised swing, so Lileja hung between him and Hugo.

"*Sveiks*, Lileja."

Lileja flinched. "Karli. You scared me, shneaking up."

Crossing her legs, she shifted her weight on the swing, taking a more neutral position between him and Hugo. She smelled boozy. "I heard you been through the wringer," she said, touching his arm with a mittened hand.

Hugo said nothing. He made no move to release Lileja and the swing.

An owl hooted from the direction of the river and was answered by one nearer the village.

"I thought your mother sent you to find Elza," Kārlis told Hugo.

"Vilz and Sniedze are getting her," Hugo said. "Appreciate your concern." Smiling and adjusting his grip on the swing, Hugo said, "I couldn't leave this rare woodland creature alone."

O spare me the poetry, Kārlis thought, longing to wipe the smile off Hugo's face.

"Hugo told me about the army, Karli," said Lileja.

Damn him. Hugo was a bone in his throat. Kārlis did not deserve this aggravation right now.

"What a rotten break," Lileja said. She flung her arm around Kārlis's shoulders, making her sweater askew and showing brassiere straps and milky white skin and collarbones. "When do you have to go?"

Kārlis didn't reply. It was slimy of Hugo to get Lileja drunk like this. Some of the mothers already accused Lileja of being a strumpet or what-have-you, making Kārlis extra protective of her reputation. He'd better get her home before further damage was done.

"And he told me," Lileja said, tittering, "about the haystack disguise." She tried to stifle a laugh and failed, "I wish I could have seen it." Then she burst out, belly splitting, "I adore you, Karli. Ha ha. Oh, ha ha ha! You're such a goofball." She almost fell off the swing again.

Hugo caught her in his arms.

That did it. Kārlis glared at Hugo, his eyes two howitzers. "I heard you say you have a Molotov cocktail," he said, hefting the snowball in his palm.

Hugo couldn't deny it. He'd been caught bragging about it to Lileja.

Kārlis watched Hugo's face carefully. The patrician features everyone thought were so handsome didn't charm him. Hugo actually had quite thin lips, and a nose like a 30-60-90 triangle from geometry. Hugo glared at him, stubbornly holding his grip on the swing, on Lileja. The clearing was negatively charged like the air before lightning strikes.

"So that must mean you didn't have the guts to throw it," Kārlis said. "Is that the way it happened? At the Corner House? You let the other guys do the heavy lifting?"

A flicker of guilt shadowed Hugo so Kārlis went in for the kill. "Let me guess, you were the first to run?"

"Shouldn't be talking about it here," Hugo said, pushing the wooden plank of the swing into Kārlis's ribs.

Ow. Pain wracked his whole skeletal frame. "I agree," Kārlis said, shoving the swing back at Hugo. "I was surprised to hear your blabbing about it just now."

"Hugo trusht me," Lileja said. "He told me all about what happened to Peters." Eyes filled with tears. "They can't just take him away like that."

"Hugo was the first one to run then too," Kārlis said.

Hugo jammed the swing into Kārlis so hard it knocked him back a few steps, saying, "Isn't what happened bad enough without your *kāpost galva*—"

Stultified with pain, Kārlis somehow regained his balance. He took aim at the white face and heaved the snowball at point blank range, hitting Hugo square between the eyes.

Staggered blind at first, Hugo then moved like a wolverine. Ducking around the side of the swing, he released Lileja, slamming into Kārlis.

Lileja screamed, groping at ropes as the swing zagged loose.

Kārlis was laid out with a jarring thud, never knowing such pain. Hugo was on his chest, icicle fingers at his throat.

Lileja's screams flayed the air.

Kārlis pried Hugo's fingers off his neck and scrambled to his knees. Then he delivered the blow he'd imagined for two days, shocked at the crunch of Hugo's nose under his fist and the immediate slickness of blood on his knuckles. Yah! That's how he should've hit that Russian Volkov! That's how he'd handle himself in the army!

Hugo recoiled, arms to head, blood blotching the snow.

In the next instant all the pent-up bitterness for his butchered life went into Kārlis's fists. He beat Hugo as if the white-haired boy were Stalin himself.

What in hell was Lileja screaming about!

Then the world turned upside-down. Kārlis tumbled over Hugo's outstretched leg, glimpsing bare branches overhead before vision was snuffed in white darkness. Hugo was on his back, twisting his arm. Snow packed his ears as Hugo ground his face downward. Ice scraped. He couldn't breathe. Rising for air, pushed down harder, ribs shrieking. He couldn't worm away or throw Hugo off however he bucked.

Smothering. About to die.

Suddenly the weight came off. Lifted by the scruff of the neck, up and over, Kārlis saw branches again. He lay there on his back, gulping air, arms raised protectively, panting.

Vilz stood over him, her black jacket and sea cap stark against the moonlit fog. "Can't you find a *kāpost galva* Commie to choke?" Vilz demanded, giving a handkerchief to Hugo.

"He's such an ass," Hugo said, holding his nose.

"Well, what if you had to go with the Russian army?" Vilz said. "You'd go crazy, too. Give a brother a *kāpost galva* break." Vilz leaned down, inspecting Kārlis for damage, and picking up his glasses from the snow. "Hugo's not the enemy, you know," Vilz said, brushing off Kārlis's fedora and giving it to him.

Vilz looked from Kārlis to Hugo with disdain, "Wouldn't they love to see you two at each other's throats? Two less Latvians for them to beat down." She patted her pockets until she found cigarettes.

Raising a foot she stamped the earth, striking the match along the side of her pants.

"What difference does it make," Kārlis said, getting up gingerly, holding his ribs and quashing the desire to cry. If he couldn't even defend himself against Hugo, how would he survive the army?

Sniedze appeared suddenly, his approach to the clearing unnoticed. "We heard screams," Sniedze said. "What's going on?"

Elza was several strides behind him. She was willowy like her mother; with the same silver-white hair as Hugo, but waist length, zigzagged as if her braids had recently been undone and wild from running.

"What happened?" Sniedze asked. "NKVD?"

Nobody answered. The quiet was finally broken by Lileja's moan. She was draped over the seat of the swing, head hanging, hands and feet brushing against the ground.

Perhaps, Kārlis hoped, she'd been too drunk to notice Hugo grinding off his face.

"Nerves," Vilz said. "We're fighting with each other because we don't dare strike at our real enemy." Her dimples deepened when she dragged on her cigarette. "We got to pull together, *cilvēks,* to bring the Ivans down."

Kārlis stood crookedly fingering his throat. Hugo was bent over, washing blood off his face with snow. Lileja was limp fur, hangdog over the swing. The notion that they might bring down the Ivans was farfetched.

"We have to recapture the spirit of the Nonchalants and stand together," Vilz said, trying to turn the debacle into a pep rally. "All we have is each other."

"You guys were fighting over Lileja," Sniedze concluded, sounding disappointed for missing it. "Who won?"

Kārlis, amid alternating waves of humiliation and euphoria, determined to keep to his plan. Going to the swing and supporting her waist, he lifted Lileja's shoulders, parting the curtain of gold hair to find her face. She looked slack and slobbery, and red as a beet from hanging upside-down.

"Let's go," Kārlis said. "I'm taking you home."

Lileja popped up like an unsteady rag doll come to life. Grabbing the rope, she said, "Yah. I have something to give you, Karli. I have to give you before you go 'way."

"Fine," Kārlis said, secretly soaring with delight. "Then let's hit it."

"Kārlis," Hugo said, reluctantly. "I want to forget this if you do—"

A beam of a light invaded the clearing. It streaked over Hugo and oak branches and the paralyzed figures of Elza, Vilz and Sniedze, and then swept away.

"Стой, или вы будете расстреляны!" The words were incomprehensible, but the shout was close, practically in the clearing with them.

Everyone scattered like shot.

Kārlis grabbed Lileja and tried to lead her into hiding. She stumbled and fell to her knees. He bent down and braced her arm across his shoulders, leveraging her to her feet, her weight a knife between his ribs. Gripped in panic, he trudged her behind the vast girth of the noble oak. She wrapped her arms around the huge trunk, as if clinging to the only stationary object in the universe.

"Shpinnin'," she said, face white. She wasn't going to make it further.

Digging his fingers into the crevices of the bark, Kārlis cat-climbed up the trunk to the lowest bough. He hung, bouncing, until the lumpy accumulation of snow on the limb slid off in a gloppy, white sheet. Dropping to the ground, he saw he'd covered much of their tracks by shaking the snow loose.

He heard a man's voice, close now. Kārlis resisted the instinct to run. He could easily get away from anyone in these woods, but what would be the point with Lileja staggering around drunk.

Sliding behind the tree trunk, he leaned into Lileja. "Get down," he said, lips against her ear.

"Wherss everyone?" she hissed loudly.

"Quiet, Lili," Kārlis said, holding her as they sank to the base of the tree. "Don't move." He opened his coat, wrapping it around her, pressing next to her and the oak. He lowered his hat brim over her head, disguising their shapes, hiding for his life.

As long as there was no dog they might get away. Please God, no dog, Kārlis prayed, too tense to breathe. If there was a dog, life was over.

Light wavered from the other side of the trunk, growing stronger in swings and sweeps. Lanterns or a flashlight, carried by someone come to investigate Lileja's screams.

Whoever it was, Kārlis sensed the intruders were in the clearing now, right on the other side of the tree. He stopped breathing, waiting for them to pass.

"Hold it," said a man. "What's this?"

Kārlis's hope plummeted.

"What?" said a second voice.

"The snow's disturbed here, all over this place," said the first voice, a Russian.

Kārlis held his breath. He imagined the man tracking him to the other side of the tree. At any moment the light would be in his face. Then would he run?

"This is where the assembly was held," the Russian finally said. To Kārlis's relief, the voice was no closer. "Quite a number of them by the looks of it." Then he yelled, "Over here!"

Ak tu kungs, more Cheka? How could they not discover Kārlis and Lileja hiding only meters away?

"I think it was just kids," said the other man in the clearing, a Latvian with deep gravelly voice, probably local militia. "See the swing?"

"I can't see my hand in front of my face," complained the Russian.

They shone light all around, but it only reflected fog's white opacity.

"This swing here," said the Latvian. "It's still swaying."

Lileja shifted. Her body sagged and slumped between Kārlis and the tree trunk.

"What's that?" said the Latvian.

In the silence, Kārlis again imagined the stalkers closing in on him.

"A cigarette butt," the Russian said.

"Who's here?" said a third voice, sounding winded, huffing. It entered the clearing with another beam of light zagging around the surrounding trees.

"Hoodlums," answered the Russian. "And don't say *just kids.* Idealistic punks can be the most dangerous of the citizens," he said, with a note of superiority. "The young tend to be intimately knowledgeable of their locale. And natural liars, too stupid to be afraid. Then they grow up to be worse."

"They went this way," said the new voice.

"I'm not so sure. Look there," said the Latvian. "Anyway, we'll never find them in this fog."

"Maybe not tonight," said the Russian. "But if there're youths like that around town, you need to handle them."

"This swing," the new voice said, "part of the religion, no?"

"Well, folk tradition I suppose, in spring," said the Latvian.

"Old pagan rite, that's what I heard. See that it's destroyed."

"Yah, Comrade."

"Get me a list of the local priests, or whatever you call the religious leaders. And round up their scripture books, whatever they are."

"There aren't religious leaders *per se*," the Latvian said. "The lore's not really written. The *dainas* are sang or recited—"

"Instead of arguing about everything, just bring in the troublemakers," said the Russian. "We have quotas to meet."

"Yah, Comrade. They're mainly grannies, but of course." Assurances became fainter, but the grating, raspy voice promising to round up grandmothers gave Kārlis a chill. The Cheka were hiking away on the same trail they had come.

Kārlis listened hard, following the rustle of clothing and jangle of gear until he could hear nothing more. A hound bayed in the distance. He didn't dare move. What if one of the crafty buggers had stayed behind, and was in the dark clearing now, waiting silently until Kārlis revealed himself? He stayed hidden until his teeth were rattling in his head and his muscles were clumsy from the cold. Finally, Kārlis leaned out to look. The clearing was empty. In the distance, nebulous spheres of light looked far away and small, wobbly in the hands of foreigners to the path.

He tugged Lileja, saying, "Let's go."

She was too weak to stand without aid. He steadied her shivering body. Her breasts felt cushy against him. As his hand pressed the dip of her lower back, Kārlis dared for a moment to feel elated by his good luck. Then Lileja buckled at the waist and vomited all over him.

K. Smiltens, 1953.

AK GAWD! KĀRLIS STOOD, JAW DROPPED IN SHOCK, arms stuck out, chest dripping with hot vomitus. A vile gurgle from Lileja's depths warned him to sidestep just in time to dodge the next projectile stream. He pivoted in panic, searching for the police lanterns, afraid the retching and coughing would draw the Cheka back, but the lights had vanished.

He didn't know how to help Lileja, so Kārlis kept his distance, wiping chunks off his shirt.

She spat and leaned against the pine, wiping her face on her sleeve. "I'm better now," she said, despite her bloodshot eyes, flaccid mouth, and hair plastered to a white cheek.

That's good," Kārlis said, trying not to breathe the sour stink. "We better hurry."

Kārlis opted for a shortcut, handling Lileja like the dangerously volatile, spewing stomach on unsteady legs that she was. The trail was steep at the end, but quickly brought them out of the woods. Kārlis disliked exiting the cover of trees, even though as far as he could see, the village was as dark and lifeless as a cemetery.

He spread the barbed wire as wide as he could and laid down his coat for Lileja, ripping it in the process. Still she snagged her clothing and scratched her arm climbing through. She was in no condition to assist him through the fence. It took him a perilously long time, slithering on his back in the snow, to negotiate the wicked coils of wire. Then, with Kārlis's frozen arm around her waist, they hurried down two short blocks to where a steeply pitched roof edged in icicles marked the sanctuary of the Bier Schtube.

Entering the dimly lit tavern by the back door, Lileja strode urgently upstairs to the family quarters, head bowed. She was filthy with vomit, mud and blood, soaked and freezing. Kārlis was relieved she was going to get cleaned up and wished he could do the same. He'd looked sketchy even before Hugo ground off his face, Lileja threw up on him and barbed wire ripped his coat. The best he could do was walk with head held high.

Surveying the public house thoroughly before entering, Kārlis found the joint empty except for Lileja's father, who sat behind the bar reading a newspaper by light of a desk lamp. Few people would let their guard down by drinking beer under the stern gaze of Josef Stalin, General Secretary of the Communist Party and ruler of the Soviet Union, whose portrait hung behind the bar. Besides, it was after curfew.

Before the occupation, on any given night Kārlis would've seen at least six sets of elbows at the bar and a gang of the usual publicans arguing amiably around the soapstone stove. Now it was so empty he noticed for the first time the pegs on the cedar walls that were usually covered by coats. Without the locals, he saw runes carved on the oak bar, and a geometric folk motif on the woven tablecloths. Wooden beer pitchers were stacked in a pyramid against the wall near a tower of ashtrays—Kārlis had never known the place to have enough of either. The Bier Schtube looked different without the people in it. Or maybe the idea that you might not see a place again made you really look at it.

Mr. Lipkis sniffed and turned a page.

Kārlis arranged his hat and gloves to dry over a chair near the stove and walked to the bar, sliding onto a stool. The day's offerings were scribbled on a slate menu in chalk, the usual misspellings.

"*Sveiks*, Mr. Lipkis," Kārlis said.

Lipkis held out the pages of *Pravda* with a stern expression. "Can you read this?" he asked.

"Some," said Kārlis. He adjusted his glasses and leaned over to look at the bold Cyrillic headlines. "It says something about starving people in the Baltics rejoicing to join the worker's paradise in Russia."

Lipkis nodded, as if that's what he'd thought. "You're lucky," Lipkis said. "You young people learn Russian in school. That's the future. Impossible to learn at my age."

Kārlis had never thought of it that way.

"I understand you've been ordered to report forthwith," the older man said, neatly folding the paper.

"Yah, that's true." Kārlis could easily imagine how the village's sole barkeep already knew he'd been drafted. Probably the man who delivered firewood to the summerhouse had overheard his mother and Tante Agata wailing about the call-up notice. The wood cutter had told the next customer on his delivery route, say the schoolmistress—she loved to blab—who in turn had trotted down to the Bier Schtube and informed Mr. Lipkis while waiting for her order of smoked eel. Or some such chain of gossip. Kārlis felt oddly warmed to be at the center of the village interest. Even though *talk* was considered a deadly habit, he'd miss these lovable rumormongers.

"Well, if you're old enough to be a soldier, you ought to be old enough to have a beer," Lipkis said, getting up to pull a draught from the tap.

"*Paldies*," Kārlis said, wondering why adults were suddenly plying him with drink. He'd have loved a hot chocolate. He hoped Lileja would be down soon.

"You're welcome," Lipkis said.

"Paldies, *Comrade*," Kārlis added hastily, knowing Lileja's father admired the reigning vernacular. "And I've been admitted to the Art Academy," Kārlis said, reaching for his wallet, carefully as his bruised muscles were getting stiff. Removing the matriculation card, he gave it to Mr. Lipkis with a knowing nod.

"Congratulations," Lipkis said, examining the card and rubbing the stubble on his chin. "But the army's the way to get ahead. Especially given the, uh, the current political landscape."

"I'll go to the Art Academy after the army," Kārlis said.

Lipkis raised his eyebrows. "You can make a good living as a painter," the older man said, gesturing at the portrait of Stalin. "Now that every bar in the country has one of these."

Kārlis knew better than to contradict Lileja's father, but the portrait of Stalin didn't belong in the same conversation as studying at Riga's renowned Art Academy.

"You've heard of socialist realism, right?" Lipkis said. "The style?"

Kārlis wasn't sure.

"That's where the money is," Lipkis said. "It's going to organize the artists. Get them all working along the same theme, so they say." He patted his newspaper like he'd just read about it. "Perfect that style and you'll be heartily rewarded. I'm talking large *dachas* in the country, plenty of work."

Kārlis listened politely, though the hair on the back of his neck was rising.

"Plus, it's the law," Lipkis said, as if detecting Kārlis's doubt.

"It's the law to paint portraits according to a certain style now?"

"Absolutely. That's why the only portrait around here will be Uncle Joe's," Lipkis said, gesturing to the dictator's steely visage.

"But an artist is not just a human camera," Kārlis said. "What about imagination?"

"Foolhardy," Lipkis said. "Draws unwanted attention."

"I want to paint what only *I* can see," Kārlis said. "What's in my head."

"Careful there, son. That's the kind of thinking that makes you a class enemy," Lipkis warned. "Gets you a knock on your door at night."

Lipkis didn't envision his daughter with that kind of thinker, Kārlis guessed. Nor perhaps, with *any* kind of thinker.

Lipkis looked at the matriculation card again. "But you must have potential, to get into the Art Academy. Main thing to watch is the subject matter. Art has to glorify the worker," Lipkis said, wiping away Kārlis's view like a spill on the counter. "You're young. You can adapt. Learn to blend in."

The faint crunch of snow on the walkway outside drew Lipkis to the window, from where he carefully peered behind the curtain.

Kārlis held his breath.

"NKVD," Lipkis said in a low voice. "Headed toward the train."

The *troika* from the woods, Kārlis thought, ready to bolt.

Shaking his head, Lipkis returned to the bar and folded the newspaper. "Well," he said, "it's getting late."

"I better get going," Kārlis said, standing. "It's just that Lileja said she had something to give me."

"That's right. I'll get it."

Kārlis felt somewhat embarrassed and a little concerned that Mr. Lipkis seemed to know what it was Lileja wanted to give him. Kārlis had assumed Lileja had some intimate forget-me-not for him alone, the departing soldier. A lock of her hair, for instance, tucked in a perfumed handkerchief. A photograph of Lileja, which he would keep near his heart through every foray to the front. Or a beautifully handwritten note, "Hurry Home to Me, Kārlis, My Heart Awaits, Swollen with Affection." He'd been expecting something along those lines. Now, however, when he heard Mr. Lipkis banging his boots on the stairway he realized he was a romantic fool.

Mr. Lipkis stomped back to the bar, red faced. Kārlis recognized the object in his hands, crestfallen. He winced as Lipkis slammed it on the bar. It was the portrait of Lileja at the beach, his masterpiece.

"You got a lot of nerve, boy," Lipkis said, glaring like his eyeballs were about to pop out of his head. "Bringing my daughter home in that condition. First I thought you's just stupid, bringing in this arty crap. But—" Lipkis was right in Kārlis's face, spitting mad. "You got a lot of nerve."

"No, Mr. Lipkis, that wasn't me," Kārlis said. "What happened is—"

Lipkis poked Kārlis hard in the chest, making ribs scream in pain and forcing him to take a step back.

"You got a taste for pain, boy, that's what you got. That and a lot of nerve. Hmmph. Coming in and drinking my beer after what you done to my daughter."

"I didn't do anything, Mr. Lipkis," Kārlis said. "Lileja will tell you."

"She's in no condition to tell anything, you saw to that." Lipkis came within millimeters of Kārlis's face. "Figured you're leaving, what the hell? Never see her again anyway. What the hell!"

"Nothing could be farther— It's not like that—"

"If she is deflowered or in any kind of trouble on account of you, so help me—"

He whacked the portrait against the bar, splintering the wooden frame. "That'll be your skull."

Kārlis backed off, hands up. "She won't be," he said, bumping into a table. "It won't be."

Mr. Lipkis balled his fists and stalked angrily toward him.

"I didn't," Kārlis said, backing toward the door. "I would never—"

"Don't come round here again, boy," Lipkis said. Raising a bulging forearm, his fist coming at Kārlis's belly.

Kārlis crunched in defense as Lipkis connected with the door handle. He banged it open for Kārlis to escape before slamming it shut.

Kārlis stood witless, exposed in the cold night. *Ak tu kungs*, he had not seen that coming. He searched the road for NKVD. Exhaling loudly, he wrapped his arms around his battered ribcage. His hat and gloves were inside warming by the stove. Freezing air staunched what felt like a deep cut inside his chest.

Everything was so *pie joda* messed up.

He turned and limped back toward the woods, yearning to be in his bedroom. Hugo was probably already there, and Kārlis didn't mind. Why had he been so angry with Hugo, anyway? And the draft, suddenly seemed a welcome distraction. Everything was so messed up.

19

JANIS PĒRKONS SAT AT THE FIREPLACE with his collar unbuttoned and his bowtie dangling around his neck, trying to unwind and hopefully doze off. But his wife managed to jangle his nerves all the way from the kitchen, where she and her aunt clanked a mountain of dinner dishes. Thinking of each person who dined at tonight's table made him sweat, everybody depending on him. How would he continue to feed them all now that his livelihood, or the *means of production* as the Communists liked to call it, had been snatched?

Be grateful you're alive, he reminded himself. For tonight, at least, we have a roof over our heads. Draperies cascaded from the high ceiling to the polished wood floor. Firelight blazed from the hearth. The homey elements wove a powerful illusion of safety. The truth was, at any moment the NKVD might notice the house at the end of the gravel drive flanked by stately linden trees. Then there would be a knock at the door.

The unpleasant thought was interrupted by a thousand jingling bells. His little girl was spinning through the hall making a red skirt swirl in a circle and shaking the coins edging a blue wool shawl. Biruta was wearing her folk costume.

Janis shot out of his chair like a scalded cat, checking that every window was covered. Heart in throat, he brusquely scooped up the silly girl, crazed knowing her innocent play had broken enough laws to incriminate the whole family.

Setting her down by his chair, Janis wanted to shake her.

She looked up at him happily. "It's almost Christmas Eve, Papu!" A gold circlet crossed her forehead. Blond braids hung past her shoulders. She was the picture of northern heritage cherished and handed down for centuries, his little Biruta. Janis tried to calm down.

"Oh, Cookie," Janis began, his heart sinking.

"I always wear my regional dress to church on Christmas Eve."

The fire crackled. A burning log collapsed into itself while Janis contemplated what would no doubt mark the lowest, most miserable moment of his career as father. He lifted her on his lap. "I thought I explained to you there would be no Christmas this year, Cookie. It's forbidden."

"No, Papu." Her jaw went rigid, blue eyes instantly submerged in pools. "You only said Christmas *trees* were outlawed. Now Christmas is against the law too!" A tear streaked down a round cheek. "Why Papu. Why is it bad?"

Because our godless oppressors want to snuff every hope of redemption.

A sickening chill spread over Janis when he thought how the Communists would punish them if the child erred. If she went to school and even mentioned Christmas, the Cheka might come to the door for the whole family. They'd show no restraint. Neither should he. He had to teach Biruta strict obedience to the Communist master, for her own safety. He'd scare the wits out of her, lock her in her room, take a switch to her backside, that's what he'd do.

No. He shook the thoughts off, knowing he wouldn't do those things. How much time would they even have together? He shook that thought off as well. Unbearable.

In a cold voice, Janis said, "Biruta, if they catch us celebrating Christmas they will hurt Mama and me, put us in jail, and we might not ever see you again."

He watched as fear and shame crumpled her face. He'd hit the mark.

She dissolved in a gush of hot tears at his chest.

Janis hated himself.

"I won't. I won't do it, Papu. Don't worry I won't do it."

"You're a smart girl, Cookie," said Janis, stroking her head. "I know you won't slip up."

The fire needed another log. But Janis wouldn't get up for anything.

"I know how to keep secrets," Biruta said, her voice distorted with the strain of trying not to cry. "I saw Kārlis bury something under the garden gazebo and I haven't told anyone. So you don't have to stop talking when I come in the room. I don't like that. And Papu, I don't like going to Soviet School on Saturdays, to learn Russian. I don't like it. I don't like it." He rocked her quietly until she burst out, "Can we at least have gingerbread?"

Janis sighed in dismay. He admired her unbuckling spirit, but it scared him.

"You drive a hard bargain, Cookie." She was so like him in that regard. "I think we can manage a secret gingerbread. But the 24th and 25th will be school days same as any other. Don't say the word *Christmas* to anyone. That's important. Don't mention the gingerbread. In fact, don't talk to the other children. You understand? Don't even talk to anyone."

She nodded.

"I won't talk to anybody, Papu."

They watched the fire burn. Then Janis gently bounced Biruta on his knees, extending his hands for her to hold as if they were the reins of a horse. In spite of himself, he whispered the forbidden lyrics of a *daina* they'd always sang together:

Run a little faster, steed of mine
Don't count your steps out one by one
Did I count your oats that way?
No, I gave you purest oats,
Clover reaped on a sunny day.

Tante Agata entered the room with a cup of coffee for Janis.

"Your mother said it's time for bed, little one," she said.

"Papu, I don't like to go to bed," Biruta protested, "because that's when they take people away."

"Where did you get that notion!" Janis said, appalled that the terror gripping the country even penetrated the consciousness of a nine-year-old. "No one will ever take you away, because we have the fastest horse in the country!" He tossed Biruta with a galloping knee-bounce that made her laugh, bells jingling. Beneath his smile he was sick with dread, because if they *wanted* to take her, he'd be powerless to stop them.

Biruta went upstairs whispering, *"Run a little faster, steed of mine..."*

Tante Agata followed her slowly.

"Agata," Janis said from the depths of his chair.

The elderly woman paused on the stairway.

"Better destroy the dress."

Tante Agata nodded, looking weary.

Janis closed his eyes.

When he opened them—he didn't know if it had been a minute or an hour later—his wife was there, putting a leather satchel on the coffee table.

"I've kept my eye out for things coming up for sale, like you told me," Anna said.

He closed his eyes again, sliding heavily back to sleep.

"These should hold their value," Anna said, her voice a fingernail clawing the blackboard of his slumber.

Janis!" She gripped his shoulder, shaking it. "I want you to get an automobile and take us away from here."

Ignore her. She'll go away.

"Janis, what do we do?"

Janis opened his eyes to find his wife sitting on the coffee table, between his knees, leaning toward him.

"Fleeing the country seemed such a drastic measure yesterday," she said, battering him with rapid-fire syllables. "Now I wish we were already gone. Is it too late? I could never go without Kārlis. What if we got him out of the country?"

Janis shifted in his chair, buffering his ears with the cushion.

"What's going to happen next? I don't think I can take any more," she said, whisking the cushion from under his head. "Can you hear me?"

"I hear you." He was awake, the moment of rest obliterated. "I hear you." What he did not hear was any appreciation for the risks he took just to put meat on the table, any gratitude for continually putting the interests of the family before his own safety. Only more demands. "You can't take any more. You want an automobile."

"Yah. Please don't fall asleep."

"I won't. You've seen to that."

"Time is running out. I know it would cost—"

"You have no idea what it would cost, Anna. If you ever stepped foot out of the house you might know how ludicrous, how risky—You have no idea what's out there. I could tell you of an incident just from my lunch hour that would curl your toes. Not to mention the horror of having coffee at the tailor's. Everybody wants something from me. Everyone has their hand out, tugging on my coattails." An unwieldy swell of anger and fatigue overcame Janis. "All I do is work to save our home, but when I'm here and this is all I get from you, I have no home."

Anna stood, turned rigidly toward the mantle and stared at the wall.

That shut her up, Janis thought sourly.

But she didn't cry. The ruffle on her blouse rose and fell with measured breaths, making Janis guess that she was already cried out. What were they even fighting about? He had no idea. She was only voicing something he'd already considered from every angle.

"Can we figure this out tomorrow?" He rose to stand by her. "I am just so dog tired." Leaning an elbow on the mantle, he tried to face her, but she wouldn't look at him. He hated arguing with her. She had the annoying habit of usually being right. "We're on the same side, you and I."

He expelled a deep breath and took his time with the ritual lighting of a cigarette.

"I'm looking at this wrong," Janis finally said. "You ask me for an automobile? I should be highly complimented you think I could get one. Where, Anna, do you suppose I might get a car?"

"Ford Riga, of course."

"Ford Riga was nationalized first thing. What else?"

"Well, there must be other cars…"

"There are about four hundred cars in Riga, Anna. We are not Germany. Though four hundred is a high-water mark for us. Why I remember after the Great War, there were six usable cars in the country. Six! for civilians - and about a hundred for the army. Even the Red Army vehicle fleet is considered poor. You better believe they'd notice something as conspicuous as us driving away in a private auto."

He began to pace in front of the fireplace.

"I have two acquaintances with personal cars. Gentlemen I play cards with, men without families. Their cars were immediately confiscated. Not that it would be impossible to get an auto on the black market, I grant you, for a king's ransom. Then there would be the challenges of getting gasoline, tightly controlled by Russians, and documents for crossing borders, all very expensive, very closely monitored."

He stopped pacing to look at her. Her hair had fallen from its pins and her shoes were off. She looked small.

"But if we got around those issues," Janis said, "Where do you propose we'd go? Where do you imagine is safer than here? You do know what's happening outside that door?" He found himself pointing toward the front door, and lowered his arm, taking a breath. There was no need to badger her. "Do you want to take your chances in the forest with a little girl? Because there'd be no coming back."

He surveyed the room. Four walls had never looked so good.

"My uncle's house in Schwerin," Anna said.

"Ah, Germany. You want to go to the heart of the hornet's nest," Janis said, smoothing his goatee absently. "You do understand *total war*? Meaning *every* resource is applied to the effort. If we were at your uncle's right now, and frankly I wish to God we were, but Kārlis would still have to fight, and maybe me too. Even so, I'd rather be in Germany now. I'd take a predictable nightly bombing by the RAF over guessing what degradation Stalin will fancy next. All of Europe—the whole *kāpost galva* world's at war. We'd have to cross Soviet-occupied Lithuania, Poland, so ravaged, it no longer exists as such. The chances of getting through in a private automobile are slim to nil. Rails are monopolized by the military." His unseeing eyes locked on a section of the baseboard. "It would have to be over the water," Janis concluded, throwing the cigarette butt in the flames.

"None of that would matter if *you wanted* to go," Anna said.

She was right, Janis admitted, feeling both outwitted and buoyed by her confidence in him. What the hell *did* he want anymore? Turned out of Riga. The business gone. Son taken. Putting his arms around her, he pulled her down into the armchair. He wanted it all back.

Anna sat rigidly under his arms, discontent to let him hold her there.

"I wish I could drive away with you this minute, dear lady," Janis said. "But it's not hopeless. We're better situated than many. Maybe we should sit tight, hold the course. Who knows? After the dust settles, maybe the Russians won't be able to maintain their illegal hold on us and they'll go home."

She nodded tentatively, unconvinced.

"We'll prepare options," Janis told her. "We'll prepare for the worst, and look for opportunities. Getting away wouldn't be a simple matter. I'll talk to Rudolfs Zales. He has connections. We'll know what to do when the time comes."

Anna exhaled, shifting in his arms, fitting like the puzzle piece that completed him. Her head under his chin, hair smelling like toasted sugar, her body pressed against his chest; their breathing synchronized for a few measures of solidarity.

"You're so beautiful. Know what you remind me of?" He stroked her hair. "Lustrous. Polished."

"Janis. Stop."

"Beautiful patina."

"Don't you dare compare me to a piece of leather."

"What?" Janis feigned dismay. "It's high praise. Since the dawn of time there's never been a material so flexible for its strength." He zeroed in on her lips trying to kiss her, but she wasn't having it.

"Goodnight, then," Anna said, getting up. "I'm going to sit with Biruta. The child's scared to fall asleep."

Janis felt cold after his wife left. He wanted to follow her upstairs, be in her good graces and get into her eiderdowns. But she was with Biruta and there was much to do and how much time was left was anyone's guess. He put on his coat and went outside through the kitchen door carrying the leather satchel.

The night air was freezing. Locking the door behind him, Janis looked up at the softly lit windows of the second floor bedrooms. Anna was already there, cracking the curtain and peering out. He felt the same way she did, protective of their home. It was a far cry from the poor house where he'd grown up with his widowed mother. But even then, and all the while working his way up from a cobbler, he'd foreseen living in a country manor like this. Nothing ostentatious, there was an understated elegance to the thick stone walls, a charm to the rustic property. But after all, it was just a building and one day the Communists would demand to have it. God let him get his family out before then.

Detecting no one in the vicinity, he set out for his workshop in the old carriage house on the outskirts of the property. He'd let the dirt road become overgrown with weeds to hide the existence of the carriage house from prying eyes. Again checking that he was alone, he ducked into the trees and fumbled his way through the woods in the dark taking care not to create a direct path to the workshop door.

Once inside, he lit lanterns and checked that no light escaped the black window coverings. He fired up the acetylene torch and used it to light the woodstove, kneeling before it for a few warming moments. Turning to the tool closet, he shoved aside garden implements and jiggled the boards of the back wall. The false back lifted out and behind it lay several bulging leather pouches on top of a metal cylinder. He set the pouches aside. The cylinder was heavy, more than half filled with gold and difficult to move. Janis wrested the drum out so he could add his recent black market acquisitions.

He emptied the secret compartments of his boots, gold chains under the fleece lining, gemstones in the hollowed heels. He might have found the skullduggery droll if the consequences of being caught weren't deadly. He removed the pouch worn under his clothes and dumped the contents of the leather satchel procured by his wife, piling treasure on the workbench. Everything was at least 22 karats pure: coins, chains, money clips, handfuls of wedding bands, cigarette boxes, diamond earrings, a ruby studded cross and a filigree tiara encrusted with gems.

As it all went into the cylinder, Janis fantasized about the prospects that would be available on the day he reopened the drum. There would definitely be enough money to fund a leather works, a tried and true enterprise, but what about polymer fabrication, plastics. The field held fascinating possibilities. He'd have the capital to enter it, if strategized correctly. These intervening months—or however long it would be before he could retrieve the cylinder—might be used to plan it out. An exciting possibility, something good might yet come of these wretched circumstances.

Igniting the acetylene torch again, Janis heated the metal surfaces of the drum until molten. He affixed the end cap and hammered delicately until it had an airtight, watertight weld. Using a

fine-tipped brush he painted the words, "Property of Janis Pērkons."
He put his tools away.

Janis had kept a humidor in his workshop ever since his first
promotion to Master Tanner. Extracting a thin cigar, he snipped the
end, lit it with the brazing torch and sat puffing, reviewing his
handiwork. He considered the leather pouches hidden behind the tool
closet to be funds for rapid flight, walking-around money. He eyeballed
the thickness of the pouches, making crude estimations of what his
family would need: passage to safety, heat, meals, possibly medical aid,
and hopefully education. Whereas the cylinder, too heavy to carry, was
the mother lode, capital for starting over when this nightmare was
over. It required a long-term hiding place.

Turning off his work lights he stepped outside cautiously,
looking to see if anyone was around. In the foggy nighttime solitude,
Janis ambled over the property considering where to stash the drum.

The beauty of his homeland never failed to charm him. From the
mossy bracken of the forest floor to the emerald flames of the northern
lights, Janis reckoned this was the most wonderful place on earth. The
thought of leaving it broke his heart, but Latvia was not the country he
loved as long as the Communists were in charge. He paused to
consider the oddity of a multi-trunked linden tree rising darkly against
the fog. Then he stubbed out his cigar and strode over to the well for a
drink of cold water straight from the bucket.

20

ERIKS GAILIS LEANED TOWARD THE FIRE, rubbing his shoulder and cursing the unyielding nature of frozen earth. He sat on a tree stump, one in a ring under a blackened chimney flue suspended from the high rafters of a stone barn that housed fifty cows. Steam issued from an iron kettle hanging from a tripod. That and a nearby box of dishes gave Eriks the impression something was about to be brewed. At least, he hoped so.

"Arm hurt?" Kristaps asked, unwinding strips of cloth from his feet and drying them near the flame.

"I'm just thankful I *have* arms after jumping off a moving train," Eriks said.

"And a tongue," Kristaps said, with a knowing air that was troubling.

"How 'bout a little advance notice next time risking limbs is called for?" Eriks said, as Caleb sat down nearby.

"Less time to fuss this way," Caleb said. "I could see you were a natural, mate. You roll like a wheel."

"Damned irresponsible," Eriks muttered. "Could've broken my neck."

Thinking he saw Caleb and Kristaps pass an amused look, he sighed heavily.

Eriks had already adapted to the stench that had bowled him over upon arrival to the barn, eagerly hailing the stinky enterprise as a haven of warmth and safety. The sun had barely risen, but a crew of boys already hummed along with pails and stools, tossing hay, squirting milk and shoveling manure among an infinite line of swishing cow tails. Eriks was impressed by the discipline and rhythm of the place, especially since most of the boys looked younger than him.

"So," Caleb said, suppressing a yawn, "everyone does chores here. We rotate. Shoveling muck is an easy way to start if you want."

Caleb got up and ambled toward the back of the barn, where ladders rose to the hayloft.

"Are you pitching hay?" Eriks asked.

"I'm sleeping in the hay," Caleb said. "My chores happen at night. Like I said before, you can help me and Kristaps if you have the stomach for it. But I warn you, some of the stuff we have to do... well, it's damned irresponsible."

"I'll go with you," Eriks said, automatically.

Caleb saluted him. "Then I'll see you tonight."

A chubby-faced youngster whizzed by, running for the barn door. Before Eriks could call out, "Where's the fire?" another boy ran past, and a third.

Eriks raised his eyebrows at Kristaps.

"They just want to carry the grub for the *Princese*," Kristaps said. "She's about to make her morning appearance at the kitchen door."

"*Princese?*"

"Hmm. Old Farmer Baron's grand-daughter or grand-niece or such."

"Wait, I know who you mean," Eriks said. "Is her name Zelma?"

"Maybe."

"Dark hair? Pretty, in a librarian kind of way?"

"Prettiest girl around here," Kristaps said, glancing up and down the row of cows.

"I have a message to deliver to Zelma Barons," Eriks said, rubbing his hair back and straightening his clothes. "She's a friend of mine from school." Checking his pocket, Eriks found the envelope Mr. Barons had told him to give his daughter. "You say she's in the kitchen, in that wooden farmhouse?"

"Is most mornings," Kristaps said.

Before striking out to meet Zelma, Eriks grabbed some stalks of fresh straw, twisted them into a loop and poked it into his lapel buttonhole. He stepped from the barn into a stinging cold morning and followed the tracks in the snow across the dairy compound.

The smitten farmyard urchins were already gathered at the kitchen door, elbowing one another off the stoop. When the top half of a Dutch door opened, Eriks understood why they vied for position, craning necks for a look inside. It was a window into a world of warm yellow light, fragrant with roasted oats. Framed by the gray-grained wood, was Zelma. Even layers of wool sweaters and work overalls couldn't disguise her curvy figure. A sweep of hair escaped her cap, dark against a long creamy neck.

Zelma handed mitts to two boys before opening the lower door.

"Careful not to spill," she said, as they carried a heavy kettle out between them. She gave a basket to the third boy. It looked heavy with jars of something, covered with a towel. Watching them leave, Zelma saw Eriks. Her eyes sparked with immediate recognition.

"You're here," she whispered, resting her gaze on him. "That can't be good."

Eriks shook his head, not trusting his voice. For some reason, Zelma's sympathy tugged loose control of his chest, making him want to pour his fears into her bosom and cry his eyes out. Instead he said, "I have a message for you. From your father."

She sucked in her breath. "What about?" Her hands shook when she grabbed the envelope, stuffing it into a pocket. "What?" she demanded, eyes wide.

"Nothing. They're fine. I saw them this morning. They're okay."

Pans clattered in the kitchen, making Zelma look nervously over her shoulder.

"Just a minute, for the bread," Zelma said, reverting to a public, businesslike tone. She turned into the kitchen and, watching her walk to the oven, Eriks saw a man in there looking around with a clipboard in his hand. He wore an olive green, wool uniform with tall black boots, and took an immediate interest in Eriks.

The two held eyes for a prickly moment. Eriks couldn't avoid it, but he instantly regretted being seen. He stood out like a cleaver among butter knives. He was taller than the official and, like Caleb had recently pointed out, guilty of being fighting age.

Zelma returned and blocked the man's view by pushing an armful of warm loaves to Eriks.

"They're collectivizing the farm," she whispered. "Tell Caleb, tonight's delivery will have to be the last." Zelma looked up at him. He saw her breath in the rise and fall of her sweater. "My room is on the second floor," she said. "The north-east corner."

"What do I look like, a squirrel that I can walk up the side of the building?" Eriks asked Caleb in the privacy of the hayloft. "Because that was clearly an invitation."

"She said *tonight*," Caleb clarified, agitated by the other aspects of Zelma's message. "Tonight's the last drop. So this is happening *now*. Christ Almighty."

Eriks examined the ladder he'd just climbed. Notches kept it from slipping, but it wasn't permanently attached to the loft. "Sometimes the simplest solution is the most obvious," Eriks said under his breath, wondering what Zelma wore beneath those farmer coveralls.

Caleb looked over. "If you think access to the *princese's* boudoir is your problem, mate, then you're not grasping the situation."

"Actually I don't think access will be a problem."

"We can no longer stay here," Caleb said, looking at the surrounding mounds of dry straw like it was the Taj Mahal. "I've seen plenty of farms collectivized. The place'll be crawling with Russians. There will be nowhere to hide. Not even under your girlfriend's skirts. They list all the equipment including every person working here. Then the state redistributes it all, to make it all so much more efficient. God help us. And if you don't want to be redistributed too, mate, and by the way I have no intention of being picked up, then we better be gone." Caleb sniffed and gave Eriks an accusatory glare, as if he knew Eriks was thinking about the strand of dark hair that had slipped from Zelma's cap. "Hey, this concerns you," Caleb said. "I guarantee after you spend a night in a frozen rail yard, trying to sleep, trying to hide, you'll take an interest in this."

"Okay, okay. What do you want from me?"

"I don't know. If we could find a small, family farm the Russians don't want. Maybe sleep in the barn in exchange for smuggling. That's the usual deal. But the Ivan's are onto every speck of dirt now.

Damned if there's a *kulak* left in this country, but we've got to find one now. Kristaps has no *kāpost galva* shoes. How's he going to keep up?"

"Well, these fellows we're taking the food to," Eriks said, sobered. "How do they survive in the woods without freezing?"

Caleb gave him a withering look. "They are the Forest Brotherhood. They have their ways and connections. I don't know what they are. All I know is, they exist to fight and if you don't have a weapon they got no use for you."

There could be any number of reasons why a fellow might be climbing a ladder into the farmhouse after breakfast, Eriks thought, as he ascended the northeast corner. If he got caught, he would feign knocking icicles off the storm drain or rescuing a kitten. He was more worried about what to say to Zelma, if she was even there. What if he'd completely mistook her cryptic remark? Looking at this in the clear morning light, how could he possibly construe what she'd said as a proposition? At school she'd been a boring, goody two-shoes. Why suddenly the seductress? Was it a trap?

The curtains were tightly shut, so Eriks had to slide the window open to see inside Zelma's room. It was unlocked. Someone was expecting him. He prayed it would be the creamy-necked vixen and not Comrade Green Wool. Parting her draperies, he took a long look. Then he pushed his head through and climbed in.

The room was dim. Zelma was sitting on the side of the bed, her hair loose. She turned her head when Eriks came in, but then returned to staring forward, as if she wanted to finish her thought before dealing with him showing up. It gave Eriks a moment to take her in. Her figure was covered from neck to ankle by light blue underwear. The soft fabric formed a Y on her lap, where the crease of her thighs met the line of her legs. Socked feet just reached the floor. Cold air from the open window had aroused her nipples. Eriks closed the window and rubbed some warmth into his hands. She looked up and he recognized a loneliness in her eyes that matched how he'd been feeling. Maybe holding her would save them both.

The bedsprings squeaked when Eriks sat hesitantly next to her. He had no idea what to say. To his relief, Zelma moved right into his arms. He kissed her on the lips. To his amazement, her fingers scrabbled at the buttons of his shirt. His skin stung with cold air where she pushed his thermal over his head. When her fingers fumbled at his belt buckle, he thought he'd burst right in his trousers knowing she was going to touch him. He dove under the blankets, naked, pulling her onto him. By the time he'd helped her wriggle out of her winter underwear, a warm space enveloped their bodies. The unsolvable problems were forgotten, none as urgent as this single, hot connection. A moan escaped Zelma's lips as Eriks entered the only place where his worries couldn't follow. Traitorous bed springs squealed like an alarm for the authorities. Eriks spurned them in pursuit of a grand, messy delirium that blew away all caution. Afterward, there were scant moments to hold one another before paranoia crawled into bed with them.

"You ever have the feeling something swift and terrible is about to happen to you," Eriks whispered, lacing his shoes and watching Zelma pull her coveralls back in place.

"You're just now getting that feeling?" Zelma asked. "Something swift and terrible has already happened to us."

"I had you wrongly pegged as a frightened little bird," he said, admiring her dark locks before she hid them under her cap.

"I had you pegged as an arrogant, reckless playboy."

Eriks waited for her to say that now she believed differently. In the silence, unfamiliar noises in the building made his mouth dry with anxiety. "I mean you don't normally seduce fugitives. Do you?"

"There's no normal anymore," Zelma said.

"Well, I think you're inordinately brave," Eriks said, feeling both swirly and serious. "Noble, even."

"Why? For having a roll with you?"

"Yah. For following your heart despite lurking farm collectivizors," Eriks said. He pointed to the wall as if they both knew someone in green wool with a clipboard skulked on the other side. "I'm glad you weren't too afraid."

Zelma looked amused. "You're taking my mind *off* the scary stuff."

"Really. What frightens you, my pretty little sandwich," Eriks said, wrapping his arms around her.

"First of all, you calling me a sandwich has me a little worried. But mainly, since you ask, today I have to go pick up supplies at this sinister village, Patikamspils. You know it?"

"No. But I saw a sign for it from the train."

"Picturesque little hamlet, scary as hell. Going there's like getting caught in a spider web."

"How so?" Eriks said, sliding his hand under Zelma's sweater.

Zelma looked down toward his hand with a tolerant expression before continuing. "It's home to the most rabid militia you never want to meet," she said. "They love making examples of errant townspeople. I have to drive the sledge right past NKVD command center, this old manor house where they're all lounging around, waiting for someone to punish."

"Well, can't you take a different route? There must be a back road."

"Nay. In winter there's only the one narrow road in and out, through deep forest. It's the only one cleared of snow. And it's edged with tall, frozen berms, so once I turn down it, I can't turn around."

Eriks nodded. "A trap." He could visualize the situation.

"That's only half of it," Zelma said, lowering her voice. "The folks living there are the worst sort of Soviet collaborators, the biggest turncoats in the country. Ready to tattle on their own mother to get in good with the Ivans."

Shaking her head, Zelma suddenly pressed her hand to her face, looking conscience-stricken. "Last time I went, I took this boy, Daniels. He accidentally broke a glass in the pub. One of the villagers got up from his beer and ran down the road, nearly two kilometers, to tell the Cheka. Trying to win favor, you know, saying something like an anti-Soviet youth was badgering the village, and that it would be easy to capture him."

"And did they?"

"Oh, yah! In a jiffy! Not just one or two guys, either. The whole *kāpost galva* outpost was raging. And guns! They came ready to take on an army."

"I'll go with you," Eriks said, retracting his hand from Zelma's sweater and smoothing her hair. "I'll take your mind off the scary stuff. Yah?" Eriks wanted to succeed where this Daniels fellow, whoever he was, had failed.

"Oh, no. I go by myself now. Keep my head down. You'd just make matters worse. They'd view you and your fancy coat as an invitation to trouble." Flashing a mischievous smile, she added, "Like I did."

Eriks felt somewhat invincible as he climbed back out the window. He leaped past the lower ladder rungs into the snow and rolled up like he'd just returned from vacation. The ladder felt light as balsa wood as he carried it back to the hayloft. Climbing up, he curled in a sun-warmed corner and slept hard, arms around a bag of oats. Hoping to conjure dreams of Zelma, instead sleep was haunted by Comrade Green Wool.

He awoke with a jerk, not knowing where he was, someone shouting. Eriks rolled over, eyes adjusting to the dark as he prepared to scramble under the straw. When a madcap peal of laughter split the air, he relaxed. Just Kristaps. Eriks got up slowly, rubbing his stiff shoulder and peering from behind a rolled bale of hay. Caleb and Kristaps were on the other side, lit by a candle in a pail, wrestling in the straw like fools.

"Stop tickling me or I'm gonna pee!" Kristaps yelled, squirming away from Caleb and springing to his feet. Caleb jumped up too, pushing his sleeves up to the elbow, and the two circled each other in boxer stances.

Eriks shook his head, once again heartened by their mettle. Stretching, he brushed straw off his coat. The barn below was dark, except for glowing orange embers at the fire ring. The cows had been released from their milking lineup and were milling freely in sociable clumps, stamping hooves, chewing cud and farting contentedly. Eriks envied them their situation. Outside, twilight was falling with the heavy fact that he had to leave the dairy before an armed man in green wool reduced him to a tally on a clipboard.

He wondered if Zelma had made it back from her errand, if he dared to look for her in her room to say goodbye. He'd never known a girl he wanted to take home to meet his parents. Now that he had, home and parents were gone. What if he never saw Zelma again, either?

On the other side of the hay bale, Caleb and Kristaps were spoofing a fistfight. Caleb punched wildly at Kristaps, shouting, "Take that you little runt!" The kid reacted with head snaps and theatrical grunts.

Grateful for the entertainment, Eriks stepped from the shadows.

Kristaps screamed.

"Shit!" Caleb said, flinching.

They were staring at Eriks as if Stalin himself had materialized from the gloom.

"What's wrong with you!" Caleb said, sharply.

"What'd I do?" Eriks said, as startled as they were. Then he burst out laughing. "Hoo! You suckers a little edgy?" His belly shook with mirth. "You should've seen the look on your faces!"

"You can't just appear from the shadows all creepy like that," Kristaps said.

"Not funny, mate," Caleb reproached. "Gave me a *kāpost galva* heart attack."

"Ah, that was grand," Eriks said, sighing and feeling human. He hunched his shoulders and popped his head up, mocking Caleb's look of fright.

"Oh, yah?" Caleb said. He grabbed Eriks by the collar and threw some swings at him, stopping his fist miles away. "That's for scaring the cabbage out of me and—"

"Looks so phony," Eriks critiqued. "If you're giving out a pummeling, make it believable at least. Like this. Here." Eriks pushed Kristaps into Caleb. "Hold him down."

Kristaps pretended to struggle as Caleb pinned his arms back.

"You both stay hidden behind my body, see?" Eriks said, pulling his fist high. "Lean in tight, Kristaps. Yah? Caleb, make these hidden palm-punches, hear that?"

The two caught on right away.

"I telegraph my punch. Kristaps, you— no, wait half a second. Now jerk your head." They got into a jaw-busting groove with convincing sound effects.

"Keep your arms back!" Eriks told Kristaps.

Kristaps's eyes, looking over Eriks's shoulder, suddenly widened for real.

Eriks's heart raced. Someone was behind him.

"Hey!" said a voice.

His fist high, Eriks whipped around, every nerve unhinged and raw, heart trilling in a drum roll. *Phew!* Zelma was standing on the upper rungs of the ladder, leaning forward on slender arms. He could barely collect his wits.

"*Sveiks, cilvēks,*" she said. "Sorry to scare you."

"Hey, Princese," Caleb said, coolly pushing Kristaps off him.

Eriks went over to the ladder and reached for her hand, hoping she wouldn't notice he was shaking.

"You've brought the expected air of sophistication to the place," Zelma said as he pulled her onto the loft.

Eriks could only grin foolishly and reluctantly release his grip on her.

"I found snowshoes," Zelma told Caleb, in a low voice. "The bags are packed, outside the kitchen door. And, since it's the last time, they're heavy."

"Wonderful," Caleb said, with characteristic finesse toward daunting tasks. To Kristaps, "Let's go get them."

He and Kristaps climbed down the ladder, leaving Eriks and Zelma alone together in the loft.

Eriks felt lightheaded, the singing in his groin leaving not a drop of blood in his brain. "Come here," he said, quickly. "I want to show you something."

He led her behind rolled bales of straw, taking small steps in the dim light to the back wall. There, a wooden shutter as big as a tractor covered the window opening, secured by a cross bar. Eriks lifted the bar out and one side of the shutter swung open. A freezing torrent of air blasted them. They melded together on their perch thirty feet up, dwarfed by a view of a gray frozen universe.

It seemed they were on the same level as the evening star. Below them, fencing outlined the dairy's property, poking up from the moonlit snow in a dashed line. The cleared easement that was the railroad tracks could be seen farther out, but beyond that... Eriks gulped. The forest loomed to the farthest outreaches of the horizon in a colorless palette of smudged lines that looked unforgiving and deceptively peaceful.

She gasped at the sight.

Eriks pulled Zelma tight, shivering to the marrow of his bones. Somewhere in that vast warren of trees, people were defying the Russians and surviving on their own terms. Tonight, he'd wend a path, under Caleb's guidance, to meet them.

"You know how dangerous it is to work with Caleb?" Zelma asked. "What they do to you if you get caught? Because sometimes you act like this is all fun and games."

In answer he held her tighter.

K. Smiltens, 1947.

21

IT WAS DARK BY THE TIME ERIKS CAUGHT UP with Caleb and Kristaps outside the kitchen door, no moon in sight. A pair of snowshoes, wood-framed with crisscrossing rawhide laces, was lying next to lumpy, stuffed burlap bags. Eriks strapped the contraptions over his city shoes and stood up, feeling empowered. He'd stay drier now, floating over the surface of the snow instead of post-holing with every step. But hoisting the heavy bag over his shoulder did make him sink lower in the snow and he had to lift his feet high as he trudged after Caleb into the trees.

The bag emitted an arousing odor. Blood? Perhaps it held freshly butchered chickens. It took every ounce of restraint he could muster not to rip into the stores. But his prospects depended on gaining the favor of whoever got these picnics. He was nervous about his appointment with the Forest Brotherhood and determined to impress them with his chicken-delivering acumen. Nevertheless, his stomach complained in a way he'd never before known. Ignoring it made him angry.

Several meters into the trees, Caleb stopped and loaded his sack into some sort of feed trough turned drag sled. It was already stuffed with the other bags and loaded with hay, probably for a horse. Kristaps sat on top of the heap, smoking.

"I can tell you from experience," Caleb said, giving Eriks one side of a leather harnass, "that it'll be fastest overall if you and I pull the sleigh." Caleb positioned the strap against his shoulder, ready to put his back into the effort.

"What?" Eriks said. "We're the mules and Kristaps rides up top like a sultan on a magic carpet?"

Kristaps looked down at Eriks, blowing a smoke ring.

Eriks noted the cardboard-wrapped feet perched against the provisions and acknowledged this division of labor was probably reasonable. But he was grumpy about it anyway.

Caleb did not appear concerned with Eriks's opinion, looking furtively in all directions and tugging the tub-travois until it started to slide across the trackless snow.

Eriks had no choice but to keep up with his side. He tried several uncomfortable strap-against-shoulder positions before catching traction and making any progress. He had never done anything so brutish in his life. Fear that a farm collectivizor or other authority might confront him whirred in his head like a flickering horror film.

They had just arrived at the dairy fence when Kristaps said, "Whoa, hold it right here." He jumped off the rig and scampered like a forest creature, disappearing into the trees.

"Where's the fool going?" Eriks demanded, toes already aching-numb and aggravated at standing still. He shot Caleb a look of annoyance. "Let's keep moving. Obviously he can keep up if he wants to."

Caleb was tolerant. "Wait a minute," he said, looking into the trees where Kristaps had disappeared.

Yoked to Caleb, Eriks could not make a move they didn't both agree on. So he waited, fuming. The moon was rising by the time he finally saw the clumsy whelp coming through the trees carrying something unwieldy. Eriks could've strangled Kristaps.

"Couldn't find where I put it," Kristaps said, coming up to the sled out of breath. He was dragging a pickax that he must've stashed earlier in the day.

He hoisted it on top of the burlap bags and climbed back aboard.

Eriks tugged on the harness, grimacing at the added weight. "This is *kāpost galva* heavy," he said. "Why add that?"

"Seems good," was all Kristaps could say.

"Oh, sure. I bet it seems great from your point of view, riding up top. I mean, it would be splendid to arrive with a gasoline-powered generator and a ripsaw, but since you aren't the one dragging this *kāpost galva* tub, don't go adding unnecessary weight to the deal." Eriks felt strangely monstrous. "And you stole a pickax from Farmer Barons? After he stuck his neck out sheltering us in his dairy?"

"Actually *the People* stole everything from Farmer Barons," Kristaps said, climbing onto the trough-sled and settling in. "I stole from the People."

"Good thinking," Caleb said.

"Well, if you're so smart, why didn't you get one for everyone?" Eriks said, now angry for sounding like an ass.

Kristaps spread his hands.

Caleb said, "We'll hafta share, mate."

"Yah, fine. I'm just the mule." Eriks didn't know what angered him more, the extra weight, that he would show up to the rebel meeting empty-handed, or that he felt powerless to stop his spirit's downward spiral.

"Here," Caleb said, opening a burlap bag and reaching an arm inside. He pulled out a cold, baked potato and gave it to Eriks.

Eriks crammed so much potato into his mouth he could hardly chew. He knew he was going to feel better now, though disheartened at how quickly he'd crumbled facing adversity. A pinch of snow slaked his thirst. He wanted to cry at what lay ahead.

It was one thing to learn in school that Latvia was forty-seven percent wooded plains. It was quite another to plod past every single pine, spruce and birch in the country, which is how the endless hike through frozen forest felt to Eriks. Steering the heavy tub between densely spaced trees and sharp twiggy thickets was a constant, inefficient, slow-going tug-and-push. Moonlight streaked branch-shadows on the snow underfoot. But through the trees, Eriks glimpsed the bright glow of the moon reflecting off what looked like an easily traversed open meadow or possibly a frozen pond.

"Why don't we cut across that?" Eriks asked, pointing his stick.

He'd quickly learned the value of a stick. Essential for pushing icy branches aside, the stick banged snow off low-hanging evergreens before Eriks passed underneath, and knocked off the sludge that kept accumulating on top of his snowshoes.

"Nay, Stupid," Kristaps said, from the sled. "Tracks."

"Lead the NKVD straight to Silent Forest," Caleb said. "They'd have our heads."

It wasn't clear to Eriks who would have their heads, the secret police or the renegades hiding in these woods. Either threat seemed remote compared to the certainty of losing toes if he didn't warm up soon.

"You give them too much credit," Eriks said, also not bothering to clarify the pronoun. He wiped his nose on an icy sleeve. "Nobody in his right mind would be out here in this weather, much less looking for tracks."

"Never said anybody was in his right mind," Caleb muttered, the words distorted, spoken from a quivering chin.

Eriks could see newspaper sticking out of Caleb's cuffs and collar. He'd probably employed this practical heat-keeping measure while Eriks had been busy making Zelma swoon. Eriks staggered forward with muscles of jelly, saying, "I should've salted my *apakšbikses*. I'm frozen stiff. Ha!"

"For once I don't mind your *hot air*," Caleb said.

"Are we almost there?" Eriks asked for the hundredth time.

Caleb sank back onto his heels looking upward, as if to study the big picture. Then he pushed forward.

"Please don't tell me we're lost," Eriks said.

"Can't you shut up?" Kristaps said in the hunted, bossy tone he'd used when Eriks first met him on the train. "They're out there."

"You always have to dwell on that?" said Eriks.

Kristaps said, "Everyone hates me because I'm paranoid."

Eriks answered with a defiant clack of the stick to his snowshoe and plodded forward. For a moment it was quiet enough to hear ice crystals crunching underfoot. Searching the dark, unnerving curtain of tree trunks made Eriks's chest feel like a tight shirt ready to rip. "The thing of it is," he gasped. "For every step we take deeper into these woods, we'll have to take a matching step to get us back out. Have you considered that?" He tried and failed to be calm and think of something funny. "If we don't find somewhere warm to hole up and—"

A wind rose up, shaking the twiggy treetops like a matchbox.

"Wait. I just caught a whiff of wood smoke," Eriks said. "Did you smell that?" He tipped up his nose, but the scent had vanished.

Caleb, paying him no attention, suddenly stopped. He glanced at Kristaps as if for confirmation, then turned the loaded trough toward a small knoll. The space between tree trunks was cramped. They had to push through the underbrush single-file, with Eriks removing his harness and dropping to the rear, head down to avoid eye-poking branches.

"Hold it here," Caleb whispered, gesturing for them to halt without turning his head.

Eriks waited.

Kristaps slid off the vehicle, and stood behind Caleb's elbow, pickax in hand, peering ahead.

Eriks strained to see over their shoulders into the woods, when something like a broomstick poked him in the back. Without looking, he pushed it away with a gloved hand, but it returned with a jab to his kidney. Suddenly Eriks knew, what he'd taken to be a branch was the barrel of a rifle. Someone was pushing a gun into his back. A roar filled his ears despite the silent forest, and his hands went numb. He felt strangely tranquil, detached, wondering if the gun were loaded.

"In dense woods..." intoned the man behind him.

The words made no sense, compounding confusion.

Steel pushed into Eriks's coat.

His brain froze. He saw his hands held empty in the air before him.

A metallic click sent his body shaking, teeth clattering in his skull.

"...the trees grow straight," Caleb supplied in a clear voice, stepping around from the front of the sled and approaching whomever stood at Eriks's back. "The trees grow straight."

After a lag, the pressure, it seemed reluctantly, left Eriks's back.

"Hell, Caleb," said the voice, suddenly genial. "Heard you yapping an hour ago. Who's the loudmouth?"

Eriks turned around, still trembling.

A man in white camo fatigues was lowering his rifle with a deliberate, measured movement. Eriks had no doubt the gunman would've blasted soul-from-body according to protocol had Caleb not stepped up at that precise instant with … what, some sort of pass code.

Burning at the callousness of it, Eriks only listened with one ear as Caleb explained to the gunman, calling him Aivars, about the dairy being collectivized. While they made mouth noises about exactly how many Russians had overrun the farm and the strength of their hardware, Eriks's eyes wandered from the partisan's assault rifle up to the black wool tam worn low on his forehead. It was studded with hammer-and-sickle NKVD cap badges that glinted dull red in the moonlight.

"Barons sent him," Caleb said, nodding toward Eriks. "He's a bona fide."

Aivars studied Eriks through narrowed eyes.

Head buzzing, Eriks only then noticed that two other men stood behind Aivars. One was portly, wearing a black beanie and a white cape fashioned from a mattress cover, over a black turtleneck sweater. The two-toned get-up reminded Eriks of the national bird, the White Wagtail.

"Tell Glamour Boy to keep his trap shut next time," Wagtail said.

It steamed Eriks to be talked over like that, rather than directly addressed. He'd get common courtesy, he reckoned, if he too were holding a gun. Without one, he was not even a person.

Behind Wagtail stood a tall, thin man, whose stick figure was accentuated by a black frock coat. Sun-leathered skin stretched over his bony face. The brim of a homburg hid his eyes. Slinging his rifle behind his shoulder, the black stick figure strode to the sleigh, where he dumped the contents of a burlap bag.

Eriks stared stupidly as rifles clattered out amid some rolling potatoes. He'd not known they were smuggling arms.

The thin man plucked a potato in long, twig fingers and tossed it to Wagtail. Then he gave one to Aivars.

An owl hooted as the men ate.

Eriks salivated, acid eating his stomach lining. Caleb and Kristaps didn't ask for food, so neither did he, but he was *kāpost galva* livid to not be included in the meal.

"What you staring at, Glamour Boy?" Aivars said, mouth full.

"Nothing," Eriks said. "If I blink my eyes will freeze shut."

"Hoo-tah!" Aivars crowed and looked at the thin man. "Haralds, you hear that? Glamour Boy is a wit!"

"This rifle has no stock," the man called Haralds said, examining the arms. "And here's one without a sight."

"The usual obsolete scavengings," said Aivars.

"Might make one usable weapon if we put them all together, but if you're thinking these will admit you to the party," Haralds said, "then you are mistaken."

"Couldn't hassle my granny with this arsenal," said Aivars, pushing items around. "Pickax looks good, though."

"That's mine," Kristaps said, with a white-knuckle grip on the pickax. Eriks was impressed with the kid's brass. His cardboard-wrapped feet were not visible, but they must've been blocks of ice by now.

"Is that so?" Aivars said, raising his eyebrows at Kristaps. "In that case, you might have a job, little Bee-in-your-Cap."

"Damn few bullets," said Haralds, searching the bags. "Are there more where these came from?"

"It wasn't easy getting even these," Caleb said.

"Did you contact those names I gave you?"

"Found the chemist and a few others. But people are disappearing, or don't want to be found. Here," Caleb said, extracting a pouch from his jacket. "Here's the collection."

"Next time spend it," Haralds said, loosening the drawstring pouch for an unimpressed look inside. "Cannot buy powder in these woods. You get a line on some morphine? Penicillin? Vodka?"

"Some. But like I said, we had to clear out of there," Caleb said. "And we can't go back."

"More to the point," interrupted Wagtail, "nobody will be arriving with anything better in this forest tonight. So let's get going with what we got."

"Let's get organized!" Aivars chimed, with queer enthusiasm.

Wagtail and Haralds assumed the lead, muscling the makeshift sledge through the trees with the energy of fresh horses. Caleb and Kristaps pushed from behind. Eriks, defrocked of the harness and suddenly light, stumbled along behind uninvited, hoping that the guerrillas' clean-shaven faces meant the proximity of hot water.

Under the high moon, branches cast black webs on the snow.

Eriks rubbed his shoulders, sore from pushing against the harness. He followed Kristaps down the bank of a creek, clutching ropey willow fronds for balance. Wagtail, Haralds and Caleb maneuvered the sled up the opposite bank without difficulty. There the trail widened and traversed a glen.

"Knock. Knock."

Eriks was dismayed to find Aivars walking at his shoulder. He hadn't forgiven the man for pointing a gun at him.

"The sheep have called," Aivars said, leaning into Eriks's face. "They want the fancy coat back."

Eriks stiffened, not enjoying the joke.

Aivars chuckled. "Just kidding. What's your story?"

Eriks's story had always begun with his family owning Riga's finest department store. But here in the woods, his pedigree was not only irrelevant, he was sure Aivars would somehow use the information to torment him. He paused walking to think. His personal decline had begun three days ago, when he'd crossed Igor Volkov.

"Communists installed this apparatchik in the neighborhood," Eriks said, still not sure how events were related. "Then everything went to hell."

"A high-level party player?" Aivars asked, standing in Eriks's path and looking keen.

"Nay. Just my age," Eriks said, stopping and recalling with disgust the memory of Volkov's heart-shaped face. "Some beginner bureaucrat."

"A colonist," Aivars said. "Starting a career and working his way up the ladder."

"Yah. Same day I laid eyes on Igor Volkov, one friend was dragged to the Corner House, another was beat to a bloody pulp, my parents were *picked up*," Eriks was becoming anesthetized to the new reality. "The Cheka came back for me, so I ran." He knew better than to try to impress someone of Aivars's experience with the story about the NKVD shooting at him. "It's been an absolute string of disasters."

"I like the way you put it," Aivars said, looking concerned. "It *has* been a kāpost galva *string of disasters* ever since those Russian tanks rolled into Town Square." Aivars held his Mosin-Nagant with an unnerving, twitchy two-handed readiness, upper body taut under the white-gray fatigues.

"How do I find out what happened to my parents?" Eriks asked, suddenly aware he could learn much from Aivars.

"You don't want to find out, Glamour Boy," Aivars said, in a sympathetic tone. "Trust me. Don't invite the specters in," he tapped at his head. "They don't leave." He sidled close to Eriks, as if sharing a confidence. "They took *my* family." Aivars swung his head toward Eriks to display the NKVD cap badges lined across his beret. "This *kāpost galva*," he said, fingering the first hammer-and-sickle in the row, "took revenge on my wife." He pointed to each of three trophies. "My son, Rainis. And little Inga."

Sweat dotted Eriks's brow and turned to frost.

Aivars said, "I sent them Russian bastards to the Shade Mother." Suddenly he whipped around and fired his rifle into the trees, hand married to the bolt action. *Bam, bam, bam.* "*Kāpost galvas!*" he shouted, into the echoing reports. "That's your *kāpost galva* ass, *kāpost galva!*"

Eriks stood frozen to the earth, electrified as bullets tore the forest air.

Aivars fired another round. "You picked a fight with me," he screamed. "I'm not a fighter, *kāpost galva*. I'm a killer."

Eriks's sensorium rocketed. Eardrums rang, pulse jackhammered in his neck, tongue tasted gun smoke. He suddenly felt eyes watching him. They'd been there all along, the hateful eyes of those who despised Aivars even more than Eriks did for aiming at them, aiming to kill. He turned with dread, wishing he were invisible.

The other Forest Brethren had not stopped for the spectacle. The glow of Wagtail's mattress-pad cape bobbed and glided through a tunnel of tree limbs, growing smaller. Haralds, stickish in his long black coat, looked like a marching tree shadow. They were pushing the trough up a narrow trail and would soon be out of sight. With a heaving breath, Eriks tried to catch up in awkward high-lift snowshoe steps, anything to avoid being alone with Aivars.

But Aivars kept up easily. "You seem like a nice fella, Glamour Boy," he said, speaking again in the genial voice. "The nicer the boy, the bigger his heart, the more he feels, the bigger killer he can become."

Eriks cringed. Cold seared his bulging eyes. Aivars was insane. Killers were criminals and he was in the presence of one.

"The person who's lost the most is the best killer," Aivars explained.

Eriks didn't reply, rushing like an avalanche was about to swallow him, trying to catch up with Caleb, who'd covered a fair piece of ground. Pushing between branches, he practically stumbled into the supplies sled, stopped right there. Caleb and the men had disengaged from pushing it and faced each other in an attitude of having arrived.

Breathing hard, Eriks took in the scene, crestfallen to see just more trees and snow, no blackened kettle of simmering soup hanging from a tripod over a crackling fire, no cabin, no tent, nothing.

"Farmer Barons let us stay at the dairy in exchange for running supplies out here," Caleb was saying to the men, sounding defensive. "That was our deal."

"Yah," chirped Kristaps, standing behind Caleb at shoulder height.

"But if there's no more supplies coming, then we won't be needing you to run them. You see?" Wagtail countered, the shape of his white cape indicating arms akimbo.

"But here we are," Caleb said. "Because we did run the supplies, including guns." He expelled a weary breath. "So didn't we earn a place to stay?"

"Look, no one wants to break faith with you, Caleb," Wagtail said. "You did your part. You hold up your end every time. Now have the good sense to get away. Frankly, we can't spare a man to defend you. We can't feed one, two, three hungry pups." He pointed to Kristaps and Eriks as he counted.

"I'm eighteen," Eriks said.

"And you eat like Lāčplēsis," said Wagtail. "Don't feed strays, Haralds," he scolded, as if he had eyes in the back of his head and knew Haralds was about to hand out spuds. "Don't encourage them. Not when I got men eating snow."

Haralds slumped. "For your own good," he muttered, tightening a burlap drawstring. He lit a cigarette and the flame illumed under the brim of his homburg, for a second showing the affable liveliness that had etched Haralds's thin face. He pointed into the dark, saying, "I know an outfit to the East has women and children."

"I want to talk to the Architect about this," Caleb persisted. "I think he'd give me a chance."

"Nay. There's no need to bother him about something so straightforward," Wagtail said. "Tell you what though. Looks like between the three of you, you got two pairs of boots and one pickax. I'll give one or two of you a job. *Temporarily.* For as long as it takes you to turn a hole into an underground bunker."

"Ground's frozen solid," Caleb said.

"Didn't say it would be an easy job. And furthermore I'll fire a laggard in a drop-dead minute. That's the best I can offer you scamps. So get some shut-eye. You can stay 'til morning. Then cast lots or in some manner decide who stays and who goes."

"We'll be faster as a tunneling team of three," Eriks said. "What if we're an all or nothing deal?"

"Then I pick nothing," Wagtail retorted. "But I'm keeping that pickax either way." He exhaled, tugging his mattress pad-cape. "Look, I wish we were in a position to help you rascals. I'm sorry you were kicked from the nest. But each orphan I adopt worsens the odds for my men by that much. And likely gets you killed. That's what we're talking about here."

Wagtail grabbed the bundled hay from the sledge and heaved it to the ground. With a nod to Haralds, they began sliding away with the groceries.

"See you in church," Wagtail said.

Eriks watched them move off, his last hope crumbling like a frostbitten toe.

"Yah. Goodnight, Captain," Caleb said, quietly.

Captain? Eriks was doubly aggrieved to learn he'd not only been rejected, but by someone of stature. "Keep them dry, Aivars," Captain Wagtail said over his shoulder. He meant the guns.

Aivars carried the rifles to the backside of a snow berm. His cap-badge trophies glinted as his head turned, scanning the environs. He bent down to unstrap his snowshoes, and didn't reappear. Kristaps and Caleb followed, dragging the hay between them. Yet when Eriks clomped to the other side of the berm no one was there. At his knees a flap of oilcloth was lifted at the corner, revealing a black hole the size of a window on a bus.

Eriks unbuckled his snowshoes and, as he squatted down to peer inside, lost his balance and slipped, sliding through the berm and down a few meters into a dark, frozen den, not stopping until he bumped into Kristaps. Sitting on his tailbone, Eriks raised his arms and touched the ceiling of the ice cave, but was otherwise unable to judge its dimensions.

Moonlight seeped through the opening and Eriks's eyes adjusted. Aivars was crouched and tugging something heavy, finally dislodging a plank. "It's not your mother's, but it's dry," he said, referring to a sarcophagus-sized hole in the frozen floor.

"Cozy," Caleb said, stepping down in the hole and helping Aivars remove another board.

Aivars handed Caleb the inferior rifles they'd brought. As Caleb laid them into some rustling material, he said, "Kristaps, prop up your snowshoes and hang your rags. They'll be freeze dried by sunrise."

Kristaps started pulling off his outer layers.

Eriks fetched his snowshoes and did the same. Shivering in his long johns, he groped his way to the sharply hewn edge of the pit before removing his soaked shoes and socks. The snowgrave-gunlocker seemed to be paneled with split pine. He stepped down into it, relieved that his numb feet landed on a thick pad of dry moss, and sat down carefully. Aivars tossed in the hay. Eriks spread it around, stretching his legs and sinking into the crackle and scratch of dry grasses and bark.

Kristaps dropped in, taking the slim spot in the middle. He grabbed an armful of leaves and straw and pulled it over him, burying his feet and legs.

"Good night, young princes," Aivars said, wrangling a plank back into position across the opening.

Eriks flattened down. There was not enough room to sit up with the covering in place.

"Sweet dreams of Russian heads on pikes," Aivars said, dropping the final board, the lid on the casket.

The darkness was arresting. Eriks lay, hands folded over chest, eyes open and seeing nothing. He expelled the breath he'd been holding. Brain empty as a black slate, whoever he'd thought he'd been, erased. Even the sting of Stalin's whip was a blurred memory from the distant land of the living. The unlikely moment with Zelma, remote as a whiff of lilac in a gale force storm. The algebraic problem involving three guys, two pairs of boots and one pickax, an abstraction with solution contained in the null set. He lay in the earth and was powerless to change anything above ground. In fact, he might as well stay here and die. Ice water splat on his face. He said, "Don't bother taking me out of this hole."

"You get really bleak when you're hungry," Caleb said with a yawn. "Your stomach will adjust, mate."

"Just shut up," Eriks wanted to say, imagining the aroma of roasted potato.

Kristaps kept bumping him.

Eriks was about to snarl at the kid to keep his hands to himself, when he rolled over to find Kristaps holding out a roasted potato in one hand, and in the other an egg!

"Kristaps, you're saving my life!" Eriks cried, wanting to leap over the moon. But there wasn't even room to sit up, so he turned on his side, head on elbow, holding the bounty with unspeakable gratitude. "While we were dragging your skinny butt through the forest you were rifling the goods?"

"You can't rely on the hospitality of partisans," Kristaps said, rustling in the grass.

"Thank you," Caleb said.

"Yah, *paldies*," Eriks said, excited but deciding to eat slowly this time. "And forgive me for ever being uppity about your tendency to steal things."

"*Loudzu*," Kristaps said. "It is Christmas Eve, after all."

That sucked the chatter out of the crypt.

Christmas Eve tugged powerful heartstrings, magnified by heritage-soaked rum-and-raisin memories of every Christmas Eve before it. Family gathered in the penthouse above the spellbinding view of the lit up park and the Opera House. The smell of his father's pipe, gingerbread, and wax while Eriks lit the candles on the tree. Last year, as Eriks had recited a *daina* to get a present, no one could have foreseen that by the following Christmas his parents would be arrested, and Eriks would be essentially buried alive, his sole gift a potato, given by shoeless Kristaps.

"There's a Hannukah saying going 'round the ghetto this year," Caleb said, cracking an eggshell. *"Where they want to bury us alive, we pull the gravediggers in with us.* Sounds catchier in Polish."

"Sweet," Kristaps said.

As Eriks nibbled, an angel's breath of music floated to his ear. "Is that a flute?" he asked, wondering if he was hallucinating.

"That's Aivars," Caleb said.

"Aivars plays the flute?" Eriks asked, unable to imagine that the man who'd terrified him with rifle blasts also produced these delicate reedy notes.

"Yah, made from the bone of a Chekist," Kristaps said. "He draws the enemy out with a tune, then he sends them to the Shade Mother."

"He's pulling your leg," Caleb said, chuckling. "Funny, though, how he blathers about that ancient lore like its real."

"He's crazy enough to do it," Kristaps said.

"He's the deadest shot in these parts, that's the truth," Caleb said. "Kristaps! Why's the dugout smell like dog farts?"

With a moan, Caleb writhed upward, widening the crack between boards and nosing for fresh air that fell inside heavily and cold.

Kristaps was squirming and hooting about stink bombs, acting childish.

Annoyed, Eriks then remembered how young the kid was. Caleb looked out for him like a big brother. Eyes moist with holiday goodwill, Eriks said, "I will strike out for that other outfit. You two are a team. You should stay together." He didn't feel as brave as he thought he sounded.

"Just hold on. You don't know the ropes yet," Caleb said. "You could get lost or stumble into a hot spot."

"Let's make our own hole and hibernate 'til spring," Kristaps said.

"This hole was made last summer," Caleb said. "When the ground was soft and a few paranoid folks, who were absolutely right, started stashing weapons. Now that it's the dead of winter, we'd have to blast and burn and thaw and hack every centimeter to dig something this grand."

"Well, then what?" Eriks asked, dispirited that even this miserable pit was beyond his grasp.

"I do not know," Caleb said, yawning again. "I just rise in the morning and figure it out fresh every day. Been lucky like that for over a year now."

"Hmmph." Eriks said, rolling over and, in so doing, forcing the other two to also shift positions. "I know a thing or two about luck," he said, "and this is not it. I may never be warm again. My face aches and a thousand burning needles are pricking my thawing feet. Nay. *Lucky* was me yesterday with Zelma."

Suddenly Eriks realized in a rush that he hadn't even asked Zelma how her errand had gone, the trip she'd dreaded making into the treacherous, Cheka-infested, one-lane village. *Fuck*! He was dense, as well as unlucky. What did it matter anyway, he conceded, sinking heavier into the earth. Nothing did anymore. His chest hurt, lungs in irons, every breath a dull stab of pain. Patikamspils. That was the place.

K. Smiltens 1943.

22

ERIKS COULDN'T SEE THE VILE CREATURE. *He felt its sharp-clawed, gluttonous presence, leering into the tomb.*

"Who are you?" it asked in a rumbling, disembodied voice.

"I was nursed by all Latvian mothers," Eriks said, and was frightened by his own utterance, which sounded like a congregation of flat voices reading in unison. "My soul is the souls of all Latvians lying under the soil of the Motherland."

"There's no such place… your Motherland." The evil thing shifted shape. Entering a suit of armor it became a knight. A wave of terror rippled across the land.

"You are Loudmouth. Glamour Boy. Pup!" mocked the knight from behind a beveled face grate. "Your so-called nation has no history, just old wives' tales, folk songs, proverbs, incanted by farmers and midwives. Hearsay!"

A muzzled dog was whining. Humming filled Eriks's ears, getting louder, buzzing like a sawmill in his head. The knight's laughter grew loud and diabolical, until the visor snapped open. Eriks saw a heart-shaped face in the helmet. A million lit candles on Christmas trees flared and were snuffed. Silence. Eriks was floating, looking down at his corpse in its earth coffin, wreathed with frost flowers and ice ribbons.

He woke with a jerk, sweating. Thank God, he thought with a gasp, it's all a nightmare. Eyes opened, still dark. Hands ran over the chilblains on his arms. He couldn't move, trapped between a slab of frozen pine and shivering Kristaps. His heart caved. This was his reality. He would die if he didn't change it.

The fibers of a plan wove together all at once in bold geometry. Muscles insisted he rise. He pushed the planks off like a pavement-cracking weed.

The hour was late morning, judging by the height of the sun bursting through holes in the clouds and making odd patches of snow glisten. A few snowflakes were falling. The world was a white canvas on which anything might be painted.

Eriks strode toward where he heard the volley of men's voices, and soon saw the outlaws at a small fire. Nearby, a thin plume of steam rose from the top of a pirts. The sauna looked smartly constructed of birch trunks, uniformly as thick as Eriks's forearm, leaning together teepee-style.

Eriks walked up as Haralds was saying, "The priority is to get some powder or make it." He lowered the brim of his homburg and tugged his black frock coat around his thin frame. "Otherwise we can do nothing."

"One thing we cannot do is nothing," Captain Wagtail said, startling Eriks who had not noticed the portly man, a credit to the mattress pad camouflage. "We either grow or we perish."

"We can keep on wire-cutting," said a new face. "Pull up rail ties."

There were several men standing around whom Eriks had not seen before. But his attention snapped to a man sitting on a tree stump, wearing boots and a towel, naked from the waist up except for a black beret. The man's skin looked flushed, like he'd just stepped out of the pirts and was steamed to the bone. He held a besom, still wet from dripping water on the hot rocks, and swatted his back with the whisk of dried birch leaves, emitting a waft of wintergreen. Executive decisions were often made in the serenity of the pirts, Eriks knew, and he bet this man was the Architect, whom Captain Wagtail had referred to the night before. This was the man Eriks must persuade.

"Just be sure we don't cut communication wires the Germans will need when they come to liberate us," Haralds said.

"I hate Nazis," Captain Wagtail said, lifting a small branch and tossing it on the fire, "but anyone opposing Stalin has got to be considered an ally." As Eriks came up to the fire ring, Wagtail said, "Labrite, Glamour Boy."

"Good Morning," Eriks replied, aware that all eyes were on him and his posh overcoat. The plan that was brilliant a moment ago now seemed idiotic. He looked at the faces in the loosely formed ring, seeing in the men's features some hardness that he'd been sheltered from until three days ago. He ran his hands over wild hair that would never lie down.

"So, you're Gailis, like the department store?" said the Architect.

"Yah," Eriks said, a lump in his throat. The moment for his proposal was now. He took a breath and straightened up, noticing as he did that he was taller than everyone present. "I—me and my friends—we could be an asset to you, if you'd have us." Faltering and feeling a fool, he spoke faster, to pitch his idea before anyone cut him off. "Granted, I don't have a gun to defend myself with at the moment, but I'm not coming here with my hand out. I have intelligence and a plan, a plan that could yield a trove of weapons."

Eriks cleared his throat and continued, "But it'll take serious nerve to pull it off. So, if you can't stomach it, I'll look for backup from that outfit with the women and children."

The men laughed at that, to Eriks's surprise.

"All right," said the Architect. "Let's hear what you got."

Eriks threw out his chest and described his "live bait" scheme, a plan drawing from everything he'd seen recently.

The Architect leaned back, listening, saying nothing.

Captain Wagtail interrupted frequently, pounding Eriks with questions.

Determined to prove that he was worth feeding and sheltering, Eriks embellished the upside potential of his plan, getting modern weaponry, and downplayed the likelihood it was a deadly boondoggle. He elaborated in a detached manner, almost forgetting that it would be his flesh used to draw out the Cheka, until he saw the white faces of Caleb and Kristaps who had come to the fire ring and stood listening to the roles Eriks had in mind for them.

"The ambush has to take place in that particular village," Eriks explained, "because the sole NKVD outpost is located two kilometers away down an isolated road, which is also the only point of access." He was betting the farm on Zelma's pillow talk. "The authorities there are known to be among the most strict and zealous of the NKVD."

"That's a fact you can take to the bank," said a snaggle-toothed man, nodding.

"I like it, Glamour Boy," said Aivars. "I say we move on it straight away."

Great, Eriks thought, nodding to Aivars. He had the insane killer's vote. The plan must be madness.

"Mayhem. Could be absolute mayhem," Captain Wagtail said. "I'd want to see this road. Surveil the village and assess the habits of the local Cheka thoroughly before committing the men."

"It's not right," said a man wearing a hunter's vest. "It's not a boy's place to hazard such a risk on behalf of grown men."

"A youngster has a better chance of getting away with it," said another.

"You have to give us a chance to prove ourselves," Eriks said. "Because if we can't find a place with you, then I don't know where we go next." He felt his eyes tingle at his pitiable situation. "Maybe Kristaps won't have to be involved."

"We'll discuss it," said the Architect. "Why don't you boys warm up in the pirts. Get a bite to eat."

Eriks was heartened that, if nothing else, his bid had earned him another morsel. He stripped his clothes and ducked through the entrance into the dry heat of the pirts, inhaling the comforting aromas of birch and tar. Warmth at last stilled his shivering core and he imagined telling Zelma about how he'd led an ambush. He pictured her admiring him holding the trophy he'd win from this gambit, his own gun.

That very morning, the Architect, Aivars and Captain Wagtail set out to verify Eriks's claims. Three days later, they had not returned. Eriks worried that the scouts would tromp into camp and say, "You and your bogus idea can hit the road." He dreaded that they would come back to say, "You're brilliant. The plan is a go." Then there was always the chance they'd never be seen again. The prickly wait was only bearable because the boys were allowed to use the pirts and sleep in the gun cache. Kristaps spent happy hours feeding slim rations of hay to the band's perky, but ribby horse. They dined with the renegades on reindeer sausage, pine nuts and birch tea, as well as the foodstuffs from the dairy, watching the stores deplete rapidly.

Eriks used the time to drill, exchanging fake punches with Caleb and Kristaps, as they'd done in the barn.

"It's got to look real," he said, swaying and holding fists in front of his face. "We got to be bodacious. Fizzing!" He ripped at Caleb with a jab-cross combo and a peppering of rabbit punches. "What we want is for some spineless jerk to report us to the Cheka. Woe-hoe!"

Caleb countered with an upper cut that would've clocked Eriks good, had it connected.

Eriks nearly slipped on ice, but regained his balance, bracing a hand against a tree bough. "We have to pose an epic threat," he said, "so every Chekist in the vicinity wants to arrest us. We need to be… disturbing."

"That's crazy!" Kristaps cried, perching on a fallen tree trunk. "We're gonna try to get caught by the Cheka? They'll fry our giblets!"

Eriks snapped his fingers. "We'll dress as mummers."

"Mummers, what?" Caleb said. "Translation, please."

Kristaps brightened instantly. "My father sang in a Budēļi group. He was a stork."

"I thought we needed to look dangerous," Caleb said. "Not like caroling wildlife."

"There's something kāpost galva unnerving about mummering," Eriks said. "Come on." He beckoned to Kristaps. "We got to find materials for making masks, and anything freakish or bizarre."

"Ask that hunter," Caleb said, "the one who makes the tasty sausage."

The hunter gave the boys a matted old black bear pelt, for what he called welcome distraction. Draping it over Eriks's head, the man fashioned laces to hold the pelt in place. He lifted tufts of fur and shaped round little ears with a razor.

Kristaps watched in fascination as Eriks blackened his eyes with charred cork. He screamed with merriment as Eriks lumbered after him Frankenstein-style, with rigid outstretched arms.

"So, this mumming," Caleb said, breaking off branches, trying to find a pair that looked like antlers. "It's a Latvian winter ritual?"

"Not what my family does," Eriks said. "I never have mummered personally. It's old, old, old-timey stuff. Folks still do it for frolic, though, as a way to visit neighbors. Not that it'll really change the next year's fortunes. But there's something mystical at the deep bottom of it, some power I can't explain. The Communists won't abide it."

Caleb held his "antlers" to the sides of his head and bellowed a buck mating call.

Kristaps copied him.

"Now, how to make them stay put," Caleb said, as the branches fell from the fold in his hat.

"Hold on," Eriks said, remembering something he'd seen in the gun cache. In minutes he was in the ice cave, under the planks, searching through the dried grass. He found the solution in the stash of obsolete armaments. It was perfect.

"Here," he told Caleb. "Try on this gas mask."

"Hot damn!" Caleb said, holding up the contraption for a look. "That's some legitimate prankster garb."

"From the Great War," Eriks said, helping Caleb don the oiled canvas mask, which completely covered his head, rendering him faceless.

Leather circles holding glass lenses gave Caleb the eyes of a giant insect. A metal filter canister hung around his chin like an alien proboscis.

"Tuck your antlers under the straps, like that," Eriks said, and stepped back to study the effect.

Caleb secured his antler branches and topped the whole affair with a fur cap, becoming a netherworld stag.

Kristaps whistled. "That'll put the frightens on them."

"Puts the frightens on me," Eriks said, unsettled where he was leading his friends.

"Just buck up!" Caleb said, his voice loud and muffled.

"Ha!" cried Kristaps, alerting Eriks to the pun.

"I can't," Eriks retorted, modeling the pelt. "I'm bearly dressed."

"Caleb's going stag," Kristaps shot in.

"Yah, well, you shouldn't run with his elk," Eriks said.

"That's not what I herd," Caleb said.

Eriks was racking his brain for an antler pun, when he heard a low whistle and spun around to see that Aivars had stealthed up.

"Straight outta the Shade realm," Aivars said, approving the masquerade.

Captain Wagtail was walking over, too.

Eriks suddenly felt like an ass in the mumming get-up, but Wagtail didn't mention it.

The captain planted his legs and folded his arms under his cape before pronouncing, "Your plan is not impossible."

The bottom dropped out of Eriks's stomach.

"Utterly reckless, but it's the best we got at the moment," Wagtail said. "If you still want to do it, we're leaving tonight."

23

IGOR VOLKOV SAT WHERE JANIS Pērkons used to sit, ensconced in a deep executive armchair. From the loft office, he overlooked the factory floor of what used to be Pērkons Leather Works. His feet rested on the desk, which was topped in supple, rich leather that made his boots look cheap as tarpaper. Life was unfair, Igor brooded, lamenting his mistake. He should have forced Pērkons to fabricate the superior custom boots *before* reporting the capitalist as a Harmful Element. The NKVD had reacted unpredictably swiftly in banishing Pērkons and his employees. Then a swarm of state shitheads had pranced in, not respecting that it was Igor who was to credit for confiscating the Leather Works, Igor who should be in charge.

He missed Pērkons. Besides having a bigshot wardrobe, Pērkons showed respect, paying tribute, cash and a 22-carat cigarette case, in exchange for Igor's blind eye. But Igor had taken the bribe and snitched on Pērkons anyway, because he despised the wealthy man. Igor had erred, he concluded, appreciating the weight of the gold case in his pocket. He should have milked Pērkons dry, amassing a small, secret fortune... in case life became drastic.

Learn from the cat, Igor told himself. The cat toys with the mouse at leisure. Igor could have dawdled long enough to make the old craftsman eat belt stew, and other pleasurable deeds. He could have raided Pērkons's closet and by wearing his shirts be seen as a powerful person to respect. There would still have been plenty of time to later gain points with the secret police.

Dealing with the NKVD had been a vile and wicked experience. The agents put Igor to grunt work. To make matters worse they installed a foreman who, to Volkov's disgust, was an Asian breed, an ugly, pig-nosed Buryat low-life scum from some backwater near Mongolia. His workers were rowdy low-class menials. Igor Volkov was descended from Cossacks. Taking orders from an oversized, slant-eyed nomad sucked all pride from him.

"Komsomal!" The foreman didn't deign to learn Igor's name, stupidly shouting the Communist youth union as if summoning a boy scout. "Get moving before I put a boot up your ass." The workers were manhandling the industrial-sized immersion drums through the rolling loading doors, snorting and swearing.

Volkov panicked at the fervent scramble to disassemble capital equipment and ship it to Russia. Such work was beneath him. It was cowardly and disgraceful to act afraid that Germans would chase Russians out of Latvia.

Tools were dumped into barrels and rolled away clanking. Someone cursed at finding that the heavy cutting table, with its massive iron underside, was bolted to the cement floor.

An intellectual destined for greatness, Igor could not degrade himself to common toil. He exalted labor as much as the next Communist. And when a job fit his extraordinary, magnificent person he would be the zenith of discipline, and would rise above all other men.

But the present dire situation was a horrific humiliation. Inside this factory inferiors from the hinterland treated him like a mule. Out on the street, beautiful blond Latvian females reviled him. And a photograph of the family Pērkons propped on the desk, mocked and tormented him. Igor had never been immortalized by a camera. Yet he'd seen this inferior insect Kārlis Pērkons, the same age as Igor, who was born into wealth and never had to fight for his rightful place in a brutal world, memorialized for posterity in at least two photographs. Igor imagined tracking down Kārlis Pērkons and executing him. One day he would be powerful enough to punish everyone who looked down on him, everyone he hated.

The wooden stairway shuddered as somebody ascended to the loft.

Igor felt giddy about the inevitable confrontation with the foreman.

The door opened without a knock. Igor kept staring at his boots, channeling rage into the look of his eye. The look alone was often enough to make these weaklings back away.

"Igor Volkov." A smart Russian accent, the speaker had authority.

Igor's head snapped up.

A uniformed soldier sneered down his nose at him. "Papers."

Igor swung his legs off the desk and stood. The soldier's haughty mien was insulting, but Igor overlooked that and hurried to show his Komsomal Communist Youth Union card, eager to know if the time had finally come.

"Sign here," said the soldier, holding out a clipboard with a list of gathered signatures.

Igor signed, forcing his hand not to shake.

The soldier handed over an officious envelope and departed.

Igor had been expecting this since he turned nineteen. He slit the envelope with Pērkons's letter opener and removed an ordinary, non-letterhead paper. The missive had fill-in-the-blank lines completed with longhand Cyrillic script.

Evidence of call to fulfill military obligation No. <u>1272</u>.

Name: <u>Igor Volkov</u>

Igor silently cursed his lack of an important sounding middle name. He should change his name, as had dear Comrade Stalin.

Date of birth: <u>November 13, 1922</u>

Seeing his birth date in print bolstered Igor's sense of destiny, as he was born the same year as the Soviet Union.

Rank or status of society: <u>petty bourgeois</u>

He bristled. That would change. This call-up notice was a step toward power, which would lead to wealth, and the women would follow.

The letter stated Igor was obligated to appear at a nearby recruitment office. Draftees were given THREE DAYS to take care of household affairs before reporting for service. Orders and consequences for not obeying were explicit. The missive bore the red authenticity stamp of the USSR. Igor felt the thrill of being swept up in the hurricane of worldwide Communism.

The door slammed open, and in sauntered the hulking foreman. "I will have you arrested for slacking," he threatened.

"I have higher orders." Igor waved the conscription notice, guessing the foreman didn't even know how to read.

But the brute's ugly features registered comprehension right away, folding arms and blocking the door. "The Army can survive without your lazy ass until you load this factory to the rails."

Heart trilling, Igor sidestepped the desk and pushed past the foreman, whose jaw dropped. "Mine is the holy duty of all able bodied male Soviets, to serve the 11th Red Army, Baltic Military Operation," he proclaimed. Igor feared the henchmen in the workshop would try to apprehend him, but they were straining to cart off the tool bench.

"Load it yourself, Comrade."

K. Smiltens, 1948.

24

THE HIKE TO PATIKAMSPILS DRUBBED THE JITTERS out of Eriks. It entailed a midnight trek back toward the dairy, and then a lengthy march beyond, this time accompanied by a phalanx of fifteen men. Eriks was buoyed by the camaraderie. There was the Architect and his two educated sons, Captain Wagtail, who'd served in the military, and Homburg Haralds. There was Snaggle-Wit who vowed to hide his two drafted sons in the woods rather than sacrifice them for the benefit of Russia, an enterprising sailor and his nephew referred to as the Hawks of Pavilosta, and a brawny fellow called Stone Hill, on account of his stubborn streak. Nicknaming abounded to avoid Chekist retribution against families. Nobody could endure the savage backlash like the one dealt to the family of Aivars the Lonely, whom Eriks secretly thought should be called Mad Aivars. Bee-in-your-Cap Kristaps travelled with the Hunter on horseback. True to their moniker, there was no chit-chat when Silent Forest was on the move.

In the dark and quietude, Eriks turned over every detail he could remember Zelma saying about the village... *the most rabid militia you*

never want to meet... lounging around NKVD command post, waiting for
someone to punish... villagers would report their own mothers to get in good
with the Ivans.

"We're not far now," Wagtail finally said, with a nod toward the sunrise. "We stop here and eat."

The last of the food had been saved for this breakfast. Eriks took the slice of black bread as turn-back-now proof that this wanna-be partisan band was hopelessly under-fueled against Stalin. He searched his universe for a source of strength besides food, some font that couldn't be arrested, tortured, deported or collectivized. Revenge didn't inspire him. He wasn't fighting for revenge. He had no choice but the course ahead. He chewed the bread, fortified by knowing the rye had been grown on this land, his country. He felt like praying. All around were trees. The trees. He awakened to their energy, even as it coursed in the dried veins of his hiking staff.

Eriks put on the bear pelt with intention suiting a ritual, not speaking as Caleb applied the eyeblack and it dribbled from the corners of his eyes. The disguise gave him a buffer of anonymity, as if it was not *he* risking his life. And the beast personna linked him with some ancient force, the one he sensed lying dormant in the tangled roots beneath the frozen ground. After all, four Baltic tribes had struggled for their territories in these woods, appealing to local spirits, tree or animal, for strength. Why shouldn't he? Not understanding the connection, Eriks quietly snapped off the end of a fir branch, and poked it through his lapel buttonhole.

Captain Wagtail was coming over, and Eriks wondered briefly if the captain felt similarly empowered by his white, mattress pad cape. Aivars, in the white camos, was with him, both hands ready on his rifle. The Architect followed, looking professional in a crisp white shirt over thermals and sharply trimmed beard and moustache.

"Let's be sure we're on the same page," the Architect said. He held out a strip of birch bark marked by confident pencil strokes. "Here's our village. The traditional layout, shops and a tavern around the town square. There's only one passable road into town, with high frozen berms on either side of it. About two kilometers down the road from the village is this old manor house." He tapped its symbol on the bark. "Command center for the local militia and NKVD. They're fully staffed and well-armed. Takes them from five to twenty minutes to ride into town depending on their level of enthusiasm."

Eriks understood the situation, theoretically.

"Keep the sun at your left shoulder and you'll reach the village square in about half an hour," Wagtail said. "Meanwhile, we'll fan out and take positions farther up along the road."

"We're all in, Glamour Boy," Aivars said. Under the camouflaged hood, the cap badge trophies on his beret lined up precisely straight. "Go out there and throw a seven."

Climbing over the tall, icy berm in snowshoes was a clumsy affair landing Eriks on his buttocks. He scrambled to his feet brushing snow off his pelt, hoping none of the men were watching. The road was empty in both directions, a snowy lane glittering like sugar in the late morning sun.

Caleb removed his glasses, upended a bottle of whiskey to his mouth, swished and spit it out, spraying his clothes. He pulled on his gas mask, and adjusted his antlers and fur hat. Eriks, likewise, doused himself with the booze perfume and handed the bottle back. Caleb exhaled a wavering stream of white vapor. He tapped the whiskey bottle with a spoon, a slow beat. Eriks calmed down, matching his breathing to the steady rhythm of the bottle-drum.

"Here we go, mate," Caleb said, pivoting toward the village. He started down the road with heavy steps, drumming evenly, the gait of a person heading where he never wanted to arrive... pretending to be drunk and wearing the eerie stag getup with the same aplomb that he approached every daunting task.

Eriks was damned grateful for meeting Caleb on the train. Now he had a brother to walk with down the road.

"There's special songs, right?" Caleb asked, his voice muffled by the mask.

"Yah," Eriks said, searching his mind, which was not in song mode. "*Nu, tetin, ziemas svetki. Father it's the winter festival.*" He couldn't remember more.

"And I've frozen a testicle," Caleb supplied. "Is there anything edible?"

Father it's the winter festival." Eriks sang.

"I call it the *whimper* festival," Caleb said, hee-hawing Eriks's every verse.

The road had been recently cleared, and it wasn't long before Eriks saw where it ended at a cluster of two-storied, half-timbered buildings. The song left his head, as he walked into the village square. Lesser roads radiated from there, more like footpaths used by townsfolk going about their business under shrouded, hunched shoulders. He and Caleb gravitated toward a dais in the center of the plaza, where uprooted cement and twisted iron jutted up, as if a statue of the village hero once honored there had been toppled. Shop windows edging the square were shuttered tight. No sign indicated which door lead to the public house, but Eriks deduced its location by following the most trafficked path, cobblestones showing through the slushy snow, to where assorted snowshoes leaned against the wall. He and Caleb unlaced and added theirs to the collection.

Entering the tavern, Eriks had to duck so his bear head cleared the lintel. While his eyes adjusted to the dim light, he took stock of the premises. A couple dozen locals appeared to be grabbing an early lunch, a joyless bunch, probably washing down bread and herring with a beer before returning to work. He filled his chest with a deep breath and sallied forth.

"Children, let's go mummering, on a winter's eve," Eriks sang, plodding toward the bar. Caleb followed, *tinking* double-time on the bottle.

"We bring blessings of fertility to this canteen," Eriks called out as he passed a crowded table. "Heavy crops! And babies! Be blessed with many *Latvian* babies." He sensed a communal intake of breath at that, and covered the awkward silence with a belch, as someone muttered, "troublemakers".

"We also frighten away evil spirits," he said, sliding onto a bar stool, "and you know who I mean."

The bartender's expression was hidden behind a plush, white caricature moustache that curled up at the ends. He faced Eriks stiffly, acting like he hadn't heard the remark.

"You're supposed to welcome us with a treat," Eriks told him. "Two Balsams will do."

"You have money?" the bartender demanded.

"My friend's buying," Eriks said. "He's a deer. Bah! My funds have been frozen."

Seeing Caleb pull out rubles, the bartender took down the brown crockery flagon labeled *Rigas Black Balsams* and poured some into two shot glasses. While he diluted each with vodka, Eriks read the ornate black and gold label.

"Distilled uniquely in Riga," Eriks remarked. "An ancient mixture of forest herbs with mysterious properties. Heard this all my life," Eriks said, sliding a glass to Caleb. "You'd think, by now, the mysteries would be solved." He lifted his glass to the portrait behind the bar. "Here's to General Stalin," Eriks said. "Although..." He opened his gullet and threw back the shot, "I like it better when he wears the pink dress."

The elixir burned going down, steadying Eriks with a worldly hand. He felt his heart beating in his neck, his precious heartbeat, and was not bothered by the bartender fussing, "I'll have none of that. And I mean Get Out. You with the horns, you too! Out!"

"All right, we'll skedaddle," Eriks said, scooting his stool from the bar. "How 'bout one quick skit first, though, for the sake of tradition." Turning to face the most populous table in the pub, he said, "Heard the one about *The Knock at Night?*"

A graybeard shifted in his seat, unable to take his eyes off faceless Caleb, who swayed behind Eriks's elbow.

Eriks put on his campiest melodrama. "One night there was a loud knock at the door of a certain house." He acted it out, pounding on the table, rattling lunch plates.

"Watch it!" roared a man in an argyle vest.

"The family inside was too afraid to answer it. So they cowered in their bedrooms." Eriks hid behind trembling forearms. "But the knocking got louder and LOUDER." Eriks moved down the table, darting between the patrons and hammering the table with his fists.

"*Kāpost galva* fool!" cursed a man with a mouthful. Eriks snagged a fried potato off the plate of a man picking his teeth, and ate it, while a fellow lighting a cigarette looked on with wooden disapproval. A man in green suspenders scraped his chair across the floor and strode to the coat rack. Eriks stared, barely able to keep talking as the man left the tavern with a slam of the door. Was that the wished-for informant? If so, how long before the Cheka came? Five minutes, twenty?

Caleb kicked him.

"Anyway," Eriks resumed, "the family pretended to be asleep, 'til finally the bastards start breaking down the door!"

The bartender was coming around the bar to get him, so Eriks puffed his chest and spoke faster.

"Inside the house, the grandfather thinks to himself, 'I'm an old man. I'm going to die soon anyway. I'll go see what they want.' So he gets out of bed and goes to the door. A minute later he rushes back shouting for joy, 'Good news, loved ones. *The building's on fire!*'"

"Ha ha!" Eriks held his belly, snorting. "Get it?"

"You're outta here," the bartender said, grasping Eriks under the arms. "Time for some fresh air."

"Oh! Be a doll and put up a couple mummers for the night," Eriks said.

But the bartender pushed Eriks toward the door, hissing in his ear, "You'll be killed, you idiot. The militia here is severe. Go home. For godssakes, go sober up."

Eriks, a head taller than the barkeep, allowed himself to be manhandled, until he passed another full table. Then he applied his feet like brakes and leaned into a sallow-faced guy, saying, "You know why the Cheka works in groups of three? One can read, one can write, and the third man keeps an eye on the two intellectuals! Ha ha ha. Buy me a drink." He grabbed the man by the collar.

The sallow man got up with surprising speed and took a swing, which Eriks barely dodged, breaking loose of the bartender.

"Comrade, if I hit you, you'll need a travel pass," Eriks said, waving his fist, everything alive and all juices flowing. He glimpsed another man get up to leave, this one in a double-breasted jacket. Then clenched knuckles hit his eye and he staggered back, crashing into chairs. He tried to regain his footing and strike back, but his arms were pinned. Caleb's buck mating call brayed over the fracas. People shoved and dragged Eriks toward the door, a zoetrope of scuffing arms and legs seen through the throbbing slit of an eye. Bright cold air hit him before he slammed into frozen cobblestones. The heels of his hands broke his skid, stinging. He righted himself, looking up in time to see Caleb ejected from the tavern, legs pedaling for balance, gas mask maligned and antlers askew.

Eriks grabbed a handful of snow and held it to his tender, taut eye socket. His head was thumping and the job was not done.

His ears pricked up at the rhythm of soft thuds coming down the road. He looked up quick, relieved and disappointed to see it was not the Cheka coming, but the flopping footfalls of Kristaps's cardboard shoes. His muffler and pointy knit cap, bobbing as he ran, caught the attention of the handful of villagers in the square.

"Well, the squirt's right on cue," Eriks said.

"He shouldn't even be here," Caleb mumbled.

Eriks strode to the center of the square, cutting through a young family, to block Kristaps's path. "Not so fast, little comrade," he said, snatching the boy's cap. He waved the cap high and low, out of Kristaps's reach.

"Gimme back my hat," Kristaps said, his voice shrill.

Eriks clutched Kristaps by the lapels and whispered, "What's going on?"

"Nothing. The Hunter's over there, behind some trees."

Eriks looked down the road. It was peaceful as a Christmas card. His plan was losing momentum. Gutted, he pushed the kid away.

"Can't quit now," Caleb said, grabbing Kristaps's arms from behind.

"Leave me alone," Kristaps cried.

"Why aren't you in school, boy, learning Russian," Eriks bullied, rearing a fist.

"Help," Kristaps yelled. "Somebody help me!"

Eriks backhanded Kristaps's round cheek.

"Cowardly brute," said an old woman walking across the square.

Eriks turned to her. "I love what you've done with your hair," he yelled, scooping a handful of snow. "How did you get it to come out of one nostril like that?" He threw a loosely packed snowball, hitting the old lady on the shoulder. Then he punched Kristaps in the gut. Kristaps timed his gasping, double-over like a pro. The attack looked real.

Eriks glanced up expectantly, and looked around. No one was watching the performance! The windows of the pub were shuttered tight. No one was coming to help Kristaps. "Will no one stick his neck out to save a kid anymore?" he muttered, swinging Kristaps by the collar. "What does it take to draw out the police in this village?"

"Destruction," Caleb said, picking up a hunk of cement from the dais and hefting it from hand to gloved hand. He took aim at a second-story picture window on the corner building and heaved it. The glass shattered in a chiming cascade to the walkway below, where a young woman scurried away with a tiny shriek. The old lady and every passerby fled the square.

Eriks turned to watch the road, expecting the militia to descend in a fury.

Kristaps was looking in the opposite direction when his face drained of all color.

A leggy black horse was stepping down one of the footpaths between the buildings, an NKVD agent in the saddle. His red hammer-and-sickle cap badge glinted in the noon sun as he looked down at the broken glass and up at Caleb, and reined his mount into the square.

Eriks's stomach flooded with acid. He'd expected the Cheka to charge from the manor house, down the road where the guerrillas were lying in wait.

"Beat it, Kristaps," Caleb muttered, shoving the kid behind the dais. But there was nowhere to hide.

The agent zeroed in on the boys and crossed the slushy cobblestones directly to where Eriks stood. A second Chekist came in on a bay, scouting the perimeter of the square at a brisk trot, followed by the third. The black horse fidgeted in front of Eriks, stamping close and blowing streams of white vapor. From the superior position of his saddle, the mounted agent assessed Eriks and Caleb. A brand spanking-new Russian submachine gun with a drum magazine hung from his shoulder. Eriks could see the wood grain on the oiled stock.

Caleb's hands rose in submission, but his stare conveyed all the frightening insolence that could be borne by a faceless, alien-eyed elk. His hand moved toward his head, perhaps to remove the mask and get some air.

"Took you long enough," Eriks told the agent, hoarsely.

The man on the black horse raised his rifle without a word, and with a *pa-pa-pa* and a bored expression, shot Caleb through the heart. Kristaps screamed.

A shot rang from across the square. Eriks dimly linked it with a jerk of the rider's belly and his slump over the saddle. The other horsemen pivoted and, banging hooves, charged the source of the bullet. From farther away gunfire peppered the air.

Staring at Caleb in horror, Eriks dropped to his knees. The black horse above him clattered against the cobblestones, nostrils flaring in panic. The dead weight of the Chekist careened out of the saddle and toppled, hanging a moment at the horse's flank before falling as the beast skittered across the square.

Eriks crawled to where Caleb lay, and wrenched the gasmask off his face. Uncut hair haloed Caleb's head on the ground. Complete surprise was frozen on his face, eyes wide at the sky, the starter moustache patchy over an o-shaped mouth. Eriks pressed an ear to Caleb's chest and heard a beat. But it was galloping horses pounding the ground. Caleb's heart was still. The snow was spreading crimson where he'd fallen, smelling like the butcher's shop.

The shooting on the road was furious. Eriks heard shouts. Aggrieved to leave Caleb, instinct bade his legs crawl to the dais and crouch, head under arms, listening. The longer he heard rifles firing, the more he knew his stupid plan had gone disastrously wrong, because his allies didn't have that many bullets. What had he thought? That those family men and their paltry arsenal would get the upper hand on the NKVD? The Cheka must've somehow taken cover and were right now rooting out and executing the brave fellows who'd been Silent Forest. His arrogance had killed Caleb. Next, the Cheka would find Eriks, the idiot mastermind, and kill him too. His parents would never know how his short thoughtless life had ended.

All fell quiet.

The stink of sulfur entered his throat.

The silence after the minutes of gunfire was unique, slowly broken by the sound of crisp, businesslike movement. They were coming for him. Too late to grab the rifle by the fallen horseman, Eriks was galvanized with fear. He saw the barrel of the gun first. At its other end stood Aivars.

Aivars eyed Eriks and Caleb, and nodded to someone else in the square, moving his hand in a series of gestures.

"Any Cheka in there?" Aivars demanded, pointing his weapon to the public house.

Eriks thought he answered, but maybe no sound came out, because Aivars kept asking.

"Just the local yoyos," Eriks finally said, as Aivars strode to the pub and kicked the door wide open. Snaggle-Wit and Stone Hill followed him inside, weapons drawn. He heard Aivars address the lunch crowd in a clear, angry tone.

"*Lab dien,* Villagers. Hear ye, hear ye. I got a message for any traitors here. To you party organizers and neighborhood spies and milk collectors. And I'm especially talking to you quiet go-along-to-get-along collaborators and lazy look-the-other-wayers. You are hereby directed to abandon your treacherous posts. The time has come for you to take a stand. I say return to your people. Join men in the forests unafraid of red scum or the cold. Swear to fight degenerate gangsters, so a Latvian can be the master of his own house."

As he listened to Aivars's ultimatum, Eriks watched Haralds, black frock coat billowing, kneel down and put two thin fingers to Caleb's neck. Then he swiftly passed his palm over Caleb's face, closing the eyes.

"Consider this your last warning," rang the voice of Aivars. "For whoever does not heed this directive, and does not return is Not Needed. And Shall Be sent straight to the Shade Mother."

The pub door slammed.

"Let's go, Eriks," Aivars called, already halfway across the square.

"Get up," Haralds said, pulling up Eriks by the arm.

Aivars picked up the dead horseman's assault rifle before leaving the square. Working as a pair, Snaggle and Stone stripped the uniform off the man who'd shot Caleb.

Haralds guided Eriks out of the village square, but when they reached the road, Eriks stopped and looked back. Caleb lay alone, but for the corpse of the mounted NKVD man who'd killed him, who in turn had been shot by the Hunter, laid out in the road just meters away, arms crossed over chest and head set to rest on a green-needled pine bough. The Hunter's killer was no doubt among the bodies strewn in the road.

"Keep going, Eriks," Haralds said, turning him firmly by the shoulders and forcing him forward. "There will be reprisals."

Eriks gazed down the road in a stupor, disconnected from its swift, methodical activity. Men were catching horses, plucking weapons and ammunition from lifeless figures in the snow, rolling bodies and peeling off their clothes. Kristaps was in the fray, tugging a boot from a leg of green wool.

Next thing Eriks knew he was standing near the Architect, who was holding the assault rifle as if weighing it against heavy considerations.

Captain Wagtail strode up leading three horses behind him. "Twenty," Wagtail told the Architect. "No fewer than twenty came out. Completely off guard. A masterstroke."

The Architect nodded. He held Eriks's eye like it was an induction ceremony, and pushed the PPS sub-machine gun to Eriks's chest, saying, "The *Papasha*."

The gun was repulsive to Eriks, still warm, and Caleb getting cold.

"That's *daddy*," said Snaggle-Wit in passing. "Don't point it at anyone 'til you're ready to shoot."

Eriks's eyes stung as the Architect and Wagtail walked away and he was left holding the coveted rifle. Homburg Haralds pushed him toward the trees.

"Well played, Eriks," said one of the Architect's sons, leading a booty-loaded horse past.

"He's a wanted man from here on out," Haralds said. "Better call him… Bear Slayer."

25

MARCH 21, 1941

THE SUMMERHOUSE

WEARING GABARDINE BREECHES OVER WOOLEN LONG JOHNS, Kārlis Pērkons cinched his belt to the tightest notch. He adjusted his glasses and watched himself in his bedroom mirror don the final accoutrement for Private, Red Army 24th Latvian Territorial Corps, a steel helmet. Before leaving, he slid his Art Academy matriculation card between the mirror and the frame. If —*when* he came home, he would find the card here and resume his studies in art. Then he closed the door to the bedroom he'd been sharing with Hugo Krumins.

His friends were in the kitchen, having caught the milk train immediately after school to be with him when he presented his head.

"Hugo's the sure bet for valedictorian," Vilz Zarins was saying, looking dark with slicked hair, seaman's cap and bomber jacket.

"Which means on top of exams I have to come up with a speech," Hugo said, white shirt, face and hair.

"Sucker!" Sniedze said, from under an oversized newsboy cap.

"If I'm not back for graduation, assume I've been killed," Kārlis said, going for merry banter but the comedy falling flat.

"With your boots on!" Jekabs Leopolds said, rescuing him. "Better than slain by Hugo's speech like the rest of us." That the Leopolds had come made Kārlis feel like a million *lats*, because he knew they always went to their temple on Friday evenings. Jekabs was rarely seen not working, but this afternoon he was in a sports coat instead of an apron and without a speck of flour from the top of his wavy haircut to the soles of his shiny shoes. His Uncle Eli was outside talking with Kārlis's father, the two avidly discussing ways to increase ventilation to the root cellar.

"Thanks for coming all this way," Kārlis said to all.

"We are the Nonchalants," Vilz said, in a fierce whisper, upholding her fist to the center of the group. "A Nonchalant will never abandon another Nonchalant."

"Or give up his name," Hugo said, copying the fist pose. "No matter how they torture you."

"Or steal his girl," Kārlis said.

"Sharply creased fedora, black-faced wristwatch, English newspaper," Jekabs said. "That was our style."

"While it lasted," Sniedze said. "Now we're the Nonchalants minus Peters and Eriks. And soon we'll be minus Kārlis."

Leave it to Sniedze to spoil the moment, Kārlis thought, forgiving him. The twit couldn't help but blurt out any feeble thought that rose in his puny mind.

"Time to go," his mother called from the front hall. "We're in trouble if you miss the army train."

"I got it," Hugo said, offering to carry his duffel.

"Bring an umbrella, Biruta," called his mother. "It's a gray sky."

Kārlis heard his little sister's running steps as the Nonchalants filed out the kitchen door into a spring afternoon where all was wet and green with new growth bursting from every earthen crevice.

A rickety wooden ladder leaned against the linden tree, and on the top rung Kārlis recognized Tante Agata's rubber galoshes. She was muttering something, her arms and shoulders among the pliable branches and leaf buds dancing in the wind.

"Tante Agata, you're too high," Kārlis said, holding up a hand to steady her.

A flutter of blue silk brushed his arm as Tante Agata finished tying a ribbon around the tree. She grasped his hand, descending, and put her palm to the trunk. "Kārlis, you know your linden sister," she said, as if introducing him to a debutante at a ball. "You've grown up together. You can find her wherever they send you."

His eyes tingled. *Dammit.* He'd acted manly up to now. Kārlis didn't want to get gooey wondering if he'd see her old gray braid and woven headband again.

"No more sacred groves, of course," she said, patting the trunk, "burned and salted by pillaging knights, but she won't be driven from this land, and you must draw on her energy." Tante Agata slipped her foraging basket over her shoulders, and adjusted her chunky amber necklaces, murmuring,

"The flowers, bee's sweet julep, bloom in May.
Five to ten drops of tincture, in water thrice a day.
Brew flowers for infection,
The leaves soothe anxious tension
Wood ash for intestine
Lifts spirit from depression
The sap abounds in mucilage

from which sugar can be elaborated,
Bilious giddiness, loose bowels
and thrumming head alleviated,
In May the yellow flowers be in bloom… "

Kārlis knew the ending and recited it with her.

"Pick most the flowers for the tea
but leave some for the broom."

It suddenly dawned on Kārlis that Tante Agata's constant chanting had never been mindless. The cunning old bird had been trying to instruct him all along. He walked with her down the drive wondering if, one day, he'd even understand her baffling proverbs. Kārlis matched his gait to Tante Agata's mincing step, falling farther behind his parents and Mr. Leopolds, who led the procession, and the Nonchalants swaggering behind them four abreast. He took time to admire the crocus, hyacinth, and daffodil spotting the drive. Gravel crunched underfoot as Kārlis left home, heart beating like a military drum.

"I don't think there's enough linden tea on the planet to calm down the world's nervous tension, Auntie."

To that she uprooted a cushiony clump of bog moss and told him, "Field dressing! Oh, my," she said, eyeing a carpet of mushrooms. "Pink Bottoms. That's what we want for dinner. I'll catch you up, Kārlis." She left him with a face-wrinkling smile and, lifting her skirt, Tante Agata crossed tangles of overgrowth to enter the trees where shafts of light hit the forest floor at a steep angle, her galoshes sinking slightly into the thaw.

Kārlis's mother called from the front of the parade, "Biruta, don't step in those puddles!" The warning arrived just as his little sister jumped on his back, flinging arms around his neck and jarring his helmet. "Giddy-up!" she said, kicking her shoes.

He caught her legs, piggyback style, and trotted to catch up with the others who had by now turned onto the road leading to the village. Biruta disproved the maxim about the cobbler's children going shoeless. Janis Pērkons's daughter always had new shoes, even during the past year when no one did. Hers, slyly custom-crafted by the leather master at his father's confiscated Leather Works, were cream-colored saddle shoes with light blue piping. Kārlis would not be home to celebrate his sister's upcoming Name's Day, or to see her turn ten.

Just as he caught up with the boys, he observed Vilz Zarins tuck a paper into a mailbox. Kārlis turned on his heel, quick, hoping his little sister hadn't seen, and set her down. She laughed at the jerky stop that made her braids fly, and ran to catch up with their mother.

Kārlis snatched the leaflet, and turned his shoulder to read it unseen, instantly recognizing the raised "e" made by Vilz's typewriter.

"*Ak tu kungs!* Vilz! My sister almost saw you. You can't leaflet in this neighborhood. Someone might think it's my family spreading anti-Soviet dirt."

"One newspaper's worth a thousand firebombs," Vilz said, without apology.

"Yah. And just as dangerous if caught," Kārlis said, reading the handbill. "You wrote this?"

"Nay, a professor hiding in the Bikernieki wrote it," Vilz said. "But I came up with the title."

Latvia on Verge of Extinction

After nine months of Russian occupation, our confusion is past. By now everyone has seen relatives and friends arrested on the slimmest of suspicion and has grimly stayed silent. We at first thought only "Harmful Elements" were to be reprimanded by the Communist regime. We now know we are dealing with cynical and cold-blooded minds that consider the whole independence-minded Latvian nation to be a Harmful Element. As individuals we bear up, tottering under injustice. Collectively, Latvia is on the verge of being erased from the registry of nations. Now that the destruction of Latvian values and order is well underway, the gloves are coming off. No longer bothering to wear the mask of legitimacy, how long before the Communists decide open slaughter is the simplest means to achieve their goal? Will Germany arrive before the planned destruction of our nation is realized?

Kārlis gulped. Was Germany coming to save them? Bringing war, war with the Red Army? Kārlis looked at his Red Army uniform, stomach churning bilious giddiness, soft bowels and thrumming head. Nazis. That's who Kārlis would be sent to fight.

"Don't be afraid of Fritzes," Hugo said, reading over his shoulder. "The average Russian soldier fears what his own side will do to him more than Germans."

"That's comforting, Hugo," Kārlis said, resuming walking. "This is nuts. Things should never have gotten to this point. I should be graduating high school and going to the Art Academy. I should be screaming, running in the opposite direction as this army train, following Tante Agata into the woods, or hiding with the professor in the Bikernieki Forest. But that would leave my family having to answer to the Ivans."

They had reached the Bier Schtube, across from the train station, and stopped walking. Raindrops fell. A few customers seated on the outside tables were taking their beers and plates inside the tavern for shelter.

"The future's a loaded shotgun pointed at our heads," Vilz said.

"But they keep everybody going to work," Jekabs said. "Cook the frog gradually. If you just drop it in boiling water, it will leap out."

"Actually, the frog's skinny legs turn into a mess of thin, white strands," Sniedze said. "I know for a fact it just dies a nasty death."

"Get out of the rain, Kārlis," his mother called, from under the awning at the platform. "Janis, he's in the rain."

"Mama, I'm not made of sugar," Kārlis shouted, loitering in the road outside the Bier Schtube, watching the door. He wanted to see Lileja, wanted Lileja to see him in the soldier uniform.

"Her father won't let her out," Hugo said, reading his mind.

How did Hugo happen to know that, Kārlis wondered.

Janis Pērkons came over twirling his umbrella. He lifted Kārlis in a bear hug and set him down gasping, right in front of everybody. "If the world were ruled by women there'd be no war," he said, tilting his head at the Bier Schtube. "Just a couple nations not talking to each other. Did you know I married Mrs. Pērkons one week before I was called up to the Czar's Imperial Army," he said. "Then I spent four years in a German POW camp before seeing her again. She waited for me. I don't know if they make them like her anymore."

No, Kārlis guessed. That did not sound like Lileja.

Then a shutter swung open from the uppermost window, at the narrowest point of the steeply pitched roof. Waves of blonde hair tumbled forward as Lileja leaned out from the Bier Schtube. She smiled, waving down at Kārlis, and it felt like the sun had broken through.

"Sveiks, Lileja," Kārlis called, holding his helmet as he tipped his chin up and waved back, feeling a measure of peace flood his soul. He looked over his shoulder. Hugo was also waving, returning the smile. So was his father and every fellow in the road, smiling up at the window. Who had her smile been meant for? It didn't matter.

"Now would be a good time to go," his father said. And Kārlis followed him toward the platform.

"Mr. Pērkons." It was the stationmaster coming around the side of the building, dressed in a dark navy uniform with two columns of brass buttons and gold cording across the visor of his peaked cap.

"*Lab dien*, sir." Janis Pērkons greeted the stationmaster with a slap on the back. His father was on easy terms with the leaders of society.

"You're coming to the card game."

"Wouldn't miss it," Janis replied. "Say, what's this business here?" He pointed down the yard, to where cattle cars were stockpiled on the sidings.

The stationmaster lowered his voice. "They are retrofitting those for people."

His father's face fell, haggard within the symmetry of his sideburns and goatee.

"More of them each day," the stationmaster said. "Shuttling them between the smaller towns. An ill omen, I tell you."

Kārlis felt his guts wrench. The train was due in minutes and he had to use the toilet. He held back from following his father and the stationmaster as they ambled toward the vacated construction site, shaking heads at the wide shelving being installed in the cattle cars. Further down the track, black smoke billowed into the gloaming. The train was coming.

"I better say goodbye to Mama," Kārlis said, excusing himself.

The Nonchalants, Biruta and Mr. Leopolds were already filling up the small platform, huddled under umbrellas and looking, Kārlis feared, like an illegal assembly. Watching them was a burly, dark-haired man in a civilian overcoat, a rifle on his shoulder, local militia, extra police. His mother was wending her way toward the "self-defense" man, though Kārlis could not fathom why.

"You clean up well," Mrs. Pērkons told the burly militia-man, as Kārlis came over to stand by her. "I almost didn't recognize you."

The man recognized *her*. His deep-set eyes, shadowed by a protruding forehead, gleamed with interest.

"The lathe-and-plaster you repaired in my entryway," Mrs. Pērkons said. "It's flaking off. Could you possibly come take a look at it?"

"Is the old lady still at your place?" the militia-man asked in a gravelly voice. "The granny with the medicinals."

Kārlis froze, his guts roiling at the raspy voice. The coarse tone hurled him back to a harrowing episode from the winter. This man had stalked him, been on the opposite side of the noble oak, at the swing in the clearing, where Kārlis had hid with Lileja. He'd been ordered by a Russian to weed out keepers of the lore, like Tante Agata.

Mrs. Pērkons began, "She could remedy that hoarse—"

"No," Kārlis interrupted. "My great-Aunt doesn't live here anymore."

Massive locomotives pounded toward the station, filling ears with the roar of engines.

"She went back to Riga," Kārlis shouted to the militia-man, above the din. "I'll write you, Mama," Kārlis said, flinging his arms around his mother's shoulders. He maneuvered her away, whispering, "Steer clear of that one. He's trouble."

The engines slowed, dragging passenger carriages past the platform, dominating space with noise and iron.

"He's my handyman," she whispered. "He's always been a pariah." His mother spoke fast, while brakes screeched. "No one would hire him when he got out of prison a couple years ago for manslaughter, except your father."

Kārlis nodded. His father was on easy terms with the dregs of society. But his father didn't know what Kārlis knew.

"Janis gave him odd jobs until he got on his feet," his mother said.

The train crawled forward amid pneumatic hisses, finally stopping. The door to Kārlis's carriage swung open. This was a whistlestop and Kārlis the only passenger.

"Well, he's militia now, so stay away from him," he told her, tersely. "Keep him away from Auntie."

Kārlis looked up, startled to see the militia-man standing right beside him. He kissed his mother's forehead and announced, "I already fixed that plaster, Mama. I should've shown you but I forgot in my rush to join the army." He met the man's deep-set eyes. "So it's not a problem."

The man lowered his head, studying Kārlis. Something further was expected.

"The eagle doesn't catch flies," Kārlis told him, quoting Tante Agata, and shrugging his eyebrows.

It was time to board.

Ak tu kungs! Convicts running the town. Grannies wanted for arrest. Artists turned to soldiers. Cattle cars for people. The world was a spinning shambles.

Hugo gave him the duffle. Someone dressed like Kārlis but with black *gorgets*, stepped onto the platform, shoulders squared, and matched Kārlis's document to information on a roster. Kārlis was admitted on board, bound for the Litene training camp nine hours hence, pure, grade-A Latvian cannon fodder.

Arms stretched out to Kārlis as he mounted the train, fingers and palms imparting the content of hearts.

Sveiks, Kārlis. *Sveiki.*

The stationmaster blew his whistle. The train left the station.

Kārlis barely had time to slough his duffle in an empty seat and crane his neck to the window where his life, standing along the platform, shot by in a blur. The Bier Schtube, the road to the village, Tante Agata's woods, the summerhouse, the linden tree, all dissolved into a budded forest about to riot.

But the light lingered. Shafts bore through the nimbus hinting at mysteries hidden in the trees. Today was the vernal equinox, with exactly equal lengths of light and dark. The sun would set precisely at 18:28. There was still that much order in the universe.

26

April 1961

America

"And that, muzais puisits, is how I learned to make this tea," Kārlis Pērkons said. He collected the empty teacup, and turned off the bedside lamp. *"Feeling better?"*

The flushed face bobbed as Kārlis moved toward the door.

"Wait, Uncle Kārlis," came the high voice from the pillow. *"Is Latvia a real place?"*

Kārlis stopped midstride. *"Of course it's real,"* he said. *"Why would you even ask me that?"*

"The Mysterious Island's not a real place." His nephew sat up, putting a small hand on the Jules Verne tome Kārlis often read. *"No one at school has heard about Latvia, not even my teacher."*

Kārlis struggled to find the right words. Events from his former life were still vivid enough to wake him in a midnight sweat. *"It's real all right."*

"So is Tante Agata still alive?" the little boy asked. *"Did Lileja marry Hugo after you left? Did Peters ever come back?"*

"I don't know," Kārlis said, "but I search every issue of the Exile Examiner for news."

"Can't you write and find out?"

"If they received a letter from someone in America," Kārlis said, "they would be arrested for spying."

"Just for getting a letter?" The boy stared, wide-eyed. "That's not proof. Then anybody could be arrested."

Kārlis leaned against the doorjamb with a sigh. Compared to his hulking frame, everything in the room seemed small. Stilts. Rockets. Dinosaurs. How could a little boy possibly understand? "Sounds crazy," he said with a half-hearted shrug. "But I promise you, it's real."

"Then where did Grandfather bury the treasure?"

Kārlis fumbled, barely catching the clattering cup and saucer.

"Grandfather Janis," the boy insisted. "That part's real too then. Right? Where did he bury it?"

Kārlis's eye darted to the window and scanned the hallway outside the boy's room. No one was there. He exhaled. "I've already said too much."

The television set was droning from the living room. Kārlis had turned it on, anxious to watch the 5:30 newscast. Cuba had been invaded by a mercenary force, which Fidel Castro claimed was organized, financed and armed by the US government. Lurking behind Castro was the tall shadow of the Soviet Union, the only nation besides America with the atomic bomb. Communism, it seemed, had chased Kārlis across the globe to the Bay of Pigs, practically on American shores. But this time the thugs would not catch him unawares.

"Don't talk about this to anybody, muzais puisits." Kārlis said, recognizing a lifelong wave of dread as he raised his finger to his lips. "Never speak of these things."

K. Smiltens, 1945.

The Knock at Night

27

SOUTHERN CALIFORNIA
NOVEMBER 1989

OXYGEN COURSED THROUGH Kārlis Pērkons's body as he ran past the final acre of orange grove. And the good news was nobody was chasing him! He smiled to himself, feeling good, a runner's high, as sinuous leg muscles pushed against the cushy soles of his Nikes. It had been over a decade since Kārlis had read the bestselling Complete Book of Running and had been, like the rest of America, swept up in the jogging craze. This morning he would take another medal. There were few athletes in the 65-and-over age division and, as he had just turned 65, he expected to be the strongest. The finish line was coming into view. Backdropped by purple mountains, a high banner stretched across the street between city hall and the library of the Victorian-era, university community he called home. More and more spectators lined the road as he approached, cheering, propelling him and the other entrants toward the win. Kārlis had never seen so many happy people in one place. He looked for the little blond head he knew was also watching for him.

"Yay! Uncle Kārlis! Whoopie!" the high voice seized Kārlis's heart.

His grandnephew was wearing the t-shirt Kārlis had designed, pro-bono, for the event. Even size small dwarfed the eight-year-old frame that jumped and waved as Kārlis ran by. Crossing the finish line, his strides slowed to a walk. Kārlis heaved a huge breath of satisfaction into exhausted, energized limbs as he turned back to find the lad.

Old enough to be engaging company, the boy still grabbed Kārlis's hand as they strode down the sidewalk, to mill through the park and adjoining downtown until the medals were awarded. Kārlis's chest felt light and bursting with goodness as he and his grandnephew ambled through the crowd, exchanging a few backslaps with some folks he knew. The public races are like a party, Kārlis thought. Everybody seemed happy and excited.

"I'd say a 10k shows American culture at its best," Kārlis remarked to Johnny. "Hundreds of people of all ages and walks of life freely attend just to be fit and feel good. Ak tu kungs, I remember a time in Europe when you wouldn't find such a crowd unless it was some power-grabbing dictator rallying the masses. Here people are just out to do their best and raise some money for charity."

A growing crowd blocked the sidewalk outside an electronics store. An eclectic gathering of runners, a mom with a baby stroller, an older couple, college students, a businessman, and even a local dignitary seemed riveted to the glass storefront where about twenty-five television sets were all tuned to the same channel. On screen, a live newscast featured guys with sledgehammers swinging at a graffiti-fraught concrete wall, the Berlin Wall. Holes had been punched to the opposite side and rays of light were shining through.

Kārlis froze mid-step and adjusted his hearing aid, forgetting to breathe and everything else as he watched. A line of men straddled the notorious wall. One man in a leather jacket stood atop the broken concrete edge, arms raised, fingers in Vs for Victory. He had to know he could be target practice, would certainly have been executed maybe as recently as the previous day.

"What's wrong, Uncle Kārlis?"

"Oh, Johnny." Kārlis pulled himself to the present moment while still watching the news. "They're tearing down the Berlin Wall." He explained, "Those countries have been ruled by the Communists for nearly fifty years. People want to be free."

"I can't believe this is happening," the young mother said. "They'll be mowed down like weeds."

"Not this time. Their economy is in shambles," said one of the college students. "They're losing their grip. The whole thing is breaking up."

"It's been a long time coming," said the dignitary.

"Some very brave people have never stopped resisting," Kārlis murmured. With the boy's hand in his, he pivoted, decided to walk the half-dozen blocks home, no longer caring to collect his award.

"Maybe those kids who were stranded at their grandma's house can get back home now," Johnny said, skip-walking to keep pace.

Kārlis was always astonished at the details the boy retained. He'd almost forgotten he'd told Johnny the story of the children who'd been visiting grandparents in East Berlin when the wall was first erected, who'd never again seen their parents or West Berlin home.

Kārlis began humming a tune. "An old song just came to me," he said. "To translate into English, it would be,

I was throwing a few flowers in the Gauja

To send greetings to my girl

It's been a long time since I remember this song

Time since my beloved is married to someone else-

("Something like that," Kārlis hedged.)

Whenever in spring flowers bloom again

I go to the river and scatter flowers there

Not asking where the waves will take them

"The English translation isn't as catchy as the original Latvian which has a snazzy ring to it," Kārlis explained as he traversed the drive to his bachelor's apartment with a jaunty step. "According to The Baltic Observer, the last couple of years has seen spontaneous singing by the masses in the Baltics. Songs that have been strictly forbidden since the Soviet occupation fifty years ago are again being heard. Songs that brought a death sentence when I lived there."

"No! You can't kill people for singing!" Johnny was incredulous. "Or everyone at church would be in jail!"

"Absolutely so! I wouldn't kid about it," Kārlis said, unlocking his front door and letting the boy inside. "But the funny thing is, those old dainas have been resurfacing in my memory lately, too. I haven't even thought of them for years, and now I hear them so clearly." One more nostalgic idea popped into Kārlis's mind. "Remember what a palindrome is?"

"Taco cat."

"Yah. And 1991."

"Borrow or rob."

"We're getting close to the finish line, Johnny. I'm glad you're here, muzais puisit, to celebrate with me. Today the Berlin Wall is coming down. Ak tu kungs, the Soviet Union is crumbling, Johnny!"

Johnny shot to the drafting table where he liked to spin around on the stool. The slanted lightboard where Kārlis worked was command center to the surrounding tubes of paints and jars of brushes, and dominated the spartan studio furnished in worn Danish modern. Kārlis took a plump folder of aged documents from a shelf, sat on the couch and spread the file contents before him on a low table. "I've kept everything waiting for this day," he said, lining up small stacks of documents, yellowed newspaper clippings and old photographs. "Everything should be in order."

"*You see Johnny, Communist logic allocates 1,000 square meters of land to every citizen, so our summer property has no doubt been subdivided beyond recognition. Half a dozen tenants and their families probably live there, each paying a token thirty-five cents a month, the price of a U.S. postage stamp. The state "pays" the lion's share of the rent, and it's not enough to cover repairs. I can just imagine the leaky roof and rotting floors. And of course, we never had indoor plumbing. We had to run through the snow to the outhouse. The place is surely out-of-date and dilapidated. But I'm getting ahead of myself. All in the proper order. First we get the house back, then repairs.*"

"*Why do you want a dilapidated, old house in Latvia?*" Johnny asked. "*To get the treasure?*"

Kārlis felt his cheeks flush, but he tried to ignore the comment. Johnny's imagination tended to get stuck on the prospect of buried treasure. "*I will need to find a lawyer,*" he went on, talking to himself more than to the boy, who thankfully had started drawing pictures. "*Reclaiming private property nationalized by Communists will probably become a specialty. From what I read in* The Baltic Observer, *we'll have to be rid of Communist tenants before a lawyer can transfer property. When the time comes I'll pay the damn Russians to quit the premises. Then ownership will be legally transferred back to the family, at last.*"

"*Kind of like how they got rid of you?*"

"*What? Nay! Not the same at all! Believe me. And they've been living in our house for fifty years, it's high time—*"

"*Fifty years!*" Johnny exclaimed. "*And how long did you live there, Uncle Kārlis?*"

"*Well, about twenty years before I had to—*"

"*Only twenty! Dang. That's not nearly as big as fifty. No wonder the Russians think they have dibs on—*"

"It's not a question of dibs," Kārlis said, disgruntled. "It's not easy to explain, *muzais puisits.*"

"No, I get it," Johnny said eagerly. "The house is sort of like a trophy."

"Nay," Kārlis said, shaking his head, annoyed. The house was no mere symbol of victory. But, come to think of it, what was he to do with the property once he'd gotten it back? He'd never been a homeowner. He owned one fork, one knife and one spoon because why would one man need more? His bachelor pad was minimalistic, except for his paintings and athletic medals, which covered every square inch of wall space.

"One of us might like to live there someday," Kārlis said, defensively. "Or spend summers, like we used to do. It's the principle of the matter, *muzais puisits.* You'll understand one day." Kārlis laid out the few existing photographs of his former life, black-and-whites of his parents, the Nonchalants, the house. "The proper order is to first get the property back," he concluded. "Once it's ours we can decide what to do with it."

Johnny leaned over the photos, his hand moving to his fair locks. "There's a lot of bald guys in the family," he said, with a note of worry.

Kārlis stacked the documents and photos precisely and laid them gingerly back in the file. He sighed, and said, "Since the war, Latvia's been all but forgotten by the western world. I never thought I'd be away from home for so long, but it was impossible to get back. And now fifty years have gone." Kārlis stood, tapped the folder smartly against the drafting table and took it to the window where he held it against his breast, surprised at the swell of emotion he felt. "In 1991, I'll be nearly seventy years old Johnny. I'm an old man."

"Maybe they'll make a Seventy-and-Over class for you at the races, Uncle Kārlis."

"If I outlast the Communists," Kārlis said, patting the plump folder, "I've won the main event."

28

A MIDSUMMER DAY, 1940

PĒRKONS SUMMERHOUSE, OUTSIDE RIGA

SOMETHING ABOUT THE LIGHT TODAY DARED a guy to try to catch it, Kārlis Pērkons thought, while obediently posing for the photograph. Solstice sunlight streaked through the breezing linden tree, dappling Kārlis and his friends in gold as they crammed onto the balcony. Not the precious-metal gold buried for treasure because it's incorruptible and still gleaming when dug up fifty years later, but the fragile kind of gold glimpsed sometimes at the end of the day that you could never hold onto.

"The Leica is the most sophisticated photographic instrument money can buy," Kārlis's father boasted from the yard below, where he aimed his new camera up at the youths. "You'll never forget this day."

"Line up according to height!" Peters Kalnins ordered, installing himself at the tall end of the balcony.

"If you insist!" Eriks Gailis gibed, bumping Peters from position. A crown of oak leaves and a leafy boutonnière made Eriks look like a sneaky, human tree of unknowable height.

Jekabs Leopolds and Vilz Zarins were doubled over in mutual headlocks, brown curls and a Greek sea captain cap bobbing in the tangle of Jekabs's biceps and Vilz's seldom seen womanly physique, as the two wrestled, circling in place.

"Get back, Hugo!" Kārlis told the white-haired boy elbowing past him. "We're the same height!"

"Yah, but I'm barefooted!"

"This is not the proper order," Kārlis shouted, laughing as he was jostled next to the youngest boy, Sniedze Krasts, but not really caring. Nobody could settle down.

School was out.

The midsummer air felt like helium in the lungs. Ahead was the final year of high school. Like each of his friends, Kārlis had plans, launch-over-the-moon dreams made of portfolios and interviews and girls and letters of acceptance and girls and dances and leaving home.

Crackle filled the air. Inside the house his mother must have dropped the needle on the gramophone, pulsing the occasion with Strauss, her favorite.

"Hold still," his father called.

Seven friends eager to prove their generation's mettle leaned over the balcony and stared down the lens, endorsed by the portentous engineering of the Leica's shutter click.

Behind his father, Lileja Lipkis walked out of the forest carrying a tray of pierogi. Kārlis watched her curves in motion, fascinated, while each boy seemed to grow taller. He suddenly felt foolish standing at the knickers-and-knee-socks end of the line next to Sniedze.

"Sveikee, Mr. Pērkons," Lileja told his father, holding up the tray. "These are for the party."

"Excellent, but we'll need more," said Janis Pērkons. "I am hosting the biggest Name's Day party ever seen in these parts." He swept an arm toward

the forest. "The whole village will be here and two hundred of my closest friends from Riga."

Kārlis turned to exit through the house, one in a like-minded, hormone-driven stampede of boys aching for a chance to speak to Lileja. He heard his father's booming promise, "People will be talking about this party for years."

Crossing his parents' bedroom, Kārlis nearly collided with his yellow-braided little sister chasing the cat out the window. "Hey! You can't climb on the roof!" he told her remaining leg before it too vanished over the sill. "That's dangerous!"

At the base of the stairs, he almost kicked the handyman, who was on his hands and knees dabbing plaster near the baseboards. The man lifted an indignant face to Kārlis, who stepped wide around the brooding deep-set eyes, apologizing.

In the yard, his father was directing caterers to the carriage house saying they were to roast at least three sucklings.

Hugo, the weasel, had beaten him to Lileja's side and was already carrying her tray. "I can't wait to show you," Hugo crowed, as they fell in behind the caterers. "Mr. Pērkons has vats of caviar, and pigs' heads roasting in barrels."

"See you tonight at the bonfire, Karli," Lileja said, dazzling him with an over-the-shoulder smile before disappearing with Hugo and her toothsome wares.

"Yah, see you there," Kārlis called. "I mean here." He stood wondering what to do next.

"Musicians around back," his father told a quartet of men carrying graduating sizes of instrument cases.

"Nay, Janis," his mother had sallied up, bouffant hair pinned with precision. "Have the string quartet in front, playing as the guests arrive."

"This is the lady of the house," Janis told a man driving a wagon with kegs of beer. "She's in charge."

"Serve the drinks under the linden tree," his mother said, waving a blousy arm. "It's shady and still in bloom. And Janis," she leveled gray eyes at her husband. "Why do we need to plaster the foyer today?"

"The plasterer needs the work today."

"He's a murky character," his mother said. "None of my friends will hire him."

"Exactly."

"He just got out of prison for manslaughter."

"We all make mistakes, Anna. But get a man on his feet, and you've got yourself a customer."

"I wish I had more input around here."

"I got your input right here, Bosoms," his father said, sliding an arm around his mother with a wolfish squeeze.

Ak tu kungs. Kārlis stared at the toe of his loafer and rued his timing. Nothing was more awkward than parents flirting with each other.

His father opened a slim gold case with the flick of a button and extended an offer of tobacco to someone standing behind Kārlis.

He startled to discover the handyman-convict had sneaked up behind him to report a job finished.

The jailbird accepted a cigarette as his mother skirt-swished to another cause. The two men shared a lit match, though his father's shiny oxfords clearly walked a different world than the convict's dusty work boots.

"I got so many guests coming," his father said, waving out the flame and tossing the matchstick. "I've built a barge to ferry wagons across the river. And I'm renting the barn down the way where people can spend the night."

"*Business must be booming,*" *observed the handyman-convict in a raspy voice.*

"*Well,*" *Janis equivocated, exhaling a stream of smoke.* "*If you only celebrate when times are good, where's the trick in that?*"

The handyman shrugged. "*If I had the capital I guess I'd ride it high, too.*"

"*More than capital, man, you need a vision of your idea played out in a set of future events. You need optimism for a future where you can manifest those events,*" *Janis punctuated his advice by stabbing the air with his cigarette.* "*Close deals and get paid.*"

His father had cleverly slipped a lecture for Kārlis into the conversation, no doubt trying to seduce him away from art school and into the family leather enterprise by the poetry of capitalism. "*That's the beauty of the system,*" *his father said.* "*Keep your mind on the big picture. And don't sweat minor setbacks.*"

Another wagon was rolling up the gravel driveway, following in the tracks of the beer delivery. The driver reined a pair of massive Clydesdales to a halt, while two men in bright blue, one-piece work suits jumped down. One said, "*Who do I speak with about settling a debt?*"

"*That pretty lady over there is in charge,*" *replied a man tapping a keg.*

His father blew smoke, crushed his cigarette, and ducked toward the house.

Kārlis and the convict-handyman remained, orphaned in each other's company. Kārlis didn't use tobacco, though he'd witnessed how smoking together formed instant cameraderie between the most unlikely men. In his case though, the acrid, curling tendrils rising between him and the convict-handyman only accented the uncomfortable, sharp divide of fortune. He felt a little bad about it, but the simple truth was that since his father had mastered "*the beauty of the system*"*, Kārlis could afford to eschew a trade and attend* the Art Academy. This convict and his son if he had one would probably always be doing piecework. But unlike his father, Kārlis was hard pressed to bridge the divide with chummy repartee.

"Where are you taking that chair?" The odd couple were saved by his mother's fierce demand.

"Sorry ma'am. The bill has not been paid," answered one of the blue work suits, not a caterer after all, as he angled a brown leather library armchair out the front door and walked it backward toward the wagon.

"What? Janis!" Anna Pērkons's eyes ignited. "Where is my husband?"

No one answered. Elderly Tante Agata heard the plea from where she'd been honoring a tree with blue silk ribbons, and doddered over.

Kārlis's mother quickly understood her furniture was being repossessed. No one had more practice with his father's risk-return continuum than she. "Just a minute, please." She strode alongside the blue work suit. When he loaded the chair, she detained him with a dainty hand. "Perhaps we are overextended at the moment. Everyone makes mistakes. But have you considered that if you give a man a chance, especially a go-getter like my husband, then you will truly have yourself a customer!"

"Who will raise the cat's tail, if not the cat?" shot in Tante Agata.

"Ma'am. I'm just the furniture removalist. You'll have to speak with people in Riga."

The needle scraped off the gramophone and Strauss was silenced. Kārlis went inside the house to save his mother's favorite record from the debt collectors. He was mortified to discover the sitting room was full of people to witness the spectacle of repo men crashing Janis Pērkons's lavish Name's Day party. A mover in a blue jumpsuit stood at the gramophone. The boys, Vilz and Lileja were crowded alongside someone with a cello. A couple of caterers lingered at the door to the dining room. His father stood at the mantel with a protective hand over Kārlis's little sister, who clutched the cat. Expressions *were grave. No one turned to look as Kārlis stepped into their midst, making room for the convict-handyman behind him. Attention was focused on his friend Jekabs, who worked dials at the radio console to tune in a broadcast that had apparently disintegrated into static.*

The transmission became clear.

"… have confirmed ruthless border post attacks. Communist NKVD troops killed three guards, and the wife and son of one of the guards, and captured ten border officials and twenty-seven civilians. Russian tanks have invaded Riga. The capital is overrun with Red Army troops."

Kārlis felt his stomach clench with shock.

His mother and Tante Agata pressed into the room. The furniture remover settled the gramophone back on its pedestal, looking frozen. Everyone seemed to hold his breath, straining to hear the disembodied voice of the newscaster.

"The Soviet Union has issued an ultimatum, to be answered in six hours. Latvia must immediately form a new government, and allow an unlimited number of Russian troops to enter the country or—"

The signal cut out abruptly. A violent gust of wind rose from nowhere and battered a linden bough against the eaves.

"—or we die!" Sniedze blurted.

"—or we fight!" Vilz Zarins said, turning to the room with defiance.

Kārlis's mother looked at the line of young people with a pale face.

"That would be a futile, bloody resistance," said the convict-handyman.

"Those border murders show how cutthroat Russians are," Eriks said, shaking his leafy crown.

"The Soviet army is huge and ready to roll in," Hugo said, like the classroom know-it-all. "Not to mention Russian military bases already in the country."

"Quiet!" Peters ordered with an outward palm.

Everybody watched Jekabs's back as he rotated knobs on the VEF with the delicacy of a safecracker.

Stomach churning, Kārlis went over and plucked Strauss off the gramophone spindle. He held the black disk by the edges, flipping it over and over, staring into the black grooves. Would Stalin's actions affect him? Politics happened in newspapers and on the radio, but just now events had banged down Kārlis's front door and placed a boot on the throat of his plans. His mind swirled as he stared at the shellacked Strauss 78. The face looking back at him was dim and distorted.

Jekabs finally settled the tuner on the frequency with the least buzz.

"—in fear of further violence," came the voice from the capital, "the seated government is ordering Latvian troops to cooperate with the Soviet forces."

The airwaves were heavily silent. Then the pronouncement, "Latvia is an occupied country under martial law."

Tante Agata gasped. Shoulders slumped. Jaws dropped. The Family Pērkons, their friends, hired help and creditors looked at one another in disbelief. Kārlis realized his father had been right. He would never forget this day. All faces turned toward Janis Pērkons at the mantel, as if watching to follow his lead.

His father nodded, pressing lips together in a hard line as the conclusion became clear. Kārlis heard the last thing he'd expect his father to say.

"We are bowing."

29

JUNE 12, 1941

RIGA, LATVIA

VILZ ZARINS WAS NOT AFRAID of ghosts. At least not of any spirits who would haunt Matīsa cemetery, situated on a pie-sliced property between Riga's Central Prison and the Central Train Station. She'd been waiting here in the dark for hours and, if anything, the local skeletons were kindred souls cheering her on. The two meters of soil separating Vilz's bones from the dead actually united them, rich, verdant soil, Latvian earth.

Take the ghost of Osvalds Martins for instance, 1900 – 1918. The flat granite rectangle marking Osvalds's grave lay at the base of the chestnut tree where Vilz hid. Osvalds had died the year the country was founded. Had he been a patriot? Dying for the land? All concerned the land, Vilz supposed. She could not detach who she was nor her kinship to the graveyard spooks, from the land. And soon enough, like Osvalds here, she would return to Latvian soil.

But not tonight! Vilz shook off the morbid thoughts that came with lingering in the bone yard, and shifted positions. Hiding on the tree limb was an exhausting balancing act, but Vilz didn't dare leave the bushy dome of chestnut leaves while in view of the prison's guard tower. The "researcher" who had preceded her in collecting the prison stats had "disappeared". Vilz did not want to follow those ill-fated footsteps. Time passed so slowly, she again turned to the deceased for company.

Osvalds Martins had been Vilz's age when he'd died, eighteen. The years of his birth and death were carved in stone, 1900 – 1918, as if that defined a life. All the living happened in the dash. Whether someone was brave or a coward, whether someone stuck her neck out for others or just cared about his own skin, all was reduced to the same dash eventually, Vilz contemplated, feeling damp and chilly.

The approach of an engine snapped her attention to the prison gates.

"This is it, Osvalds," Vilz whispered to the late co-conspirator. A cape of cold air settled on her shoulders, raising the hair on her neck. While she didn't mind the local ghosts, monsters came from Russia. Of them, Vilz had the good sense to be terrified.

She pushed binoculars to her eyes. The chestnut tree afforded, from a distance, a limited view over the tall brick wall surrounding Riga's Central Prison. A truck pulled up to the prison intake door, a knobby-wheeled Soviet GAZ-AA. Barely breathing, Vilz brought the rear of the wooden-railed truck into focus, and watched as two men walked into the black-edged circles of her binoculars and outwrested a trunk.

NKVD. Two agents lifted the military style footlocker by the handles and muscled it into the prison like it was heavy. Vilz craved to know what was inside the secretive midnight cargo. Or who. The disappeared researcher? She didn't move a muscle as six more brass-latched, leather-bound trunks were carried inside the prison.

On high alert, Vilz watched the prison door. Hours passed. Nothing happened. Restless and stiff, she debated leaving. But in a few hours she'd exchange intel with the fishmonger, who would expect Vilz's piece of the puzzle to be accurate and complete. The fishmonger was tasked with following one of those midnight prison trucks to find out the story on the heavy footlockers.

At last the prison doors opened and the agents reappeared, again lifting a heavy trunk between them. Altogether eight trunks were loaded back into the truck. The engine growled and the vehicle rumbled away.

Vilz hid the field glasses in the lining of her black leather bomber jacket and considered what she'd seen. Thirty trunks had been carted in and out of the prison this week during the dark of night. She waited a long while before daring to climb down from the tree and drop to the ground. Pulling the Greek sea captain's hat low over her eyes, she raised her collar and got the hell away from the prison. Matīsa cemetery was built for invalids and the poor, affording few monuments or tombstones to hide behind. Vilz was relieved to cross into the train yard.

She cut through lines of cattle cars backed up as far as the eye could see.

Interesting, there was not a cow in sight.

Striding swiftly toward the river, Vilz squatted on the grassy bank, wet from dead-of-night mist, and rolled a cigarette. She smoked, alert to any surrounding whisper or twitch. After minutes, the tobacco and the tonic of River Daugava's spray settled her stomach. Nobody had followed. Nobody watched. So she went home, walking dark blocks to the University district and quietly climbing stairs to the apartment. After sleeping a couple of hours, Vilz left again without even seeing her parents.

The sun was not yet up, but the fishmonger would be. Vilz set off to find him at the Central Market. The old zeppelin hangar bustled with night seamen bringing their catches to the fish pavilion. Vilz fell in behind an eeler's sloshing buckets, passing aisles of stalls to a wet counter heaped with silver-bodied mackerel.

The fishmonger, old enough to be Vilz's father, wore an oilskin apron with thermals shoved up to his elbows. He was laying fish in straight rows across a shallow wooden box. He glanced up and, seeing the Greek seaman's cap and bomber jacket, wiped his hands and stood across the counter from Vilz, looking impassive.

Vilz gave him thirty rubles, standing for the number of trunks she'd observed. "Whatever's fresh," she said.

The fishmonger counted the rubles. At the total, his eyes got pink. He grabbed a pike by the tail and slammed the big fish on the cutting block.

"Tortured bodies," he uttered, striking the base of the head with a cleaver.

Vilz felt ill. Not that she was surprised to confirm that the NKVD was torturing guys and stuffing them into trunks. But because she'd been so close and still unable to help. That could be *her* stuffed in a trunk if she didn't watch it. Instead, she was burdened with the sickening knowledge, one of few alive to tell the tale.

The fish merchant sawed until the head was severed. "—shallow grave," he said, relaying the grisly details in a low voice that rose and distorted in the hangar's rafters and was lost in the market's hum and din. "Rumbala forest."

Staring at the pike's open round eyes, Vilz committed the detail to memory, afraid she would never forget it. "Who?" she asked.

The fishmonger shook his head, lopping off fins. "Couldn't tell."

He sliced a strip of flesh along the backbone, and wrapped the filet in paper. "When the Germans come," he said, handing the purchase to Vilz, "we'll identify them, notify families."

Turning his back to Vilz, the fishwife put a hose to the bloody mess on the floor, rinsing away evidence of the exchange.

K. Smiltens, 2001.

30

June 14, 1941

Red Army Training Camp

Litene, Latvia

He would die young. The boding that he would die soon infiltrated his sleep. Kārlis Pērkons woke in a sweat. He pushed the scratchy blanket off, cursing the metal crossbars of his narrow bunk. Then he was instantly chilled, and tugged the blanket back under his chin. Surrounded by fitful snores, he gazed past the sleeping soldier an arm's length away and through the stacks of conscripts down the length of the dark barracks. Soviet command had sequestered the entire 24th, every Latvian in the Red Army, practically every fighting man in the country, here at this camp in Litene.

Kārlis rolled over and came face-to-face with a wide-eyed soldier on the next bunk. The fellow was propped on his elbow, whispering to the guys below them about the German Army's standard service rifle. "… a Kraut gets trained on his Karabiner semiautomatic at the age of ten," he said. "That's why they're the deadest shots in the world."

Kārlis nosed over to the edge of his bed, eavesdropping on commentary from any number of faceless bunks.

"They haven't taught us shit here."

"The Reds mainly terrorize civilians. They're no match for the *Wehrmacht*."

"They don't train us to fight, because they don't intend us to fight."

Kārlis nodded in the dark. He'd only been taught latrine maintenance so far.

"They keep us here where they can watch us. So we don't go fifth column."

"They'll use us to slow down the Nazis while they make their getaway back to Moscow."

"As long as they're leaving, fine with me."

"Unless they drag us along."

"They took away my piece as soon as I got here."

"The entire 24th was disarmed."

"So what do we do when the Krauts arrive?"

Kārlis squirmed, wrestling an impossible quandary. First he'd been conscripted to serve the brutal regime terrorizing his life. Now the Russians would force him to fight the coming German liberators.

The whole country was praying for a swift German invasion to drive away the Communists. But when the *Wehrmacht* came *blitzkrieging* through on a killing path to Moscow, Kārlis would be ordered to fight them and he'd be gunned down, like countless, nameless soldiers killed daily. Nothing special. Life over. The unique body that was him, *Kārlis Pērkons*, put under dirt at age seventeen. Hugging himself, he seized a lungful of air.

"I say you're lucky if you make it to see a German on Latvian soil," said the fellow on the lower bunk. "'Cause I notice something around here. The Latvian troops are *disappearing* every day. Especially the older guys. You notice that? Ten fellows leave for an exercise and eight come back."

"Yah. What's the story there?"

The door at the end of the barracks slammed wide open. Cold air hit, and the concerns of the bunk bed conference were obliterated by a bugle blast.

The next second, Kārlis was out of bed, pulling gabardine trousers over long johns. He cinched his belt to the tightest notch, vowing to eat every drop of lumpy porridge he was served in the effort to gain weight. He extracted his black wire-rimmed glasses from inside his boot before shoving a foot in and lacing it tight. Pushing his garrison cap over clipped hair, he hustled out the door to line up.

Kārlis headed toward the side of the line where the ethnic Latvians tended to muster, apart from the Russian soldiers. They didn't much mix, so it was obvious to see that there were fewer Latvians now than when Kārlis had first arrived. He wondered with a twist in his gut what *had* happened to those that disappeared.

Since the Red Army had swallowed the former Latvian Army whole, renaming it the 24th Territorial Rifle Corps, Latvian officers now answered to Russian commissars, and Russian recruits steadily infiltrated the rank-and-file. Kārlis had seen rival colonies of ants mashed in the same jar with more camaraderie than this band of stepbrothers.

The sergeant barked announcements in Russian. Kārlis listened hard, but didn't fully comprehend, and froze with dread when the sergeant stepped toward him, pointing at him with a rigid arm. Then the sergeant moved down the line of soldiers, counting out about ten of them.

"Report to Logistical Support by 0700 hours," said the sergeant.

Kārlis exhaled with relief, though dismayed to note that he was the only Latvian in the detail. Was that a mistake? Or maybe Major

Kristovskis in Logistics had specially requested Kārlis Pērkons. He'd been praised for some scale drawings he'd prepared for Major Kristovskis in a previous assignment. He hoped that was the case. The Major was a fishing enthusiast from Jurmala, and the sort of man who might advise Kārlis about impending doom.

Dismissed from roll, Kārlis went directly to the mess hall and stood in another line. He'd barely gotten his ration when he saw the other grunts on the Logistics detail already leaving. Scarfing the contents of his bowl, he jumped up to follow them—under the watchful eye of the guards. The guards were never Latvian. Always Russian or Soviet Asian.

Walking to Logistics, Kārlis felt small amid the vast compound. Spring wildflowers dotted an expanse of grass that stretched to towering pines at the forest border. Except for a cluster of pointy-topped white tents and soldiers everywhere, the setting reminded him of his high school campus, where he and his friends, the Nonchalants, raced over the lawn. How naive they'd been six months ago when they'd named their secret fraternity. *Ak tu kungs!* It was June 14. Tomorrow was, would've been, his high school graduation. Kārlis stopped walking, crestfallen, picturing his friends all together for commencement exercises. Not only was he not with them, but without a diploma he couldn't attend the Art Academy.

As Kārlis gazed wretchedly, a man darted behind one of the distant trees. Kārlis sucked in his breath. NKVD. Even at fifty meters, by God, Kārlis knew the tall black boots and red hammer-and-sickle cap badge of Stalin's secret police. A man could be arrested by the Cheka for any reason or for no reason, before disappearing permanently. Kārlis turned his eyes straight ahead, pretending he'd seen nothing. He hurried to blend in with the other drab green uniforms, not wanting to be the hapless deer that looked easy to the wolf.

As if entering a better neighborhood, tents gave way to wooden structures. Kārlis hustled behind the other soldiers, cutting between the buildings, at the last moment looking back to where he'd seen the NKVD agent. Deeper behind the trees, he saw a line of trucks, the kind used for transporting troops, snaking into the forest.

He tramped over a gravel walkway, where the aroma of eggs and coffee hung in the air, sharp as any barbed wire that might separate the officers from the enlisted men. Minutes later, the crew filed up a short flight of wooden steps and entered the Logistics offices.

Kārlis and the Russian recruits stood at attention against the wall. A lieutenant was already there, seated at a typewriter behind a steel desk. The Commanding Officer was not Major Kristovskis, Kārlis saw with disappointment. Instead, a wide-faced, narrow-eyed Soviet officer dominated the room. He was talking on the telephone, and appeared to size up Kārlis's crew in one second while replacing the receiver in its cradle. Turning to the typist, he dictated, "To: All Officers. Regarding: Mandatory Assembly at 0830 hours."

The typist responded with the rapid striking of keys.

"For a lecture by Chief of Staff Miljevski," said the Soviet, raising his voice above the clacking, "on the topic of battalion attack tactics."

Finally, thought Kārlis, the camp might get a handle on something that could save his life.

"At Strohm Hall, Comrade?" asked the typist.

"*Nyet*," the Soviet said. "The officers will gather in the open-air cinema."

That was where Kārlis had just seen NKVD. The coincidence didn't feel right, making his stomach curdle.

The typist didn't miss a beat. "I assume chairs must be set up for the officers?"

"That won't be necessary," said the Soviet. "But it is imperative that every officer is present. There are over seven hundred. Therefore," he turned toward some of the soldiers standing by, "half of you will distribute this memo to the officer list immediately." To Kārlis and four others, he said, "The rest of you will dig a pit."

Kārlis disguised his annoyance as he followed the CO outside to a stand of shovels. Running the mimeograph or delivering messages throughout the compound wasn't even work compared with Kārlis's unlucky task, which he guessed was setting up latrines.

The Soviet officer led the digging detachment past the grass where the assembly would convene, and indicated a dirt area off to the side and behind some trees. Kārlis saw no further sign of the NKVD, and, from this angle, he couldn't observe the line of trucks he'd seen either. Marking the corners of a jumbo rectangle with the heel of his boot, the Soviet said, "At least one meter deep, preferably two. You have one hour." Then he strode away.

The other soldiers immediately began stabbing the earth with their spades, but Kārlis stood where he was, perplexed. The dimensions were wrong for latrines. If not a pit toilet, then … His mouth went dry. The gathering of the Latvian officers and the presence of the NKVD was a parallelism that knotted his guts.

A large dirt clod thumped Kārlis in the chest. He gasped in pain, caught completely off guard.

"Get those toothpick arms moving, Stickbug," said the rock-thrower, a slope-shouldered brute picking up another clod to heave. His compatriots laughed.

Kārlis hated them. He hated how a rush of liquid anger threatened to seep from his eyes. He started outlining his side of the pit with sharp vertical thrusts, trying and failing to curb his macabre imagination. He was digging a grave, a huge one. His? His arms trembled as he tossed shovelfuls of soil in a pile well away from the edge.

Kārlis envisioned bodies, *his* body, lifeless and far from home, under cold, airless dirt. The other men were skeletons, knee-deep in the pit, carelessly flinging soil that tumbled back into the hole. He had to get out of here. He kept digging, shaking. Was this just another case of his imagination running wild?

The other soldiers were now into Kārlis's end of the rectangle, eight elbows and four flying steel shovelheads that Kārlis took care to avoid.

"Time's up," said the rock-thrower, breathing hard, and surveying the work.

Obviously, they had not dug two meters deep all around, but Kārlis was not going to be the pit critic. The Russian grunts didn't include him in the ritualistic passing and lighting of tobacco, so he kept digging with his head down. Kārlis felt foolish when his crew started walking back without him, so he stepped behind some trees, pretending like he had to relieve himself anyway.

Holding his shovel to his chest, Kārlis rested against a stout pine. It was shockingly quiet, except for birds chirping a litany.

Peering from behind the trunk, Kārlis realized there was absolutely no one around. Where were the guards? An idea hatched that drenched him in sweat. His legs didn't want to cooperate, but he forced them to move to a farther tree. He hid behind it. The sky didn't come crashing down. The birds didn't miss a tweet. The voices of the digging crew had faded.

The brazen idea had its fists in Kārlis's face. Now. Do it now! Right. Wrong. Has to be now. At any moment, every officer in the 24th would gather in that field, surrounded by Russian commissars and probably the Cheka. The premonition of evil prickled hot on his skin. The compound was not fenced. Evaders were executed on sight. *I'm going to die anyway.* He took a deep breath and thrust his jaw forward. *I'm going home.*

After the first step there was no turning back. Twenty trees deep, walking turned to running, shovel in two hands, heart in throat.

Kārlis had a map of the area in his head because he'd made scale drawings for Major Kristovskis. He knew nearby rail and supply roads made Litene strategic for a training base. But Kārlis strove to avoid the thoroughfares, instead scrambling through the trees and over willow-shrubbed bumps on the rough terrain, though it was slow going. The forest was a dense, green cavern, larger than he ever imagined by looking at the map.

Wood snapped and Kārlis jerked his head around. He heard crashing in the underbrush hundreds of meters away. Someone else was running. Chasing him? Kārlis's heart nearly popped. Nay, bypassing him. The distant figure ran jerkily behind a scrim of thin, dense trunks that made his fleeing shape flicker like a movie. Another evader, probably. Kārlis waited, leaning against a tree, heaving breaths, until the man ran out of sight.

A shot scudded the air, dull and distant. Birds and buzzing insects went silent. Another *pop*. Kārlis heard the gun, clutched the shovel in both hands and counted bullet reports. Ten. Eleven. He lost count. The shots came from the open-air theater.

Taking bearings from the gunshots, Kārlis kept moving, behind the cover of bushes. He'd rest when it got dark, and hide in the forest until the Germans came.

31

JUNE 14, 1941

RIGA

VILZ ZARINS SAT HUNCHED OVER HER TYPEWRITER on the pantry floor at the Leopolds Family Bakery, between the wall and a rampart of fifty-kilo flour bags. She couldn't decide on a title for her article, so she hit the return lever thrice, leaving blank lines that she would fill in later.

It was previously reported that dozens of trunks have been arriving at the Central Prison, spurring conjecture that patriots are locked inside them, suffering an agonizing journey to the jail where the Communists use interrogation tactics too ghastly for even them to openly admit. Within the past week, the NKVD have been observed removing no fewer than thirty such trunks from the Central Prison at night, and taking them to forested areas outside Riga for secret burial.

The night was pleasant, but Vilz was in a cold sweat, as if each typewriter key she struck banged a gong, alerting every Bolshevik in the vicinity to the presence of a Harmful Element. Not to mention Mr. Leopolds, who was baking in the next room and did not know the publishing arm of the resistance operated from his pantry. But the typewriter ribbon was worn thin, so Vilz had to hit the keys hard, nearly punching holes in the flimsy paper.

Exhumation of the shallow graves has proven they are the bodies of tortured prisoners, with evidence of smashed skulls, contusions, gaping horrified mouths and facial disfigurement beyond recognition. It's presently too dangerous to attempt further identification of the corpses and notification of family. Editor's note: The reporter originating this research, a regular contributor to Free Latvia, has since disappeared, presumed arrested, but not confirmed.

Vilz looked around the pantry shelves, trying to come up with words. Her personal lexicon didn't have enough synonyms for evil. She chose the title Hideous Sufferings, hoping it wasn't sensational - the mark of an amateur. Wiping sweaty palms on her trousers, she centered the title in the blank lines. It was always like this, she noted. The tightness in the chest, the queasy stomach wouldn't go away until the printed bundles of *Free Latvia* were picked up for distribution.

"Vilz."

Vilz jerked, stomach lurching, irate to see Sniedze Krasts poking his freckled face through the barely opened door.

Sniedze's ever-present newsboy cap further shadowed the dark half moons under his eyes.

"What is it?" Vilz said, hands trembling on the keyboard.

"What do we do if they catch us?" Sniedze whispered. "You know with the typewriter? Would they pull out our fingernails? I would never say nothing, Vilz, no matter what, if they did catch us. But what's our line?"

"Sniedze, you don't need to be involved in this. So scram, pal."

"I'm a Nonchalant, aren't I?" Sniedze mouthed in a stage whisper. "I'm already in deep."

Vilz could not deny that Sniedze had been present the day the Nonchalants had formed in this very pantry, one of seven who'd drank from the flask of distilled courage and made brazen pledges of fealty to one another and to the downfall of the Communist occupation.

"I told Jekabs I'd keep lookout while he goes to the toilet," Sniedze said. "I'm gonna say *harmonicas* if Mr. Leopolds comes. But what if the Cheka comes? Shouldn't there be a different code word for them?"

"I'll take my chances until Jekabs gets back," Vilz said. "Why don't you go read your comic book or something. For chrissakes, Sniedze, I'm trying to concentrate here."

She tried not to let Sniedze get under her skin. The kid was just scared. Vilz was always scared. Isn't that exactly what the Communists wanted?

"Sniedze, in or out," Vilz said quietly, tugging the paper out of the roller with a zip. "Just decide and close the door." She drew a small little fox-face at the bottom of the article with the flourish of her fountain pen. Hidden in the signature icon were her initials, VZ. Picking up the Adler, she gingerly outlined a steel key with a safety pin, cleaning gunk from letter "e", which always gave her problems. "What time is it?"

"Midnight," Sniedze said. "Even though it's not that dark."

"Almost Midsummer." Vilz cranked a fresh sheet of paper under the roller.

"You should see it," Sniedze said. "Take a break and go look out the window."

"After this last article," Vilz said, straining to read the penciled submission under the pantry's sole hanging light bulb.

"Lenin Street's all silvery and glowing," Sniedze said.

"Freedom Street," Vilz said. "Call it by its true name."

"Nay! You could slip up and say that in front of the wrong person," Sniedze said, "and wind up in the Corner House. When the German's get here we won't have to worry about slipping up. When they coming, Vilz?"

"Any day," Vilz said, clacking away. "Any minute, according to the professor hiding in the forest who wrote this."

German Troop Buildup Along the Soviet Border

A reliable communiqué reached Free Latvia on June 1, 1941 stating that the unstoppable Wehrmacht downed four hundred Bolshevik planes and would be here in two weeks. According to the source, panzer units are already rolling into position, preparing to crush the Soviet Union in what will one day be known as history's biggest military operation.

The door opened and a theatrical, deep voice said, "What's going on in here?"

"Jekabs! Thank God you're back," Sniedze said.

"What's going on out there?" Vilz answered, peering over the flour-sack parapet.

"Me and Uncle Eli are baking extra batches, so we can take off tomorrow for graduation."

"Well, keep clanking pans," Vilz said. "So he can't hear me typing."

"I wouldn't worry about that," Jekabs said, stepping inside the pantry and closing the door. "He does have other things on his mind besides what you're doing."

"Yah, well, don't let your guard down, anyway," Vilz said, anxious not to bring the NKVD down on the Leopolds bakery. "I'm not gonna repay your uncle by being sloppy." The bakery was Vilz's second home. She paused typing to examine Jekabs Leopolds, who was leaning over the typewriter to read.

Jekabs displayed the usual bulges of muscle dusted with flour, and yet... "Something different about you," Vilz said. "Your neck is stockier. No brown curls. You cut your hair."

"So you noticed!" Jekabs exclaimed, modeling, accenting each turn of his head with an alternating bicep flex. "You're in your own world back here. I got shorn for graduation."

"Looks good," Vilz said, suddenly dispirited that she was bound to look scruffy at the ceremony. She pulled a comb from her back pocket and slicked down the black wave grazing her shoulders. "My beauty operator was deported," she joked, feeling hollow.

Vilz did not have two centimes, much less money for a haircut. Publishing a treasonous newsletter took all her time, so she had no job. Her father was a plumber with neighborhood customers always wanting to pay with *lats*, if not bushels of beets. By the time lats were traded up to rubles, the money seemed to vanish. Self-pity taunted her, but she banished the useless leech from her mind.

"Think anyone's going?" Sniedze asked.

"To graduation? If we don't go, that's just one more thing the Ivans have stolen from us," Vilz said. "I'm going for myself, and in the name of everybody that can't go."

Names were important. Correctly spelled names. Every one deserved to be accounted for. Not just her fellow Nonchalants, but the scores of other students who'd been drafted, arrested, or otherwise disappeared.

"You only graduate high school once," Jekabs chimed. "I can't remember the last time we got dressed for a good time. I got a shirt here that'd fit you," he told Vilz. "In case you don't have time to go home."

"*Paldies.*" Vilz appreciated the tact. She did not want to go home and lose another argument with her mother about the safety of ever leaving the apartment.

"After the ceremony we'll print this baby bomb." Vilz gestured at the article, still in the typewriter.

"Yah, about that German invasion," Jekabs said, looking disgruntled. "*The unstoppable Wehrmacht downed four hundred planes.* I thought you weren't supposed to use words like *unstoppable.*"

"The German army is unstoppable," said Sniedze. "They took Poland, Denmark, Norway, Belgium," Sniedze counted on his fingers, "the Netherlands, France, Yugoslavia, Greece. The *Luftwaffe* is bombing England to—"

"Just because no one's stopped them yet, doesn't mean they're unstoppable," Jekabs said. "*Unstoppable* is an opinion."

Vilz was silently annoyed at the criticism.

"It's a wish. A prayer," Sniedze said. "God bless the *Wehrmacht*, let them get to Latvia before Stalin slaughters every last—"

"Well, maybe they are stoppable," Jekabs said. "I just question whether your source is one-sided. I'm not keen on being rescued by Nazis. I don't know any Jews who are. You know what the Nazis do to Jews?"

"What," Vilz said, loathing a re-write.

"First thing when they occupy a country, they make the Jews wear an identifying star. Then they herd us into a ghetto."

"Where'd you hear that," Vilz wanted to know, peeved that Jekabs had pointed out a cloud darkening the German-invasion ray of hope.

"Uncle Eli," Jekabs said. "Word gets around in a tight-knit community."

Vilz nodded. She'd noticed the baker on more than one occasion, in guarded conversations with yarmulke-clad customers, no doubt from their outlawed synagogue. It seemed strange, Vilz mused, that Mr. Leopolds was also hiding a secret, but nowadays, being an upstanding man meant sneaking around like a criminal.

"Don't repeat that," Jekabs said, pointing at Sniedze.

"Well, the Germans want you all in one place to keep an eye on you," Sniedze said. "The Jews are all for the Bolsheviks."

"Why you little fink," Jekabs said, rounding on Sniedze, fists on hips. "How can you stand there and say my uncle and me are for the Bolsheviks." He opened his mouth, then stopped short, taking a deep breath of restraint.

"The top guy at the NKVD is a Jew," Sniedze blabbered on. "And they say the worst torturer in the city is a Jewess."

"I don't know about that, but even if it's true, you don't judge a whole nation by what a few individuals do," Vilz said. "There are former Lutherans in the Cheka!"

"The Jews come out full force at the labor rallies, *most* Jews anyway," Sniedze amended, as if for Jekabs's benefit. "They're all singing and full of enthusiasm for Stalin."

"Everybody's required to attend labor rallies," said Vilz.

"But the Jews are singing the loudest," Sniedze said, "You can just tell they mean it."

"People have been executed for *not* singing the *Internationale!*" Jekabs said, voice rising.

"I'll scratch out *unstoppable*," Vilz conceded, reaching for the typewritten draft. "Otherwise I think my source is pretty objective for—"

The door opened and, moving faster than Vilz had ever seen him, Mr. Leopolds was inside the pantry. He doused the light and closed the door behind him to a crack, peering out. "Quiet," he ordered.

No one spoke. Vilz didn't even breathe.

By the light seeping in the cracked door, Vilz saw Mr. Leopolds hold up a finger indicating they were not to ask what was happening.

"What's happening?" said Sniedze.

Mr. Leopolds shook his head. "Car door," he said.

Vilz's heart was pounding in her throat. Silently she slid the typewriter along the ground under a shelf, shoving it back out of sight as far as it would go.

Then they heard a car door slam out front on Freedom Boulevard. No one moved. A man's voice called out, Russian, speaking fast.

At the rear door of the bakery, tires screeched in the alley. Now automobiles blocked both exits. Something started tumbling inside

Vilz, plummeting from her head to the pit of her stomach. Her guts and knees went weak. Another door slammed. Vilz raised the papers she'd just typed. They rustled in her shaking hands. She opened her mouth and pushed in a corner of a page. Afraid of noisy tearing, she softened the page in her mouth and started to chew.

Someone pounded at the front.

Mr. Leopolds had his face to the crack in the pantry door, his arm thrust back in *stop* - a needless gesture. No one intended to answer the knock.

Vilz wadded half the article in her mouth and chewed furiously.

Raised voices and heavy footsteps got nearer, thundering up the stairwell on the other side of the wall.

"It's not us," Mr. Leopolds whispered. "They're at the apartment building next door." He nodded at the wall the two buildings shared in common. "God forbid. It shouldn't happen."

Vilz heard pounding and shouts through the ceiling and could easily visualize the gloved fist of the NKVD beating someone's door. She forced a choking dry lump of paper down her throat. The knock was answered. They heard the sleepy voice of a doomed neighbor, who'd come to face whatever issue the secret police didn't want to address during the light of day. Vilz heard orders, protests, panicking footsteps, the banging of cupboards and closets, a sob. After an unbearably long fifteen minutes, the stairs on the other side of the wall thudded with the footsteps of people departing, and the bump, bump, bump of their suitcase.

Sniedze's skin shone ghostly white. He had the wide eyes of a trapped animal.

"They're leaving," Vilz said, intoning calm.

But as soon as the words left her mouth, pounds and shouts reverberated from elsewhere in the building, echoing through joists and plaster like a nightmare infestation of rats.

Vilz's spirit sank. There was to be a repeat of the demoralizing scene. A vehicle door slammed from out on the boulevard and, again, boots clomped up the stairs. She started to eat the second typed article.

"They're coming for us," Sniedze said through clenched teeth. "We gotta run."

"Do not go near that door," Mr. Leopolds whispered. "They work from a list. As long as we're not on the list, nobody'll know we're here if we don't give ourselves away. Jekabs, we better unload the ovens." It went without saying that anything smelling delicious or charred would attract attention.

Vilz admired Jekabs's grit as he went unhesitatingly with Mr. Leopolds, dropping to his knees and crawling from the pantry. She prayed the front counter would block them from the view of anyone who might be on the boulevard and looking through the bakery display windows in the half-dark of Midsummer.

Minutes dragged by while noises of misery seeped through the walls. An argument bellowed from somewhere above them. On the street, engines revved and vehicles drove away. New arrivals flashed headlights in the bakery window. Stairwell thumping was nonstop.

"They're raiding the other side now. Hear that?" Sniedze said, pointing to the opposite wall. "We're surrounded."

Trapped, Vilz and Sniedze sat with their backs against the wall, listening hard. Every sound conjured a picture of terror. A deep pop was followed by a high scream. Sniedze began to hyperventilate, and burst into tears, doubled over, shoulders heaving in sobs. "We're next." He banged his head against his knees in a deranged fetal position.

"Aw, Sniedze, don't!" Vilz patted Sniedze's back, repulsed, really wanting to slap some backbone into the kid. She couldn't stand such unraveling.

Jekabs came crawling back into the pantry. "I would never have believed such meshuganas if I hadn't seen it with my own eyes. There're at least twenty trucks out there, armed units. They're arresting everybody on the block." He pointed in the direction of Freedom Street. "Cheka are swarming like—ants in a downpour. It's insane."

Mr. Leopolds crawled through the pantry door next and carefully closed it, leaving them in pitch black. He exhaled audibly. "Our best bet will be to wait this out."

Vilz couldn't think of a single other option.

"Barricade the door with those flour sacks," Mr. Leopolds said. "Don't make a sound."

Vilz and Jekabs formed a line and passed the bags to Mr. Leopolds, who stacked them behind the door. The reinforcement muffled sound, sealing them off from mayhem, and trapping them completely. Vilz regretted losing the option of running, even though it would be a desperate play if it came to that. When the door was fortified, they all sat, privately interpreting whatever reached their ears, an occasional yell, a horn honking, splintering boards.

Sniedze flinched at every noise.

But what disturbed Vilz most were the silent parts, the creepy quiet of cooperation, the muffled pattering of sleepy disoriented footsteps. Folks following directions to avoid an ugly scene in front of the children as families were forced into the vehicles of the NKVD and driven away. She would've rather heard a massive fight, taken part in one, would've rather lost one.

"I thought you said the Germans were coming," Sniedze whispered.

"They are," Vilz said.

"The Germans are coming. The Germans are coming," Sniedze chanted under his breath.

Vilz heard Jekabs shift his weight and sensed his dissonance. The statement was true. The Germans were coming. But by saying so Vilz had somehow betrayed the very friend who sheltered her. There was no winning.

Time made no sense. There was no looking forward to an end.

At length Mr. Leopolds sang quietly, *I'm going, yah, I'm going to Canaan land ...*

"I'm not going nowhere," Jekabs whispered, "I'm graduating high school tomorrow."

Sniedze and Vilz stifled giggles. Then they settled into the silence known mainly by dry bones inside tombs. At least that's how Vilz would describe it, wishing she knew better words. Thinking of the article she'd written and eaten, it wasn't sensational after all. It had been understated. She tried to think of stronger words to describe the wrongness of tonight, while the acid bath in her belly digested Hideous Sufferings.

32

KĀRLIS PĒRKONS PLODDED THROUGH the forest, lost, hungry, penniless, and without leave papers. But he'd dodged a massacre, he felt sure. Rays of setting sun backlit the canopy like emerald stained glass in a leafy cathedral, warming fragrant cedar and pine, casting shadows of freakish branch-impaled creatures and bog fiends lurking just out of sight. *Ak tu kungs.* Stop it! The situation was dire enough without his dark imaginings. A brook gurgled a beguiling plash.

He'd read that the average human walking speed was five kilometers per hour. "That's without blisters," Kārlis rectified as he unlaced his boots and dipped his feet into the cold water. "Or wading through swamps."

Oh, if Lileja Lipkis could see him now, he thought, ever the rugged and feral man, surviving the wilds with only the rustled Red Army shovel. He pictured her, curvy and golden and selfish, waiting tables in her cobalt dress. Serving a beer to Hugo Krumins, who was smiling and saying something witty. Wait! What? How did Hugo's white face worm into his fantasy!

Kārlis stood in angst, picked up a stone and skipped it down the creek. Of course, Hugo and Lileja would console each other in his absence. Hugo's family had been unhoused by Soviets and forced to move in with the Pērkonses. Hugo was probably in Kārlis's room at this moment, no doubt making love to Kārlis's girl.

What a rotten year.

But he missed them both. The likelihood of dying in the woods inspired him to forgive them. He just wanted to be home and have a loud laugh with Hugo over the whole ridiculous rivalry. Who he would never forgive were the Communists. The vast foreign regime boiled down to two hatable faces, Josef Stalin, the ever-devouring butcher of the eastern world, and Igor Volkov, the local boot who'd personally stomped Kārlis. Those two had fouled all he'd ever cared for, obliterated any proper order to his life, and put simply, wanted him dead. He felt the same about them.

The wind was kicking up.

Through swaying branches, Kārlis glimpsed a bright green grassy slope—he sprang up and crouched behind an oak, clearing his head. Slopes were chimeric in the flat Latvian countryside. He slid on his boots and slinked to the next tree for a fact check. The "slope" turned out to be a steeply pitched, thatched grass roof, covered in bright green moss, with olden style jerkinhead gables, covering a barn.

Before going closer Kārlis circled the building, eyeing it from every angle with distrust. He saw nobody. Oddly, the barn wasn't part of a farm and didn't have a house nearby, or a road leading to it, at least not anymore. Cat-walking closer, Kārlis stood on tiptoe to look inside. The window was meticulously blacked out and the interior, still as a salt lick.

Double wooden doors were chained and padlocked. Kārlis wedged his shovel tip between them and pushed. The chain had some slack and the doors parted with a creak. As he squeezed through, Kārlis was glad he had the physique of a stringbean.

The barn was pitch black inside and wonderfully dry. It even smelled good. Kārlis stamped the shovelhead twice on the dirt floor. The *clank* seemed absorbed by an interior full of things, rather than echoing into empty space. Walking a few feet, he bumped into something smooth, hard, and covered in canvas. Turning, he took small, blind steps until his hand found some irregularly shaped protrusion under another fabric. Patiently, he wended a path deeper into the stacks and stores of … *furniture*, he deduced. That's what it was. Smelling like his mother's wood oil, the barn no doubt warehoused fine furniture.

Kārlis explored until he found an appealing nook in a back corner. A drop cloth draped over a table, formed a sort of pup tent. Taking off his bog-soaked clothes, he spread them out to dry. Then he shook one of the canvases vigorously, to evict any creepy crawlies. Foolish to survive an officer massacre only to be taken out by a spider. Wrapping himself in the canvas, he ducked under the makeshift tent. Leaning against some sort of wooden surface, he curled his legs beneath him and listened to the wind.

Too exhausted to sleep, Kārlis began to catalog his worries from greatest to least. Foremost, he feared that his family would pay the consequences for his desertion. The Red Army was said to execute entire villages related to an evader. Heavy eyelids dropped, shutting out the lesser worries. Cupping his balls, he tried to dream of Lileja. He yawned, and sensed again the exotic fragrance of the barn-sanctuary. Possibly an article was crafted from sandalwood or was from the Far East, settling his mind with a mysterious peace.

K. Smiltens, 1949

33

JANIS PĒRKONS STOOD AT THE WINDOW on the seventh floor of an abandoned office building, looking down at Riga Central Rail. Traffic engulfed the train station in a nonstop stream. Lanes were jammed with military jeeps, civilian automobiles, horse-drawn carts— a bizarre assortment of vehicles.

"Cheka driving a hearse," Janis uttered, pointing with a hand-rolled cigarette. "And there's a school bus coming in." He watched as suitcase-laden passengers exited the school bus, unloaded at gunpoint. "Apparently the NKVD have commandeered anything on wheels, and are dispatching repeated loops to pick up Harmful Elements." He blew a stream of smoke at the glass. "But what do they want with the children?"

"We're on the brink of a war," said Mr. Lapsins, who stood at a desk behind Janis, his neck craning from vulture-like shoulders to examine the label on a bottle of 1889 French cognac. "The Russians want to deal with anybody who might turn against the regime from within."

The victims looked small, vague in the dim light, indistinct in the aggregate. Their sheer number boggled the mind. Janis had to remind himself that each was an individual. A shifting, undulating mass of humanity covered every square meter of the depot's vast concourse. People were prodded, separated, regrouped and herded along. All channels of movement ended on the platform, where cattle cars were lined up in either direction as far as he could see. "Yah, but why the children," Janis said again.

"The Russians have very little time left to accomplish what they came to do," Lapsins said, returning the bottle to its raffia nest in the case and pulling out another to inspect. "They want to finish on a high note."

Janis was acutely aware of his rarified position, watching the miserable masses from above instead of hustling among them. Likewise, he was relieved his family was thirty kilometers outside of Riga, at the summerhouse.

"We're witnessing the death throes of our Soviet occupiers," Lapsins said, with clinical detachment. "Are you familiar with the violent, heightened energy an animal unleashes before giving up the ghost?"

"This took planning," Janis said, standing a careful distance from the window. "An eleventh-hour police surge of this size indicates coordination on an unheard of scale."

Janis turned from the glass to face his colleague, the gem trader, and the business at hand. A case of Three Star Courvoisier he'd won at a card game that night was on the desktop between them. If the desk had been the fulcrum of a scale, as Janis sometimes imagined it to be during negotiations, then the advantage was clearly tipped to the side where Lapsins—and his lurking bodyguard—stood. On his own side, Janis sensed the erosion of presence and position, diminished over the past six months since the Communists had nationalized the company that was his life's work.

His goatee and moustache were still precisely trimmed, but by his own hand, not the barber's. His cheeks had hollowed to planed angles that shadowed his face. His epicurean zeal had been replaced by something harder. Janis wore a baggy canvas coat and cap, identical to those of a million other workers in the city. The garb hung on a lankier frame than had his tailored suits. Sobering, he reflected, how quickly a man his age withered without the refreshing flow of cash. Furthermore, his resolve to liquidate all but bare-bone essential assets was a cloud of desperate cologne, easily detected by a fox like Lapsins.

Lapsins looked as suave as Janis had ever seen him, new pinstriped suit, shiny shoes. He'd actually gained weight. Janis didn't begrudge the black marketeer his profit. Risk merited reward. But the dealer had dominated their recent trades, making Janis accept a pittance for the radio and the sewing machine, and establishing an unfavorable precedent for tonight's transaction.

"So how are things going at the—what is it you do now, Pērkons?" Lapsins said.

Janis noticed he was no longer *Mr.* Pērkons.

"They assigned me a job in a tannery."

"Right. And how's that going?"

Janis felt like decking the arrogant bugger. "Swimmingly," he said.

"Well, I'm happy to take a few bottles of booze off your hands," Lapsins said. He slid some gold coins across the desk. American Liberties.

Janis regarded the offer without moving. His limbs still ached from carrying that case of cognac four blocks over from the card game, and up seven flights of stairs. A low boil jangled him. He stubbed out his cigarette, letting the anger pass.

"This cognac was liberated from the plunder of Paris," Janis finally said. "One can only imagine the trail of dubious transactions marking its passage north. It's worth ten times that amount."

Lapsins suddenly sounded impatient. "I see a lot of this kind of thing, Pērkons. Go ahead and take it elsewhere." The dealer waved a hand toward the pandemonium outside the window. "You'll find this is what the market will bear."

That was a lie. Janis knew aged French brandy was absolutely unavailable. But what choice did he have? He couldn't very well carry the case to another bidder.

"I'll throw in a night on my couch," Lapsins said, tipping his head in the direction of some pallets strewn in the corner. "You don't want to go out into that maelstrom." He turned to read something from a little black ledger, looking bored.

A sour taste turned down the corners of Janis's mouth. "Thank you," he said, aligning the wooden top to the crate and snapping the metal latches closed. "But if that's your best offer, I'll be on my way."

Lapsins looked up, an incredulous and wily expression on his face, as if intrigued Janis dare test him. "Come, man," he said, smiling like the game had turned interesting. "You can't go out there with that. You won't make it ten steps walking around with a rare case of cognac."

"Ah ha!" Janis cried, wrapping his coat around the crate and tying the sleeves together. "A *few bottles of booze* is now a *rare case of cognac!*" He heaved the case onto his shoulder and, ignoring the startled bodyguard, stalked to the door. The empty office shook from the force of his footsteps.

Janis regretted the decision almost immediately. Under the bulky burden, he footed uncertainly on the dimly lit stairs. His slow egress was embarrassingly anticlimactic to his parting bravado. He was only beginning the third flight when Lapsins called from above, "All right, Mr. Pērkons. For you I will double my offer. You've been a good client for a long while."

"You've followed me down two stories," Janis said, aggravated and short of breath, "telling me that this," he patted the case, "is liquid gold." Somehow, his last drop of dignity was in that case. Lapsins's next offer had better be astronomical.

"You'd be a fool to leave the building," Lapsins said. "It's after curfew. We're on the brink of a war, and the whole city is under arrest. Something catastrophic is unfolding out there—beyond what we've ever seen or imagined. If you go out that door, Pērkons, you won't be able to hide!—not skulking around with a valuable case of spirits."

Janis shifted the case so it rested on his right hip, grasped the handrail on the left and kept going, propelled by a ridiculous stubborn energy. It was an ordeal just to reach the ground floor where he set the case down, huffing, and leaned against the door. Through the wood, he heard engines rumbling like a monstrous swarm of hornets. Lapsins was wrong about one thing, Janis thought. He would not skulk. Lifting the case to his shoulder, he took a deep breath and pushed through.

Outside, the air hung eerily—a vacuum where a thousand useless screams should have echoed. Was it self-respect that made everyone go quietly, that made him carry this *pie joda* case of pride?

He considered staying the night at the Riga apartment of elderly Tante Agata, but Janis wanted to go home. So lowering his head as if opposing a gale force, he pointed himself toward the pontoon bridge and strode down the sidewalk.

He'd gone a block and hadn't been stopped.

The stutter of a machine gun reached his ears, clamping his chest and beading his skin in cold sweat.

He did not turn to look.

Ten paces later, he swung the case off his shoulder and rubbed where the wooden slats had pressed into his neck. He lugged the box with both hands, anxiously looking around, girding his nerve to walk past the rail yard.

The line of vehicles unloading prisoners stretched out of sight. He'd never seen so many NKVD in one place—easily spotted by their red hammer-and-sickle cap badges—goading mayhem. One grabbed an elderly woman climbing with difficulty from a maroon sedan. She dithered over to her husband, who held hastily bundled necessities in bony arms. They looked frozen amidst the surrounding melee, thoroughly bewildered, until the Chekist rifle poked the man to move deeper into the chaotic throng.

Another Chekist pushed a woman struggling to hold both a wailing baby and a fuzzy-haired toddler. Then he swung his cudgel to the ear of a round-faced man who'd refused to leave the young mother. The round-faced man was in his thirties, wearing a brown suit, and carrying a little boy and a stuffed duffle bag. The man fell to his knees, dropping the boy to protect his head from the cudgel. Janis's view to the grim vignette was suddenly blocked by a military transport rolling up to unload more victims. He turned his head away, eyes frozen wide. Walking on, he felt despicable, as if he'd personally split the young family. He balanced the cognac case on his shoulder, a blinder, pointing one foot after another toward the pontoon bridge.

Limbs quailed, but he didn't risk ducking into a doorway to rest. Tempted to ditch the unwieldy crate, Janis realized it provided useful cover. His physical struggle to carry the case was authentic, lending veracity to his overall incognito. Many workers were out, especially as he neared the water, men dressed just as he was, moving swiftly. Some were pushing carts or wheelbarrows, footslogging materials in the double and triple shifts of heightened defense that would brace the country for the German invasion. That he might blend in with the fray was unexpectedly lucky.

He paused, shifting the case to the other shoulder. If he could get to the pontoon bridge, if he could cross the river and get past the checkpoint on the far side, then he could get out of Riga and hike the thirty kilometers home.

Janis leaned the crate against a kiosk to catch his breath.

Grinding engines roared in his ears. Vehicles embarked, Janis supposed, on fresh orders. Three identical looking military trucks rumbled past, with benches running the length of the beds, each manned by six soldiers. The school bus passed him next, followed by a farm truck with tall wooden planks around the back of the wagon, a florist's van, a couple more military transports, the maroon sedan that had abducted the elderly folk, and finally, a bevy of jeeps. Janis shifted the cognac again and marched alongside the unholy parade, which was also headed over the bridge and which ought to get swift, unquestioned clearance at the checkpoint.

At the pontoon bridge, traffic was bottlenecked to a standstill. Janis walked past the army trucks, treading the iron gridwork as the bridge swayed over River Daugava. He peered over the rail, scanning the waterway for a chance ferryman who could help him. But a daunting military presence blocked access to the river. Obviously, control of the waterway would be critical for the victorious army, German or Soviet. Surely soldiers secured the riverbanks for twenty kilometers downstream to the prized Port of Riga.

The bridge would be the only way across for Janis. Perhaps when the convoy started moving again and sailed through the checkpoint, Janis could glide along in their slipstream, unseen by the guards. He had no better plan. The pedestrian walkway was narrow. Janis had to maneuver the case sideways to avoid brushing the green, woolen elbow of an NKVD agent protruding from the passenger window of the farm wagon. He walked by the school bus slowly, nervous to be only steps away from the armed military transport. Suddenly traffic loosened. The military transport lurched forward and away. The school bus rumbled to life and grinded past in low gear, followed by the farm truck.

Something jabbed his ribs. Janis didn't see what hit him, but stepped sharply away.

"Hey you, Citizen! Hold it right there," said a deep voice, heavily accented.

Janis's fingers trembled, nearly dropping the cognac.

An NKVD agent leaned out of the passenger side of the florist's van. Again he jabbed Janis with a clipboard.

Janis stopped, hoping the florist's van would keep moving with the flow of traffic. But it also stopped, choking the line of cars behind it. The van door opened, to Janis's dismay, and an oversized NKVD agent unfolded from within, dwarfing the flower delivery van. He said, "You. Citizen. I'm talking to you."

Janis lowered the case from his shoulder with shaking arms and put it on the ground. The NKVD man was a head taller than he was, with hair and beard of yellow-black stubble, and a face snorting with irritability. Janis followed the diagonal line of a leather bandolier across the agent's broad chest to its terminus at a holstered revolver.

"You know this address?" said the stubble-faced giant, pushing the clipboard at Janis. *"Daina Iela, Ikskile.* Where is this?"

The clipboard held a long list of names and addresses. Janis raised his eyebrows, dumbly. "Across the bridge, Comrade," he said, his throat so dry it stung to speak. "About twenty kilometers."

"Obviously," the Chekist said, hand out. "Identification."

Janis drew his papers from his pants pocket. "I work at the tannery," he said, presenting the ID. "Over the river."

The army truck they were blocking honked.

The Chekist straightened to full monster height and shouted, "Kiss my asshole!" Then he leaned into the cab and chewed out his own driver, saying, "Don't be steamrolled just because we got assigned a stupid flower truck!" He banged the van with his fist, giving Janis the horrible suspicion he might be executed just for show, so the giant could compensate for riding shotgun in a vehicle with headlights like two watermelon halves mounted on the front grill, and painted with daisies and the slogan, *Love Blossoms with Flowers.*

"What's in the box," the agent demanded. "Open it."

"Alcohol," Janis said, hoarsely, kneeling by the crate and picking at the knot tied with the covering coat sleeves. He pretended the knot was impossible to untie. "Used by tanners, Comrade. I'm to get it to the factory." It was at least two a.m., so Janis said, "Running shifts around the clock to prepare, you know," Janis looked up, "for Barbarossa."

Did Janis imagine it, or did the agent squirm at the name, shift his weight uneasily and pass his hand over his gut. Operation Barbarossa, according to a man at the card game, was what the Germans were calling their invasion.

Behind them, the army driver leaned on his horn.

The goliath agent kicked the crate. "Hurry up."

"Comrade, I know that address," Janis said, fumbling at the knot. "You keep straight after you cross the bridge. But the tricky party is finding *Skolas Iela.*" He ignored the case, gesturing directions. "Turn on *Skolas* after about five or seven kilometers, but it's easy to miss if you aren't watching carefully for an opening in the trees. If you pass that old tractor repair yard, you've gone too far."

A sustained, blaring horn drowned out Janis's advice.

The giant Chekist leaned in the window to confer with his driver. Then he said, "Get in, Citizen. You're taking us to this address." He pointed to the open cab. "Hurry up. We got a quota to meet."

34

WHILE THE HERCULEAN NKVD agent made obscene gestures at the honking army truck, Janis Pērkons hefted the case inside the cab. He slid across the seat toward a skinny driver, settling the cognac onto his knees. The driver was a young soldier with a fringe of brown hair zigzagging across a white forehead. He scowled at Janis. The big Chekist got in and closed the door. Janis sat as compactly as possible in the tight space, awkwardly sandwiched between Russian bedfellows. A small rectangular window opened to the back of the van, and Janis heard the movements of a couple of men riding back there. The lane before them was open clear to the checkpoint. The driver struggled with the double clutch, wiggling a long-shafted gearshift in the floorboard near Janis's feet, grinding gears and lurching forward.

Through the windshield, a glass that didn't slope up from the hood but was a smack right angle to the dashboard, the guard shack appeared brightly lit. Soldiers there stared at the flower delivery van, scrutinizing whatever was holding up the convoy. The sentries grew ominously larger as the van approached, looking surreal viewed under the exterior visor's colorful, decorative scalloped edging, and over the engine hood extending like a big shoebox. One guard shielded his eyes from the glare of headlights. Another exchanged a salute with the driver as the florist's truck sailed past the checkpoint. Soon the sound of tire thumping abated, marking the end of the pontoon bridge and the start of the highway.

In the side mirror, Janis could see the tail of the convoy arcing behind them. Lights from the capital's iconic skyline grew smaller, but Janis made out the crenellated façade of the castle, the circular battlement of the "powderhorn" munitions vault, the spire of St. Peter's dome, and cranes and masts lining the river. He regarded the view as if he'd never see it again.

The giant Chekist spoke to the skinny driver in Russian. Janis knew enough to catch the gist. "Can't you go faster?"

The driver made a disgusted face, saying something like, *What do you think? I'm driving a kāpost galva flower truck here!*

There was no sign of the vehicles ahead of them, while the military transports behind were tailgating.

The density of commercial buildings was thinning along the highway. By the time they'd passed the airport, only trees framed the white line down the middle of the road.

The big Chekist reviewed the clipboard, cursing. "Our list is as long as everyone else's," he said. "How can they expect us to hold as many …" He set his jaw, looking dangerously moody. "We'll be making trips all night."

Meanwhile the kilometers sped by, taking Janis toward home faster than he would've ever dared hope.

"Where's the turnoff?" the Chekist asked, turning to Janis. "And you better not ball this up because a fleet of trucks is following us."

Janis, straining to read signs, indicated the turn east was coming up.

Despite advanced notice, the driver took the turn too fast, making things bump and slide in the back, and pushing Janis up against the driver's shoulder where he got a close-up view of tissue paper pressed over shaving nicks on the young man's jaw. The driver reminded Janis of his son, Kārlis, also new to shaving, also wearing that uniform, though not willingly.

Not knowing how to get out of it—alive—Janis navigated to the first address. The van pulled into a picturesque neighborhood with baronial style townhouses built during the colonial German period of the previous century.

"Five pages to be collected from this same neighborhood," said the giant Chekist, thumbing papers on the clipboard. He tipped his straw-stubbled head to Janis. "So we will not be needing him anymore."

Then the big agent squeezed out the door.

The driver faced the windshield, as if he didn't want to look at someone who was no longer needed.

Out on the sidewalk, the Giant conferred with the two agents from the back of the van. One was highly agitated, twitchy and nervous. The other slouched. Preparing for the night's task, they straightened uniforms, organized weapons and reviewed the clipboard, nodding to one another. The Giant gave the pre-bully pep talk, vesting Twitch and Slouch with the demon to dominate the unarmed and unsuspecting.

Janis studied his captors for any signs of weakness or humanity to which he might appeal, finding none.

Pumped up, the Giant returned to the cab. "Get out," he told Janis.

Nay. His legs refused to move his body toward that lethal triad. Grabbed by the collar, Janis was forced to slide across the seat. He pulled the case of cognac behind him—his last card to play. He found footing on the running board, and tried lifting the case.

"Leave the box there," the Giant said, moving a hand to his pistol.

"Yah," Janis said, pointlessly. "You can have that."

Feeling naked, Janis climbed from the cab and stood on the sidewalk at the mercy of Stalin's henchmen.

"Get in the back," said the giant Chekist with a shove.

Janis obeyed with wobbling legs, relieved to escape the sidewalk firing squad. The cargo doors slammed behind him.

The van was dimly lit from the small window to the cab where the driver sat. Janis stooped across the cargo hold, over a few stems and leaves crushed into the metal floor. A bucket had rolled to one corner, probably used to transport gladiolas during happier occasions. Benches ran along the sides. Janis found his way to the far end of one, where he crouched behind the driver. From there he could look out the small window and see a sliver of what was happening outside.

The *troika* was stalking, presumably, the first names on their list. Deep voices and slamming car doors from the street gave Janis the impression other trucks from the convoy were nearby doing the same. Sure enough, another trio of uniforms came into view farther down the street, headed toward the rear of a building.

The driver also seemed engaged in watching the NKVD deliver what folks had whispered of with dread for the past year, the feared herald of doom, the knock at night.

As the banging of a gloved fist echoed through the neighborhood, a dog yapped an alarm, and Janis slipped silently to test the door handle. Locked solid.

He returned to sit behind the driver, depressed by the gravity of his plight. He was caught. An hour ago, with the black market dealer, he'd looked down at the trodden masses from safety. Now, thanks to his own stubborn impulses, he was among them. He couldn't explain why he'd acted so rashly, except that it was the only way he knew to live. He'd have crossed some line eventually, he reckoned, but he should've kept his head down tonight for the sake of his family. The question of how they would manage without him rapped on his conscience, and he had no answer, except to admit that sometimes he was just an ass.

"My son is in the army," Janis said to the driver, "same as you."

The driver looked straight out the windshield.

"He was sent to Litene for training," Janis said.

The driver reminded Janis of his son. Perhaps Janis would remind the driver of his father. "It can be good for a young man, being in the army," Janis said. "But not easy."

The driver shifted his frame, so skinny, the seat engulfed him. "You're even stupider than I thought," the driver said, "if you think your son has been sent for *training*."

Janis considered the remark. The kid was probably terrified, hiding behind a taunt. He decided to prod.

"You mean, you think the Latvian boys were just drafted to dispose of them? You're probably right about that. But aren't all soldiers expendable? Isn't that the point?"

He watched the soldier wipe the palms of his hands on his trousers and return them to the steering wheel.

"I don't blame you for being scared, son," Janis said. "Anyone facing the *Wehrmacht* would be. Fighting Germans will be different from harassing defenseless families." Janis let that sink in. "Stalin purges his own best officers... then he sends amateurs here to face seasoned Germans. You boys couldn't even handle the Finns! Huh? Wait'll you meet the Nazis."

The soldier's hands left the steering wheel and fidgeted uselessly over the dashboard.

Janis kept wheedling. "And then, when the Krauts do kick your ass back to Moscow, if you survive, you've got to deal with your own command. They execute losers, isn't that so?"

"Shut—" The driver cut off when a door opened at a nearby residence.

A gray-haired man, professorial looking, hurried down the concrete steps, barefooted, in a t-shirt and pajama pants.

A moment later, the giant stubble-faced NKVD agent appeared. His hulking form was silhouetted in the doorframe by the interior yellow light.

Seeing the escape, the driver yelled, "Halt!" He pushed the van door open, fumbling for his gun. "Halt, I say!"

The barefoot professor cut across the grass, running.

The Chekist descended the concrete stairs in two swift steps. Appearing unrushed, he aimed his pistol at the running man's back. The muzzle flashed with a businesslike crack that echoed off the neighboring houses.

The runner fell forward, sprawled headlong in the road.

The dog barked frantically.

The Chekist went back inside.

The professor, or whoever he was, was left lying where he fell, without examination.

The driver looked frozen, standing on the running board, halfway out the door.

Janis forgot to breathe.

A man's life was over.

A man like him—wouldn't move again.

Whatever the point of this life had been, whatever came next, Janis teetered between the two planes. He felt keenly aware of every moment comprising his fragile lifespan, grateful, even for the mistakes that brought him to this, his final predicament. Acting on the impulses that inspire is what defines a life. The poignancy flashed and was forgotten in a crush of panic. The killing got everyone moving like the starter gun at a race.

Townhouse doors opened and people were ushered out, wearing odd combinations of clothes and carrying disorganized bundles. Chekists hustled a family down the sidewalk. The mother shielded her children's eyes as they passed the splayed professor.

The cargo door opened with a metal clank, and the agitated agent whom Janis thought of as Twitch stepped aside to admit the family of four. Despite the hour and scant warning, the man climbing in had managed to put on a suit jacket and a fedora. His white shirt was unbuttoned over a t-shirt. He helped his wife up; she wore a housedress. Janis guessed she'd spent her allotted minutes outfitting the two boys in layers of clothing. They looked about ten and twelve years old. The family sat on the bench across from Janis, arranging two suitcases and two stuffed pillowcases at their feet. When the door closed, the man asked Janis, "Where are we going?"

"Probably to the main rail yard in Riga," Janis said, quietly, "to be deported." Information was key to any saving coordination. Otherwise, Janis wouldn't have spoken in front of the boys who were already wide-eyed. "Thousands of people are being moved right now," Janis whispered. "The Cheka have commandeered every vehicle in the city." He dropped his voice. "This van is armed by four men.

"I saw heads of household separated out," Janis said, hoping the youngsters might not catch the oblique reference to their father. "Everyone's loaded on cattle cars."

The woman's face went white.

The rear doors opened. Janis stopped speaking as a lady around fifty was pushed inside, a leather case behind her. She wore a turban-style scarf that didn't quite cover her curlers. She sat on the bench near the cargo doors. Fluffy blue knitting poked from the handbag she clutched on her lap.

"What do we do?" the man asked.

Janis shook his head, waiting for the doors to close. He didn't want the guard to catch him conspiring.

There were many voices outside now, probably dozens of people surrounding the florist van and military trucks. It was difficult to know what was happening with only the small window to see from. But as people arrived, both rear doors were kept open, presenting a wider view and a different angle of the street. One of the military transports was parked at the curb behind them. Slouch was posted between the two vehicles, holding his rifle like a backslash across his body, watching as people from the nearby houses filed into the back of the van. The two boys moved to the floor, making room for an elderly couple to sit on the bench. The boys were soon joined by other youngsters, shifting their positions with each addition of luggage.

As the van became crowded, Janis sized up the captives, counting able-bodied men. There were four at the moment, though he didn't know what good they might do. There were also three elderly, five women, and ten children—some very small. The smaller the victim, the larger his corresponding luggage, Janis observed. The baby proved the theorem true, bringing satchels of nappies, blankets, and clanking little jars of special food. One woman carried in a tub of groceries and kitchenware.

"Cram more in there." Janis overheard the deep voice of the big NKVD agent explaining his logic. "Fewer trips."

The baby began to cry. The dog, from a window of a nearby home, barked with fury. The rising hubbub, tinged with panic, was unhinging Twitch, who stood at his post biting his lip.

"Quiet back there!" Twitch roared, brandishing his weapon when the baby didn't comply, and frightening a toddler to tears. The center of everyone's attention, Twitch made a show of raising his gun and aiming it at the dog in the window, as if he could threaten the children into calm.

Dog and baby kept up a desperate racket.

"Watch them," Twitch told Slouch, "while I handle this." He stalked off ominously.

Slouch turned his rifle, an old-model Nagant bolt-action piece, toward the cargo hold, watching the captives under heavily lidded eyes.

The wait for Twitch to discipline the dog was sickening, broken by the shatter of glass. Barking stopped with a yelp. Yelp turned whimper, and then nothing. A child screamed. Sobs stifled by pressed hands. The young mother was frantic in quieting her purple-faced infant.

Twitch returned, eyes darting, black and shiny.

"Idiot," an agent from the military transport told him. "Do you not know the meaning of stealth?"

"Reksis is okay," a sniffing woman whispered to her children. "I can see him upstairs, wagging his tail at the window." She was a good liar. "Good boy, Reksis."

K. Smiltens, 1975.

35

THE ENGINE REVVED ON THE MILITARY transport behind them. Weirdly, Janis Pērkons looked forward to also getting underway.

Slouch planted his big, black boot in the florist van. He was coming in to get situated for the ride. Twitch stood behind, his hand on his revolver. Bodies scrambled clear as Slouch stooped and plodded over children and luggage, to sit on the bench behind the cab. The woman in the housedress made room, moving between the knees of the man with the fedora.

Slouch settled in directly opposite Janis. They were of a similar size and build, but the NKVD agent was ten years younger and bulky with protective clothing. Catching Janis looking at him, he raised his rifle and panned it over the passengers while Twitch the Dog Killer took his seat. Twitch sat near the doors, next to the knitting lady.

Outside, the big Chekist who'd originally confronted Janis on the bridge leaned into the van, peering at the night's handiwork. With a final nod to Twitch and Slouch, he slammed the doors closed, barring fresh air and hope. The click of the latches marked a horrible descent into helplessness. In the dark, tightly packed cabin, shortness of breath and fear were pressurized like bottled hysteria.

Janis was near the only window, the small rectangle to the cab. He watched the big agent squeeze in up front, eyes bright, cheeks rosy under the stubble of the black-yellow beard, looking exhilarated as he propped a rifle between his knee and the door.

The military truck behind them moved out with the growl of a powerful engine, lunging in front of the florist van. Its canvas-covered, mammoth frame easily caged its captives. Two soldiers positioned at the rear held weapons ready, looking professional, regarding the flower delivery vehicle in their dust.

"What in hell?" said the Chekist giant. "He's supposed to follow *us*." He pounded the dashboard with a fist. "Never mind. Let's go."

"Shouldn't we wait 'til the other truck's ready?" asked the driver.

"No. Just go."

The van pulled away from the curb with sagging heaviness, accelerating jerkily. Taking the first turn at a reckless speed, the driver was oblivious to the passengers' gasps. He sped up on the highway completely focused on catching the lead truck. What difference did prudent driving make anyway, Janis thought, as the road rushed beneath the floorboards, now that they were headed to Riga.

"Will you be taking me back to my factory now, Comrade?" Janis said through the window. It was worth a try.

The big Chekist huffed, and mimicked Janis with a snide voice. "No, I will not be taking you back to your factory now." He rolled down his window with alacrity. "You, Citizen, are going on a long trip." He took out cigarettes and settled into his seat, one arm resting on Janis's crate.

"Comrade," Janis whispered. "That's valuable cognac in that case. If you like it, I can get you—"

"Nay!" cried one of the boys, making Janis look up just before Slouch smacked him with the rifle butt.

Whipping up his forearm, Janis's ulna took the brunt of the blow, meant for his skull. He collapsed in the corner, shrunk to the throbbing of his forearm.

Everyone in the van was silent, schooled by example.

The giant in the cab struck a match across the dashboard, chuckling. He held the flame before the tip of his cigarette, letting the match burn. "Thank you, Citizen," he said, directing the remark to where Janis had sunk against the cab, cradling his injury. "I'll toast your good health when I drink your valuable cognac." When he touched the flame to his cigarette, it flared slightly with his first puff.

The windshield exploded. A torrent of air rushed through shattered glass.

The big agent slumped in his seat.

"*Sheist!*" the driver cried, hitting the brakes in panic.

Slouch thrust his face to the cab. "His neck!" he shouted. "He's shot in the goddam neck!"

"Go! Go! Floor it!" Twitch yelled. "Get us the hell out of here."

Foundering mismatched gears and rpm, the skinny driver pushed for speed.

Thunk! The van listed hard right, careening from a front tire blow out.

Someone was shooting at them! Janis's brain tumbled the logic.

The driver yanked the steering wheel, overcorrecting. Captives screamed as the van skidded and toppled out of control.

Unless… a rescue? The thought sparked and snuffed as the flower delivery van crashed into something with unyielding finality.

Newtonian force threw the passengers on one side of the van into those on the other side. Janis butted heads with Slouch and landed on top of him. Reeling, Janis lifted his face away. The agent looked vacuously at him, head lolling on a flaccid neck.

Janis felt the outline of the rifle and yanked it out of Slouch's hands. He struck the Chekist's head with the stock, and doubled, tripled the action for good measure.

Slouch didn't get up, but Janis rose, lost his balance and fell on his backside, landing on one of the boys. Guns fired outside. Bodies moved around him like an ocean swell.

"Let us out!" a man shouted, banging on the vehicle wall, now tilted above them.

Gripping the rifle, Janis found a place to kneel, fingers feeling around the trigger, trying to see.

A desperate fight thrashed near the cargo doors. In murky light, black-on-gray figures rode Twitch's back—clung to his legs and arms as he staggered from one side of the crooked van to the other.

Janis strained to get a bead on the embattled NKVD agent. Too many innocents—

Twitch's gun went off, rupturing eardrums inside the metal box. A woman shrieked. A man coughed out the sting of sulfur. Crying filled the air.

The cargo door handles rattled.

The mass of figures attacking Twitch collapsed. The struggle winnowed to a sloggy pounding and sobs of exertion.

Battering thudded the latch and the door cracked open, lifting with the screech of mangled metal. Fresh air met Janis's lungs, smelling of the forest and burnt rubber.

One of the boys scrambled to get out, but Janis restrained him, anxious to know first, who had shot at them.

The shooter stood hidden behind the door. "How many Cheka back there!" he called with the voice of a strapping young man.

"Two," a woman answered. "Knocked out, I think. And two in the cab."

The door flung open revealing a strange sight. By the moonlight, a tall shaggy figure with a rifle surveyed the deportees. After a moment Janis saw that it was a black pelt hood with ursine ears and snout that gave the man an unnerving and unidentifiable appearance. The bear-man raised a steady arm, pulling the elderly fellow out of the wreckage.

Rescuer, Janis decided, releasing the boy who clambered up the jilted metal floor to freedom.

As captives helped one another get out, a second stranger leaped into the back of the truck, pistol drawn. He wore a black tam that mocked the NKVD with a display of stolen red hammer-and-sickle cap badges, that glinted as he darted his head, taking in the situation.

"Forest Brethren," the fellow in the fedora whispered to his wife, pressing her toward the exit.

Janis knew of the Forest Brothers, men determined to give the Russians a fight.

The man in the studded tam stepped warily to Slouch and fired a perfunctory bullet into the Chekist.

Passengers hardly reacted to the execution. Janis's senses were already fully taxed as he groped his way to the door under orders to *hurry*, stepping over the woman with the curlers, who lay motionless, staring at nothing.

When he came to Twitch, Janis froze. The dog killer's face was purple, strangled by a silk stocking embedded around his neck. His skull was bashed, an iron skillet in its pooling blood. A knitting needle skewered his cheek. On his hands were scratches and the curved indentation of teeth.

The partisan in the studded beret autopsied the corpse with a practiced eye. "My kind of gals," he concluded, sounding tender.

"Keep moving," came the order. "The Cheka could be here any second."

Janis was among the last to exit the crashed vehicle. Rifle upright, he sat for balance before swinging his legs over the upended fender. The fellow in the bear-eared hood steadied the final victims clambering out. Something about his boutonnière seemed familiar, oak leaves poked through the lapel of a dirty, but once expensive coat. Before fully formed, the memory blanked as the bear-man lifted a limp little girl, draped her over his shoulder and, her long yellow braid trailing down his back, rushed her into the trees, frantic parents gimping behind.

Stepping out, Janis saw that the shot up delivery truck had hit a tree. Rescuers ushered passengers to wooded safety. A gaunt man in a black homburg and frock coat knelt over a prone boy, pressing pulse-seeking fingers to his neck. Another kid, a forest urchin of no more than ten or eleven, was at the gas tank siphoning fuel into a jug.

A portly man wearing the fatigues of the former Latvian army, including a captain's three-star collar insignia said, "Bring your things if you can." His bass drawl intoned calm and authority. "Food, medication of any kind, bring it." His eyes pegged the bolt-action Nagant Janis had seized.

"There's a military transport behind us," Janis said, "manned by six soldiers."

"You hear that, Aivars?" the captain called to the man in the studded cap.

Aivars was already on his belly in the van, steadying his rifle between propped elbows, peering toward the highway. "What is it, Christmas?" he said.

"I'm in your debt," Janis said, giving the rifle to the captain.

340

"You're not staying for the party?" Aivars asked.

Janis shook his head, and the motion flooded the space behind his eyes with pain.

"That's too bad," Aivars said, gazing down the length of his rifle. "We're gonna kill some Russians."

Janis started for the cover of the trees. No one else was in sight, but he knew the forest hid dozens of people. It was probably about 2:30 a.m. Sunlight was already seeping into the celestial sphere, backlighting trees. With the solstice only a week away, the sun barely dipped below the horizon at night, instead circling the sky in a tightening noose around the planet's northern theatre.

Glancing back at the wrecked florist delivery truck, Janis saw the big NKVD agent who'd accosted him on the bridge. He lay face down outside the cab. He'd been rolled, and stripped to his underwear. As if recalling something from a previous life, Janis trotted back to the truck, stepped on the running board and looked inside. On the floorboards was his cognac, still wrapped in his jacket, now shiny with blood. Leaning through the window, he lugged the case over and up onto his shoulder, embracing the familiar burden with some kind of satisfaction. He hurried back toward the trees again, until he noticed something out of the corner of his eye that made a chill ripple up his spine.

Not far to the side of the road lay the driver, nearly naked. He seemed especially boyish without the disguise of the army uniform. It looked as though he'd tried to run away during the ambush.

Janis was rooted to where he stood. Down the road, a rumbling engine approached, but he was paralyzed.

Anguish surged from guts to chest to eyes, swamping reason.

He saw his son left lying on the highway like a rolled carpet.

And banished the delusion from his head.

The coming army truck roared louder. Janis moved as quickly as he could. He clanked the cognac down on the road and ran to the driver. Grasping the boy at his armpits he dragged him off the asphalt and into the trees. The soldier was light. His bare feet and lifeless hands skidded and bumped against the dirt. Janis trudged backward into the sanctuary of the forest, stopping in a cloister of tightly spaced, straight white trunks. He ran a hand over the bad haircut, the crooked brown fringe across the white forehead, closing the soldier's eyes.

36

THE COGNAC WAS WHERE HE'D LEFT IT. Hoisting it to his shoulder, Janis Pērkons loped across the road, head down, the weight stabbing him with every step. He fled the vehicle wreckage, where he sensed Death hovering over freshly vacated corpses, watching his escape with resentment, and anticipating the coming soldiers with relish.

In an icy sweat, Janis glanced back and saw headlights of the oncoming Russian army truck. Some brave ambuscade fired a shot. God help us! Janis's heart was thumping out of his chest by the time he made it into the trees. He ran fifty trunks deep before he stopped, gulping dank, earthy breaths, while firefight drummed the air.

Janis interpreted the pattern of shots with a sickening conclusion. Well-armed Russian soldiers were not rolling over for a ragtag band of highwaymen with hand-me-down weaponry. Under a crush of guilt, Janis walked on. There was nothing he could do for anyone, except get home.

A field of yellow rapeseed blooms glowed eerily in the pre-dawn of midsummer. He'd seen this field before, from the train, and knew where he was, though the meadow was far vaster on foot. The wind pushed against him, rushing at his ears. He hiked into a pine forest and nearly dropped the crate when a monstrous stork rose up, catching him completely off guard, squawking loudly and winging him in the face.

"Just a bird," he exclaimed, setting the box down, heart racing at the speed linked with sudden death. His head thudded with dehydration. How long since he'd had any water? His hand went to his waist and plucked at air, forgetting he no longer wore the vest with the gold-chained pocket watch. He wore a scratchy unbleached cotton shirt, full-sleeved for the workingman and damp with sweat, and canvas trousers.

The wind died down. In the calm, Janis smelled smoke and froze. He would not survive another run-in with the Cheka. What if he'd stumbled upon them burying bodies in the woods? Listening hard, he heard voices. A melody wafted on the night air, the delicate vibrations of horsehair dragged over catgut. Janis crept toward the strains of a violin, careful to avoid snapping twigs and rustling leaves. Peering past enormous pines, he saw a campfire, and around it… He stood a long time watching, drawing closer.

The Romani.

Their carts and tethered donkeys were on the other side of a clearing.

Harmonizing strings drifted from two men. One stood at the fire, with a full black beard and a headscarf, clenching a violin under his chin. An older fellow in a misshapen fedora sat on a log, hunched over what looked like a folk zither, a *kokle*. Youths were entwined in twos and threes. One couple stood in each other's arms, swaying dance-like near the low flame. Some slept, blanketed lumps on the fire ring outskirts.

Janis cleared his throat to announce his presence. The *kokle* player stopped thrumming. The violinist drew his bow across the strings and held it up like a rapier. Everybody was staring at Janis as he lowered his crate to the ground.

"Good evening," he said, exhaling wearily. "Or good *morning*, as the case may be."

The fire crackled.

"State your business," said the violinist.

"Can you spare a drink of water, please," Janis asked, tucking in his shirt.

The violinist looked ready to slit his throat.

"Mr. Pērkons?"

It was the girl who'd been dancing by the fire. She had white-blonde hair that cascaded in zigzags, as if freed from a tight braid.

"Elza?"

Elza Krumins, fourteen-years-old was staying at Janis's place. The whole Krumins family was sheltering with him, since the Russian occupation had left them jobless and homeless. "I didn't recognize you under all that lipstick," Janis said, lifting the girl in a bear hug and setting her back on the ground where she stood a whole head taller than her brown-eyed boyfriend.

"I must be closer to home than I thought," Janis said, elated. "Especially if you walked here in high heels." He didn't care that the girl looked dressed for a cabaret, with loose hair and crooked black seams down the backs of her stockings, though he knew Elza's father worried that she ran wild.

But looking around, Janis saw nothing that would tarnish Elza's reputation. The encampment was tidy, and well, enchanting. And thank God he'd run into Gypsies, and not the Cheka.

"Evening, Campers," Janis told the young folk seated around the fire that cast each in a variant shade of orange. Faces looked familiar, but he did not see any of his son's close friends, especially those who had gone missing. Young fellows were spending more time in the woods, lest the Cheka came calling. Tonight was a good night to not be home.

"Gentlemen," he said, turning to the adults. "I'm Janis Pērkons, I live nearby, in the village."

The *kokle* player didn't get off the log, but offered his waterskin by way of introduction. The horn nozzle was undone and dangling by a string.

"Thank you," Janis said. "Good Lord, I'm thirsty." He squirted a stream of water through the air into the back of his mouth. Then he wetted his neck.

"Have a sit if you like," said the violinist, gesturing with his bow to the log.

"*Paldies*," Janis said. "A brief rest, then it's urgent I return to my family. I'll escort you home, Miss Krumins," Janis told Elza, who slumped at the news.

The log might've been made of feathers for how good it felt. Janis sat next to the kokle player. His fingers moved over the strings like spider legs, evoking the ethereal, tinkling soul of the folk songs. The songs were illegal under Article 58 of the Russian Criminal Code, and hearing them again sparked a tender memory.

"I don't know if you men have had any contact with Riga tonight," Janis said in a low voice. "I've just got out of there. There's a massive deportation campaign underway. You should know. The Cheka are pulling out all the stops tonight."

The old zitherist nodded knowingly. "The closer the Germans get, the more murderous the Bolsheviks."

"It's absolute lunacy tonight," Janis said. His report seemed absurd in the serene forest. As if the violence of the capital couldn't reach this campfire, surrounded by pines, under the pastel sky, but Janis had to warn them. "The NKVD are up to some mind-boggling purging. I cannot emphasize enough the scale of what I saw."

A frog croaked.

"It's a miracle I escaped," Janis persisted. He could not account for how he'd walked out of the net, even as it tightened around the people of Riga.

"I said, what's in the box?" repeated the violinist.

"The box?" Janis strode over to the cognac case, ignoring the ache of every muscle again called upon to lift and carry. Setting the crate on the log, he worked the jacket off and sloughed it to the side with a bit of a flourish.

"Gentlemen, this box contains the best goddam French brandy we'll taste in our lifetimes," Janis said. "I've carried it on my back from Riga, and I for one feel like lightening the load."

The *kokle* player abandoned his zither and joined the violinist to peer over Janis's shoulder, as he unfastened the metal latches and raised the wooden lid. Twelve circles of red foil were visible amid a dense nesting of raffia. Adjusting his glasses first, Janis lifted out a bottle and displayed on extended fingertips, Three Star Courvoisier.

"Care to join me for a snifter?"

The Romani gents were enthusiastic. The zitherist rummaged through a box producing two jelly jars and an enameled cup, while the violinist offered his knife for cutting through the wax seal and the foil.

"Let's see if it's worth its weight," Janis said, grasping the cap and pulling.

The cork left the slender glass neck with a quiet *pompf*, emitting a prescience of age and splendor, hinting of sandalwood, like releasing a genie.

"Pity not to let this breathe," Janis said, pouring liquid gold into a jar and examining its clarity against the firelight. "Soft legs," he pronounced.

"That bodes well," said the zitherist, nodding.

"It certainly does," Janis said, pouring for each. "What'll we drink to?"

The three turned to one another—the headscarf, the misshapen fedora and the laborer's cap—in conference, as if they'd been asked to name a baby.

"Freedom," said the old zitherist.

Janis agreed. Raising their vessels, they looked one another in the eye. "To freedom."

All partook at once.

The first sip was a playful velvet paw awakening the senses. Janis didn't try to articulate the attributes. He just swirled the jelly jar and inhaled the vapors that, for some reason, made him want to cry.

The next swallow was less like tasting, more like meeting a beloved friend. More questions were raised than answered as the fluid danced over his palate, heating his throat and chest. Janis sat back on the log with improved perspective, savoring the long finish.

He would've carried that case around the world.

"Mama," said the violinist. Finishing his cup, he threw a massive log on the fire, which spewed a fountain of sparks. Then, bracing his foot on a rock, the violinist began to play with stirring serendipity.

Janis poured three more measures of drink. When the zitherist offered him a cigar, he thought he'd gone to heaven. "Just a few puffs," he said. The tension in his shoulders was just starting to melt away from the knot in his neck."Then I really must hit the road."

They smoked in quiet fraternity.

"A purging, you say," said the old zitherist, pulling the *kokle* to his breast.

"Yah. Of historic proportion," Janis said. "Historic."

"Like the Trail of Tears, perhaps," said the zitherist. "That was horrendous."

"What's that?"

"In America, about a hundred years ago. The Indian tribes were forced to march across the continent. Deadly. Sixteen thousand started out."

"Well, I can't guess at the numbers I saw, but I assure you, this is momentous."

"Maybe more like the Babylonian Exile," said the zitherist, "twenty-five thousand."

"Holy cow," Janis said, puffing his cigar. "You're a man who knows his deportations, sir,"

"It's more like family stories," said the old man, modestly.

"Bear in mind," Janis said, punctuating the air with his cigar, "that Stalin, making use of modern rail, could accomplish in *one night* what no doubt took those other fiends years."

"Good point."

"You should've seen it," Janis said, suddenly giddy. "A few hours ago, I actually escaped past an NKVD checkpoint in one of their own commandeered vehicles." A chuckle bubbled up. But then the other sights from the night barged in: the professor gunned down on the sidewalk, the dead lady in curlers, the Russian boy who'd reminded him of his son. He drained his glass, rinsing away the perversions. "I don't know why I should be the one to get away."

Janis refilled and handed the cognac to the zitherist, who likewise topped off and passed the bottle to the violinist.

"We don't know what is happening," said the old musician. "We only see a small corner of the puzzle. What if the people on those trains are to be the survivors?"

"Ha!" Janis raised an eyebrow. Had he been looking at this wrong?

"Within the week this place'll be German army stomping grounds," said the zitherist.

"I see what you mean," Janis said. "While I can't wait to be rid of Russians, war between Russia and Germany will be a meat grinder."

The old fellow nodded. "Those here to witness it will be the meat."

Janis missed talking. For the past year, he'd policed every word out of his mouth, walking an exhausting line of silent, untrusting secrecy. Now, he felt his opinions ripen with each sip of cognac. How refreshing to converse with this *kokle* player, a pundit of current events. Really fortifying! Iron sharpens iron, Janis thought, as the old fellow belched and launched into discourse about America's Lend-Lease Act.

"The funny thing is the name," the zitherist said. "Lend-Lease. You think the Cheka will return the weapons after they've slaughtered everybody?"

Janis laughed. He hadn't laughed in ages, but now he let it out, jiggling the diaphragm muscles never required by sobriety. "Hah! America'll arm anybody fighting Hitler," he said.

The bottle had made its way to the other side of the campfire, where some of the older boys were having a nip. One of them was beating a drum shaped like a large hourglasss. The zither plucked. The fiddle aired. Janis moved his foot to the shared heartbeat. Damned if music didn't hearten the spirit, he thought. No wonder the authorities feared it. Rebel leaders, the folk songs.

Janis could see Elza's luminous locks through the flames. She seemed to be avoiding him, the wet blanket who would escort her home. Now that he saw how it was here, he wouldn't deprive the girl of dancing 'til dawn. How many such nights are there in a life, really. Too damn few. He got up to open another bottle. The notion that his wife stood at a window watching for his return—stuffed in a pocket. She was probably sound asleep. *He liked feeling unafraid for one minute!*

Janis was pouring a shot at the log, like some rustic bartender, when a door to one of the wagons banged open and in its frame appeared a lady. She surveyed the party, settling her gaze on him. Gathering her skirt revealed toned, bare legs as she climbed down the wagon, hopping off the last step. She traipsed over to the drummer, raised one arm in a curlicue, and began lifting and dropping a hip, dancing.

She is not wearing a shred of humility, Janis thought, smoothing his goatee.

From the waves of her long black hair, to the mounds of a white blouse barely contained in a little black vest, to her petite waist, the dancer flowed like sea grass. Her hips were the province of the drummer, while her corsage seemed intimate with the haunting melody of the violinist. The blue skirt mesmerized as she swirled, presenting a view of herself to Janis through the flames. The more Janis watched, the less able he was to pry his eyes away.

One of the youths trilled at her, a wild, shrill birdcall.

Janis moseyed over—cognac in one hand, cigar in the other—to see what she'd do next.

She flicked a turquoise veil at him, sending a whiff of pine perfume. "I think you like my Chiftatelli," she said, sounding like wind chimes on a breeze.

"Ya-ah, indeed." Whatever it was, Janis liked it. "May I offer you some brandy, miss?"

She tasted. Smile lines sunlighted from the corners of her eyes.

"Sit down, Papu," she said, as if decided about something. "You've seen much." Squeezing his shoulder, she pushed him to a seat on the log.

His aching muscles cried in ecstasy. Her sympathy was better even than the cognac, which she quaffed with a little shudder.

"Is it too early to celebrate Midsummer?" she asked.

"Never," Janis said, pouring more.

Her bodice was adorned with silver circles and wolves teeth. Her veil had slipped to the crooks of her elbows. Her skirt brushed the insides of his knees.

"I find the predictability of the heavens comforting," she said.

Janis agreed. "What happens on Earth is much harder to figure."

To Janis's surprise, the Gypsy removed his cap and pressed a cool hand to his injured forehead, making a *tisking* sound. Tsk. Tsk.

Oh, it was right that someone attend to him, Janis thought, melting at the nearness of her bosom. She slid her veil behind his neck with the sleight of a magician's hand and slowly pulled one side. The silk tickled like faerie breath.

Just then the drummer struck a new rhythm, turning her head.

Before the vixen could get away, Janis stood up, slightly unsteadily. He took her hand and held it out like the prow of a ship. Wrapping his other arm around her, he pressed her and her little vest closer.

The Gypsy looked amused. Janis figured the rhythm for a cha-cha. She followed his lead with fun-loving grace. The band riffed an unruly anthem. The whole camp moved to it, as if following in the shadow steps of the ancient Baltic tribes. Janis felt his partner's softness, her firmness. He felt her skirt swirling around his legs. Otherwise, he was wonderfully anesthetized.

He had not forgotten the night's barbarities. But for whatever reason, he was alive right now, when other people weren't. He was dancing in a forest with a dirty-footed and beautiful woman in a slippery veil, and she was everything he loved about life—ripe peaches, the taste of something fine in his mouth, freedom. This was his short moment to live.

The tempo grew hot and they bumped bodies to keep time, her laughing, her arm around his shoulder. The kids were cutting up in one grand, bacchanal wingding. There was some commotion at the other side of the fire, but Janis didn't want to stop—until he recognized Elza's voice raised in protest. So he turned to see what had happened.

An intruder. Krumins was there. Elza's father had come to collect her. His ridiculous lamb chop sideburns were the last thing Janis wanted to see right now. It was bad enough Janis had to put up with Krumins and his neurotic wife at home, the perpetual houseguests. Now Krumins had spoiled his Gypsy dance.

"—been searching for you all night," Krumins stormed at Elza. "And here you are scruffing around with vagabonds!"

The youngsters ebbed away from the killjoy. The drummer quit. The violinist petered out mid-song and vanished.

"—why you have to make such a stink about everything," Elza said, in the high-pitched, tight-throated voice of a girl about to cry publicly. Her eyes looked like puffy inkwells, giving away the child beneath the makeup.

To Janis's dismay, the Romani woman left his arms and went over the Kruminses, saying, "Please don't be angry, Papu. We all need a little distraction from our troubles."

"Thank you, Madame Indra," Krumins said in clipped syllables, piously not watching the heave of her breath. "I know you mean well."

Indra. So caught in her magic, Janis had not asked her name. Imagine Krumins knowing it.

"But these woods are crawling with soldiers and outlaws," Krumins argued, "and my daugh—"

"Akshully, Kruminss. I thinkits shafe here." Janis blurted his slurred opinion from across the campfire.

Krumins turned, squinting. "Pērkons? Is that you?"

"Yah," he uttered thickly, coming closer. "I've witnessed absolute h-h-horrific night."

"I daresay," Krumins replied, looking judgmental.

Janis realized he was swagged in the turquoise veil and yanked it off. "There's uh massive deport- you wooden believe- worse than Trail of Babylon."

"Pērkons. I'm grateful to be under your roof, so I'll say nothing of your choices," Krumins said. "But, *if it's of any interest to you,* your wife and daughter are accounted for and well under my watch. Though Anna is miserable with worry."

"Wait a—H-how dare—" Janis was flummoxed. "F'yur information I barely escaped."

"Let's go, Elza," Krumins said. "You have to consider your reputation in this community."

Indra tried to stop him, saying, "Papu, the young ones, they have no future here." She reached for Elza's hand and turned it over, gazing at the girl's palm. Shaking her head, Indra said, "Let her at least have tonight."

"How dju do that?" Janis said, nosing over for a look at Elza's fortune.

"Madam, nothing could be farther from the truth," Krumins said. "As we speak, *panzers* are rolling to the border. Germany is coming, thank God, to run the Russians out and restore the country. It's just a matter of days now, maybe hours. Life will be the way it was. And you, young lady," he took Elza's hand from the Gypsy's, "have excellent prospects."

"I hate you," Elza said, whipping her hand away from her father. She stalked away, tottering down the path in her high heels.

Krumins absorbed the bitter words silently.

Janis couldn't decide how he felt about the exchange.

"Heed the signs, Papu," Indra said. "Latvia will not know freedom for a very long time. Not until a year," she looked significantly from Krumins to Janis, "a year named by numbers that read the same forward as backward."

Janis wracked his brain. "Like *Alus ari ira sula!*"

"Oh, goodnight Madam," said Krumins, turning to march after his daughter. "See you, Pērkons."

"Beware, Papu," Madam Indra called to his back. "Hard times ahead."

The spell was broken. Janis saw the magical forest clearing to be, obviously, just an overgrown dirt crossroads dotted with piles of donkey dung. The old fellow was slumped on the log staring at a pile of ash, his fedora impossibly crushed. Janis and Indra were again adults with responsibilities. She rattled some dishes, saying she'd boil water. But Janis took his leave. Latching the crate and hoisting it back on his shoulder. He thanked the Romani for their hospitality, and walked on, thirstier than ever.

Walking home, Janis tried to focus on the predicted year of independence, which would read the same backward as forward. He drew numbers in the air, calculating, and staggered once on uneven ground.

"1991? Or it could be 2002. That changes everything."

The walk took forever. He'd never felt worse in his life. At the river Janis stripped off his shirt and splashed water over his head. Hoo! Blood rushed in new directions, thumping as it passed his temples.

A rooster crowed.

"There's a word for it," he said, toweling off with his shirt and having to put it back on.

He cut over to the village, ever circumspect. One early commuter stood at the rail platform. The Bier Schtube was, of course, closed. The church was boarded up.

When he turned off the road and onto the gravel drive, the house came into view, with its stone-block edging. The linden tree, covered in huge green leaves and butter-yellow blossoms, waved in the breeze like a flag at a finish line. The curtain at an upstairs window moved, Anna watching for him.

He entered through the back door into the kitchen, finally home with the hard-won case of cognac. Groaning, he collapsed in the chair by the wood stove. There was a dinner plate, probably set out for him the night before.

Anna came in, but she didn't offer to heat it.

He wolfed down the potatoes, cold.

His wife wore a Chinese-inspired peignoir of pale peach, and foolish slippers she referred to as scuffs. Janis stood and gathered her in his arms. "Anna, put something practical on," he said. "We're leaving this place."

She turned her face to the side, "Ew. Cigars," she said, nose wrinkled.

"Right now. Get Biruta."

"She's asleep."

"I'll carry her. You have to trust me."

"You've been drinking."

"Yah, a little. I din't have any dinner and—And my arm might be broke. Anna, what dya call a word that's the same forward as it is backward?"

"A palindrome?"

"That's it," Janis said, snapping his fingers. "Go get ready. I'm gonna dig up my gun."

"Is it really nece—"

"It's necessary," Janis said, even though he didn't know if it was. "Do it."

She started for the stairs, saying "I hope you take time to bathe."

He opened the icebox and swigged a hangover-curing shot of sauerkraut juice, straight from the jar.

"Nay. No time," Janis said. "We gotta vacate the premises. At least to the carriage house. We should tell the Kruminses, too."

"You do that," Anna said, over her shoulder.

"I'll be a hundred and two in 1991, Anna," Janis said. "The year 1991, I mean. A hundred and two years old. That changes everything."

He guessed she was upstairs and didn't hear him.

Janis lifted the trap door to the root cellar and carefully carried the cognac down the narrow stairs. The cellar was dimly illuminated by light streaming from the kitchen. Stone walls and an earthen floor kept the space cold and dank. Stashing the cognac in a corner for now, Janis set to work moving cases of preserved food. He cleared the spot where he'd buried his hunting rifle several months before to avoid having it confiscated.

Janis jabbed dirt with his spade, seeking the waxed canvas covering when Anna interrupted. She was kneeling on the kitchen floor, leaning her head over the trap door opening.

"What is it?" Janis said.

"Probably nothing. A mistake," she said hesitantly. "But it's odd. A school bus just turned off the road."

37

LIFE BECAME THAT SUSPENDED SPLIT second before certain death, after the floor drops from the gallows, but before gravity collects its due.

"God! Anna! Run!" Janis said. "Get Biruta. Get out of the house."

Anna drew back, looking more horrified by what she saw in Janis's eyes than by the apparition of the school bus.

"Wait," Janis said. "Don't let them see you running from the house. They'll gun you down. Gun you right down. I've seen them do it. Hide. Don't let them find you!"

Anna froze, whipsawed in confusion.

"Get Biruta and hide down here. I'll cover the trap door."

"Then where will *you* hide?" Anna said.

"Just get her. Don't be seen."

Anna fled. He heard her thumping up the stairs.

Janis abandoned getting his gun. At this point its presence would likely result in the execution of his own household. He flung some dirt back over it, and climbed out of the root cellar still gripping the shovel, praying there'd been a mistake, that they'd not come for his family.

Gravel crunched outside on the driveway. Headlights panned the front windows.

Hurry, Anna. Janis waited for her at the hole to the cellar, sweating. *What was the hold up!* He slinked into the dining room, nearer the entry hall, and was staring at the front door when he heard it.

Five sharp knocks on a solid oak door.

Janis couldn't move. Crushed by the weight of his mistakes and their dreadful consequences. God, stop time. Let Anna and Biruta creep swiftly down the stairs. Let them slip past the NKVD, now rapping insistently on the door, now banging with fists or cudgels. They must. Let them disappear into the cellar, and he silently lower the trap door to hide its existence. He ghosted back to the kitchen and leaned the shovel in a corner, so he'd be ready to slide the rug, with the kitchen table on top of it, over the outlines of the root cellar. But the girls didn't come. Janis ignored the door pounding, a man's voice shouting. This plan would work. It had to work. *Where were the girls?* He swallowed dryly, and took a breath.

Men on the stoop cursed the thick beams and sturdy lock hindering their entry. One was battering the door, probably with his rifle. Janis would not open it. He heard footsteps coming down the stairs. That would be the girls, he expected, crouching at the cellar steps to speed them into hiding. Once Anna and Biruta were concealed, he would let the Cheka in. Appear to cooperate. What else could he do?

But the girls didn't come. Pounding ceased. The front door opened. Janis recognized its familiar creak with a clenched jaw. Then the oaken door slammed against the wall.

Janis was stupefied. What fool had opened the *kāpost galva* door! Who would dare— Fury that someone had compromised *his* house was expelled by straight horror. The Cheka were inside his home.

Where were the girls?

Peering from the dark kitchen, Janis looked through the unlit dining room, gaining a surreal view of armed men striding into his entry hall. Amidst the influx of uniforms stood Krumins! Valise in hand, the pompous retired cop wore a wool coat in the same gray-tan as his overgrown sideburns.

"Here I am, Comrade," Krumins said, calmly, but looking from man to man, unclear whom he should address. "I am ready to go."

Janis tried, but from this angle could not see up the stairway. Where were Anna and Biruta?

Krumins edged toward the door, looking eager to lead the invaders away.

The raiders showed no inclination to leave. One soldier bounded through the sitting room, rifle butted against his shoulder, eyes darting in all directions. He kicked open the door to Kārlis's room, where eighteen-year-old Hugo Krumins slept.

An NKVD agent with a red hammer-and-sickle cap badge strode up several stairs and turned to read, holding a clipboard like it was the Lamb's Book of Life. Clipped there was, as Janis knew all too well, The List.

"Citizen Pērkons, capitalist, and Citizen Krumins, police officer. For harboring anti-Soviet attitudes, you must come with us immediately," the List Man ordered. "Bring your entire families. Head of household, Janis Pērkons; spouse, Anna Pērkons, and daughter, Biruta, age 10. You have fifteen minutes to pack travel necessities. Head of Household, Konstantins Krumins, spouse, Egija Krumins, Hugo, 18, and Elza, 14. Get going. You will sign documents on the bus."

"Comrade, I, Konstantins Krumins, am ready," Krumins said. "We can go now."

"Not so fast," said the List Man, running his finger down the index of names. "Where are the wife and two children?"

"They know nothing," Krumins said. "They never had connection to my work."

"The son, Hugo Krumins, is here in this room," yelled the Russian soldier from the boys' bedroom.

"Families Pērkons and Krumins," announced the List Man. "I warn you to use your allotted minutes to gather practical essentials. I'm being generous." To the soldier, he ordered, "Go find the others, Volkov."

Volkov? Janis registered the name with a start. Igor Volkov had been the name of the so-called apprentice planted at Janis's business last winter. Right before it was nationalized. Was he the same? Had Igor got his wish to join the army?

The soldier in question moved with a frightening energy never displayed at the Leather Works. His wavy, brown hair was buzzed short, but Janis recognized Igor's heart-shaped face and high cheekbones. His symmetrical lips pursed as he swung the nose of his weapon in an arc before him, panning the dining room where he found Janis.

"Igor," Janis whispered to his former employee. "Igor, please help me."

Volkov recognized Janis and reacted like he'd stepped in shit. "Here you are, you fat pig. Here is Pērkons!" Volkov announced, pointing at Janis. "Capitalist. Enemy of the people." He moved on, poking his head in the corners of the room, glancing in the kitchen. "Nice place you have here, Citizen," he said, passing Janis on his way back. "I mean *had*."

Volkov leapt up the stairway two or three steps at a time, with Krumins scurrying behind. A door crashed at the Krumins' room, sounding like Volkov had needlessly kicked it open - the upstairs rooms were not even equipped with locks.

Janis resisted the urge to run upstairs. Searching for his wife and daughter would just lead Volkov to them. Instead he went to see the man with the list. The front door had been left open, and a glance outside showed several Russian gunmen guarding a full school bus.

The initial shock subsiding, Janis saw that three men had raided the house. In addition to the List Man and Igor Volkov, a burly, dark-haired man squatted in the entryway. His uniform looked like local militia. He was scowling at an uneven patch of plaster on the wall with the unhurried authority of a ranking officer. The observation flit unfittingly with the other thoughts whirring in Janis's head that refused to coalesce into a plan.

Another door was kicked in upstairs, coming from the room Biruta shared with Elza. Janis tried to ignore that a goon might be dragging his little girl from her bed, saying to the List Man, "My family is not here, Comrade. My son deployed with the 27th Rifle Corps months ago. The others are visiting their Tante Agata Smiltens, in Riga, at 717 Elizabetes Iela." Janis didn't care if he was caught lying. He had to keep his family off that bus.

"No kidding," said the List Man. "I've heard that crap all night. No one's ever home. You refuse to comply. No problem." He moved his hand to the gun at his hip. "Just say so."

Janis kept quiet, lest his entire life be reduced to the squeeze of a stranger's trigger finger.

A woman upstairs screamed like her voice was a weapon. Mrs. Krumins. "No," she shrieked. "I won't go."

Hugo Krumins, messy white hair, rushed from his room, pants over pajamas. Puffy eyes searched the direction of his mother's screams, ready to charge up the stairs.

Janis cut him off, a restraining hand to Hugo's shoulder. "Your father's up there," Janis said. "He'll handle it."

Hugo relented. His face drained of color.

"Pack your things," the List Man told Hugo. "No more than one hundred kilos per family. Get food, clothes, valuables."

But Hugo, hand on the banister, was fixated on the commotion upstairs, where yelling escalated, and something crashed to the floor.

"I have her." Mr. Krumins's voice boomed above the melee. "She's ready, Comrade. There'll be no problem."

The List Man frowned and cast his eyes to the entry hall. The ranking officer stood and walked toward the stairs. "Can't you fools pick up a few citizens without this circus performance?" he said with a raspy voice.

"We're almost finished here, Comrade," said the List man, standing straighter. "Get them down here now, Volkov," he called. "Find the others."

Janis panicked at *find the others*.

The Kruminses appeared at the top of the stairway. Mrs. Krumins wore a fitted wool coat with dress shoes and wrist-length gloves, her cheek bearing a pink handprint. Mr. Krumins helped his wife down the stairs, her knees buckling in a stumble-walk. Volkov jabbed her from behind with his rifle barrel. Elza followed, wearing a ruffled summer frock and dragging a suitcase, her face streaked with tears. Little Biruta was not with them. Janis exhaled in relief.

It pained Janis to see what Elza had packed in her allotted minutes: a doll and a bottle of fingernail polish were visible in her open bag. Janis lifted his overcoat from a hook and wrapped the garment around the girl's shoulders, smelling the smoke of the Gypsy campfire still on her hair.

"Aren't you coming, Mr. Pērkons?" Elza asked.

Janis shook his head. "Nay, Elza."

She looked aghast, bewildered at his words, betrayed.

The List Man scratched his pencil over the clipboard. Elza was a checkmark to him.

At the bottom of the stairs, Mr. Krumins said, "Hugo, get food." He thrust a pillowcase to his son, "As much as you can carry."

Hugo obeyed instantly.

Mrs. Krumins looked subdued as she went out the door. But at the last minute she grabbed a vase from the foyer and flung it at the List Man, missing him by a kilometer. The vase shattered on the sitting room floor.

Volkov hooted loudly. "Now was that nice?" he asked, raising his rifle and aiming at Mrs. Krumins. Then he lowered it, grinning broadly.

Krumins picked up his valise and hurried to get his wife outside.

Volkov ran back upstairs, bashing the only unopened door, that to the master bedroom.

Janis refrained from following him, maintaining the pretense that his family was in Riga. But he forgot to breathe, listening so hard.

Volkov reappeared at the upstairs landing a second later, looking perplexed. He jogged downstairs and crossed to the kitchen.

"Time's up, Pērkons," said the List Man, not looking at Janis.

Janis didn't budge, wracking his brain. If they shot him, would they then leave without finding Anna and Biruta?

"Let me see that," said the Ranking Officer, holding his hand out for the clipboard. "You go check the bus."

The List Man did as instructed. "Hurry up in there!" he shouted toward Hugo in the kitchen before going outside.

The officer studied the list. Lines creased a protruding forehead as his deep-set eyes darted from Janis to the list, and back to Janis again. "You look different," the officer said.

Janis went slack with astonishment.

"Guess I do too, though," said the officer.

Janis rummaged his mental files and suddenly matched the gravelly voice to someone he knew. The man in charge here was a convicted felon, guilty of manslaughter. Two years ago, he'd returned to the village from prison, a pariah, unable to find work. Janis had hired him. Paid him to restore the lathe and plaster in this very room, and had offered the convict other odd jobs until he'd got on his feet. Then along came the Russians who used outcasts, those with no stake in the game, promoting them to leadership. Janis barely recognized the man now, a clean-shaven, high-ranking representative of the Communist militia. The cards had been shuffled and a new hand dealt.

"What is this?" Volkov burst from the kitchen with the shovel. "The basement hatch is open, and there's dirt on the floor."

Janis stayed focused on the convict-officer, speechless at what might be a blessed turn of fortune.

"Answer me," Volkov demanded. "Why is this shovel in the kitchen?"

"I've been baking," Janis uttered.

"He buried something in the basement," Volkov contended to the convict-officer. "I want to know what it is."

"It's time to go," said the officer in his gravelly tone. "Get that kid and get on the bus."

Five seconds passed before Volkov obeyed, tossing the shovel. "Doesn't matter," he said to Janis, "I'll find it out after you're gone." Then he went to lay hold of Hugo.

Hugo came out of the kitchen carrying a heavy sack of goods.

Janis met Hugo's eyes, bright blue, brimming with tears, knowing that the look was goodbye.

The List Man poked his head in the front door with a report. "Ready to roll. Dispatch Pērkons," he told Volkov, with a nod toward Janis.

Volkov almost at the door, turned back, his eyes shining black, titillated at the order.

"I'll deal with him," said the convict-officer, returning the clipboard to the List Man. "You get the bus moving."

"Comrade, I—" Volkov exclaimed.

"I said I'll handle it," repeated the convict-officer, his gravelly voice rising.

Volkov slumped, redoubling his persecution of Hugo, jabbing him from behind with his rifle.

After they left, the convict-officer nudged the door closed. He unholstered his *nagant* in a businesslike routine that chilled Janis, who knew he was meant to die now. An infusion of anger, sorrow and gratitude surged in Janis's veins, pricking hot and cold. Trying to figure a way out, he could only think how heavy his skin felt, hanging resignedly over utterly exhausted bones. He saw the hand wrapping the gun - just an arm's length away from his body. But his spirit was already outside, looking down on his murder from the highest bough on the linden tree, his broken house under his wing.

The deep-set eyes turned to Janis. "You once gave me a break," the convict-officer said. Pointing his weapon downward, he fired into the floor with a jarring blast that rattled the windows.

"Now we're square."

A certain click of the bedroom door woke up Biruta. She had fallen asleep on Mama's bed with Katkis, and woke under the slippery, silver blanket. The click scared Katkis, who skittered off the bed, leaving a cold place by Biruta's legs. The pale light showed Mama leaning against the door, breathing like she was playing tag.

"Katkis!" Biruta called.

"Quiet!" Mama snapped, high and brittle. She swooped down on Biruta and grabbed her by the armpits. A whimper came from Mama's chest as she lifted Biruta from the bed and squeezed her against her chest. "We have to hide," Mama whispered. She moved in jerks, head darting, looking for a place, under the bed, behind the wardrobe.

Downstairs, someone was banging at the front door.

Biruta turned to ice. It was the middle of night. That's when the Cheka took people away. Everybody at school said so. Hot tears flooded her eyes. They'd come to get her. Or Mama. Or Papu. Or Katkis.

"Here Birute," Mama whispered, parting draperies.

"Nay." Biruta knew about hiding. "They'll find us there." She unfastened the window latch and pushed the glass up. Hoisting herself over the sill, Biruta swung a knee onto the roof. She turned back to help Mama, whose eyes glowed so big. Mama never went on the roof.

Angry voices and stomping boots echoed from inside the house.

Mama raised the window higher and gathered the layers of her nightgown. Biruta wanted to scream *hurry!* Mama took her scuffs off her feet and set them on the roof. *Get Katkis!* Biruta wanted to cry, but her fingers covered her mouth and no sound came out.

"Go, Biruta," Mama whispered. "Go on." To Biruta's horror, Mama turned back into the room.

Nay! Mama! Biruta was rooted to where she stood, unevenly perched on the angled slate tiles, suddenly alone. Her insides bubbled with poison. She should go back with Mama. She should hide. She didn't know what she should do. She stepped to the branches of the linden tree that hung over the roof and held one for balance, waiting, tears dripping from her cheeks.

Beneath the overhanging branches was the window to Krumins's room. Mr. Krumins's big voice thundered into the night. Mrs. Krumins wailed. Strange voices were in there too. Biruta was too afraid to move in any direction.

Oh! Biruta heaved a breath of relief. Mama was finally coming out. Her tumbled hair was outside the window, and then her arms. Her body lay against the roof tiles as she crawled out on elbows and knees, and slid the window closed.

Inside, the bedroom door slammed the wall with a crash! The Cheka was in Mama's room! Mama scrambled over and Biruta moved aside branches with a terrible rustling of leaves. They crouch-walked to a corner made by the roof and the dormer of Krumins's window, and huddled behind the leafy green, yellow-flowered shield. Mama wrapped her arm around Biruta and held her tight against her heart, covering Biruta's ears and eyes.

In the muffled dark, Biruta was alone inside her head. What bad thing had she done? Where was Papu? It seemed Papu was not the one in charge! That tumbled everything she knew. Breath stuck in her throat. Mama's skin was wet. She was still as a statue, except her chest rose and fell, rose and fell in a kind of rocking. Biruta stopped shaking. She tried to match Mama's breathing. The linden blossoms smelled good. The hurt in her chest eased up. The house was quiet. An engine rumbled in the driveway, sounding like her school bus. The Cheka was leaving!

A blunt gunshot rattled the window. Biruta screamed, shrill against Mama's shoulder.

Mama squeezed her tight.

Biruta's hands and arms shook. If it weren't for Mama she'd slide right down the roof. Her heart thudded in her ears, but she heard it—no mistake, the slide of the wooden sash.

Somebody was opening the window.

Many moments passed before Janis Pērkons could master the alternate waves of fear and relief in his belly. He heard the bus's engine turn over outside.

He waited for the wheels to move, crunching gravel, before mounting the stairs with trembling knees to look for Anna and Biruta.

The small room the Biruta and Elza had shared was in its usual disarray, and empty.

A chair was knocked over in the Krumins's room. Janis couldn't look at the disorder of their personal items, sickened by the story it told.

The master bedroom was eerily vacant. The bed was made. Anna must have had the wits to do that. No feet showed below the curtains. Think! They must be somewhere. Where did the little girl like to hide?

Janis raised the window, pushed his head into the morning breeze and gulped the scent of linden flowers. To his right, the tree arched over the housetop, hiding a section of the roof behind a screen of dark leaves and yellow blooms.

Janis climbed out the window and traversed the tiles in a crouch. "Anna," he whispered. "They're gone."

He pushed a leafy branch to the side, and saw his wife and daughter huddled against a dormer.

Janis let out a huge breath, eyes looking toward heaven. The pink morning sky was plumped with buttermilk clouds. Clutching the branch for balance, he peered over the roofline in time to see the school bus turn off the gravel drive and onto the road, loaded with its cargo of misery.

Parade of the Dead. K. Smiltens, 1948.

38

HUGO KRUMINS WAS THE LAST of his family to be loaded onto the school bus. He stumbled down the aisle, the soldier rifle-jabbing his back. Elza was sitting next to their father. Behind them, Hugo saw an empty seat next to his mother. He settled beside her, the pillowcase of food at his feet.

"We're all going to hell," she told him, staring out the window.

The engine started. Hugo looked around at the rows of passengers and back to the house, bewildered. The bus was ready to depart. Why weren't the Pērkonses on board? "How did they manage to get out of it?" he murmured, trying to get events straight in his head.

When Hugo had gone to bed last night, Mr. Pērkons hadn't even been home. Mrs. Pērkons had said her husband was detained in Riga on business, though she'd never left the window, where she watched for him. But fifteen minutes ago, when the soldier woke him up, suddenly Mr. Pērkons *was home,* claiming it was Mrs. Pērkons and Biruta who were in Riga.

"Pērkons has no doubt swung some deal," his mother said, following Hugo's gaze.

A gunshot from the house punched the daybreak, making passengers gasp.

"No deal, Mr. Pērkons," the soldier standing behind him said, sounding upbeat.

A hunk of ice formed in Hugo's belly as he watched a burly, dark-eyed officer slam the door to the summerhouse and climb aboard. The officer sat near the driver and the bus rolled down the gravel drive. Hugo twisted his neck around, watching the linden tree grow smaller, until the bus pulled onto the paved road. Had Mr. Pērkons refused to obey?

"Don't feel badly, Hugo," his mother said. "If we're headed where I think we are, Pērkons got the easy way out."

"Did you know him well?" The soldier leaned over Hugo and spoke in a conversational tone that was bizarre and chilling. "He was once my so-called employer, you know." As if to prove it, he removed a cigarette from a gold case. Mr. Pērkons was the only person Hugo had ever known who possessed such lavish trappings.

As the soldier lit up, Hugo noticed they were the same age, and knew who he was. The Nonchalants spoke with hatred of the Russian spy who'd be assigned to apprentice for Mr. Pērkons. His name was Volkov. In the last fifteen minutes, Volkov had roused Hugo at gunpoint, terrorized his mother and sister, forced his family from home, and been party to Mr. Pērkons's murder. Hugo hated him too.

"I like his house," Volkov said with a wave of the cigarette. "Tonight was the first time I've seen Pērkons's summer place, very charming, baronial, and all that." Grabbing the seat, he leaned down as if he were watching the sunrise over the fields. "So, what was going on back there?" he said to Hugo in conspiring tones. "Why the dirt in the kitchen? And the shovel?" The rifle dangling from his neck banged against Elza's head.

Hugo's father turned around and glared.

Volkov straightened up and pointed his rifle at Mr. Krumins. "*Ack-ack-ack-ack-ack.*" He mimicked automatic fire at the base of his throat.

Hugo started with horror.

Volkov burst out laughing at Hugo's response to the faked gunfire.

Hugo's father, however, a veteran of the former Latvian police force, did not flinch. His face florid beneath overgrown sideburns, Mr. Krumins faced front again, looking disgusted.

Hugo's cheeks burned.

His mother reached a gloved hand to Hugo's shoulder. "Don't worry, son. There's nothing we can do." Returning her gaze to the window, she said, "We're all going to hell."

Sighing and still chuckling, Volkov started a lap up and down the aisle of the bus, bullying the passengers to face forward and stop talking.

Hugo studied the sadistic soldier, his heart-shaped face, the high cheekbones and haughty expression, his fingers stretching and curling nervously over the rifle, burning the features into his memory, as if on Judgment Day he'd get to point him out in a line-up. Volkov patrolled back and Hugo steeled himself for more abuse.

Grasping the seat back, Volkov leaned down and said, "Pērkons was burying something." He sniffed, looking at the passing farms, practically cheek-to-cheek with Hugo. "Rich man like him had piles of trinkets he wouldn't want to put in a bank. Now he's dead, somebody's going to uncover his stash."

The gunshot from Pērkons's home still rang in Hugo ears.

"Question is do I dig in the cellar or somewhere on the property outside that kitchen door?" Volkov said. "You might as well tell me, because no one else is left. You're being deported. Pērkons is dead."

He was being deported.

Mr. Pērkons was dead.

"The son's gone," Volkov said, frowning thoughtfully. It took Hugo a moment to realize he was talking about his best friend, Kārlis.

"So that leaves me," Volkov said. "I'm the last man standing and, to the victor goes the spoils."

39

KĀRLIS PĒRKONS OPENED CRUSTED EYELIDS TO FIND himself in total darkness. Where— Oh yah, the thatch-roofed barn. How long had he slept? He listened hard, fearing someone would hear the canvas rustle as he crawled out from under his makeshift tent.

Morning had arrived and entered the barn through knotholes and splintered cracks, lighting shafts of dust in the air. Wearing only his *apiksbikshes* Kārlis made his way to a window. He pulled back a corner of the blackout fabric and was blinded by the sun. He winced, eyes adjusting, and gazed out at the trees. Hearing nothing but birds, he relaxed.

Kārlis tucked up the curtain, admitting enough sunlight to survey his surroundings. Turning for a look, he shrank back in fright.

A large man was right behind him, taller than Kārlis, eyes fixed in a wooden stare.

Kārlis gasped.

Dead, he knew, in shock. The pasty, lifeless body behind him was not alive.

The man had been tortured. His head hung down and to the side, blood had dried in a trickle down his face. His arms had been stretched out and hands nailed to a roughly hewn...Kārlis exhaled in amazement...cross. He nearly chuckled with relief. Jesus Christ.

"*Ak tu kungs!*" Behind him stood a larger-than-lifesized figure of the crucified Christ. Kārlis looked up at Him. He ran his hand over the sculpture's timeworn wood.

"You are a magnificent One," Kārlis uttered, as his heartbeat slowed to normal. Intricately carved and painted, gold-leafed in places, the Figure was sublime. "You could've hung in a famous cathedral."

Behind the altarpiece, another canvas draped to the ground. Kārlis lifted it and discovered another Crucified Christ, of equal gravitas. Stacked behind that was one more. And another one behind that. Altarpieces, the crowning glory of the Christian churches, each unique, each looking historically and artistically important were lined up ten deep to the wall. Kārlis cast his gaze over the dimly lit barn, where ghostly knobs of canvas poked up at various heights from wall to wall.

"What is this place?" he muttered to the first Crucifix. He gandered along, peeking here and there under the carefully mantled oilcloths and protective blankets. Discovering a stash of triptychs, Kārlis examined a hinged panel dated 1581. When he laid a hand on a faded portrait of the Prince of Peace, a galvanizing current flooded him, plugging his weary soul into a million-volt spiritual power outlet.

"Masterful art has always moved me," he said to the anguished eyes under the thorn crown. "That's why I wanted to study it." Kārlis turned away, vexed. He ambled among pews and communion tables, whistling at a stack of ornate platters and chalices, stained glass and a collection of icons decorated in Baltic amber. Climbing spiral steps to the top of an elaborately carved pulpit, Kārlis stood in his underpants and leaned forward to address the standing room-only crowd of Christs.

"There must be hundreds of you sacred art pieces here," Kārlis said, gauging the dimensions of the barn. "Someone has gone to a lot of trouble, not to mention risk, to save you from the marauding, church-burning Commie atheists." The NKVD would find inspirational art of this caliber as threatening as machine guns.

Kārlis didn't usually go in for public speaking. He was an observer, a watcher of details and eccentricities, eventually saying his piece with ink or a paintbrush. But a deserter's path was a lonely one, and he was grateful for the company of other fugitives, especially such skillfully crafted treasures.

The pulpit's ornate tracery caught his eye. "So is this Baroque?" Kārlis followed the pattern with a finger. "Or medieval Gothic?" He looked out at the congregation. "I'd know if I'd been allowed to graduate high school and attend the Art Academy. I'm not complaining." Not when close friends, like Peters and Eriks, had been arrested and probably tortured and killed. But venting to wise, sympathetic listeners felt good.

"I have tried to conduct my life in the proper order, as You know," he shook his head, smiling without mirth. "Fat chance a deserter has getting into the Art Academy. *Ak tu kungs!*" He slammed his palms down on the lectern. "Tonight is commencement! My friends will be together celebrating. At least I hope they made it. I would give anything to be there." He looked toward the peak in the rafters. "That is *not* a prayer," Kārlis clarified. "I'm saving that for *real* dire straits." He returned his gaze to the wooden audience. "We needn't disturb God about the Art Academy. Still, as long as we're all hiding here, we may as well talk. Keep each other from going nuts."

He stretched and contracted his arm, elbow inflamed from mass grave digging.

"But it's not prayer," Kārlis repeated glumly as he descended the pulpit.

"I'm going out to find a white willow," he told Them, taking the shovel and squeezing through the barn door.

Willows grew at the water, so Kārlis backtracked toward the stream in his underwear as if he were the sole survivor on earth. The moon was still visible, white against the early blue sky, though dark clouds were building at the edge of the horizon.

A willow was easily spotted, pliable branches shimmering in the breeze. Kārlis recognized the narrow silvery leaves and deeply fissured gray bark with certainty. Carefully gouging away the outer corky layer, while swatting rampant mosquitoes, he cut the pink inner bark and peeled it from the tree in rough strips. He began chewing the end of one immediately, knowing the juices would soothe his aches and pains.

The flavor made him miss old Tante Agata, a dab practitioner of herbal medicine and the one who had taught him the white willow remedy. Tante Agata was an old bird. What if she didn't survive the Commies, who were rightly threatened by crones like her who knew the forest lore? Worry, worry, always worry under the Russians. For anxiety, Tante Agata would brew linden tea.

A bird flew overhead and Kārlis imagined its view. A few kilometers away in any direction, the world was going crazy. What was the rush to join in? Especially when he could stay at the barn? It wasn't the Art Academy, but here he was free to study a secret archive of meaningful art. Let the Nazis tackle the Reds. He'd know when the Germans arrived. Their cannons would make thunder sound like his grumbling belly.

Black clouds promised a downpour before long. He could set out those communion platters and chalices to catch some drinking water. Then he wouldn't have to come all the way to the stream. Suddenly a burning idea seared Kārlis's brain.

Rushing to the barn, he squeezed between the doors and found his way to the section where he'd seen a communion table. He looked under canvases in an eager and systematic search of the sacral inventory, checking trunks and crates, sliding open a cabinet door— Ak tu kungs! As he'd hoped! A case of crackers. Paper thin, round, stale tasteless wafers. Kārlis tore the box open, munching with gusto, ever grateful for the body of Christ, broken for him.

JUNE 15, 1941

JEKABS LEOPOLDS AWOKE WHEN something heavy hit the floor next to him, emitting a puff of white dust. He opened his eyes to find the light on, the naked bulb harshly artificial in the confines of the pantry. Uncle Eli was dismantling the barricade, schlepping bags of flour away from the door. Jekabs got up to help, stretching muscles stiff from cowering in the pantry all night.

Grabbing one end of a fifty-kilo sack of flour, Jekabs said, "Put 'em in a U-shape." He caught himself before divulging that Vilz liked to type in the middle of the bags, as they made excellent soundproofing. His uncle would pop a vein if he knew Vilz regularly wrote illegal articles on the premises. "Heaven help you, if I should find that you're bringing that Secret Meeting schlok here!" had been Uncle Eli's view.

Jekabs didn't like deceiving his uncle. But he agreed with Vilz that abetting the clandestine press was their best chance for kicking

Russian ass back to Moscow. Last night's violence underscored the penalty for getting caught.

Until last night the NKVD had never come to the Leopolds Bakery, except for coffee and rugelach. Last night had marked some kind of turning point, from bad to… Jekabs didn't see what could be worse than last night.

Sniedze was awake, but slumped in the corner not offering to help, and smelling faintly of urine. Jekabs wrinkled his nose, feeling sorry for the pisher.

"That was one helluva carnival, eh, Sniedze," Uncle Eli said, hoisting bags.

"I hate Cossacks," Sniedze said hoarsely, watching the labor with red, puffy eyes from under the brim of his newsboy cap. "They almost got us. Only a matter of time."

"Give us a hand with these bags, Sniedze," Jekabs said.

Without getting up, Sniedze said, "Vilz likes them arranged like a foxhole, so—"

"Yah, she can do that herself," Jekabs said, quickly. "These are heavy."

"So what?" Uncle Eli asked, "What were you going to say, Sniedze?"

"So no one can hear her," Sniedze said.

Jekabs shot Sniedze a look and held his breath. That was exactly the kind of thoughtless comment that could ignite Uncle Eli's suspicions.

"Hmm," Uncle Eli said, looking at the stack of flour bags and sizing up the dimensions of the pantry. "Smart."

Sniedze shrugged.

"Yah, she's a genius," Jekabs said, waving his hand toward Vilz, who, sleeping on a low shelf, snored lightly, as if on cue.

As Jekabs moved the last bag away, Sniedze cried, "Don't open the door!"

Uncle Eli froze, hand on the doorknob.

Jekabs's stomach jumped to his throat.

Sniedze was suddenly all choked up. "We don't have to open it yet," he said, his voice high and tight. "What if there's Russians out there? We should stay hidden a lot longer."

Uncle Eli exhaled. "Don't worry, Sniedze." He sounded irked that he'd been riled by Sniedze's false alarm. "I'll be very cautious."

Jekabs was not thrilled about walking out of the pantry either. The door had separated them from a living nightmare. However, the boulevard had been quiet for a couple of hours. Memories of squealing tires, gunshots, screams and sobs seemed unreal.

"Nay, don't let them in," Sniedze said, clenched with emotion. "Please."

Uncle Eli was not the kind of man who didn't care if someone was on the verge of hysteria. He looked at Sniedze and again around the pantry. "What you need, Sniedze, is a roll-up-your-sleeves project. I'm reorganizing this place today and you're going to help me."

"I'll scrub the whole place if you want, Mr. Leopolds," Sniedze said, "only please don't open that door."

"Men don't hide in pantries for no good reason, Sniedze," Uncle Eli said, cracking the door. He looked carefully in all directions before widening it and stepping out. Jekabs followed him, meeting the fresh air with equal parts dread and curiosity.

The kitchen was wrongly untidy and cold. Uncle Eli shook his head at the pans of ruined bread, the batch they'd aborted at the start of the NKVD raid. Jekabs followed a few steps behind as Uncle Eli started walking toward the storefront, lightly running his hand across the wall and counting his steps under his breath, like he might be measuring for a carpet. The hallway was long, on account of the large pantry and the bakery's narrow, deep lot.

Before stepping onto the retail floor, they paused, peering cautiously through the metal bread racks to the street. Jekabs saw no one. Uncle Eli lifted the hinged section of the counter between the cash register and the display case and passed through, going closer to the window. They scrutinized Lenin Boulevard where all the deportation tummel had taken place. Jekabs saw no evidence of the insane roundup. No bodies in the street. No splashes of blood and bullet holes against the walls of the tall, silent buildings. No patriots hanging from street lamps. Just a beckoning spring morning.

A man in a suit was hurrying down the sidewalk across the way. A couple of women left a building, walking arm in arm, small felt hats angled over their brows. Jekabs watched these test canaries for several moments, waiting to see if anything awful happened to them. A cat strolled past on the sidewalk with its tail in the air.

"Quiet out there," Uncle Eli said, in conclusion. He flipped the sign hanging in the window to Open, and turned on the lights. "I think the best plan is to stick to our routine."

Jekabs nodded. Taking the broom and a deep breath, he opened the front door. Long rays of the summer sun slanted up the sidewalk, giving the morning a warm golden glow. He started sweeping the sidewalk same as he did every day, knowing it wasn't at all like every day. Last night his neighbors had been yanked from their homes and taken who knew where. Still, sweeping seemed a better move than hiding in the pantry.

By the time he finished there was a steady trickle of commuters on the street, but nothing like the usual onslaught of the morning rush. Going in, Jekabs wiped down the aluminum counter, always proud of the spiffy way it reflected the lights hanging from the stamped tin ceiling tiles.

Back in the kitchen, Vilz was up. She'd put wood in an oven and was pumping the bellows. "Come on," she grumbled, trying to get a flame out of the surviving embers.

Jekabs held cigarettes to the small fire.

Uncle Eli was already groomed to his daily standard. Brown, receding hair combed neatly under a white skullcap. He'd put on a starchy white collarless shirt, that didn't show the flour, under his usual white apron. "What a waste," he said, shoving the night's ruined loaves into the bin.

Vilz took a deep drag, activating dimples. "I'm going to tell the world what happened last night," she promised softly.

"Dangerous to discuss such matters," Mr. Leopold said, "You never know who's talking to the Cheka, whether by choice or for survival."

"Dangerous *not* to discuss such matters," Vilz said.

"Dangerous either way," Jekabs quipped, "This whole *kāpost galva* situation is fucking fraught with peril."

"Good thing we started the rye sour yesterday," Eli said. "We'll make *Rupjmaize*. Everybody in the neighborhood is broke and black bread is a crowd-pleaser."

"One loaf is dense enough to withstand a siege," Jekabs said. "Or break a window if we run out of bricks."

"You think anybody in their right mind will step outside their cellar today?" Vilz asked.

"We all gotta eat," Uncle Eli said, scooping coffee from a tin and filling the basket of the percolator. "Fresh bread puts the world right."

"I don't have to eat," Sniedze called from the pantry. "I'll fast 'til the Germans get here."

"*Vor der Kaserne*," Jekabs sang, "*Vor dem großen Tor*." He peeled off his grimy t-shirt and pelted it at Sniedze, translating,

"Outside the barracks,

By the corner light."

Sniedze had made lousy marks in German.

"Stop singing that sleezy Marlene Dietrich," Sniedze retorted.

"You're just jealous her voice is deeper than yours," Vilz said.

"I'll always stand and wait for you at night," Jekabs crooned, splashing at the bathroom sink. He dressed, wrapping a white linen towel over his trousers and tucking the ends tight. He perched the envelope-style baker's cap over his new haircut and studied the effect. "Should I shave?" he asked. "For graduation?"

"Definitely," Vilz said. "Both hairs."

"I find it hard to believe you have graduation on your mind after all that happened last night," Sniedze called. "Graduating won't make any difference. No grand new horizons will open and if we go out we could get arrested. So what's the point?"

"The point is they earned it," Uncle Eli said, pouring from a heavy sack of rye flour. "If we weren't on last night's *list*, I think we're in the clear. So don't stop making plans for your future or else all of this," Eli waved his arm around the bakery, "is for nothing. You youngsters got your whole lives ahead of you."

Eli reached for the honey jar, a rationed ingredient that was near empty. "What're you gonna do, Vilz?" He lowered his voice, "When these crummy Communists go home." Eli thinned the honey with warm water. "Let me guess. Prime Minister? Ambassador?"

"Ha!" Vilz hopped up to sit on the counter. "Beekeeper."

"What? One of those schmoes with the net over his head? And you so good looking?"

"Bees are the most artful communicators in the world," Vilz said. "A honeybee never sleeps!"

Eli thrust his chin out, nodding. "That's a nice trick. What about you, Jekabs?"

"Oh, you know. I already got it all right here," Jekabs said, meaning the family bakery. Chatting up a rosy future was delusional, but pleasant. "After a year or so, open my own shop. Maybe we make a chain."

"That's the spirit! That's why we go to graduation," Uncle Eli said. "Don't rob me of a chance to kvell at your achievement."

"And a huge accomplishment it is," Vilz remarked. "We've not been drafted, tortured, deported, arrested or executed *and* we've completed the coursework."

"Been a miserable year," Uncle Eli said. "But it's *your* miserable year. So you must go. What about poor Kārlis in the army? Think he would hide in a pantry if he had a chance to go to graduation? Or Peters Kalnins or Eriks Gailis? Wouldn't they give their eye teeth to go to graduation?"

"Hugo's valedictorian," Vilz said. "I'm sure his whole family will be there."

"Imagine that," Uncle Eli said. "Valedictorian. Coffee's ready."

"Thanks, but I better get going," Vilz said, hopping off the counter and shrugging into her black bomber jacket.

"You're sure you want to go out there?" Jekabs asked, suddenly emotional about his independent and unique soul-friend.

Vilz slicked back her hair and pulled on the Greek sea captain's cap.

Whomever Vilz was meeting, Jekabs figured, had probably been told to watch for the cap.

"A honeybee can pass complex instructions without saying a word," Vilz said.

"We just don't want you to get stung, Vilz," Uncle Eli said.

She acted cool, but Jekabs saw Vilz take a deep breath and clench her jaw before she left by the back door.

K. Smiltens, 1947.

41

GRIPPING THE PILLOWCASE OF FOOD, Hugo Krumins stepped off the bus.

Riga Central Train Station, the terminus for five lines as well as the line to Russia, teemed with unwilling travelers. In every direction, red hammer-and-sickle cap badges bobbed like drunken demon eyes.

"What a fiasco," Elza said, this magnitude of bedlam beyond her vocabulary.

"Proceed to the sorting area," a Chekist shouted. The crowd before and behind Hugo forced him forward in small, lurching steps.

"Stay together," Hugo's father bellowed, shepherding Hugo, Elza and his mother in a tight cluster. "That's the imperative."

"Heads of household, men, this way," insisted another green uniform, inserting the muzzle of a machine gun into Hugo's family, separating him and his father from the females.

"No!" cried Hugo's mother, wheeling around so fast her coat swished. "Don't go!" She stood eye-to-eye with her husband on account of her dress shoes.

Hugo was used to his mother's hair in a strict bun, not white tendrils snaking over her shoulders and face.

"Heads of household are going ahead of their families to prepare lodgings," the green uniform deigned to explain.

"Save that for some idiot," Mrs. Krumins snapped. "Where are you taking him?"

"That will be disclosed at a later time," the soldier said, resuming his original rigidity. "Women and children over there."

"Don't go, Krumins," Hugo's mother said.

But his father, bending mechanically, kissed Elza on the top of her head and leaned toward his wife to do the same.

"Don't leave us," Mrs. Krumins pleaded. "Or we'll never see you again!"

But with a nudge for Hugo to follow him, Mr. Krumins turned away, following orders with a stoic air, as if by taking more abuse on his shoulders, he would somehow lessen the burden for others.

Mrs. Krumins lunged for her husband, falling on the ground with her arms around his legs. A Chekist kicked her ribs, but she held on. A boot kicked her white-gloved hand, which finally let go. Hugo dropped his pillowcase and knelt where his mother had collapsed, sliding his arms awkwardly under her shoulders. Frantic, he looked up in time to see his father's tall, erect bearing already disappearing, one step at a time, into the marching throng of heads of household.

"Mark my words," his mother gasped. "We won't see him again." She cradled her ribs, which Hugo prayed were not cracked. "I knew this would happen," she said. "We're all going to hell."

The Chekist left to harass others.

A parade of legs and several minutes passed before Hugo was able to help his mother to her feet. Holding her with one arm, Hugo picked up his pillowcase and marched with his mother and sister in the direction opposite from where his father had gone.

As they were absorbed into the pressing stream of families, Hugo realized that he was now in the women and children's group, and wondered what, if any, difference that, or anything, made at this point. He did see one elderly man, clutching his bundle, tottering around, looking for somewhere to sit. Hugo stepped carefully around mothers crouched on the ground holding babies and trying to keep small children near.

Eventually, the deportees ceased moving forward, only crowding closer together, until finally corralled tightly in one place. Most people eventually put down their things, sitting on or near them, getting up periodically to shift with the stream as it inched forward.

The concourse was a hopeless mass of human distress, so Hugo searched the sky. He prayed to see a saving spearhead of German Stuka out of the west, commencing the German invasion with dive-bombs to the rail network. But the blue sky was calm, dotted with undisturbed rows of altocumulus.

42

THE MALTED RYE LOAVES WERE RISING, their brushed egg-white coating turning shiny. The sweet-sour aroma wafted enticingly to the boulevard. Every time the door jingled Jekabs's heart lodged in his throat, afraid for Uncle Eli who went out to meet the customers. Many were regulars from the neighborhood, but a few came in wearing the terrifying green uniform. Jekabs steadied his nerves with the muscled rhythm of kneading and forming loaves, timing it so the next batch would be ready before the last batch was sold out.

The door jingled and, again, Jekabs's ears pricked up in worry. He was relieved to hear someone say *shalom*.

Uncle Eli responded to the greeting in a heartfelt tone that made Jekabs leave his duties in the kitchen to see who was there. A respected man from the temple had come, a mensch in Uncle Eli's view. Wiping his hands, Jekabs stood behind his uncle in greeting.

"Shalom, Jekabs," said the black-suited visitor. He had curly grey hair and a long scraggly beard. The fringes of his *tzitzit* dangled visibly from under his shirt.

"Jekabs, take the register for a minute," Uncle Eli said, lifting the counter.

"What about last night's meshugas, Eli?" the mensch said, passing behind the counter and following his uncle toward the back.

"Life goes on," Uncle Eli replied. "My nephew graduates high school today."

"Mazel tov."

"Thank you. And you?"

The visitor lowered his voice, saying, "It's getting dark in my eyes, Eli."

Jekabs tried to focus on the subdued conversation behind him, while attending to a couple of customers standing in line at the register. He said to a kerchiefed lady, "What can I get you, ma'am?"

"*Auschwitz... massive expansion...* " The murmurings reached Jekabs's ears.

"Young man, I said, is this fresh?"

"*... can now hold a hundred thousand prisoners...* "

"This is yesterday's bread, isn't it?" said the kerchiefed lady. "I don't see the usual loaf I buy here."

"No ma'am, we don't have the white loaf fresh today."

"*Guess who's forced to do the labor?*"

"*Oy-yoy-yoy.*"

"Well, I can't use this brown bread. And I'm not interested in day-old."

"*—planning a facility outside Riga. Maybe even bigger than Auschwitz.*"

"*What does it mean? There aren't that many Jews in Latvia.*"

"I'm sorry about that, ma'am. We'll have the white fresh tomorrow."

"Paris. They're rounding up… "

"Tomorrow. Well, that doesn't help me today, does it?"

"No ma'am. Excuse me please. Are you ready, sir?" Jekabs's ears were burning so hot he could barely think as he mechanically wrapped the next customer's purchases in paper.

"They'll be here within a week. Maybe two."

"God forbid!" said Uncle Eli, again lifting the counter for his guest.

Before the mensch departed, Uncle Eli said, "Take some strudel, friend. May your strength continue."

Uncle Eli stared after the mensch with a stony expression. Jekabs's heart was palpitating.

"Is the strudel fresh?" the kerchiefed lady asked.

Uncle Eli resumed the front counter duty and Jekabs went back to the kitchen, knowing he'd eventually learn the details of the temple gossip. He had the gist of it and his hands shook as he formed dinner rolls. He'd been raised not to kvetch about whether life was fair. It wasn't. With Germany coming, everyone else in Riga was coming up for air, the end to the Russian occupation in sight. Yet he had to fear pograms, violent attacks for being Jewish, something his friends never thought about. He wiped his eye with a sleeve and focused on preparing a slew of long trays, identical with tidy matrices of uniform blobs of dough.

The morning rush tapered off to the ever-thinning lunch crowd. Uncle Eli walked in the kitchen and Jekabs avoided his eyes by wielding the long paddles that slid trays to the back of the oven.

Uncle Eli cleared his throat, but then, as if he was putting off saying something, went into the pantry and started banging pots. That was Uncle Eli, facing problems with action, Jekabs thought, hearing the rattle of shelf reorganization. Sliding the last tray into the oven, Jekabs noted the time. Then he noticed something else. All was quiet. The silence in the storeroom shook him by the shoulder.

The typewriter! No!

Rushing to the pantry, Jekabs saw he was too late.

Uncle Eli stood among stacks of pans on the floor, hands on hips, red in the face.

An innocuous-looking dark green box with latches and the name *Adler* stamped in gold sat on a little table, under the light bulb as if it were being interrogated at the police station. Uncle Eli's gaze bore into Sniedze who stood rigidly, the whites of his eyes as big as plates. When Jekabs came in, his uncle turned the furious eyes to him, square on.

"You have something to tell me, Jekabs?" Uncle Eli said.

Jekabs teetered on the high wire of a moral dilemma. He couldn't be loyal to Vilz without betraying Uncle Eli, and the opposite was distressingly true as well.

"About what?" Jekabs asked, slowly. "Just... that typewriter?"

"Do I look like a schnook?" Uncle Eli said.

"I'm just not sure what the problem is," Jekabs said. "A typewriter in and of itself isn't—"

"After I have welcomed your friends here at my own risk, now you give me this blather. Whose is it?"

"Sorry, Uncle Eli. I should have trashed it. I should have thrown it into the sea before I let anyone store it here for one night." Jekabs was talking out of his keister, avoiding answering the question.

"It's Vilz's," said Sniedze.

The pantry went silent.

"Oy," Uncle Eli finally exclaimed, turning appalled eyes toward Sniedze as if he'd just discovered weevils in the flour. "What's on his mind is on his tongue!"

Sniedze looked confused, like he'd expected praise for providing the correct answer. "It's true," Sniedze said.

Jekabs leveled a steely gaze at the pipsqueak.

"I'm just being honest," Sniedze said. "It *is* Vilz's typewriter."

"I don't know what troubles me more, Sniedze," Uncle Eli said. "That Vilz has been lying to me, or how fast you were to give up your best friend in the world."

"Yah! Send in the rat patrol," Jekabs said, glad but guilty to deflect Eli's wrath onto Sniedze.

"You don't want to be a mosser, Sniedze," Uncle Eli said.

"A squealer," Jekabs translated.

"Is Vilz collaborating with Nazis?" Uncle Eli asked Jekabs, pointedly.

"No, Uncle. She has nothing to do with them. Or I wouldn't have covered for her."

"Vilz undermines Commies," Sniedze said.

"Oy! Pimples should grow on your tongue!" Eli clutched his cap. He poked his head out the door then, reassured no one was listening, turned to Jekabs for an explanation.

"Vilz is for a sovereign Latvia," Jekabs said. "Democratic—"

"Yah, I've heard her schtik," Eli said. He stared at the typewriter, and Jekabs wished he knew what his uncle was thinking.

Uncle Eli took a breath, calming down a bit. "She's a purist." Eli nodded, then shook his head. "Naive, but well, she's young. Has ideals. I'll say that about Vilz Zarins. Scruples." His tone suggested no one else there had any. "And chutzpah."

He pointed at Jekabs, saying, "When she gets back we're gonna have a sit-down."

"As for you," Uncle Eli said, pointing at Sniedze, "I hope you won't be such a nebbish if someone ever questions you about me." He sniffed the air. "Those loaves are ready."

Jekabs rushed to the ovens, glad for an excuse to get away. One of the ovens was stoked to over 200 degrees and its contents had to be quickly transferred to the other oven to finish baking at around 80. Jekabs used mitts and long handles to maneuver the pans in the deep, coffin-sized, brick-lined kilns.

As he did his uncle came over, stood at his shoulder and spoke quietly. "Here's the deal. We're gonna build a false wall in the pantry."

Jekabs stood stunned. Uncle Eli must be scared witless to hatch such an extreme plan, which, in turn, scared Jekabs.

"You and I can't go around buying materials," Eli said. "But Vilz, her father's in the building trade, right?"

"He's a plumber."

"Close enough. Vilz can get us what we need. If she wants to keep her private typewriting office there among the flour bags, she has to do that for me."

"She would do that for us anyway, Uncle Eli. That's Vilz."

"Yah. I know. We're gonna need a friend like that." After a moment of gazing at the embers, he said, "Leave Sniedze out of it."

Jekabs nodded. His uncle was right, though it saddened him.

"Schtuk coming down the pipeline, Jekabs."

Given his way, Sniedze wouldn't have left the safety of the pantry at all. But his stomach cramps signaled a desperate need for the toilet. He burst into the kitchen headed for the small bathroom near the back door. Mr. Leopolds and Jekabs, leaning heads together over bowls of dough, obviously didn't expect that. He could tell they'd stopped talking about something as soon as they saw him. Maybe they'd been calling him names in their secret language again. Maybe they'd been bad-mouthing the Germans as usual.

It came out like when he'd had the flu. He sat dejectedly, listening hard for fear the NKVD would raid the bakery, discover him, and drag him off the toilet. He'd got an upset stomach listening to Uncle Eli and that scraggly-bearded man saying the Germans wouldn't be coming for another two weeks. That was a long time to hide here, especially since the Leopolds were clearly mad at him. Sheesh, the way they'd jumped all over him you'd think Sniedze had been the liar instead of Vilz. But *no*, he's the one to get chewed out for being honest, for getting the facts straight, for telling Mr. Leopolds the truth about the typewriter. That was not moral.

Neither was their view of the Germans, Sniedze reasoned from the porcelain thinking chair. Sure, Germans didn't allow Jews to go to the cinema or own land. But the Russians didn't allow *anyone* to own land. Small price to pay for an army that crushed Communists like cockroaches. They even looked like heroes, all blond and big and good-looking. Two weeks. They'd be here in two weeks and this Russian nightmare would be over. Sniedze could stay hidden that long, if the Leopoldses didn't stay mad. Sheesh, anyone wearing a skullcap and a tasseled shawl is sure welcomed like a lost brother with hugs and free strudel. Remembering his mother's rule to wash up afterward, he didn't. His life depended on getting back to his hiding place.

As he dashed through the kitchen, Mr. Leopolds said, "Sniedze, you could use something to eat."

"No, thank you, Mr. Leopolds."

"You need something solid in your system, boychik. Have a piece of bread. Come on, just a shtikl."

Eating was the last thing Sniedze wanted to do. It would require more risky trips to the toilet. He curled on the bottom shelf completely blocked from view by the pantry stores, his innards a poisonous, bubbling stew. Willing his bodily functions to shut down, he felt paralyzed, except for a knee-jerk surge of fear every time the bakery door jingled. He closed his eyes, wanting to turn off every sense, and restart life in two weeks.

"Sniedze."

Sniedze opened his eyes to find Mr. Leopolds kneeling in front of him. He wondered how much time had passed, because Mr. Leopolds was now wearing a brown suit with a black tie. "What do you say we take the trolley over to your house and check how your mother fared?" Mr. Leopolds said. "It's more or less on the way to the school, anyway."

Sniedze thought for a moment, picturing the tiny apartment where he lived. "We wouldn't be able to tell by looking whether the NKVD had been there or not," he answered. "You know how it is? My sister moved out. Mama is gone all the time with her new fellow. So, nay. No point in going there."

Was Mr. Leopolds trying to get rid of him?

"Okay. But either way, it's time to get moving," Mr. Leopolds persisted.

"I'm not going anywhere," Sniedze said.

"We're leaving for graduation," Mr. Leopolds said. "I'm closing the shop. If you really don't want to go, like I said, we can take you home."

They were kicking him out! Turning him over to the Cheka, practically!

"I'm getting my diploma," Jekabs said, peering down at him from over his uncle's shoulder. "You'll understand when it's your turn. You should come to the ceremony. But you can't be seen with me looking like a shlump, so wash up. You're covered in dust balls."

Sniedze could see he had no choice, but as soon as he stood up, he needed to rush for the toilet again.

The sun blazed an arc above Riga's Central Rail Station. There was scant shade, and leaving to find a toilet risked separation from his family. Hugo looked for weaknesses in the guarded perimeter, remembering six months ago, how he'd outrun the Cheka at the Corner House. There was a chance he could get away again, but never with his mother and sister in tow, so he didn't think about it anymore.

"That lady has a seriously big bottom," Elza said, pointing out a woman who looked like she had pigs wrestling under her skirt. "If I have to sit by her, I really will kill myself."

"And that couple over there," she said, pointing, "living reminders of the Stone Age."

Elza nodded at a fancy looking lady. "Mutton dressed as lamb."

Hugo saw what she meant. The once-pretty lady had, too much loose skin drooping from her arms for such a girlish, summer blouse.

His sister's sense of humor was childish, but she made him feel like a human being.

At three o'clock in the afternoon, Hugo was eating bread and cheese from the pillowcase, when he realized his high school graduation ceremony was starting.

"Hey, graduation is happening right now," he told his mother. The family had planned to attend the ceremony together. The recollection came with a stab of worry for his father. Then, with another kind of ache, he thought of his friends gathered, probably dressed up and going forward with their futures, while he was here, the future on ice. He stuffed the remainder of his lunch away in the pillowcase, not hungry.

Mrs. Krumins nodded. "Congratulations, Valedictorian."

43

SNIEDZE KRASTS SCURRIED ALONG BEHIND the Leopoldses, aiming to reach the high school's massive wooden doors before the boogeyman got him. Commencement exercises were held every year in a big echoing auditorium with stained glass windows that reminded him of church, a worrisome notion since church was outlawed. Mr. Leopolds sat down in the audience area with a few other parents, but Sniedze felt like a heel sitting with the oldsters, where other kids might think he had no friends, so he tagged along backstage behind Jekabs.

Expectancy bubbled backstage, Sniedze noted with a snort of disdain, as if the graduation candidates thought in an hour they'd suddenly turn into adults. They tittered like fledglings about to fly, complete with mushy sentiments and inside jokes. Sniedze never had anything to say to Jekabs's peers, who were two grades above him, though he longed to jump into all the small-talk chatter with a ripping clever line. His knees knobbed from between his shorts and tall socks like white signposts saying, I'm an idiot! He lowered his newsboy cap over his eyes.

A redhead with sculpted wavy hair and her blonde friend came over, practically throwing themselves at Jekabs, who seemed to take for granted how well his suit fit as he hugged them.

"Jekabs! I would never have survived trig without your help!" the redhead said, batting her eyelashes. "Am I ever going to see you again?"

The girls were a stupefying swirl of perfume, gloves and curls, in dresses dipping down nearly to their ankles. In their stacked heels, Sniedze could barely see over the crest of their corsage-stuck bosoms. He didn't know where to look.

"Jekabs, you're here! I was afraid you were missing too," the blonde said. "Half the class is gone."

Sniedze looked around at where half the class should be, stomach churning.

"I almost didn't come either," the blonde said, "but who knows when we'll see each other again. Look at this." She pushed a scrap of handwriting under his nose. "My mother and I came home to an empty house and this note."

Sniedze leaned in front of Jekabs's shoulder to read it.

Your husband has left to pursue opportunities elsewhere!!!

He sends heartfelt regards to you and your daughter!!!!

Signed, Colleagues

"What do you make of it?" she whispered. "We don't know what to do."

Jekabs shook his head, a vertical crease between his eyebrows, as if he didn't want to break the bad news to her. He finally said, "It's as if they're mocking you."

The sinister note made a ripple of sickness run up Sniedze's intestinal tract.

A blond, tanned fellow, one of the athletic types, sidled over to see what they were looking at, though Sniedze thought he was probably more interested in the pigeons flocking around Jekabs than in the note. His name was Hans Something. Sniedze had seen the fellow heralded at school sporting events.

"There are bizarre notes stuffed in the cracks of doors all over my apartment building, too," the redhead said. "Has everyone been, you know ... what's happened to everyone?"

"Did you hear about the missing children?" whispered the blonde. "Their school bus took them directly to the rail yard. And when their parents went to find them they were all detained there as well. Can you imagine?"

Sniedze could.

"We shouldn't talk about it," the redhead said primly, suddenly buttoning her mouth and standing like a coat rack.

"First I've heard of this," blond Hans said with a superior air.

Hans was just miffed that the girls liked Jekabs better, Sniedze reckoned.

"Nothing about it in the papers," Hans said.

"No, well there wouldn't be," Jekabs said.

With a snide look at Jekabs, Hans said, "It was peaceful in my neighborhood last night." Then he sidled over to another crowd, one looking unburdened by knowledge of the deportations.

Another cluster of students were laughing loudly and coming backstage together. Sniedze couldn't see over their heads, but he knew that voice from the center, and his heart swelled with relief. Pushing his way through the circle, he saw Vilz in the middle of her classmates, cracking jokes. Sniedze hardly recognized her without her trademark bomber jacket. Her hair was slicked back, and she'd put on a simple blouse and a trouser suit, like that American Katherine Hepburn!

Vilz didn't ignore him. "My good man, Sniedze!" she cried, grasping Sniedze's hand and pumping it. "You came to witness my graduation!"

"Heads up," Sniedze whispered, pulling Vilz close. "Mr. Leopolds found your typewriter. He said you were a liar and you need to have a sit-down."

Vilz raised her eyebrows. Then she lifted her gaze over Sniedze's shoulder. Jekabs was standing there.

"Cat's out of the bag?" Vilz said, quietly.

Jekabs nodded.

"Sorry," Vilz said. "Did I get you in a cesspool of trouble?"

"We'll talk later," Jekabs said.

Sniedze stiffened, sensing Jekabs meant they'd talk when Sniedze wasn't there. "You seen Hugo?" Jekabs added hurriedly.

Vilz looked around, shrugging. "Where is everybody else, for that matter? Twice as many students were here at rehearsal."

The approaching click of dress shoes on the auditorium floor cut short the questioning.

"Here comes the Dean," someone said.

"Show's about to start, Sniedze," Jekabs said. "Why don't you go sit with Uncle Eli?"

There it was, Sniedze thought, Jekabs giving him the brush-off again.

"That way you can get the full effect of us walking across the stage to get our diplomas," Jekabs said, in a more coaxing tone.

"Yah," Vilz said, dimples giving away her cheer. "Witness a little-known and soon-to-be-forgotten moment in history."

Feeling stupid, Sniedze separated himself from the excited tangle of graduates. He headed toward the rows of chairs in the auditorium, a dolt among grownups.

Then he saw Frieda, a girl his age who lived in his apartment building. Even with long yellow braids, sturdy shoes and no lipstick, Frieda didn't look the least bit self-conscious standing by herself. Sniedze expected her to ignore him like all the other girls had, but she acknowledged him with a little smile and a singular gesture, a straight, outstretched, palm-down arm. She was brazen, and pretty. Her notice made Sniedze feel not only included, but somehow wiser than everyone there.

He would not sit down with Mr. Leopolds and the old folks after all. He would stand by Frieda. Heart racing, hoping no one saw him, Sniedze returned the gesture. It was the hand signal that meant you were for the Germans. "Hold onto your hats!" the motion shouted. They were coming to square things, and the world would quake under their jackboots.

Footsteps clicked rapidly across the stage, making everyone look to where the Dean strode into view carrying a stack of large envelopes. Walking briskly down the steps to the backstage anteroom, he confronted the students.

Sniedze expected the Dean to announce last minute directions such as *Walk Tall* across the stage. *Stand with Dignity* at the podium while he presents the diploma. *No Talking* as you file into the chairs across the back of the stage. After all the diplomas are handed out, *Sit Still for Speeches and Pose for the Group Photograph.*

But, instead, the Dean didn't even look at the students. "Berzins? Uldis Berzins?" he said, scrutinizing the first on the stack of envelopes.

The group looked at one another, shifting weight from foot to foot.

"He's not here, sir," someone replied.

"Kristine Bukss?"

"Not here either, sir."

Sniedze hoped the Dean would clarify for any doubters why so many students were missing, and give them some advice about where to hide, but he didn't.

"Ludvigs Circenis?" said the Dean.

"Here, sir," said a boy in an immaculate, starched shirt. Stepping forward, he offered a single stemmed lily to the Dean.

"Very good." The Dean handed an envelope to Ludvigs Circenis and took the lily without looking up. "What about Hugo Krumins?"

Sniedze's throat went dry. Where was Hugo? Sniedze tried to exchange meaningful looks with Jekabs and Vilz, but to his dismay, they weren't even paying attention! They were whispering. The way their heads tilted close together roiled jealousy in Sniedze's heart.

"Hugo Krumins?" the Dean repeated.

"He's Valedictorian… " a girl murmured.

Shaking his head, the Dean announced the next name, working his way through the stack of diplomas, finding that only one student out of every three or four called was present.

Where was Hugo? Sniedze thought, panic rattling his ribcage. What were Jekabs and Vilz talking about? Him? Jekabs showed Vilz something in the palm of his hand, something written or drawn on a scrap of paper.

"Jekabs Leopolds."

So intent was Jekabs, he didn't hear his name called, didn't realize everyone was staring at him.

"Leopolds," the Dean repeated.

Jekabs's head snapped around and he strode forward. As he reached for his diploma, someone with a loud voice said, "Parasite."

Sniedze couldn't believe it.

It was blond Hans, who wasn't even trying to hide the fact he'd been rude.

Sniedze held his breath, awaiting the disciplinary smack sure to follow.

The Dean looked up at Hans, then his eyes returned to the stack of envelopes, as if he hadn't heard the dirty crack.

Jekabs was frozen, his hand grasping his diploma. Reddening, he looked pointedly at the heckler.

Hans smirked, unruffled.

Sniedze suddenly felt embarrassed. What if Frieda knew he was with Jekabs, had seen them come in together? Right now Jekabs looked such a spectacle. Foolish, the way he'd gotten all dressed up, like his graduation was so important. Thank God, Jekabs took his diploma without further drama, returning to his place. A small, worm-sized part of Sniedze felt it somehow served Jekabs right, for calling Sniedze a squealer. Clearly Sniedze wasn't the only person thinking Jekabs was too coiffed and bossy. Maybe he'd have more humility now.

Vilz stepped up beside Jekabs, arms folded and eyes blazing.

The Dean worked his way to the "Z"s, finally calling Vilz Zarins. Vilz went forward and snatched her diploma, giving the Dean a hard eye, but the Dean never even looked at her.

Every envelope had been read.

"That's that," the Dean said, turning to the milling students. "So, please go." He turned on his heel and strode out of the building, dropping the unclaimed diplomas in a backstage waste bin.

"How does he come up with such pearls of wisdom?" Vilz said, passing around cigarettes as they stood on the cement terrace outside of the auditorium. "*That's that.* Does he give the same address every year I wonder? Or is this special advice for the class of '41?"

Mr. Leopolds looked preoccupied. Probably going to lay into Vilz at any second, Sniedze thought, secretly looking forward to it so he wouldn't be the only one called a nebbish.

"Allow me to address the graduates with advice for the future," Mr. Leopolds said, stepping forward with his lighter. "Be noble. Be fearless. But avoid trouble whenever possible. So with that in mind, let's walk home by a different route, because I don't like the looks of Goldilocks and the three thugs over there."

He nodded to where Hans and a few other boys, all athletic types, were laughing loudly, looking primed for some sporting event, watching the Leopoldses and blocking access to the sidewalk.

Yah, let's please avoid trouble, Sniedze thought, noticing Jekabs and Hans locking eyes across the campus, the hatred between them sizzling even though they used to be friends. Sniedze couldn't tell which one broke away first, but Jekabs finally turned his eyes to the clouds that had crept up.

"Looks like rain," Jekabs said dully. He turned to walk with Mr. Leopolds in the opposite direction from where they wanted to go.

Vilz exhaled a stream of smoke. "Yah, and that's that," she said, stepping in with Sniedze behind the Leopoldses.

As he followed along, Sniedze had the uneasy feeling he was running with, who his mother would call, the Wrong Crowd. The last thing he needed right now was more enemies. Nor did he deserve to be painted with the same brush as Jekabs, whose popularity was nosediving. Maybe Vilz felt the same way, because they hadn't gone very far when Vilz, walking with her hands in her pockets, quietly said, "Sniedze, you were right. I can't type at the bakery anymore."

"What?" Sniedze whispered, casting a look around. "Did old Leopolds give you an earful?"

"Hey, I was wondering," Vilz said, a few steps later. "No one's ever home at your place. Want to slum it over there?"

"*My* house? When?"

"Right now."

"Sheesh. Mr. Leopolds's really steamed at you then."

"Yah," Vilz said, nodding. "That's it." She looked sheepish.

Sniedze suspected there was more to the story. Maybe Vilz would spill the details when the Leopoldses weren't around. "So," he said. "Just be the two of us?"

"Right."

That appealed to Sniedze. Though, again, he felt he didn't have the complete picture. "Did the Leopolds say they wanted me gone? Are they throwing me out of the bakery along with you?"

Vilz didn't answer. She was frowning at the rustling branches in the hedge before them.

With a crackling of foliage they jumped out of nowhere, Hans and some muscled-up buddy of his, already free of coat and tie. Hans stepped directly in front of the Leopoldses, trying to halt them with an outstretched palm and a malicious eye. Sniedze glanced behind him.

The rest of Hans's gang was already there. They'd been surrounded before Sniedze even knew it was an attack.

"Hold up, Jew-boy," Hans said. "You're not allowed on the sidewalks in civilized countries."

Fear zinged Sniedze to his toes. He hated fights. Run, he thought. He could dart between them. He could get away. Run, before someone caught him, before his guts liquefied. Too bad for old Mr. Leopolds, who was practically forty. He'd never be able to outrun the likes of Hans and his track-team cohorts. But Sniedze, legs flexed for a getaway, could make it.

Jekabs and Mr. Leopolds stubbornly kept walking, forcing Hans to walk backward.

"Why do you suddenly want to be an ass, Hans?" Vilz asked, soldiering on behind the Leopoldses. "We've all been walking on this sidewalk together since Grade Three."

"Shut up, Zarins," Hans said. "This doesn't have to involve you."

"For someone who just celebrated an education," Vilz said, "your stupidity is appalling."

"I'm stupid? You keep company with clip-tips and you think I'm stupid?"

"Christ-killers," said a guy coming from behind. He pushed Jekabs, who stumbled but regained his footing.

Hans got right in front of Mr. Leopolds, cleared his throat and spat on him.

Mr. Leopolds stopped. There was a pop of fabric, the rustle of Mr. Leopolds's sleeve, and Hans was suddenly lying where he had just stood.

The other attackers shrank back, staring at their leader silently, shriveled like a mouth after false teeth removed.

Mr. Leopolds took out his handkerchief and wiped his shirtfront. He bent over slightly, examining Hans's jellied figure. When Hans's eyelids fluttered open, Mr. Leopolds stood up, straightened his suit and kept walking, resuming the rhythm of his previous stride.

"Sidewalk's all yours, shitheel," Jekabs said over his shoulder, as he kept pace with his uncle.

"Let's rethink this, Hans," Vilz said to her former classmate, stepping over his body without pausing.

Sniedze skittered around Hans's legs. Walking with his head craned backward, he saw Hans roll up to sitting, covering his face with his hands. It didn't look like Hans was going to chase them. Mr. Leopolds had punched him down like a rising blob of white dough.

Following the others as they crossed the street, Sniedze said, "I knew we shouldn't a come." They walked down Lenin without speaking. Rain began to patter.

When they got to Sniedze's street, Vilz said, "So I'm going to Sniedze's, like we said."

"Okay, let's call it a night," Jekabs agreed.

"Congratulations, Graduate," Mr. Leopolds said, clapping Vilz on the back. "*Ar labinacht*, Sniedze."

"Good night," Sniedze returned. *What in hell is happening?* He swirled in the delirium that had unhinged him countless times in the last twenty-four hours. This morning he'd sworn he wouldn't set foot outside the Leopolds Bakery or leave their protection until the Germans arrived, but now he felt the Leopoldses themselves were somehow the dangerous ones and he couldn't wait to get away.

"See you around, Sniedze," Jekabs said.

The crack of a summer lightning storm split the sky, and a wall of water poured out even as the thunder pealed. Branching away from the Leopoldses, Sniedze and Vilz started running, water rivulets coursing their faces, shoes slapping on shiny sidewalks with puddle reflections distorting streetlights and signs. For a moment, a blip of fun tried raising its head above the flatline routine of terror. Then something snagged Sniedze's mind, something Vilz had said. "I'm going to Sniedze's, *like we said.*"

Sniedze's suspicions had been correct. They *had* been talking behind his back.

44

JUST WHEN HUGO KRUMINS THOUGHT matters could get no worse, a swiftly moving cloudburst drenched him and his belongings. Now the crowded, exposed deportees were also soaked.

"Hey Valedictorian, why didn't you pack an umbrella?" his sister said, tenting the overcoat Mr. Pērkons had given her above her head.

Hugo was way ahead of her, upbraiding himself for not bringing more water jugs, more canned goods and nuts, a sturdier knife, fishing hooks, and heavier clothes. In the panic of the NKVD arrests, he had not maximized the hundred kilo limit allotted his family. And his father had been separated without taking practically anything.

The beleaguered deportees stagnated miserably into the night.

"I'm sick of waiting around," Elza whined, stir-crazy. "Let's board the stupid train and get where we're going!"

"Careful what you wish for," their mother muttered. "Whatever special place the Russians have prepared will no doubt make us yearn for this wretched train depot.

Hugo sat on the wet concourse, arms folded over his knees. Inured to the ambient dirge, the tense silence of bucked up courage, children crying, the sporadic shout and gunshot, he fell asleep.

The leaden cloud in his head refused to budge at first. But Elza kept shaking him. Hugo opened his eyes to see his mother's chunky square heels. She was already standing with the crowd. Hugo got up and picked up their things, yawning. Now that he'd been roused, he wanted to get going. But nobody was moving. He was forced to just stand amid cranky children, jostled and pushed by centimeters toward the platform.

In the morning sunlight, Hugo saw for the first time the rail cars they were to board. They were not even meant for humans. He was herded past carriages already loaded with people, fear filling his lungs along with the stale stench of livestock. Some cars were still open, the victims crowded inside somehow cowed into silence. Other cars had been sealed, their wooden rolling doors heavily shut. Disembodied laments and a sour terror seeped from small, high windows.

Guards blocking his path indicated Hugo was to board the car on his right.

"All the way to the back of the carriage," the guard said. "Step to the back!"

Elza obeyed, whispering, "I do believe someone may have peed in here."

Hugo gulped fresh air and, feeling weirdly lightheaded, stepped over the gap into the car. He tried to look calm, in hopes his mother would remain so.

But Mrs. Krumins caught one whiff of the dank wooden box and dug her heels in. "No! No, no, no, no, no!" she cried. "I'm not getting into this rolling casket. Why are we going along with this?"

Hugo dropped the pillowcase inside the car and stepped back out to take his mother's arm. "Quiet," he said into her ear. "Do you want to be taken away from us too? Then get in here. Don't give them any reason to notice you."

He finessed her on board, looking for a way to make her comfortable as the car filled with people. One end of the car had two wide shelf-like benches where people were stacking their bags and kids were climbing to get near the windows. Elza plopped her suitcase on one, staking a claim as it were, but the notion of reserved seating was trampled by the surge of refugees, crushing them against the back wall.

Hugo heard his mother snipe, "Watch it. For godsakes, that's my foot." A baby was inconsolable. Bodies packed shoulder-to-shoulder like a densely crowded elevator.

"We'll suffocate," Mrs. Krumins announced, her eyes crazed like a drowning swimmer's. The next second she was frantically squeezing her way between shoulders, clawing her way back toward the open door. Once there she clutched the frame in both hands, thrusting her face into open air. She clung there, disobeying the order to move to the back of the carriage. "We'll bake crossing Russia in this oven."

"We're going to Russia?" a girl said. She appeared to be in her mid-twenties with a round face.

"We're full," Mrs. Krumins told the guard. "This car is full."

Hugo winced at her imperious tone, which carried clearly to the back of the car.

"Who said they're taking us to Russia?" the girl repeated.

"Not *to* Russia," Mrs. Krumins said with disdain. "*Across* Russia. They've banished Harmful Elements to Siberia since the czars. Did you think we were going to the Crimean Riviera?" Mrs. Krumins clung to the doorframe as more people crammed in. "We're going to the gulags, dearie."

It was one of those unlikely moments, when the fear chatter had died down in unison right before Mrs. Krumins uttered her poisonous prophecy. Everybody heard it.

"What's a gulag?" a little boy with blond ringlets asked, tugging on his mother.

The child's mother was a robust woman around thirty with a baby in one arm and a bulging diaper-bag in the other. She looked daggers at Mrs. Krumins. "Keep your opinions to yourself, lady."

"It's not an opinion," Mrs. Krumins said, dourly. "We're all going to hell. Mark my words."

"Mother!" Hugo reprimanded from behind several rows of heads. Catching her eye for a moment, he shook his head vigorously trying to stifle her noxious attitude.

"What's hell?" the little boy said, blue eyes huge and shimmery.

"Stop scaring him," the diaper-bagged mother ordered in a loud voice. "I will strangle that old woman if she opens her mouth again," she promised to the car at large.

"Get back," shouted the green uniform, as another wave of unwilling newcomers crammed on board, met by resentment from those loaded moments before. "All the way back."

More bodies squeezed in, shoulder-to-shoulder, until finally, there was room for no more.

Hugo kept next to Elza. He had to stretch and lean to see around the heads and the toddlers held against shoulders, but he tried to keep an eye on his mother where she stood in the open doorway, watching her with worry.

A green uniform filled the doorway, hands on hips.

"Here is deal," the uniform announced, silhouetted in the opening holding up a bucket. "If you wait quiet. If you do not put one toe outside of carriage, I leave door open to fresh air until we go. If I close door, it won't open again for long time."

Gasps and horrified twitters of consent rose from the boxcar victims, as mothers desperately silenced children. Hugo prayed his mother would not choose this moment to tell the soldier that he was a loathsome *kāpost galva* or announce that they were all going to hell. He could see her chin quivering from the effort of reining in her jaw.

Seeming satisfied with the intimidated passengers, the soldier pushed the bucket to the woman closest to him, who, to Hugo's consternation, happened to be his mother. "Use this until we get moving," the soldier said. "Then use the hole."

Mrs. Krumins, comprehending that she was to excrete in front of a rail car full of strangers, looked at the bucket as if it were already full of shit. She pushed it far from her body, holding it outside the carriage.

The guard was incredulous at her nerve or stupidity, staring at her like a vicious dog meeting a nasty polecat. Hugo tried squeezing between bodies, to head off a misunderstanding, but before he was near enough, he heard her low, venomous voice say, "I will bite off my fingers before I work Stalin's mines, so you might as well shoot me now."

The guard grabbed the pail and knocked Mrs. Krumins's head so hard it clanked, before flinging it into the car.

"Close it," he said to his comrade, who yanked the sliding door.

At the last moment, he grabbed two women crossing the platform, and pushed them into the already crowded car. Each was followed by a scurrying bevy of children, desperate to stay together, to find floor space for tiny feet.

Hugo roared as bodies crushed inward for the final compaction needed so the rolling door could slam shut. He couldn't breathe.

Protests echoed in the dark. Children cried like a nursery school was on fire. Mothers' high-pitched, panicked voices couldn't calm them. The only source of air and light were small rectangular windows, high up and barred.

After minutes, a sort of settling rested the passengers. A sense of acceptance set in. This is what it would be. They'd feared this. But with a jittery apprehensive fear, now supplanted by a heavier dread. They were already acclimating to this latest circle of hell.

Whether from practice or weight loss, Kārlis Pērkons easily squeezed between the barn doors and crouched against them silently. The midnight sky was dross silver. The forest was full of noises, but he did not detect the presence of another human. His stomach growled. He'd consumed most of the communion wafers, and every berry and mushroom within foraging range. Kārlis was on a mission to find food.

He struck out through the trees, seeking the nearest road to the nearest town.

"You are dragging me down," he told the shovel, reluctantly stowing it behind a pine.

The first byway he encountered was dirt. Kārlis followed it to a paved road, his north star to civilization, someone's garden, a chicken coop, trash bins, or a refuse heap. His mouth watered. He hiked along the road ready to flee at the first sight of a blocking detachment, a unit charged with shooting evaders or stragglers. A sign said he was walking into Gulbene, population 16,000.

The forest ended abruptly at a field of uniformly spaced trees.

An orchard. Kārlis ran to the nearest fruit tree and yanked at its branches. The small greenish whatever-they-weres were hard as stones. He chewed one anyway, the unripe flesh souring his mouth, eyes stinging at the failure to get an apple. He tried another and spit it out. Inedible. He swallowed his disappointment and put a steadying hand against the trunk. He would rather be hungry than sick.

At the far edge of the field, steel screeched. Lights glared eerily over the treetops. Kārlis heard the hissing hydraulics of a locomotive. The orchard was adjacent to a rail yard that was roiling with commotion. Strings of carriages groaned and chattered over the tracks. What were the Russians up to at 2:30 am, buzzing around the trains like evil bees? Probably scrambling to make ready for the German army. Yah! That would explain the frenetic pitch. Probably running back to Moscow. And good riddance!

Kārlis regarded the rail complex with anxiety. It sprawled over both sides of the road into town. Tracks and platforms on one side, on the other high fencing topped with coiled barbed wire outlined a yard of lit up warehouses. In the distance, a man shouted. A dog barked. Though he longed to enter the town where he imagined milk bottles on door stoops and pies on windowsills, this place reeked of the military and the thought of taking one step closer killed Kārlis's appetite.

He could backtrack and bushwhack a circuitous, safer route into the town. But by the time he went kilometers out of his way, why not just point himself toward Riga and hike home? He could be sitting down to his mother's home cooking in a week.

An auto engine whined, growing louder until it changed up gears. Kārlis knelt at the base of the trunk, watching for headlights in the gray light, debating what to do.

Nay to striking out for Riga on a whim. Strategy shouldn't be decided on impulse. He couldn't just leave his shovel behind. Things should be done in the proper order. He didn't know if he was cowardly or wise, but angrily, Kārlis turned back, retreating to the barn of outlawed art. He would rather be hungry than caught.

The sleeping alcove was sunny by the time Sniedze Krasts woke up and shuffled for the kitchen end of the studio apartment. Right away, he was disappointed to see Vilz's blanket folded on the empty sofa. Vilz must've already crept out, as she had done every morning since graduation.

Sniedze put a pan of water on the hotplate, knowing that somewhere among the empty bottles and salami rinds Vilz had left a note saying she was going to "get her typewriter," "find a bloke," "scrounge groceries" or "work for her father". Always a reason to leave early and not return until the end of the day.

Sniedze had warned Vilz it was foolhardy to leave the safety of the apartment. But it was just as dangerous to stay put, as everybody now knew the NKVD plucked their victims right from their homes. Given such bleak prospects, Sniedze saw no point in clearing away garbage, stuffing clothes in a corner, or washing dishes. His mother wouldn't be nagging him about cleanliness, wherever she was, inseparable from her new fellow.

He was searching the cupboard for another packet of tea, when he came across a small bottle labeled *phenobarbitone sodium*, prescribed for his mother's nerves. White tablets rattled when he shook it, more than half full. Pouring hot water over the tea strainer, he considered taking some medicine. He was certainly overwrought with nerves worrying if he would ever see Vilz again. Every day, paralyzed with fear, Sniedze watched the world from the window of the second floor apartment, knowing he'd be either the next one taken or the only one left.

He threw the teacup across the room. How had things got twisted around so he was here alone, helpless and furious, waiting for Vilz's return like a jealous mate? He missed the bakery, the Leopoldses razzing him and the fresh bread. Those times were through. He knew it.

Shaking, Sniedze shook out a few of the sedatives, for bravery, and chased them down his throat with water. He flopped on the couch and lay looking at a crack in the ceiling. He'd spent much of his life waiting in this apartment for things that never materialized, for his mother to check in on him or for his older sister to drop by, and now for Vilz to come back and for the German army to make things safe again. Waiting for nothing, sick of life, he hated it here. Sniedze wondered if he'd feel like living again even if the Germans came today. He slept like the dead and woke up not giving a damn about Vilz.

Slap'n scuff, slap'n scuff, slap'n scuff.

The sound drew Sniedze to the window where the sun shone high in the sky. He felt eerily out of touch with the world, but pleasantly surprised to recognize Frieda on the sidewalk with her jump rope. Though he knew Frieda lived in his building, he hadn't seen her since they'd chatted at graduation. Sniedze watched her yellow braids catch air and fall with each beat, mesmerized.

He shook out a few more tablets but then stopped. He'd better save them. The white pills could be his solution to the Russian problem, really the only one he had. Everybody ought to have a plan, Sniedze thought, feeling shrewd. If the Germans didn't come soon, this would be his.

The Victors. K. Smiltens, 1945.

45

CHUBBY FINGERS STRETCHED TOWARD the small, high, barred window of the rail car. Round-faced toddlers were held up, bleating for light and air. Hugo gave up hope for a place at the window. He sank down, resting on his haunches, overlapping his knees with others trying to find space to sit. Constant motion surrounded him. *Kinder* crawled and careened over every surface, babbling, squealing, screaming, trespassing like Hugo was more luggage. How did this happen? Not just the bogus arrest, but being incarcerated with the women and children? Hugo dropped his head over folded arms. He should be with the men.

"He's cutting a tooth," said the mother of an inconsolable, to whomever she thought was listening. "Suffering dreadfully."

Hugo recognized his mother's voice from across the car. "We're going to suffocate." She sounded subdued, and Hugo remembered the guard bucketing her head.

"Well, if we do, it's your fault," said a loud woman, whose voice rang above the other curses aimed at Mrs. Krumins.

In contrast to Loudmouth, another lady started to sing,

Hush-a-bye, hush, my bear cubs, hush-a-bye, hush,

as if she might soothe the bickerers.

With your little brown bear feet, hush, hush, hush.

Many of the children calmed right down, scooting closer to Lullaby Lady. Hugo felt weight slide off his shoulders at her lilting voice. *Father brought a honey pot, hush-a-bye, hush.* Elza joined in and singing picked up through the carriage. By the second verse, the women were breathing slower. By the third verse some were harmonizing. Disparate notes blended into spontaneous fleeting enchanting music, making it seem that the deportees could handle, even outfox, the Cheka.

Then the charm wore thin, and the imprisoned children resumed fussing. Lullaby quickly tossed out her glove, starting a game of the Old Man's Mitten.

The kids swamped her, climbing over each other for a make-believe animal role.

"Dear, dear! Everybody wants to be in this mitten," Lullaby said with romper room aplomb.

Hugo thought Lullaby was clever, making the overcrowded children think it would be fun to cram into an even tighter space.

"Ruta's feeling left out," Loudmouth said, pushing a child forward by the shoulders. "Can't she play?"

"In you go then, Ruta! You're the frog," Lullaby said. "But don't say we didn't warn you! It's crowded in there."

"We'll go bonkers before we ever leave the station," Elza said to Hugo.

Not everyone was enthralled in the game. Some tikes were fingering and mouthing every surface within reach of their pudgy arms. In the corner, someone went potty in the bucket to the cheers of an adoring audience. Someone named Oliver had put a "diamond" up his nose. A bobble-headed baby was learning to hold up his neck.

"Make room for the Bear!" Lullaby said, over spasms of laughter. "See, we can all fit!" Lullaby addressed the point of her allegory to the broader congregation. "There's room for all."

"Idiots," Hugo's mother cried. "That wretched mitten story is Marxist propaganda."

Hugo pictured her clutching fistfuls of her white hair.

Loudmouth said, "Lady, you are damned lucky to be over there where I can't get my hands around your bony neck."

A scream went up. The frog had pulled the mouse's hair. Someone poked an eye. Mothers of injured parties got involved. Lullaby refereed, her tone growing sharper until the mitten game boiled over like scummy milk.

"All the nursery rhymes in the country can't help us now," Mrs. Krumins moaned. "Has no one here ever heard of the Road of Bones?"

"Shut up!"

"Pass the water, please," said a grandmother.

"Sorry," was the polite answer from the mother of a gold ringlet clan. "I have three children. I have to make mine stretch."

"Here. Take mine," said Lullaby, thrusting her jug over pointedly. "I say we share food and water and diapers and so forth in a civilized manner. How many of us have water?"

Hugo felt his grip tighten on the pillowcase of stores. He admired Lullaby's spirit, but a base voice told him that those who shared their water would soon run out and find themselves at the mercy of those who didn't want to share. Such a situation would bring out the worst in his mother. So he ignored the question. No one could really see the show of hands, anyway, in the semi-dark.

"I know what water's made of."

"What?"

"Clouds! And I know where water comes from."

"Where?"

"Pipes!"

"Why don't you like beets?"

Lullaby shouted over the children's chatter. "We're going to have to trust each other," she said. But her confident tone was already wavering. "Small sips," she told the grandmother.

A slender lady with a long brown braid lifted the jug to her grandmother's mouth. Hugo felt something primal stir as he followed the flow of water with his eyes. After Grandmother drank, the jug went to a mother whose blouse was rolled off her shoulder exposing a breast larger than the head of the baby sucking it. She upended the jug with one strong hand and chugged, before finally passing the remainder to another guzzling wet-nurse.

A green glass bottle was also opened and, with much wiping to prevent germs, the youngsters were watered. The "wolf" insisted on lapping his from a bowl on the floor.

At this rate of consumption the train had better get moving.

Hugo shifted cramped legs.

"Oooh, I can hardly wait to get somewhere, anywhere!" Elza said, looking longingly at the windows, where the backs of fluffy heads blocked light and the flow of air.

"Elza, these might be——" Hugo stopped. He'd been about to tell his sister that these could be the last moments in their homeland. Try to savor them. Instead he said, "The longer we tarry, the more likely the Germans will get here."

Hugo imagined a Nazi rescue. The likely scenario froze his blood. *Stukas* dive-bombing the rails while he and these fluffy-headed innocents were trapped inside this cattle car.

"*Sveiks*," Kārlis Pērkons whispered to the barn of wooden fugitives. He pressed a reassuring hand against the speared belly of the nearest altarpiece. "The Germans are coming."

Kārlis squeezed through the barn doors, prepared to not return, though the prospect of hiking two hundred kilometers across the country was daunting.

"Must be about nine," Kārlis deduced, polishing his glasses on the cleanest part of his shirt. He couldn't actually see the sunset, but its scarlet hue seeped through the trees surrounding the barn. An acrid note, like burning-tire smoke, met his nose.

In five days of hiding Kārlis had seen no sign of the barn's caretakers and he worried that the rebel docents had been caught.

He'd taken one of the canvas coverings, rolled it tight into a bedroll and made a strap for it. This he slung over his head. His military buzz cut had grown to a short, straight blonde cap. He'd ripped the insignia off his clothing, and turned the dark-blue shirt of a private in the Latvian 24th inside out. But these tricks wouldn't fool a Red hunting a deserter, or a German hunting a Red soldier, or some partisan sniper exacting justice from a distance, to name a few of the threats to his life running around the countryside. He'd filch someone's laundry first chance he got.

Shovel in hand, Kārlis left the hidden barn, making no disturbance that would attract attention to its illicit cache.

He set off through the forest much as he had two nights before, even following the dirt road toward Gulbene. But when he reached the paved road, Kārlis crossed it, going for the trees on the other side, following a deer trail to avoid the imbroglio he'd seen at the Gulbene rail station. He aimed to meet the railroad track at some unwatched point outside the town, and follow it west to the major line leading to Riga.

The actual forest was so much larger than it appeared on the map. After hours of hiking, he still saw no sign of the tracks. Doubt made every footfall heavier, until the distant whistle of a locomotive to his left gave him a bearing.

Forest gave way to farmland, monotonous fields of flax. Inedible.

He kept north, making a series of tacks on a grid of minor roads, and found himself going through a residential area. Modest plaster houses were set back on a gently curving road. Someone here probably had a delicious garden, Kārlis thought, searching the dark yards between structures. A row of mailboxes glowed in the midsummer penumbra. Kārlis opened one and immediately a dog started barking. Sweating, he checked every mailbox, finding nothing of use.

Before running off, he answered a curious calling and poked at a heap of burlap on a tree stump. A stirring aroma met him as he lifted the fabric and looked inside. To his amazement, it contained bread and something promising that crackled as he grabbed the whole bundle and ran.

Leaves crashed underfoot as he ran back into the woods. His heart leaped, his feet were dancing! What were the chances that food would be just sitting there, as if put out for him? It was a miracle. He bit off a chew of the bread while running, the whistle of a locomotive guiding him through the trees and toward the tracks.

Behind a pine's broad trunk, Kārlis ripped into the bag and found a parcel of caraway seed cheese, Jānu Siers! Just like what his mother always made for Midsummer. What a feast! He ate solemnly, only allowing himself a fraction of the bounty.

Fortified, Kārlis trekked until he saw the railroad track, a black zipper running up a green corridor between walls of trees. Seeing no one, he jogged out of the woods and up a gravel embankment to walk on the tracks. The sidewalk home. Now that his belly was full, he practiced the story he would tell Lileja, imagining her blue eyes huge with admiration, and walked faster.

"Hmmph. About time," Sniedze Krasts muttered from the window, at last sighting the Greek sea captain's hat and black leather bomber jacket coming around the corner. He sniffed and checked the wall clock, nearly midnight.

"Where's the typewriter?" Sniedze asked, opening the door before Vilz knocked.

Vilz pushed her lips together in a line that passed for an exhausted smile. "Hello to you too, Sniedze." She set a loaf of black bread on the table. "Whatcha wanna know?"

"You said you were going to get your typewriter," Sniedze said. "Does that take all day? Have you just been twiddling your thumbs at the bakery all night? What's going on?"

"I got some bad news," Vilz said, removing her hat.

Sniedze smirked. "No shortage of that." Vilz was hiding behind bad news to avoid his questions.

"Hugo's been taken by the NKVD."

Sniedze didn't move. Behind his eyeballs, a smug voice in the dank cell of his mind said, *Told you so! Guess who's next?*

"Your eyes look glassy," Vilz said. "You all right?"

"No! They're picking us off like sitting ducks," Sniedze said. "What do we do?"

"We hold the course, I guess," Vilz said, running hands through hair. "I don't know. The fellows who organized the meetings and told me what to do, they're gone too."

"Look who's next," Sniedze said, pointing to himself and to Vilz.

"The Germans are coming. Things will change," Vilz said, pulling a can of Vienna sausages from her jacket. "I just hope they get here in time to help Hugo." She pried the can opener from her pocketknife. "You better eat something."

"How do you know this about Hugo?" Sniedze said, not at all hungry.

"I was afraid that's why he didn't show up for graduation," Vilz said, slicing bread. "And Mr. Pērkons came by the bakery."

So, you all had a cozy reunion at the bakery without me, Sniedze thought acidly.

Vilz ate her portion of sausages and bread like a lumberjack.

"We're down to three," Sniedze said. "Just three of us left. You, me and Jekabs. Tomorrow, I'm going with you wherever it is you go."

"Sure," Vilz called from the bathroom. She came out damp-faced, in pyjamas, folding her trousers and draping them over the sofa.

"Don't skive off without me."

"Course not." Vilz stretched out on the couch, fluffing a sheet. "You're one of us, Sniedze. An original, founding Nonchalant. It's just that people have to trust—" she yawned widely. "Trust that you can keep your mouth shut, you know? So, don't talk about anyone, especially one of us. If you see something, just keep it under your hat." She punched the cushion and dropped her head on it. "Give the

Leopoldses some time to rebuild confidence in you. Could you turn off the lamp?"

Sniedze switched it off, but he didn't want to sleep. He'd been semi-comatose all day. So he sat dazedly, staring at Vilz and thinking about what she'd said. Rebuild trust. What had he ever done to destroy trust? The others weren't treating him square. He got up to swallow a couple of tranquilizers, to settle his nerves.

"Hey Sniedze," Vilz said quietly. "Remember when we made the Molotov cocktails?"

"Yah, but I never had nothing to do with that Corner House business."

"Right but, I'm just thinking... Hugo never threw his," Vilz said. "Do you happen to know where he stashed it? Did he ever tell you?"

Sniedze did not know. "If I did, you think I would tell you?" he sniped. "No! I would keep my trap shut to rebuild trust!"

Vilz rolled over, burying her face in the couch and moaning. "Oh brother! We got to work together, Sniedze." She yawned again. "That's how we beat this." Her voice trailed off. Soon Vilz was asleep.

Sniedze puzzled over the dust on Vilz's trousers. It wasn't the usual flour. It was flecks of sawdust.

46

A SOUND LIKE ROLLING THUNDER woke him. Hugo couldn't remember where he was at first, until his eyes found the high rectangle of light. Outside, the doors of rail cars were slamming shut in a series.

He'd been dreaming he was with Lileja, in her room above the Bier Schtube, a place he'd never been except in dreams. Waking to reality he bolted upright, drawing in his limbs, finding he'd sleep-slouched against the shoulder of a red-lipped lady, his first deep sleep in days. Hugo tugged his shirt over his crotch, embarrassed he was hard from the happy fantasy in Lileja's boudoir. The red-lipped lady, the one his sister had dubbed Mutton-Dressed-as-Lamb, was watching him. She raised a seraphic eyebrow, as if she knew all about Hugo and Lileja.

The car jerked beneath them.

The captives looked at each other, electric with hope.

"Hallelujah," Elza called out. "We're moving at last."

Cheers went up at the jostling and slight movement of air, a chance to use the toilet hole instead of the bucket. Everyone stretched, shifting positions expectantly, blessed to be finally moving closer to, what Hugo's mother kept calling, the death camps. Anywhere would be preferable to this endless waiting on the tracks.

"*Sveiks*," said a lady holding a little girl to the window for good-byes. "Send kisses to Papu."

Then Hugo heard the engines decline. The train glided to a standstill after maybe a hundred meters. Moans rose and the carriage fell silent. Hugo thought everyone, like him, was listening hard, craving to hear steel engage and feel forward momentum. But the train was at a dead stop.

The teething baby screamed.

"What's the *kāpost galva* hold-up?" Loudmouth yelled to the outside world.

Could it possibly be a rescue?

"Did anyone bring a thermometer?" someone clucked, oblivious to the bigger picture.

"*He should be quarantined.*"

"*My head tickles.*"

"*Wanna wiggle my tooth?*"

"*My Grandpa can take his teeth out.*"

"*I won't be your friend anymore.*"

"*Yah, but you'll still be my cousin. You have to have an operation to stop being my cousin.*"

The teething baby wailed.

"*Can't you make him stop? I just got her to sleep. Are you just going to let him cry?*"

"*He'll stop in a moment.*"

"Rub his gums."

"Mine have always slept through the night."

"Someone's hiding under the blanket. Peek-a-boo!"

"I wanna go home."

"My arms are burning," said a girl, holding a tot to the window. *"Pie joda."*

"Still full of people with suitcases," reported a boy from where he perched on the shelf. "And green uniforms and guns."

"What color does the other team wear?"

"They can't get in through the windows, can they?"

"Hold on to me, Mama. Blanket on me!"

"At least we're not in Father's car," Elza said, scratching her scalp. "Can you imagine the chainsaw snoring of the Heads of Households?"

What Hugo imagined for his father was unbearable. His cheeks burned at being trapped with the women and children.

"Why did you pack food in a pillowcase?" asked a boy around eight. "Why are you tall? Why? Why?"

Hugo turned his head away, accidently locking eyes with Mutton-dressed-as-Lamb.

"You're the only actual man among us," Mutton said, before Hugo could disengage from the tractor beam of her smoldering eyes.

"Why aren't you in the fathers's car?" Eight-Year-Old asked.

At Hugo's elbow, a round-faced girl around his age turned to gape at him. Hugo said nothing and she returned to wiping dribbles of gruel from her baby's chin with a rubber-coated spoon.

"Does anyone have something for fever?"

"I can see how you slipped through," Mutton said, nodding. "You have refined, aquiline features. And so attentive to your mother.

That's a nice quality in a young man." Mutton's legs were extended sideways from her hips, like interesting parallel lines intersecting the tangle of bodies pressing around her. She leaned against a stiff, palm-planted arm, arching her back slightly. "One arm around your mother. Luggage in the other arm. Lovely white hair flopped over your forehead. They never noticed those nice broad shoulders."

"It's not as if I had a grand plan to sneak into the women's car," Hugo protested from under her measuring eyes. Oh, who cared what this bag thought.

"You wouldn't have gotten by me," Mutton said. "Why, you even shave."

Breathing unevenly, Hugo was embarrassed to find his hand at his chin, rubbing peach fuzz.

Mutton winked.

Behind her, the thirsty grandmother sat propped up in a corner, looking wan.

Someone shrieked. Young Leonids had smuggled his pet toad on board. For this, he was made to face the corner.

"You'll be glad he did when you wind up eating it," Hugo's mother said.

"You want that filth bucket on your head again, Shrew?" Loudmouth blustered from across the car. "Just keep it up."

"She's entitled to her opinion, same as everyone else," Elza quipped.

Lullaby started singing, *Hush-a-bye, hush, my bear cubs, hush-a-bye, hush*. But to no effect.

Trying to avoid Mutton, Hugo crawled carefully over and between bodies, pushing his way to the window where a toddler teetered, arms outstretched. He picked her up and held her to the window for air.

"Out!" the toddler demanded.

Loudmouth came up beside him, blasting his eardrum as she yelled through the window. "Open the door! *Loudzu!* We need some air. We won't do anything. We'll do whatever you want."

Kārlis was making some time! Striding over the evenly spaced railroad ties was much faster than gimping around the forest edge in the half dark. In the distance another train was coming, a pinprick of light growing bigger, so Kārlis scrambled down the gravel embankment, dashed into the forest and waited for it to pass. Every train was going in the same direction. Were these Russia-bound cattle cars the beginning of a retreat?

"That's right! Get outta here you stinking red *kāpost galvas!*" Kārlis shook his fist at the receding caboose, a hop in his step. "Back where you came from! Begone!

"With you assholes out of the picture," Kārlis said, climbing up the gravel, "I'll be home in four, five nights tops—*Ahhk tu kungs!*"

He'd nearly stepped on a snake, stumbling to avoid it.

The Northern Viper thrived in tall grass, like that growing along the sides of the track.

Wielding his shovel, he approached the creature cautiously. For a snake, it was unusually still. *Nay*, not a snake. Splayed on the ground, whatever it was might have been tossed from a railcar. Poking it from as far away as possible, he scooped his shovel under the serpentine body and lifted it.

A long braid of gold hair hung from the shovel.

Kārlis was stunned, revolted, unable to move, wishing it *had* been an adder. That would have at least been natural. He stared at the loop of braided hair, his eyeballs doubling in size, comprehending.

There were little girls loaded in these cattle cars. Not retreating Russian soldiers. Little Latvian girls.

His sister was of the age that wore hair braided like this. With a shaking hand, he took the hair off and dropped the shovel. A light blue ribbon was still tied at the braid's narrow end. The wide end was a loosening fringe of roughly cut, fine hair.

His chest heaved. The straight lines of the tracks swirled around their vanishing point. Naïve to be shocked, he told himself, trying to calm down. There was no depth to their evil. No boundary marking the limits of human decency that a Communist wouldn't cross. He had to get home to his sister and parents. But his feet wouldn't move. What if his family were on one of these trains? He clutched the braid in his fist, teeth clamped together.

Kārlis saw two headlights coming. From so far away, he couldn't hear the engine yet, but it was obviously a vehicle patrolling the tracks. His muscles were stiff when he staggered down the embankment and hid in the bushes. He didn't worry about snakes. They were relatively harmless.

The next afternoon Sniedze woke up feeling disgusted with himself. He remembered Vilz trying to rouse him at an early hour, but Sniedze had fended off his friend with a shoulder like a roadblock. Why couldn't Vilz sleep in for once? Parched, he staggered to the kitchen sink, his head a cracking cement block.

A note on the table read, "Be right back." Vilz had signed it with the little fox-faced design that by-lined her secret articles, made by overlapping the letters V and Z, for Vilz Zarins.

Sniedze's heart palpitated with a sense of doom. He'd been left behind again. Scared to go out in public, he was a sitting duck if he stayed home. Then they know right where to find you—no place is safe, he thought, eyes darting around the room. Bolting to the cupboard, he reached for the phenobarbitone and felt better just rattling the bottle. Drugs in hand, he held the power to end the daily spiral of fear for good.

Slap'n scuff, slap'n scuff, slap'n scuff. Going to the window, Sniedze squinted, irritated to find the sun so high. Frieda was there again, jumping rope. She glanced up and, seeing him, made the German hand salute.

Sniedze opened the window wider.

"Hey, what are you doing?" she called.

"Nothing," he croaked.

"So boring around here," Frieda said, her rope cutting the air into evenly spaced slices. "I'm hoping when the Germans come we can have Young Maidens or some kind of Youth meetings."

Sniedze kept silent for two reasons. First, because it was not safe to speak—anyone might be listening. And, secondly, he didn't want to sound like an ignoramus because he didn't know what the heck she was talking about.

"Back home, the boys all had Hitler Youth," Frieda said, braids bouncing. She phrased her speech to fit the rhythm of jumping. "There were camping trips. We'd divide into platoons and storm trenches, and make bonfires and sing."

She sang:

When Jew blood spurts from the carving knife,
Oh, it's that much more okay

Her optimism was refreshing, Sniedze thought, intrigued. He must've misunderstood the lyrics.

"I went all the time when I used to live in Germany," Frieda said. "See?"

She stopped jumping and turned toward Sniedze, opening her cardigan. Sniedze's jaw dropped at the sudden display of her mounds under a vanilla-colored blouse, thrust at him like scoops of ice cream. Closing his mouth, he saw that Frieda wore a dagger on a belt under her sweater. She unsheathed it and lifted it up. "See the inscription?" she said. "Blood and Honor."

"Hghhah, put those away!" Sniedze said, nearly falling out the window. "Shhh!" But apparently no one was watching, so he asked, "Does everyone who joins get a dagger?" That would be more impressive than an old high school diploma in an envelope.

"Not everyone gets to join," Frieda said, replacing the knife and flipping the rope over her head in a high arch. "First you have to prove your bloodlines are clean. Mine are Aryan back to 1650. Then you have to pass certain tests, prove yourself worthy. Then you get the dagger."

All this had been explained while Frieda jumped rope, never sounding out of breath. Sniedze nodded, slapping a mosquito on his cheek.

Chatting with Frieda, time passed swiftly. Before he knew it, Vilz was back with another unlikely excuse instead of her typewriter. Tonight, mysterious specks of paint dotted her dark hair. Sniedze didn't know what to make of it. Vilz was obviously trying to trick him.

She'd been painting somewhere, maybe having to do with her sneaky newsletter, though Sniedze didn't see how that fit. But mainly, he was grateful Vilz came at all.

"Guess we'll just be panivores tonight," Vilz said, searching the barren cupboard and settling on the remains of last night's bread. "So what did you do all day, Sniedze?"

About to tell Vilz about Frieda, Sniedze bit the words back. His friends all thought he was a blab. Fine. He wouldn't tell anybody anything anymore, to prove he was trustworthy. The problem was, how would they know he could keep a secret if he never told them what he knew?

"What in hell is this?" Vilz said, discovering the phenobarbitone and holding it up to the light.

Sniedze spun around. "That's mine! My nerve medicine," he said, thrusting his hand to the bottle as Vilz raised it out of reach. "Works too."

"Boy, you're not kidding it works," Vilz said, reading the label. "There's enough here to kill a horse." She looked at Sniedze's eyeballs. "This explains a lot. How much have you had?"

"I said that's mine, Vilz!" Sniedze cried, snatching the bottle. It was his one weapon. His ticket out and he could not spare a single tablet.

"Okay." Vilz held up empty hands. Turning to slice the bread, she shook her head, saying, "It has not been easy. But you're not alone in this. I've been interviewing people and I can tell you. Nobody sleeps. Everybody panics at every bump that could be a knock at the door. We all know we're not safe at home or anywhere else. People are building hiding places, if they have the means. You have it pretty good compared to a lot of folks, Sniedze. I tabulate every murder and abduction I hear of, thinking one day somebody will be held accountable. So I can tell you with absolute certainty that all around us, families have been ripped apart, left without providers, paychecks. Neighborhood after neighborhood is left without leaders, caretakers. Those with the wisdom to advise us have already been deported or are well hidden. Everybody else is just holding on. I don't know for how much longer. But we just have to hold on."

Sniedze declined the plate of bread Vilz held out, feeling queasy.

Vilz chewed in silence, dry black bread with a swig of water.

"There's work out in Ogre," Vilz finally said. "I'm going tomorrow. You should try to get hired on, too. Even if we have to split the pay, you'd best have a job so the Russians don't draft you."

"What about the Germans?" Sniedze said. "You said they'd be here by now. That's what everybody said."

"Well, I guess my crystal ball needs calibration," Vilz sighed. "Get a good night's sleep, Sniedze. I'm not leaving you here alone to mope with a jar of sleeping pills."

The next morning, Sniedze followed Vilz to the trolley stop feeling heavy-headed. He sat dully for the commute, as if lead curtains had been drawn over his eyes that were finally yanked open during the long hike to a town outside of Riga. After a day of muscle-tearing work digging a trench along a quiet residential road, Sniedze was clear-thinking enough to be terrified again by nightfall. He "slept" at the construction site—eyes wide waiting for Vilz to return from wherever she'd sneaked off to for her so-called "investigative reporting". Sniedze kept his drugs at hand, vowing, in case of a spot search, to swallow the whole bottle before the NKVD could take away either him or the pills.

47

HUGO FELT THE LOCOMOTIVES RUMBLE to power, shudders vibrating the cattle car floor where he sat pinned between Mutton-Dressed-as-Lamb and someone getting a diaper change. As the carriage creaked to acceleration, he didn't display his relief and excitement. Nor did the other exiles. Fooled before, they did not, especially in front of the children, raise hopes to have them dashed. The Harmful Elements sat dully, jostled in unison as the train pulled from Riga Central Station, chugging toward where the sun rose, with frequent stops they did not know the purpose of.

Hugo had been stagnating in the train for over two days. His muscles screamed to stretch. Twisting the neck of the pillowcase closed, he stood, wide-stanced for balance, and stepped through squirming tots over toward his mother. She leaned against the door. Her hands, still in wrist length gloves, were flattened at her sides, absorbing bumps and rumbles. In the ill light, she stared into the carriage, seeming to register nothing, long white hair dangling around her blank face like strings in a mop.

"Mother, are you all right?"

She turned a disappointed eye to him. "Did I raise you to ask stupid questions?"

"Have you had anything to eat?" Hugo showed her an apple, blocking its view from others.

She shook her head. "As if I could with this stench."

"Keep your strength up," Hugo said. "You'll feel better."

"It doesn't matter whether I'm jolly or ghoulish, son. Regardless of my feelings on the matter, I'm headed for a hard labor camp that squeezes the life juice out of prisoners within three months."

A girl pouring water on a cloth overheard Mrs. Krumins's malediction and her hand faltered, spilling.

"If we're strategic, some of us might survive," Mrs. Krumins said, with a scathing look at the wasteful girl, "but somebody has to take control of the water."

"She's at it again," the spiller reported to Loudmouth, across the car. Then, ignoring Mrs. Krumins, she pressed her wet rag to a toddler's flushed forehead.

"Opportunity makes the thief," Mrs. Krumins retorted, watching the damp cloth like it was a gushing pipe burst.

"Somebody make her stop." The girl sounded at wit's end.

Narrowing her eyes, Hugo's mother leaned toward him. "Forget every manner, every civility I ever taught you, son," she said. "Just remember the vulture. Efficient. Conserving energy. Surviving off others until their inevitable failure also nourishes it."

Hugo looked away from his mother with a bad taste in his mouth. She'd already travelled down the dismal road she sometimes wandered and it would be difficult to escort her back, especially without his father's help.

The train banked suddenly, knocking him against a twenty-something lady holding a long-legged boy baby to the window.

"I beg your pardon," Hugo said.

"It's all right, *paldies.*"

Hugo couldn't tell the ages of babies. This one was old enough to hold up a chubby finger and identify sights with a babble vocabulary. Hugo recognized *flower, bird, dog,* the jibberish that passed for conversation in the women and children's car.

"*Can rabbits swim?*"

"*No.*"

"*But can they row?*"

"*Is a power plant really a plant?*"

"*Mama, I thirsty.*"

"*Airplane.*"

What? Hugo jerked his head toward the chubby finger pointing out the window. He elbowed his way in front of the young mother so recklessly the carriage chatterers shut up.

Treetops. Through the high, small window Hugo only saw the tops of an emerald forest jagging into the sky.

Above the forest, in the distance, planes. Five. No, a sixth edged into the tight frame. Nose propellers lined up with formidable precision. Gull wings, spatted undercarriage, Hugo knew the single engine, two-man dive-bombers from photographs. "Stuka!"

Passengers held their collective breath. In the silence, droning plane engines grew louder.

The women rose to their feet, pressing behind Hugo.

"Is it—?" Lullaby ventured.

"The *Luftwaffe!*" Hugo announced.

"Oh, God! They're here!" cried someone. "Oh, thank God!"

"We're saved!" another shouted.

A cheer rose, "The Germans have come!"

Hugo watched the ominous squadron prowl across the sky, and trembled. The whole ordeal might be over in a second. The Stuka were deadly accurate. They would bomb the rails, snuffing a Russian retreat and he was glad of that. They'd also bring a swift and terrible end to the deportees and their suffering, collateral damage. Hugo tasted in that moment, how he wanted to live. He wanted to again be in the air and light, wanted to go home.

The train took a curve too fast, pushing the deportees into one another. No one complained. Loudmouth and Lullaby were holding each other up, hugging in laugh-sobs.

Hugo regained his balance. The Junkers were flying beyond the tiny window frame. But he could still hear the engines.

Voices from the next cattle car were singing, *Dievs, svētī Latviju!*

The ladies behind Hugo joined in, God, Bless Latvia.

Prayers had been answered. Help was here. Hugo pictured what those Stukas meant for the people he cared about, Lileja, the Nonchalants. Salvation. Independence. War.

Gradually the overhead engines faded. But the singing persisted with defiance because the Russians had banned the national anthem, and now that would change. Everything would change.

But the train chugged on.

Blisters burned like live coals in Kārlis's boots.

To take his mind off the distance ahead, he was scouring the rails for anything else that might have been thrown from the trains when he heard a single, distant boom in the west.

The muted blast gave him pause, changing the direction of his blood flow, bringing a new heart to life. His chest swelled with expectation. He heard it again. *Ba-boom!* The blast graduated to a series of sky-pounding reports. Artillery. *Yah!*

Kārlis skipped on the tracks, punching the air. *Yah!* He whooped to the trees around him. "They're here! That's Germany!"

A train was coming. Kārlis ran down the embankment to hide.

The distant explosions were ramping up as he crawled deeper into the foliage. He listened, exultant, counting the cattle cars pulling past, sixty-four, sixty-five, sixty-six. Must tell these numbers to Vilz, he thought, proud his friend documented all that happened with facts and figures. Now that the Germans were here, the world would be informed of the ghastly year. *Whoever is in those cattle cars, listen to the cannons! We're saved!* Seventy-one, seventy-two, seventy-three. Kārlis turned his head. He couldn't bear to see the length of the train.

The day promised to be a back-grinding, trench-digging variation of the one before. Sniedze opened his mouth to ask Vilz when the Germans were coming, but caught himself. He was practicing keeping his thoughts to himself, and getting better at it. Anyway, he'd be a fool to believe Vilz, who'd probably just sugarcoat the fact that they were doomed.

Sniedze leaned on his shovel and wiped his brow with his sleeve. "I heard one of those old geezers working down the line say rumors of a massive German invasion was just wishful thinking."

"It's real," Vilz said, without stopping work.

"The old man says it can't be true," Sniedze retorted, "since there's absolutely no sign of the Russians preparing a defense."

"Stalin's afraid to provoke Hitler," Vilz said, tossing dirt to the top of the ditch. "Doesn't want to get caught moving a single tank, give Hitler an excuse to invade."

Sniedze said nothing, not knowing where to take the discussion next. Vilz could be very self-centered, he concluded. Always down on Sniedze's nerve meds and only thinking of her own problems, such as finding paper for the printing press.

The tedious morning of work was still hours from lunch break. Tired and bored, Sniedze looked up to see something he'd not seen before.

A woman was running toward them across the fields.

She had a low center of gravity that brought to life a blunt, dark skirt. "They are leaving," she yelled, waving her arms. Sniedze looked around. She was calling to him and Vilz, and to some men working farther up the road.

Vilz stopped shoveling as she ran up.

"Not just leaving." She spoke like a person who'd just found she had a voice. "Fleeing!" Grabbing Sniedze, she crushed him with her big, flabby arms, pressing wet cheeks against his face. He didn't even care. Her words were sinking in. "Germans have crossed the border!

"They are burning their party cards and running away!" She ran farther up the trench, where grown men had heard her and were already dancing, fist-pumping and yelling out.

"Oh, God!" Vilz cried, "Sniedze!" Vilz wrapped her arms around Sniedze and lifted him off the ground.

"The Germans are here," Sniedze said, breathlessly. Vilz let him go and Sniedze started jumping, tears dripping from his eyes and down his face.

"Thank God!" Vilz cried, looking around him. "Thank You, God! I want to remember every detail of this day."

Puffy white clouds crested the tops of the pines. Green grass sprouted from every possible crack amid choirs of wildflowers. Vilz reached down to scoop handfuls of soil, letting it fall through her fingers. Then she pushed a fist in the air. "Free Latvia!" she yelled at the top of her lungs. "Yah!"

Sniedze felt like laughing, so he did. "The Germans are here to save us!" he called like a playground taunt, feet dancing. "I will never live under Russians again!" He shot out his right arm in proud Nazi salute. "Heil Hitler!"

Kārlis Smiltens, 1946.

48

JUNE 24, 1941

THE SUMMERHOUSE

JANIS PĒRKONS LEANED THE BICYCLE against the side of the house. He flicked a rag at spider webs in the frame and pinched the rear tire. Explosions rumbled dully like the distant thunder of a storm coming his way. Air sirens wailed to the west, over the thin whine of *Stukas* dive-bombing Russian battleships in the port of Riga. War helter-skelter had a way of making the whole nation feel like his personal backyard.

Above him, the curtains at the kitchen window parted, framing his wife's face. Anna frowned in the direction of the artillery, and craned her neck to see up the gravel drive, vertical worry lines between her brows. Still a face Janis liked to look at over a cup of coffee. Smelling some, he went through the back door to the kitchen.

His wife seemed trying to compensate for the loss of each household member with increased cooking. After Kārlis had been drafted, she undertook an ambitious canning production. And since the Kruminses' deportation ten days ago, every kitchen surface had been engaged with something boiling, sizzling, simmering or rising. Though her garden was abundant, the country was now at war, and Janis was already worrying about future food shortages.

Tante Agata sat by the stove pitting apricots. She was wearing a long skirt, with an embroidered vest and shawl, and a wreath of fresh wildflowers over her long grey braid. Normally, Janis would have been amused at the old bird's plucky little act of defiance, putting on her national costume as soon as she'd heard of the Russians' retreat. But he was just too worried about his son to find joy in symbolic gestures.

"Happy Name's Day, Papu," Biruta said with a grin. She was at the all-teeth-and-ears stage of ten years old. Sitting at the kitchen table, where her feet barely reached the ground, she was busily twisting a green mound of vines and leaves. Then she scooted her chair back and rushed at him with an oak leaf wreath. "Look what I made for you."

Janis bent over so she could crown him with the headpiece. It felt like he was wearing a bush three times the size of his head.

"Well, that's real fine," Janis said, standing tall and posing like the star of the play. "Fits perfectly. What do you think, Tante Agata?"

His wife's elderly aunt cleared her throat, as if she'd been waiting for someone to ask her opinion. "*We have rowed well, said the flea as the fishing boat arrived at its mooring.*"

A crack of artillery split the air, rattling the dishes. The cat streaked out of the room.

"Hoo!" Janis exclaimed, despite his intention to model confidence.

"Oh!" Biruta cried, eyes popping. "Katkis is afraid!"

"Tell Katkis not to worry," Anna said firmly. "Today is a happy day." But Janis noticed her hand shaking as she poured his coffee.

"That's right," Janis said, taking the chair next to Biruta. "That's the German 18th Army!" To amuse her, he raised curved fingers like panther claws and growled, "*Panzer* tanks!" They laughed.

After a sip of coffee, he said to Anna and Agata in a more somber tone, "It's the *blitzkrieg* all over again."

"Now that the Germans are here, will Kārlis be coming home?" Biruta asked. "And the Kruminses? Are they coming back? Is that why the good china's out?"

Janis twisted around in his chair for a look at the dining room. Indeed, the table had been laid as for a company feast. He couldn't understand why his wife prepared this ghost banquet, but if it helped her deal with the pain of loss, fine, it wasn't hurting anyone else.

"It's Midsummer," Anna said, tight-lipped. "Anyone might come by."

She was bundling about a dozen hot *pierogi* in a towel and put them in a bucket with a loaf of bread and a hunk of caraway-seed cheese. Then she carried it out, leaving by the kitchen door.

"What you doing with Kārlis's bicycle?" Biruta asked Janis. "You don't ride a bike."

"What!" Janis said, feigning indignation. "I admit I'm a little rusty... " His thought trailed off momentarily, watching his wife through the window. She and her bucket were headed toward the road with a determined stride. "But since the blasted Russians have sabotaged the rail, bicycle's the only way I'll be going anywhere." It felt wonderful to curse the Communists out loud in his own kitchen after abstaining for a year.

"Russians wrecked the rail so the Germans can't use it," Biruta said, in a prim, high voice. "Now no one gets to ride the train."

"It's so obviously senseless when you hear a child say it," Janis said, watching the window. "Where is she going with that bucket of food?"

"Mama leaves out picnics for the soldiers," Biruta said.

"Well, goddam," Janis said to his coffee. Gulping the remainder, he stood. "Let's go ride that thing."

"It's a beautiful day," Tante Agata rejoined. "Biruta should not be stuck inside on Midsummer."

"But the Communists forbid Midsummer," Biruta said.

At that, Janis laughed so hard his leafy crown shook. He left by the kitchen door. "They have bigger problems than the summer solstice on their hands today, Cookie."

Balancing Biruta on the bicycle seat, Janis pushed the cycle toward his wife's kitchen garden. She had apparently deposited the savory contents of the bucket somewhere near the road. Now she was in her garden filling the bucket with tomatoes, taking time to arrange the vines on their supports. Deita the cow watched companionably. A breeze scattered the scent of wisteria from where the purple blooms climbed over her gazebo. A beautiful summer day, Janis thought, inhaling fully, sensing its fragility. Beneath the sweetness lurked an unbearable duality of hope and dread about the fate of their son, of whom they rarely dared to speak. Knowing his wife was brittle with anxiety, Janis chose his words carefully.

"You're cooking up quite a spread," he said, amiably. "Enough to feed the proverbial army. I hope that's not your intention."

"I'll thank you not to trample my dahlias, sir," Anna said with a polite smile, nodding to the green shoots under his oxfords.

"Oh, sorry." Janis patiently moved off her flowers, knowing that's not what had her on edge.

"Anna—about these picnics you are setting out. You better let me handle any Ivans straggling through the area. They're desperate. Word is they are running away and deserting in a panic. Then we've got partisans coming out of the woods full force, actively hunting them before they can escape over the border. You don't want to get in the middle of that. Setting out provisions might attract trouble."

"What if someone—needs food?" she said, her voice going husky.

Janis understood that, in her mind, she was setting out something for Kārlis to eat. She was superstitious, thinking her kindness to a stranger would cycle around to a stranger being kind to Kārlis. Janis knew the grim truth of war lacked such romance. But he decided not to press the issue this morning. They were, after all, just fleas on a fishing boat. Damned lucky fleas.

"Let's go, Papu," Biruta said, tugging his shirt.

"All right," he said straddling the bike's frame and poising a boot over the pedal. "Anna, remember what I showed you about the gun?"

She nodded. "I'll be fine. Anyway, you'll not be far," she said, looking at the bike.

"Oh, we shall see about that!" Janis said, with a grin to his daughter. He pushed forward, stepping on the pedal. The bicycle veered wildly to the side. Then when the second boot found the other pedal it zagged hard in the opposite direction.

Biruta screamed with delight at the wobbly start.

"I'm taking you to the biggest oak tree in the forest," Janis announced. "You'll never see another one like it in your life."

"Janis!" Anna called.

He turned back to see what she wanted.

"*Vārda dienas*," she said, smiling.

"A Happy Name's Day indeed!" Janis said. He took in a deep lungful of air and belted out:

All year round I gathered songs,

Waiting for Midsummer Night

He heard Biruta singing along. Good. After a ghastly year, she still knew the words.

Midsummer Night is here at last,

IT'S TIME TO SING EVERY SONG!

49

BLUNT, DISTANT BANGS WERE A CONSTANT herald to the arrival of the *Wehrmacht*. Kārlis didn't know the exact point of entry or path of the German invasion, but its blast wave rippled eastward across the country in the mayhem of fleeing, pillaging Russians. The railroad tracks, edged in places with low orange flames, seemed the favored route for retreaters on horseback and foot, headed the opposite direction as Kārlis. He avoided the desperadoes, repeatedly running into the forest, and returning when the tracks were clear.

"Getting nowhere fast," Kārlis thought. Blisters on the backs of his heels were popped and raw. New ones were forming on his palms from his constant handling of the grave-digging shovel he'd taken from Litene, swinging it like a hiking staff or sometimes upholding it like the rod of Moses. It was all he had.

Smoke and panic were in the air, infecting Kārlis with a lawless fervor. Using chunks of charred wood he wrote in large letters across a railroad tie *Russian Murderers Go Home!* On a tree, *Free Latvia*.

A railroad sign indicated that the next station was for Patikamspils. Kārlis veered away from the whistle-stop, taking a forest-lined road toward the village and an irresistible white plaster wall. Ambling over, Kārlis lingered at the wall, nonchalantly looking around to see if anyone was watching him.

Swiping his lump of charcoal in wide fluid strokes, Kārlis drew a caricature of Stalin, moustaches bigger than his arms, blood dripping from his mouth, Purge List in fist. Kārlis had perfected the defamatory character at school for his friend Vilz's underground newsletter. The drawing took him all of three minutes, while constantly looking over his shoulder. *To the Gulag with you!* He sentenced with a flourish and ran away.

The road turned cobblestone and wound into a lush, picturesque, inward facing village with old buildings of wood, stone and creamy plaster. One was on fire. Hellish flames pulsed from the upper story, a billowing, black inferno. Kārlis stopped running and stared. He'd never seen a force so powerful. He helped a line of men dragging a hose, the front liners turning their faces from the intensity of heat. When it was clear the firefight was hopeless, Kārlis cut out and headed toward the village center, seeking something to eat, information, maybe even a telephone. Whatever town this was, a foreboding sense of chaos roiled from its yelling citizens and blaring traffic.

Motorcycle riding was the closest to freedom Eriks Gailis had been in a year. Thus the '37 Pandera was his prize among a regime-change avalanche of plunder. Wiping sweaty palms on trousers, Eriks steadied the idling bike, pushing mammoth boots, recently acquired from a corpse his size, into the roadside's grassy shoulder. Aivars the

Lonely was seated behind him with raised field glasses. Stukas whined overhead. They were hidden behind a dairy truck loaded with milk cannisters, but Eriks felt naked outside the forest. He wished Aivars would hurry.

Instead, Aivars just handed him the binoculars and nodded toward the hotel. Eriks didn't need field glasses to see the new flag hanging over the art nouveau façade. The gates were festooned with the black swastika emblazoned in a white circle on a gash of red. He focused the lenses on the balcony where an officer spoke on a telephone, one of the blue-eyed, fair-haired stock prized by Nazis. The swastika graphic recurred with brio on the officer's bicep band, intensifying his sleek, tan tunic to a powerful statement. Black gabardine breeches tucked into gleaming knee-high boots completed a devastating profile.

"Hugo Boss."

"Hell, you know that fellow?" Aivars demanded.

"No. His uniform is made by the couturier, Hugo Boss," Eriks said, lowering the binoculars.

Aivars looked at him with pity.

"Before the Commies, my father was Riga's premier retailer," Eriks said.

"I forgot you were such a blade," Aivars said, flicking Eriks's shirt where the stems of sweet woodruff poked through a hole, like a boutonnière.

Eriks trained the binoculars on a detail. "See the runic, lightning bolt SS collar pins?" He remembered how good it had felt to swagger about in a clothes-make-the-man hubris. "Those *kāpost galvas* are rife with élan."

Aivars sniffed. "*My* beret is decorated by the stolen cap badges of thirty-seven dead Chekists," he said. "Can Hugo Boss make one like that?"

Eriks almost smiled. "Let's get out of here," he said, returning the glasses to Aivars and positioning his riding goggles.

Before Eriks could wheel away, Aivars jumped off the seat without warning, jogged to the hotel gate, and yanked at a flag.

Damn him. Eriks felt his heart rate surge. How typical of Aivars to commit mischief exposing them both to unnecessary risk. A guard could spot them at any moment. Eriks had no choice now but to push the motorcycle behind Aivars to speed their getaway. Seconds seemed hours as Aivars tugged fruitlessly at the flag in full view and broad daylight, finally slashing the grommets with his knife. He slid back on the seat, stuffing the banner in the saddlebag as Eriks pulled into the road.

"No, go the other way," Aivars said in Eriks's ear. "I want to know what's thumping."

Begrudgingly, Eriks U-turned toward a dull noise, which he expected to be a trudging, clanking herd of livestock. The road ended at an intersection, where some civilians wearing straw fedoras stood, hands in pockets. They were spectators to an olive green procession.

A column of soldiers, no—prisoners, some in chains—was being herded to the end of the street, into an enclosure outlined by double rows of shining barbed wire.

Eriks couldn't see the end of the miserable queue. Russian POWs, torn clothes, bruises, cuts, and swollen bent faces, marching— if that's what the exhausted stumbling could be called—three abreast. Shirts billowed over pants tucked into dirty boots, the only accoutrement a small tin pail hanging from some waistbands. One fellow somehow kept his legs marching, while his upper body slumped over the arm of a comrade.

462

A bedecked German escort strode alongside. The captives within his reach watched with sidelong looks of terror as the German raised a tall wooden stick and crashed it down hard over a man's head, picked a new target, and immediately whacked again, ceaselessly beating the prisoners.

Eriks forgot to breathe. If anyone deserved a good skull-cracking, it was a Red as far as he was concerned. Pay them back with their own coin. But the hard treatment of already beaten men was degrading to watch, lowering the value of all human currency. Behind his goggles, he blinked hard. Clopping horse hooves signaled the approach of a higher rank. Aivars nudged him and Eriks turned the motorcycle around and accelerated into the wind, smoke from a burning country stinging his lungs.

He passed fields of pale blue flax blossoms waving in the noxious breeze of scorched industry, and turned up a dirt road bisecting a field of rye, where a shiny black sedan was parked under a chestnut tree. Eriks pulled up to find Captain Wagtail, Homburg Haralds and Bee-in-Your-Cap Kristaps, key guerrillas from Silent Forest, the band Eriks considered family. They sat smoking inside the 1939 Ford-Vairogs, looking already acclimated to this latest trapping of automotive luxury they'd gotten hold of. Seeing Eriks and Aivars, they exited the car and lit a fresh round of tobacco.

"Our observations concur with the intell," Aivars reported. "German Army Group North has captured a surfeit of prisoners. POW roundups are in every district, including a stone's throw from where we stand, marching prisoners into open-air *stalags*."

Homburg Haralds nodded, his namesake hat casting a penumbral shadow over his bony frame. "We also can confirm: everywhere are pockets of resistance that still need dealing with. The Krauts advanced so damn fast they *by-passed* thousands of Red Army troops who are roaming around wreaking havoc. Dangerous waves of stragglers. On the other hand," Haralds waved a hand of long, twig fingers, "there's a deluge of Latvian citizens wanting to assist the partisans."

"We got a roomful of new recruits and it's about time," Aivars said.

"We need to organize the green-noses," said Captain Wagtail, portly and aptly nicknamed after the fussing bird. "We can't have a vacuum of power. Local Latvians must visibly occupy every town, hold down the civic positions, and take care of day-to-day business. The Communists are no longer in charge."

The gold cup comment rested in the air a moment, hovering above the other agenda items before each man recognized it to be a statement people had died for.

"Hell no, the *kāpost galva* Communists are not in charge!" Aivars roared.

Eriks placed a hand over his heart. "Hear, hear!"

"Latvians in charge of Latvia!" Heralds chimed.

Kristaps danced a jig. And silliness looked good on the eleven-year-old, whose face was still caked with mud-painted runes from his last maneuver.

"At least for now," Wagtail said, hedging like a cheesy politician. "I mean, ideally, Germany will allow us to administer our own affairs, but some degree of cooperation, er, collaboration will be expected."

"I'm not trading one dictator for another," Heralds said, ramrod stubborn.

"I don't know we have a choice," said Wagtail, ruffling chest feathers as it were.

"We fight for choice," Haralds said. "That's the point—"

"I'm fighting *against* Russia," Eriks said. "Not *for* Germany."

"Understood, brother," Aivars said. "When choosing between two evils, I always pick the one I haven't tried before. I think we can agree the sinking-ship Russian rats should be flushed out and exterminated, *toute suite*."

"Why not just let them run for the border and good riddance," Kristaps said, lighting another cigarette and tossing the match. "They gonna get worse for losing from their own army when they get home than even what the Germans dole out."

"Without a doubt."

"Many stragglers are Evaders anyway," Eriks said.

"An Evader sort of achieves the same goal we do," Kristaps said. "Undermining the Red Army."

"Nay. Not the same," Aivars said.

"Some of them never wanted to be soldiers to begin with," Kristaps said.

"Yah, well Bear Slayer wanted to be a fashion whore. Maybe I wanted to be a librarian," Aivars said, warming to a lively discussion. "We all wanted to be something else, but —"

"They execute you for disobeying a call up notice," Kristaps argued. His voice hadn't even dropped yet.

Eriks felt certain the boy's deported schoolteacher parents would be appalled to hear him back-talk his elders.

"We disobey," Aivars said, tolerating Kristaps's feral manners. "Wasn't easy last winter was it? Before the cozy underground bunker was built. You sleeping in an ice pit and no shoes."

"I'm just philosophizing about how a fellow's ideologies don't always match with his predicament," Kristaps said. The boy was a sponge for big words.

"You can have your ideologies until you put on someone's uniform," Wagtail said, "then you're their man."

"The Jews are a special case," Haralds interjected. "No uniform, but Nazis say they've been Russian allies all along, Bolshevik masterminds."

"They are fleeing to the woods like guilty parties," Aivars said.

Eriks stiffened with disagreement. "I'm not fighting along those lines."

"Me neither," said Wagtail.

"Caleb was a Jew," Kristaps said, about a fallen brother.

"Well, we can't interview every *kāpost galva* case by case to determine his sympathies. I agree with Aivars," Wagtail said, ruling with finality. "All uniformed Red Army will be put down. They're out to destroy every resource of possible value." He added, as if for Kristaps's education, "So the Germans don't get it."

"We'd be damned careless to not cut off a retreat," Aivars concurred, planting feet and looking impassable in his trim, military jumpsuit. "We want to impress those Russian *kāpost galvas* with the steep price of coming back."

"Coming back!" Eriks blurted. Leave it to Aivars and his paranoid hatred of Russians to take a line of argument one step too far. "God forbid."

In silence they all watched a flock of starlings shapeshift in the sky.

"Aivars, go back to Patikamspils and take charge," Wagtail said, in a tone that marked the meeting's end. "Organize the locals. Route the resisters. Occupy the district thoroughly. No Russian toeholds."

As Wagtail headed toward the car, Aivars said, "Captain, I appreciate your confidence, but you know my mission's more spiritual in nature. Please leave me to work in solitude. A proper leader ought to have more, you know, I'd say … élan. Anyway, that's the Bear's town."

"Oh, fine," Wagtail relented. "Bear Slayer, your élan better be up to scratch."

Nicknames served to disassociate deeds from names on a list. The mythological root of Eriks's sobriquet was also a secret source of inspiration to him. He felt his chest swell at the field promotion.

"Crazy times," the Captain muttered, shaking his head. "Two saboteurs in charge of establishing order."

As they climbed inside the automobile, Kristaps pipsqueaked to Haralds, "Last winter, it took some damned élan to go into the woods. Now everybody and his grandmother are hiding out there."

Eriks wished he were going home with Kristaps, to the new split birch-lined, wood-stove heated, ventilated underground bunker. But the motorbike would forge a visible trail to the hideout's door, so if he wanted to keep riding he would have to contend with city jobs. "Hey, Kristaps," he called. "See if you can sneak up on a bar of soap."

"Aw, Foxtrot Oscar."

Incorrigible.

Rushing into wind on 750 ccs cleared Eriks's head. He watched for landmarks, retracing the morning's route through a web of narrow farm and forest roads, examining his thoughts, trying to pinpoint the turd in the punchbowl. Why wasn't he elated by all the good news: German salvation, mobilized townsfolk, his new motorcycle and a tank of gasoline, not to mention the field promotion. Why was he so glum?

Had the Forest Brethren's splintered political views soured the hard-won victory? Nay, hashing out complicated problems in the open was a good thing. Though Aivars's notion of Communists returning was unbearable. Couldn't be simple envy of that Kraut's slick tailor, could it? Was he still that foolish? Or did Hugo Boss prick at wounds from deeper losses. That gossip about the Hebrews troubled him. And guilt was still raw where Caleb was concerned … the friend who'd paid with his life for Eriks's admission to Silent Forest. He was going back to where Caleb—

Eriks overtook the bicyclist the same instant he saw him. Pumping along the edge of an open field, the soldier was the tail of three bicyclists—no five. Reds. Pedaling hard, they didn't have time to turn their heads before Eriks zoomed past and came up on another cluster of bikes in a string that stretched out—Eriks couldn't see how far.

Aivars tensed and shifted on the seat behind him.

Eriks braced for gunfire, never knowing what Aivars might pull off. With a lurch of adrenaline and a sudden idea that the retreating soldiers might shoot at him, Eriks swerved in an S across the lanes, becoming a more difficult target.

Aivars clutched his ribs to hang on, cursing.

Ahead, bikes spread across the narrow road, the motorcycle pulling behind them. Steering tight, Eriks buzzed between two cyclists, each within an arm's length, close enough to smell sweat.

The road turned sharp. Going too fast, Eriks rolled off the throttle. Sand. Wheels slid out from under, laying the motorcycle low, careening toward the shouting riders. At a moment of settling, tires grabbed. The Pandera rose and accelerated out of the corner, trailing Aivars's maniacal laughter. The whole encounter lasted mere seconds.

Eriks's hands trembled as he checked his rear view mirror where Red Army stragglers on stolen bikes shrank into the distance. He sped down the farm road, soon swallowed by forest on both sides.

Would this country never end? Igor Volkov fumed with rage as he fled toward the border on a stolen bicycle, a clunker with a bent rim, every inefficient down-stroke chapping his ass. In the course of the retreat, Igor had met up with other Red soldier cyclists on the straight forest roads, and maneuvered into their slipstreams. Since yesterday, about twenty rogue cyclists had thus glommed together, but Igor understood he was alone. Each man was out for himself as his fear pumped him across the monotonous course, spiked with the terror of capture by the *Wehrmacht*, rushing toward certain Red Army punishment. The other Russians, like he, would never take reprieve inside the forest, its dark interior crawling with vengeful Latvians.

The locals hated him and Igor vowed he would one day return that hatred a thousand fold. His year of duty in Latvia had not rewarded him with a position worthy of his eminence. He liked the look of the girls here, but they would always revile him, proof of their inferior brains. He would return one day for the pleasure of stabbing them to death while they slept. If he could not thrive here, he wished to destroy it utterly.

One regret plagued Igor, one man, Janis Pērkons. Wealth on the scale Pērkons possessed could have bought quick solutions to the injustices Igor suffered. Not that Igor would be a filthy capitalist. He only needed money to rise above his enemies. Once in a venerated station, he would wield terrible power, advancing Comrade Stalin's agenda further than had any *apparatchik* in history. And the beautiful women would follow. So where had Pērkons stashed his obscene wealth? It had never been found in the confiscated Leather Works. Igor should've beaten an answer out of the wily businessman before the NKVD had shot him and sent both Pērkons and the secret of his treasure to the grave. Igor should have returned to Pērkons's house and pried the knowledge from his family.

The whine of a two-stroke engine was getting louder. All cyclists turned a head toward an approaching motorcycle, fearing partisans. Igor glanced back, recognizing an opportunity. The soldier at his flank was staring at the motorcycle, which was coming too fast into a bend in the road. Making a stiff "V" with two fingers, Igor poked the soldier's eyes with a hard jab. He screamed and crashed to the ground as his arms, too late, shot up to protect his face. Everybody else was watching the motorcycle, shouting as it slid low, nearly losing control at the corner. Igor jumped off his wretched bike, kicked his victim in the neck, and in an instant pirated the better bicycle. He mounted and pedaled away with force. The motorcycle averted disaster at the last moment, rising up and speeding off. Igor now rode an Erenpriess, a superior bicycle. He pressed his fingers together, feeling the tacky, slime of stupid blue eyes.

Eriks did not stop until he reached the outskirts of Patikamspils where he pulled over in view of an old manor house.

"Why're we stopping?" Aivars said, riled about the bicyclists. "Let's handle those picnickers." His shoulders were squared in the professional yet twitchy posture he adopted when thirsty for Russian blood. "Eighteen qualified Russian stragglers. Target practice for the new recruits. At least one has a potato masher up his sleeve."

Eriks didn't doubt that. The stiff-arm movement caused by a stashed grenade was obvious to detect once you knew what it was. But equally menacing was the ivy-twined manor house looming behind a tall hedge, which had recently served as the local NKVD command post.

"If they stay on course they'll be pedaling straight into town and right under our noses," Aivars said. "We got minutes to set a trap."

"But what if they stop *here?*"

Aivars looked up, the significance of the sinister old mansion registering on his weather-beaten face.

"What's the status of this joint? Is it empty?" Eriks peered through an opening in the hedge and past the geometry of a dead, formal garden. "If the stragglers go inside, they could gain a staunch toehold. They might even find some loose comrades."

Eriks weighed two bad options. If they took time now to scour the premises, the bicyclists would ride by before they'd organized the green-noses into an ambush. But if they didn't, the stragglers might settle into defensible accommodations. It could be costly to get them out, especially with that grenade. Every decision has consequences, Caleb reminded from the grave, a warning that prevented Eriks from ignoring the thorny problem and riding on.

Aivars slumped at the dilemma. Then, cocking an eyebrow, he bent to open the saddlebag.

Eriks understood at once, as Aivars pulled out the filched Nazi banner. They rolled cautiously toward the manor. Eriks steadied the motorcycle while Aivars stood on the seat and tied the flag's ripped corners around gate vines at a stately height, though the result was distinctly un-German in its slight crookedness.

"Russian repellant," Aivars said, dropping back onto the seat.

"It will have to do," Eriks said, wheeling onto the road with mongrel satisfaction from pissing on the corner post.

From here, the road to Patikamspils zipped straight through the woods. The bicyclists would likewise cover the straightaway in no time flat. Through the trees, Eriks glimpsed men hanging from their necks, swaying above ground. He couldn't stop to investigate, suddenly embroiled by the opportunity and duty to harm the enemy.

A couple hours ago, Eriks and Aivars had met a roomful of townsmen lit up with torch-and-pitchfork vengeance who wanted to "join" Silent Forest, or at least beg the partisans' protection from further scorched earth mayhem. They had gathered in a flat overlooking the village's main thoroughfare, which was an ideal spot for waylaying passing cyclists, assuming the townsmen were still there and ready to get their hands dirty.

He would have to explain to the green-noses that he'd been put in charge, Eriks thought, feeling slightly sick. Maybe Aivars would do that for him, make an introduction as it were. Yah. Men respected Aivars, or were at least wary of him. Then Eriks would relay Captain Wagtail's instructions. Wagtail had authority. The men would follow the Captain's orders even if they didn't know who Eriks was.

But what if they didn't? The Forest Brothers could barely agree even among themselves about Evaders and Germans and Jews. Why should pillars of the community listen to some upstart who hadn't even graduated high school?

Approaching Patikamspils, the forest road widened to a tree-lined avenue. Black smoke billowed into a gunmetal sky. A building was on fire, the curvy forms and flourishes of an elegant facade collapsed as hellish flames pulsed from the upper story, an inferno. Lines of people stood, arms hanging as if watching a lost cause. Eriks rode past barely noticing the catastrophe, cursing Wagtail's snap judgment to leave him in charge.

The half-timbered apartment building where the novices were assembled was ahead. Eriks threaded the motorcycle through chaotic traffic, toward the driveway to park in the courtyard. Turning in, his attention was yanked across the street by bold, black-lined vandalism.

A caricature of Stalin dominated a wall. The mockery grabbed Eriks's heart. He jerked handlebars toward the side of the road and straddle-stood for balance, boots rooted to the ground, chest about to explode.

"What now?" Aivars demanded.

Tongue-tied, Eriks pointed.

"That's a good one," Aivars said, nodding at the graffiti. "Hurry up."

"I know that hand." Eriks twisted in the saddle to face Aivars. Eriks wanted to explain, *That's my brother Nonchalant and childhood friend. He illustrated Free Latvia.* But he'd never admit that out loud. "He's one of us," Eriks said. "He's here. That drawing wasn't there when we left this morning." *Kārlis Pērkons is somewhere in this godforsaken, ransacked town,* he thought, acid flooding his guts.

A Nonchalant will never abandon another Nonchalant.

The pressure of Aivars's stare could've turned limestone to marble.

Eriks didn't buckle. "I'm finding him."

Aivars stood, looking ready to dismount. Eriks expected him to sprint to the apartment and organize the ambush on his own. Then the older marksman seemed to change his mind, settling his weight back on the seat with a nod at Eriks and a salute.

Eriks didn't waste time trying to figure Aivars. On a mission, he nosed into the road, weaving through jammed, horn-honking traffic, around loose goats and past people boarding a bus, feeling overwhelmed and desperate, the Pandera sputtering, barely in second gear. The front wheel bumped over cobblestones before the village tavern where Eriks had executed the reckless plan that killed Caleb.

Circling the town square, he recognized the exact place he'd left Caleb bleeding.

Where are you Kārlis? I know you're here. This time I'm getting it right.

He paused before turning up a side street, the knowledge of oncoming enemy bicyclists squeezing his chest.

"There's a faster way," Aivars said. "You got men."

Aivars was right. A path to a solution cleared.

Eriks bee-lined it back to the apartment building, parked the Pandera in the inner courtyard and vaulted stairs two at a time to the third floor. He knocked in the prearranged sequence and when the door was cracked, thundered inside.

Men were seated around a table covered with ashtrays, cheese rinds and an empty growler. Partisans Snaggle-Wit and Stone Hill, left in charge of an arms stash, stood, acknowledging the brothers. Five townsmen who probably hadn't smiled in a year stared up at Eriks.

Striding to the window, Eriks stuffed the blackout curtain over a rod and jimmied up the sash. He could see where the road emerged from the forest and became the main street to the village square. He saw no bicyclists, and exhaled. Stalin's bloody jaws grinned at him from the wall across the road.

Turning to face the men, Eriks drew himself up to full height, nearly bumping his head on a ceiling beam. "That Stalin picture was not here one hour ago," he said, pointing. "I need to find the person who drew that." He looked in turn at each unknown, indignant face. "One of you saw something."

A man with a plush white moustache and mournful pouches under his eyes took up most of the space at the table. He leaned back and raised his eyebrows at a greybeard in a double-breasted suit, who shrugged. Then he put a cigarette in his mouth and flicked at a lighter with the cleanest fingernails Eriks had seen all year.

Eriks boiled. Why should he put himself out for this decrepit skin bag? Kārlis Pērkons, on the other hand, deserved a chance to grow old.

Without looking at Eriks, the mustachioed man blew out a stream of smoke and asked Aivars, "What's the situation out there?"

Aivars went to the window's edge and raised his field glasses toward the forest.

Eriks leaned toward the handlebar moustache and, with a forceful middle finger, flicked the cigarette clean away from the white whiskers. "The situation is that a gang of Red Army stragglers on a run-for-the-border spree of murder and mayhem will ride through this village at any minute," he said. "I am prepared to send them home in boxes, but only if I find that artist." He stared hard at incensed eyes. Straightening up, Eriks addressed the room. "One of you saw him. Think! Thick black glasses. Poindexter nose. Skeptical expression."

A man in suspenders spoke up. "A skinny Red soldier defaced that wall."

Eriks shifted, folding his arms and staring at the new speaker as the room kept silent. He had not expected that: that Kārlis would be wearing the uniform the partisans agreed qualified him for summary execution. The weight of another moral and eternal decision crushed Eriks's chest. An impossibly complex spectrum of grays dizzied him. During the insane months since Eriks had last seen him, Kārlis must've been drafted. *Dammit.* A man *was* more than the uniform he put on. Eriks clenched his jaw, careful to not display the slightest doubt in front of the men. Aivars watched him with narrowed eyes, Aivars and his enviable, simplistic, unquestioned and total hatred of Russians.

"Your friend in cahoots with Russians?" Aivars asked, *voce sotto*.

"Not on your life," Eriks said.

Tasked with killing eighteen men in the next few minutes, Eriks reviewed what he knew for sure. The bloody Stalin was Kārlis's signature lampoon. Kārlis Pērkons was here.

"I vouch for the artist, my friend, Kārlis." Saying the words made the earth feel solid under Eriks's feet again. "Which way did he go?"

The suspendered man shook his head. "I don't know. He was carrying a shovel."

Aivars looked through field glasses at the edge of the window. "They're coming."

Snaggle and Stone rose for their weapons, but Eriks motioned them to wait. Drawing a long breath, he addressed the townsmen unhurriedly. "I don't know what you late bloomers have been doing for the past year. I suspect you've played it safe, waiting for Germans to arrive and now you want to get your property back. Well, the man who marked that wall has defied the occupation from Day One, risking his neck for *Free Latvia* while in high school. As far as I'm concerned he's worth ten of your towns."

Men sat up, stood, flexed, alert to the window. The air felt quick as a dog bite.

"There was a skinny fellow with a shovel helping put out the fire," said a sallow faced man, rushing his words. "Black glasses. Looked like he was wearing a Red uniform inside out."

Eriks nodded. "This is an order," he bellowed. "No harm comes to anyone carrying a shovel. If anything happens to this artist, if Kārlis is hurt in any manner, we are finished with this town. You understand? I will turn my back, wash my hands, shake the dust off my feet. You can find someone else to save your property from cinder and ruination."

"Understood."

"Got it."

"Yah. Aye aye, Sir."

Eriks was stunned by murmurs of agreement. But he didn't let it show. "Set it up, Aivars," he said, going for his rifle. "Send those pedalers to the Shade Mother."

With few words, Aivars assigned Snaggle and Stone key positions around an L-shaped kill zone. Three of the new recruits followed them from the apartment.

Eriks unpocketed a black pelt hood, with stitched-on lucky bear ears, and pulled it over his head. He made his station at a corner of the window. Cheek welded to buttstock, he watched the first bicyclist spin into the iron sights of his Mosin Nagant.

Hold into the breeze. Shoot between heartbeats.

He waited for Aivars's signal to fire.

Where are you, Kārlis?

50

KĀRLIS PĒRKONS WAS FAMISHED. He headed toward the center of what had no doubt been a quaint village last year. The type of village that would have fed Midsummer celebrants fresh herrings in cream with warm bread at woven cloth-covered bistro tables in the town square. His mouth watered at the fantasy, but from where he stood, the plaza hadn't seen a fried potato in months. At its heart rose an empty pedestal with exposed rebar, as if the statue of a local hero had been ripped away. A crescent of wood and stone buildings formed a jagged skyline, where slate roofs sloped low like a fedora pulled over the eyes of blackened windows.

Traffic was clogged. Someone leaned on a horn. The incessant honking upset a carthorse. Doors on the street were shut tight, except one battered off its hinges. A man strode past carrying a pig across his shoulders. A bicyclist whizzed by. Glass from a nearby streetlight shattered and tinkled to the pavement. Guys ran from it in all directions. Rough types whom Kārlis wanted to avoid.

An engine revved loudly behind him, and dread punched Kārlis's chest as an open-topped sedan full of sloppily uniformed men pulled over to him. The driver was a Chekist, wearing his hat backward. Three bruisers sat in the back seat crammed among some paintings. Gold gilt frames and a lampstick poked up at jumbled angles.

The front passenger wore a white undershirt and Red Army trousers like Kārlis's, except the butt of a pistol protruded from his waistband. Kārlis tried not to stare at the weapon, but he could foresee how quickly the soldier's hand would find it when he discovered Kārlis was Latvian. And an evader.

"Прыгнуть на," said the front passenger. *Jump on.* He indicated Kārlis could ride on the running board. The occupation's front-line brutes were offering him a ride home to Moscow.

Hammers pounded between his ears. Without speaking, Kārlis leaned on the shovel and raised his eyebrows, trying to look like he had some consideration that prohibited him from accepting this ride to the border with comrades.

A girl screamed from some building or alley behind him.

A bicyclist pedaled up yelling, "Крауты здесь." *Krauts are here.*

"Obviously," the driver seemed to say, gesturing at the car full of loot.

The cyclist abandoned his bike, pushing it to the curb, and clambered onto the sedan's rear bumper, breathless. "No, I mean SS are not far from here. Just saw them." He nodded to Kārlis, or at least to his uniform. "Parading prisoners. Go. For the love of God get us out of here."

"Поторопитесь, если вы придете," the driver told Kārlis, looking expectant. Sounding like, *Hurry up, if you're coming.*

Kārlis shuffled the mental flash cards of his pigeon Russian in a panic, heart pumping a stymieing dose of fight-or-flight.

Thunk! A body hit him hard, shoved him nearly off his feet, blindsided.

Regaining his balance, Kārlis saw that a damned bicycling soldier had run into him full bore. The son of a bitch had purposely rammed Kārlis like a wrecking ball, to get his spot on the running board!

Kārlis used the opportunity to attempt his escape, staggering on in the direction pushed, headed for the corner of a building when a slew of bicyclists suddenly wheeled in, swamping the sidewalk and hemming in the car, shouting in Russian. Twenty or so steel frames, foundered and askew, blocked movement.

"Go!" The pushy ass of a soldier who now dominated the running board was yelling at the driver. "Krauts in jeeps are coming."

The dire news made Kārlis glance at the assailer. Their eyes locked, sparking recognition that ignited a bottle bomb of hatred.

Igor Volkov.

"You!" The black eyes snapped, transporting Kārlis back to his father's workshop last winter, where Volkov had savagely beaten him to a pulp.

Kārlis gripped the shovel tight, every muscle quivering.

"You're the punk from that leather factory," Volkov accused. His rosy, heart-shaped face was the sort that looked to be laughing when agitated. "Your father is dead. I was there when they shot him."

The words were a bullseye, piercing like truth.

Kārlis's heart faltered, as if liters of blood had gushed out. His spirit parted and he felt someone else was lashing out in his voice, saying, "You'll not get away with it, kāpost galva." Not himself, he swung the shovel like a battle-axe, aiming to sever a knee joint.

"Het!" Volkov cried, stumbling off the running board to dodge the steel spade. The shovel clanged against the car, drawing the attention of every bloodthirsty Red wanting a ride home. The front-seat soldier heard fluent Latvian and, fathoming Kārlis was not one of them, drew his gun.

"Shoot the fascist!" Volkov cried, fending off Kārlis with a bicycle frame.

Fascist? That was not he, Kārlis thought, feeling unbodied, nor was this Soviet uniform he wore. He raised the shovel, looking for the chance to impale Volkov's liver, while whoever was living his life was about to be shot.

Gore splattered the convertible's windshield.

Kārlis nearly collapsed from shock as the front seat soldier's head smacked the dashboard and bounced backward, baring neck to sky, face torn like rags around a star-shaped exit wound. Shouts rose.

Kārlis reflexed, hand to head—his was still intact.

Gunfire hailed down, echoing off architecture.

Kārlis came acutely alive, back in his own skin, eyes everywhere. Men scattered in panic. Engine roaring, the convertible jerked away from the curb, knocking over a bicycler. Soldiers rushed the auto, fighting for a ride, piling in over the gilt frames, the lampstick, shrieking comrades. The Chekist on the rear bumper dropped onto the road, skull chunked apart.

Move, move, mooove! Screams of the ambushed, the same in every language.

Wielding the shovel, Kārlis tried to dash for cover, path blocked by felled, jammed bicycles, wheels spinning, soldier-riders at cross-purposes to escape the unknown source of shots fired. He didn't know which way to run or who was shooting at them. Expecting the burn of a bullet, he footed through steel and over a prone, screaming body, as someone shoved past him.

The sedan convertible failed a U-turn, veered over the opposite sidewalk and crashed into a display window. Glass shards guillotined from above as the slumped driver was yanked out by a replacement, who slid behind the wheel and jammed the transmission into reverse without looking back. Back seat riders hid from bullets beneath fresh corpses. Ambushed Reds scuttled and crouched around building corners, pistols extended like steel eyes searching the street and its windows for the snipers.

"In there!" Volkov pointed to a half-timbered apartment building. "That window!" A comrade produced a wooden handled grenade from up a sleeve. Volkov grabbed the so-called Potato Masher and started unscrewing.

Danger upshifted as Kārlis watched the ceramic ball of the detonation cord drop out.

"Hold up!" Volkov called to the car. "Don't leave me here!" Volkov cursed the retreating marauders in his alien tongue as the car sped past. Then he turned toward a window giving the boom cord a yank.

The Potato Masher was hot. Volkov retracted his throwing arm. Kārlis swung with all his might. The shovelhead smacked the grenade with a solid transfer of energy that drove the explosive on a long, tight trajectory into the open back seat of the escaping automobile.

Astonishment crossed Volkov's face, then his eyes widened with fear. He dived to earth, covering his head.

A knee-buckling explosion knocked Kārlis down, a scalding, violent airwave. The space between buildings concussed. Windows crashed. Ringing seared his every nerve. Kārlis clung to earth on hands and knees, head bursting with hell's harmonics. Time jolted to a surreal, grim meter. Broken, he wanted to collapse and vomit at the stench of burnt rubber.

Kārlis was nearly home.

The Germans had come.

But it didn't matter anymore.

Papu...

Unthinkable.

Don't think.

Kārlis crawled. Scraped palms pushed jellied muscles over the cobblestones. He passed a severed hand, innards, burning scraps of metal, a heap of debris, a bicycle. Pushing himself to sitting, he rested, inhaled poisoned breaths of scorched air, and wrapped his bloody fingers around a handlebar. The street was eerily silent while a siren blared inside his skull.

Fifteen or so meters away, the sedan convertible was engulfed in fire, black smoke billowing, inert soldiers burning. The chassis could be seen through orange flames in places where body panels were blown clean off. The speeding car had saved his life, Kārlis reckoned dully, rushing the grenade away so he'd been on the outer edge of the kill radius. And he had annihilated the sedan.

Ringing ears divorced him from the surrounding carnage, coccooning him weirdly. He surveyed the hellscape, wondering what to do. Thoughts moved like sludge, warning him to be quick, to be afraid. But he was muddled and clumsy. Where was the shovel? His hands throbbed from having grasped its wooden handle so tight as he'd batted the grenade. Look. The heap of debris had moved. It was gone.

Kārlis scrambled to knees and stood.

Volkov had staggered over to him, looking less like a harmless pile of debris and more like a brawny heap of filth.

Absent the shovel, Kārlis dragged up the bike in defense.

Volkov grabbed his lapels and pushed his face into Kārlis's, a cartoonish blackened face with eyes white, and pretty-boy looks slid into crookedness.

"Tell me one thing," Volkov wide-mouthed.

Kārlis felt the volume more than heard it. Meaning lagged.

"Where did your father hide his fortune? He buried it, didn't he? Every greedy capitalist has a stash." Volkov shook him. "Gold cigarette boxes and the family silver. Tell me. For I promise I'll find it." He looked over Kārlis's shoulder and let him go.

Kārlis couldn't think, gutted by Papu in the past tense more than the bone rattling.

Volkov snatched the bicycle and Kārlis didn't stop him from mounting it. The Russian pedaled directly into trash bins, quickly regained balance and rabbitted down an alley.

Kārlis grabbed a hunk of brick and threw it at Volkov's back. Fragments shattered uselessly on the deserted street. He watched with an ominous sense of his bad timing.

A faint humming had grown louder. Kārlis whipped around, heart in the pit of his belly. A string of German bucket-wagons had driven up to the blazing sedan. Soldiers offloaded and, too late, he realized with a stab of remorse, one had spotted him and shouldered a rifle.

Kārlis turned to run.

"*Hände hoch. Dreh dich um,*" came the order.

The one thing he'd learned at the Litene training camp stopped him. *"... a Kraut gets trained on his Karabiner semiautomatic at the age of ten...they're the deadest shots in the world."*

Lips pressed hard together, Kārlis did as told, turning slowly with hands raised.

The trooper capturing him seemed about the same age as Kārlis, but fresh, well fed and somewhat bored. His muscles rippled under a crisp green shirt. A leather and wool kepi cap, the flat circular hat with a horizontal visor, protected his haughty eyes from the sun. He pointed a Karabiner 98k, a Mauser, at Kārlis's chest.

The liberators were here at last.

Mouth dry, Kārlis said, *"Guten tag."*

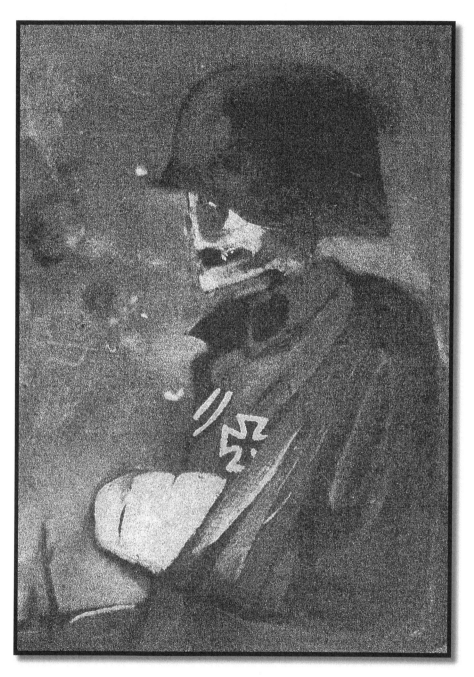

K. Smiltens, 1947.

51

JANIS PĒRKONS PEDALED HOME FROM the village post office with seam-splitting determination. At the gravel drive, he dismounted and rolled the bicycle alongside his strides toward the house, finally propping it against the linden tree near the kitchen door.

Anna must've seen him from the window, from where she watched, white-faced, ever since learning of the massacre at the army training camp where Kārlis had been sent. She came out, drying her hands on her apron. Biruta tagged behind at her elbow.

Janis rushed to meet them, arms wide. "He's alive," he said, lifting his wife in a bear hug. "He's alive," he repeated when he set her down. "There's a letter."

Anna's hands fluttered to her throat. Then she wiped her eyes. "Oh, thank God!" she murmured, looking up as if the Creator resided at the tops of the pines.

"A letter from Kārlis!" squealed Biruta, who started jumping.

"He's okay, then?" Anna said.

"Yah, well, it's not exactly a letter from Kārlis," Janis said, equivocating. "It's a letter from the *Wehrmacht*."

"The *German* Army!" Anna gasped.

"One of its departments, a staff division apparently," Janis said, pulling the envelope from the shirt pocket under his vest. "Army Group North, Area Headquarters, Rear Services, Office of Ostland Affairs, with an address in Riga. I gather they picked him up and are—"

"He got captured?" Biruta said.

"Well, they are holding him… at this facility," Janis said, rereading the missive, *"pending proof of citizenship.* Sounds straightforward enough." Actually, the letter was vague and impersonal, but Janis wanted to fan their only spark of hope. "He's alive," Janis said. "That's the important thing. Find his birth certificate, Anna. I'm going to get him out."

She was already running inside, Janis following her, Biruta following him.

"Papu, what do Germans do when they capture you?" Biruta asked, her voice in the range of a worried soprano.

Janis stood over his desk, gathering necessities for a trek to Riga: keys to the confiscated apartment over the leather workshop, his wallet, money, rubles, deutschmarks, lats, whatever he could put his hands on.

Her question sickened him. "Cookie, there are rules to follow, even in a war," Janis said, pulling his pocket watch up by the chain and winding it. "The Wehrmacht is not the Nazis, if that's what you're afraid of. Nazis are a political party. The Wehrmacht is an army, and considered to be a square institution, as far as armies go." He took his hat and went into the kitchen to find a canteen. "I myself was *four years* at a German POW camp after the Great War. *Das ist wo ich gelernt fließend Deutsch!*"

"Yah, but Kārlis already speaks fluent German," Biruta said. "So he doesn't need to be there that long."

His hand moved to his gut at a visceral memory of a horrific typhus outbreak at the filthy camp. "I agree," Janis said tersely.

"It's thirty kilometers to Riga," his wife said, picking through documents in a drawer.

"A long ride." Janis had never ridden anywhere near that far. "But it's only ten o'clock." He spread out a map of the capitol and the letter from the Office of Ostland Affairs. Tracing various routes with his finger, he said, "I want to be able to find this address even if the road's one big automotive embroglio."

"Here's Kārlis's birth certificate," Anna said, handing Janis a plump envelope. "And other records you may need, as well. You're riding that bicycle?"

"I know of no other way." Janis tucked the right leg of his trousers into his sock to save it from chain grease. "I'm leaving now."

In the kitchen, Tante Agata stood at the icebox, placing wax paper-wrapped items in a canvas bag, and muttering, "All that flows is wholly holy. What is given and what is taken away..." She gave the bag to Janis. "It's all the same."

Cycling along the muddy ruts of a tree-lined road through a combat-ravaged patch-quilt of farmland was slow and nerve-wracking. The earth was gouged with knobby, dried-mud imprints of Panzer tank crawler tracks. Janis could easily imagine machine gun-toting jeeps rousting the horse-drawn Reds from their nests of resistance. And the Russians, for their part, destroying everything in their wake to slow the German pursuit and leave nothing of value for the Nazi victors. But Janis did not know the current hot spots, so he kept alert to avoid them. He also did not know the conditions under which his son was being held, and as far as he was concerned, every minute mattered.

Hearing a shout, Janis turned to see a small band of Russian soldiers across a field. One was staring at Janis as if he'd seen a ghost. Janis feared the desperados would try to wrestle his bike from him. But, after yelling at one another, the comrades moved on.

More immediately, Janis was about to overtake some halted wooden wagons that were stopped on the road. Cycling past the first one, he found himself among the remains of a convoy, stopped in its tracks. Horses, shot dead, still harnessed to the wagons, lay along the road. A nauseating, fly-buzzing stench marked at least a couple days of death. Janis covered his mouth and nose with his handkerchief and pedaled forward. Some wagons were loaded with the twisted, blackened molten remains of Soviet anti-tank guns and other heavy weaponry. The convoy of corpses stretched for kilometers.

Then the trees dropped away and Janis saw he would have the advantage of a flat, paved road. Shifting his sore rear end on the bicycle saddle and repositioning his grip on the handlebars, Janis determined to cover some ground before a tire went flat. He passed a dead Russian soldier lying in a field of rye. His limbs were askew, lying as he had fallen. The soldier's rifle was erect, barrel-down, in the soil near his head, a slender steel grave marker against the waving grain.

An hour later, Janis faced a roadblock of crashed vehicles, still burning. He grumbled, bushwhacking a path around it, resenting the lost time and energy. Smoke stung his throat and eyes. Lungs burned with every breath. His canteen was nearly drained.

Making his way back to a paved road, Janis pumped harder, traversing an industrial district. Blocks and blocks of abandoned factories with empty windows and derelict-looking machinery proved a report he'd heard at the Bier Schtube. Industries had been disassembled into heaps of steel, loaded onto trains and taken to Russia as the Communists gave up Riga to the Nazis. His city would never be the same.

According to foreign radio and from what Janis had gleaned at the pub, capturing Riga had not been a chief objective of Germany's Operation Barbarossa. Rather, the Wehrmacht had swept through Latvia's western regions on a path to Leningrad. All but a few NKVD units had been swift to abandon the capital, anyway, people said. Riga had been cleared of Bolsheviks after a few hours, leaving firefighters with the main challenges. Janis had no idea what to expect as the familiar skyline of Riga came into view. He was simply glad he'd made it.

Then he stopped. Planting his feet on either side of the bike, Janis stared incredulously at the place where the gothic architecture of St. Peter's Church had been the cherry of the view since medieval days. Thick black smoke unfurled ominously from where the highest church spire in the city had apparently collapsed in flames. Janis's mind's eye wanted to recreate the image of the slender, tiered steeple with the gold rooster on top, but the sight wouldn't materialize. Braced for other casualties of war, he took a deep breath and pushed forward, entering the capital, determined to get his son.

Janis pedaled under the crenellated castle walls, expecting to be stopped at any moment by someone demanding to know his business. Instead, faint strains of music met his ears, the reedy, organ-like notes of an accordion. He rolled freely over the cobblestones of a narrow street. The music grew louder. Janis definitely heard a trombone. Turning into a small plaza, he stopped to register what he was seeing.

Whatever he'd expected to find inside the capital, it had not been this. People were dancing in the streets.

A jaunty band of musicians was playing a polka. A stand-up bassist and some brass blowers seemed to take their cues from a big fellow in a black vest and his squeezebox. A woman, rosy and wrinkled as a dried apple, set the beat by whacking a cowbell. A stylish lady, in a trim purple suit and beads, had her hands on the shoulders of a smudge-faced laborer. A little girl and a man, old enough to be her grandfather, sashayed around the periphery of the other dancers. One couple had the lightning-struck appearance of having just fallen in love. There was foot stomping and hand clapping by nearly every person filling the plaza, unfazed by the German soldiers milling about with rifles against their shoulders and the bass booming of artillery from the southeast. The Latvian flag, its broad white stripe running horizontally through a field of carmine red, waved from various heights for the first time in a year. Faces were wet and looking upward, hands brushing away tears and ashes that fell from the sky.

A sprightly fellow in tails and a top hat, looking like a concierge who'd strayed from his hotel doorway, popped a bottle of champagne and was filling the cups of all within reach. The concierge pressed the bottle and its remaining bubbly contents to Janis with a fierce hug. "From now on, sir, we keep wine in the cellar. The people are coming out!" He spun around like he was going for another bottle.

Janis still had a few bites left of a sandwich Tante Agata had packed. He ate, standing with a leg draped over the bike seat, washing down his dinner with the champagne. Since he had to catch his breath and establish his bearings anyway, he was glad to be a part of this street scene, with his compatriots as they awakened together from a communal nightmare. It was hard to believe the Communists were gone.

Deep down, Janis didn't think it was over.

They'd been hurt too deeply to simply heal. Some scars would be glaringly obvious, every family knew someone who'd been deported or killed for political reasons in the past year. Other injuries would be subtle, an anxious and pessimistic peasantry, mistrust and suspicion among neighbors, in the long run as crippling as the outright hammer and axe beatings by NKVD sadists.

Be that as it may, today was a time for joy.

"Russians on spikes!" The cry was followed by a brick crashing through glass, the looting of a liquor store down the block. Unable to ride, Janis pushed his bike between the revelers in the crowded street, determined to find the building for Ostland Affairs before the close of business. Turning onto a major boulevard, he wheeled through smoldering rubble, past broken gothic façades and an eerily freestanding gabled wall pouring smoke from an upstairs window. A Soviet tank was abandoned at a harried angle to the curb. The House of Blackheads was in ruins, the magnificent 14th century hall where trade met wealth and hedonism.

On the other side of the esplanade, people of all ages packed the Freedom Monument, piling up flowers in homage to Mother of Latvia, who towered triumphantly in her green gown of oxidized copper. The traditional flowing skirts and richly embroidered bodices had come out of the closet, worn by women in hammered gold forehead circlets who were giving a flower to everyone in arm's reach.

An impromptu choir was forming on the steps leading up to a church. Voices were praising God and singing the old folk songs with abandon. Suddenly, the singing tapered off as people became excited by an approaching military parade led by a flower-strewn German tank decorated with leafy, green branches.

Janis strained to hear an announcement blaring over loudspeakers from an open-topped vehicle driving slowly amidst a stream of casually marching soldiers. Next to the driver, an adjutant wearing field fatigues announced that the commander of the advancing German units, Field Marshal Wilheim Ritter von Leeb, would now greet the populace of Ostland, and handed the microphone to his superior. Janis bristled at the German's refusal to call Latvia by name, but the fact didn't dampen the enthusiasm of the crowd on the sidewalk, twenty-people deep and more pressing forward to see and hear the words marking this moment in history.

Field Marshal Von Leeb sat symmetrically on the top of the backseat, a compact figure in a precisely tailored gray-green uniform. Hairless, but for a trapezoid moustache, his head was dominated by a peaked officer's cap. An Iron Cross hung from between his collar tips. His breast eagle—the German national emblem—and the arabesques of his collar patches glittered in the sun, probably hand-embroidered in gold bullion.

"To those within the sound of my voice, and beyond to the very borders of Ostland," the commander said in clipped tones, "this country is declared liberated from Soviet occupation."

Cheers rose from every person on the crowded sidewalk. *Sieg Heil!* Victory! Janis listened hard to hear the commander's next words.

"The fame-crowned German army is extremely pleased to liberate the ancient Riga from Bolshevik bondage. We promise that, side-by-side with you, we will fight until the last Bolshevik is thinned out of this land."

Amidst loud applause and the waving of hats, some young women rushed out to kiss the parading soldiers—even men rushed out to kiss them. The heroes were given sweets, lit cigarettes, and flowers. People held up babies. Some fellows in suits were lifting a soldier to their shoulders, lauding him with a bouncing "hep hep hurray!"

"As we unshackle your country, province by province," Field Marshal von Leeb said from the crawling vehicle, "we are astounded by the unspeakable atrocities now uncovered, perpetrated against you by our mutual enemy, the Soviet Union. This morning your German liberators have uncovered proof of shocking mass executions. All citizens are urged to come to the Central Jail to identify the bodies of loved ones brutally murdered by Stalin's forces, and to dispose of them with dignity. *Heil* Hitler."

The address faded in volume as the car advanced down the boulevard repeating its message to new sections of the city. In its wake, a grateful, cheering throng sang the Latvian national anthem, *Dievs, svētī Latviju,* God Bless Latvia, convinced they'd regained independence, a seven hundred year hatred for pillaging Teutonic knights and oppressive Prussian barons, suddenly forgiven.

Up the boulevard, civic buildings had been draped with red swastika-emblazoned banners hanging from upper windows, so huge they could be seen from several blocks away. Janis pedaled toward those buildings, which likely housed the administration of the Third Reich.

This was the place, he concluded, checking posted addresses. To his bitter disappointment, a *Closed* sign hung from the glass doors of the office he needed. Six, no seven, armed guards patrolled the block. He stared at the building, too exhausted to rethink his vision of leaving here with Kārlis, the stubborn hope that had fueled him over hard kilometers and hours. Finally here, Janis was as far away from his objective as ever.

Swastikas billowed from windows seven stories up. Was his son somewhere in there? Or were they holding him at a POW *stalag*? He realized with a drooping spirit that he would have to wait until morning to find out. Leaving in resignation, he saw a man inside a lit office through the ground floor window, and turned back. Bursting with angst, Janis pushed his bicycle against the building and stalked to the door, banging on it with his fist. He had to know now. He pounded hard for attention.

"*Halt!*" a guard yelled from the sidewalk, holding his weapon diagonally before him and running toward Janis. "*Lassen sofort!*"

Janis obeyed, desisting at once. Squaring his shoulders within his suit, Janis explained in cogent German, "I have been ordered by the duly assigned representative of Army Group North, Area Headquarters, Rear Services, Office of Ostland Affairs to immediately and personally present certain documents." Turning toward the window, Janis repeated the explanation, loudly enough to be heard by the man inside the building.

There were several men in the office, staffers busily removing folders from cardboard boxes, except for one man leaning against a filing cabinet. His supervisorial scrutiny drifted out the window toward Janis's authoritative tone of voice, spearing Janis with a suspicious eye. Janis immediately displayed the letter from the Wehrmacht, holding it up toward the cabinet-leaner as if it were understood; this was the sheet of stationery for which they'd all been waiting.

"I am working side-by-side with Field Marshal von Leeb," Janis declared loudly, bandying the name he'd heard in the parade and hijacking a line from the commander's speech.

Walking to the window, the supervisor said, "Let me see that." But being too far away to reach it, he gestured to an underling clerk, who disappeared.

Acknowledging the guard and his submachine gun with a stiff nod, Janis watched the glass doors with a veneer of confidence. If the clerk came to personally see the letter, Janis had a fifty-fifty chance of charming his way inside. But that had to happen before the guard decided to run him off.

To his relief, the clerk appeared at the door, unlocked it and curtly snatched the paper. Janis stepped inside uninvited while the letter was read. Shrugging his eyebrows, the clerk led Janis down an asbestos-tiled hallway lined with bulletin boards and directed him to sit in an interrogation room. Then he demanded to see the documents Janis had so boldly touted, flipping through them with a critical eye: Kārlis's birth certificate, and the Red Army call-up notice proving Kārlis had been forcibly conscripted. Anna had also thought to enclose Janis's birth and marriage certificates, business licenses and deeds to properties. The clerk left with the vital records, and when the door locked behind him, Janis began to worry that the brash exaggerations that had got him through the door might backfire and prevent his ever leaving.

He used the interminable wait to gather his thoughts, putting himself in the shoes of the man deciding Kārlis's fate. He'd be a mid-level bureaucrat, albeit a swift, unerring, formidable German one. Janis could barely fathom the mountain of paperwork that must be generated by taking over the world. What was the bottom line for a nation-invading administrator? Sorting out who was who, that's what. Classifying people. It would be paramount for Janis to prove that he and, especially Kārlis, were not Communist sympathizers; but that they were reliable Lutherans, connected people with inside knowledge pertinent to running this small country in particular, and dominating the planet in general.

Finally, when the door opened, it was the Cabinet-Leaning supervisor who came in. Looking put out, he sat in the chair opposite Janis. With a steely glint in his eye, he began grilling. Where had Janis, his parents, and even his grandparents been born? Riga, all the way back, Janis stated. Occupation? From a humble cobbler, Janis had risen to become the nation's most prominent manufacturer of leather goods, until their mutual enemy, the Soviet Union, had confiscated his enterprises.

In a manner of speaking, this was true. He hadn't been the nation's *largest* leather manufacturer by a hell of a long shot, but *prominent*—Janis was arguably more illustrious than his mealy-mouthed competitors. Given how he'd blustered his way through the door, this was no time to be modest.

The Cabinet-Leaner looked hard at Janis before leaving the room.

At length, he returned with a different form. This time he interrogated Janis in detail about his factory capacity, supply connections and products. Janis answered expansively, with technical specificity and bravado, the sales pitch of his life. Top-of-the chain predators like the Germans attacked at the first sign of weakness. He'd have said anything to save his son from Nazi clutches. His private holdings and affinity for commerce had to prove beyond a doubt he was a true capitalist and therefore a natural enemy of the Soviet Union.

On a subordinate agenda, Janis couldn't help but appreciate the way the German kept referring to the shop as *Pērkons* Leather Works. What the Russians had taken away, the Germans could restore.

The interrogator left abruptly. Janis was left alone in the room for so long, he thought everyone else might have gone home, or wherever it was Nazis went at the end of the day. He closed his eyes to refresh mind and body, but did not rest his head on the tabletop. The evident cheapness of human life these days afflicted his imagination and made the passage of time torturous. He smoked his every shred of tobacco, all he cared for, more and more resembling the pile of ashes.

When the door finally opened, the clerk he'd met initially gestured that Janis should follow him out. In the hall, to his immense relief and amazement, stood Kārlis. His shirt, stained stiff with sweat and dirt, was tucked into pants loose from weight loss. Overall, he appeared unharmed, though the blue eyes peering through black circular frames conveyed a locked diary of anxious, dreadful days. Kārlis's face seemed set in cement, as if the boy didn't trust himself to make an expression, lest he crack. Likewise, Janis quashed the urge to cry, to dance down the hall and out the door.

Taking Kārlis by the elbow, Janis made the perfunctory courtesies to the military clerk and led his son directly from the Office of Ostland Affairs before anyone could invent a reason to stop him.

Outside, he hastily retrieved the bicycle from where he'd left it leaning against the building.

Kārlis stood staring at him, transfixed. "You're alive," he uttered, hoarsely.

"Barely," Janis said, wrestling the bike out from bushes. "My ass is throbbing after riding this contraption from the summerhouse. Here. Take it, will you?"

Kārlis took hold of the handlebars with solemnity, as if accepting the passing of his father's mantle. "Ak tu kungs, Papu. I'm grateful you're alive."

"*I'm* alive! *You're* the one who was deployed to a massacre and then captured by Nazis. I've got to get word to your mother. Let's get away from here."

"Mama's okay?" His voice was deeper than Janis recalled.

"She will be once she hears you're in one piece."

"And Biruta?" Kārlis looked ready to collapse with relief.

"Yah, of course," Janis said, thinking the boy was feeble with hunger. "Tante Agata is probably cooking your welcome home feast as we speak."

"Because I heard... I heard," Kārlis lowered his eyes, exhaling hard, unable to express whatever grievous rumor he'd heard.

Janis wrapped his arms around his son in a bear hug, lifting the boy's lanky frame right off the sidewalk. Then he produced a boiled potato from his lunch bag, which Kārlis wolfed in an instant.

Father and son high-tailed it from that district and its glut of martial authority, pushing the bike into a wide boulevard, now nearly empty. The cheering throngs had dissipated. An eleven p.m. bell began to toll when they turned down Freedom Boulevard. Janis had never called it Lenin. Kārlis threw a leg over the bike and was soon pedaling in a wide, lazy serpentine crossing all four lanes, no hands! Joints smarting, Janis hasted behind on the sidewalk, feeling overwhelmed by good fortune. The word *freedom* was invented for a moment such as this. If he never again sipped another cognac or owned a cubit of private property that would be fine. Nothing compared with getting his son back. His family could be together for one more supper. They had made it. The ghastly year was over. Janis expelled the breath he'd been holding. His footfalls echoed off the five-story stone buildings he passed, beneath gargoyles and wizened marble faces gazing down, stoic witnesses, unimpressed by the manifold human dramas of another regime change.

After several blocks, they skirted the Freedom Monument, where Mother of Latvia stood over a mound of fresh flowers, holding up three gold stars to a waning gibbous moon. A roving pack of drunks passed by, shrieking with laughter and belting out the smutty verse of some ballad. Kārlis cut into Bastion Hill Park and pedaled vigorously up the hill, not noticing as he passed the body of a dead woman who lay face down near bushes. Janis stepped quickly down the winding walkway, remorseful that any strength he might offer a fellow being had been fully tapped. The brutality of the past year had ripped and dirtied his soul to the point where the coming world war seemed civilized in comparison, if that weren't patently absurd. Janis climbed the hill, taking heart from the notion that he and his son would join forces, regroup and survive the next storm.

"Ak tu kungs, Papu, look!"

What?" Janis gasped. *The Cheka? Gestapo?* His heart leaped to his throat.

"Look at the light!" Kārlis said. His hushed voice was reverent.

Janis exhaled, prickly with wasted adrenaline. At a time like this, he never would've thought about the *light*.

Moonlight and the glow of midsummer cast a bluish hue over the panorama of steeples and spires. Heavy-hanging smoke from the conflagration at St. Peter's Church lent a dreamlike quality to the moment.

Kārlis gazed with rapture.

Janis shook his head, gravely worried that his son would not survive the realities of the German occupation, impractical as he was. Kārlis was sensitive to something Janis couldn't slow down enough to see amid the rush of ambition. Janis was broadstroke. Kārlis was a detail-obsessed stickler. Janis was lavish, Kārlis, minimalist. Janis got the job done, not belaboring the means to an end. Kārlis was walking into his future on a knife's blade, admiring the light. The two of them were simply cut from different hides.

"Thank you for coming, Papu," Kārlis said, thickly. Water crashed over boulders, splashed into the canal that had once been the city's moat and circled through another season. "They were going to send me to a labor camp."

Janis nodded, throat constricted.

They stood on top of the favorite sledding hill.

"Have you seen any of my friends?" Kārlis wanted to know.

It was a simple question. But rather than answer it, Janis found it easier to slap his pockets in search of tobacco that wasn't there.

"Hugo," Janis confessed. "I saw Hugo the night he was deported."

Kārlis nodded dully, staring down the sled-run now carpeted with lush grass.

Janis guessed his son could see the capering ghosts of friends now gone, young people who'd unluckily come of age under Stalin's boot. O, the times that might have been. How would Kārlis handle the injustice and raging grief, and come to terms with the horrors he'd seen without wallowing in a dark quagmire.

"I've always found that pouring myself into a project is a good way to take my mind off desperate thoughts," Janis said. "You know, a man's got to pick himself up. Regroup! The Russians have pillaged the Leather Works. If we can get that running, well, that'd help us leave the past behind as well as provide income for weathering life with the Nazis."

Janis began mentally compiling contacts, ones that Kārlis might like to acquaint.

"I've been thinking a lot about the Art Academy," Kārlis said. "Now that the army's behind me, there's no reason why I can't start the program in the fall."

Janis felt slightly ill. He took a deep breath, smelling moist earth tinged with lilac. "Still the Art Academy," he said, chuckling with surrender. "Son, what you lack in practicality, you make up for with a stubborn streak."

Stubborn optimism was also the hallmark of Janis's creed.

Had he glimpsed the rare reflection of himself in Kārlis? He suddenly felt very close to his son, tied by priceless heredity that threaded through everything that had happened, stitching between them and beyond, binding them to each other, to the tribe, to the land. He wanted the connection to last. So he stood shoulder to shoulder with the young man, smoothing his goatee and overlooking the park and the skyline silhouetted by smoldering Riga, trying to understand what was so special about the light.

"Don't let go of that dream, boy."

EPILOGUE

MIDSUMMER'S EVE, 1992

WHILE HIS GRANDNEPHEW SKIPPED stones over the river, Kārlis Pērkons scanned the woods for landmarks. It was like searching an old woman's face for a trace of the girl you knew in high school. Was he out of his mind, to be searching a dense forest for one particular tree? Birch trunks mesmerized with uniformity, blurring familiar and strange. But somewhere, at least in his mind, was a meadow with the noble oak.

"Look Uncle Kārlis, cherries!" Johnny said.

Kārlis didn't remember any cherry trees and wondered if he was completely lost. He joined the boy in picking and eating.

Brush rustled and Kārlis snapped his head up to see a man, fifty meters away. Hardly the police, he looked rakish and lusty, and was holding a young lady's hand. Kārlis relaxed. The man just looked wild because of solstice headdress, he under a dense wreath of red oak leaves, and she wearing a crown of wildflowers. Evidently the two revelers had to pass near the cherry pickers.

Kārlis chuckled. "They're searching for the fern blossom."

Innocent to the Midsummer lovemaking euphemism, Johnny called out, "We're searching for the giant oak tree."

The man pointed over his shoulder before leading his lover away behind the leafy curtain.

Kārlis recognized the outcropping of boulders now that the randy hiker had pointed it out. "Yah, this is the way," he said, taking strides. "So overgrown I would have missed it."

Johnny scrambled down the rocky ledges like a goat. Kārlis proceeded more carefully, saying, "These seem much smaller than I remember. We're almost there." At the bottom of the boulders, the land rose to what Kārlis expected to be a meadow. The clearing, however, could no longer be called such. He recognized the aura of the revered site more than anything visual, though he was not one to put stock in vibrations. A startled drumming of grouse beat feathers and fled skyward. Kārlis stopped. "This is the place. The tree should be here. Oh, there it is. It's dead."

The tree was down. On its great, gray side and covered in places with creeper, the enormous fallen trunk was as tall as Johnny, who'd already climbed up and was stalking its length. Bark had been stripped away by the gleaning of industrious birds and beavers. The swing that had metered the passages of Kārlis's youth was only a memory. Limbs that had nurtured a scampering woodland ecology jutted up like behemoth skeletal ribs. Johnny grabbed one and swung around it, saying, "Wow! This could be a pirate ship!"

"Well, I expected—" Kārlis was grief stricken. He leaned against the trunk, feeling rootless, laying hands on the dead oak. "I should have known better. It's dead." He was at a loss to explain why this hit him so hard. "There's no fool like an old fool," he muttered.

Johnny was poking a stick into every rotten cavity. "Avast!" he cried, thrashing a dead branch in a swordfight.

Kārlis reached down for a handful of soil, crumbling peat between his old fingers and watching it fall to the ground.

"Aren't you afraid of the police, Uncle Kārlis?"

Kārlis sighed. "Compared to what has happened already, no. I'm not afraid." If he was apprehended for the murder of Igor Volkov and sat in jail until his lawyer rescued him, so what? "I suppose living in a free country all these years has given me some sort of confidence." Not only was he unafraid, Kārlis felt numb. His love of home and hatred of Volkov had been so intertwined, now that Volkov was out of the mix the remains of his heart felt foreign. What if the place he'd tried his whole life to return to no longer existed? And he belonged nowhere.

"That detective has a mystery to solve," Johnny chimed. "Who killed Agent Volkov?"

Kārlis watched a butterfly on the breeze, resentful that, even dead, the Russian made trouble for him. "More people were killed in World War II than in any war in history," he said. "Fifty-three million dead, mostly young men in their late teens and early twenties. Now some career-climbing detective and his cronies won't quit until they find who killed one Russian thug. It's not moral or logical to me. They want a tidy report. A proper Agatha Christie wrap-up with alibis for all the suspects and the villain's monologue explaining how he did the deed." Kārlis was warming to a good rant.

"I don't like that Volkov counts. And the other 53 million are lumped into one sick statistic. I don't like that he lived to be an old man, while so many—"

"Ah ha!" Johnny cried, fishing in the hollow trunk. "What's this? Buried treasure! Yo ho! Yo ho!" The kid pulled his arm from out of the tree trunk, grasping a filthy wad and the glint of glass. He flicked off dead leaf detritus and spider webs. "This is the top," he said, uprighting what looked to be an old milk bottle stuffed with rags. Kārlis sucked in his breath. The gold fringe spilling from the bottle's mouth reeked of danger.

"Careful, Johnny." He came over. "I've seen that before. Ak tu kungs. It's a Molotov cocktail." Kārlis took the relic and held it against the sky. The contents were evaporated. The wax seal looked undisturbed. His hand trembled. An oily kerosene smell connected Kārlis to a day in a bakery, it seemed in someone else's life.

"That rotten fringy thing was once my mother's blanket."

"Your mother made Molotov cocktails?"

"No. We --- my friends did."

"Will it still work?"

"For our purposes," Kārlis said, piling dead wood. The wax seal disintegrated as he pulled the impregnated fabric out of the bottle and laid it over the stacked kindling.

"Stand back," Kārlis warned. He tossed a match on the rag fuse, which lit with a poof, emitting a black shimmer of heat.

Those long ago events were as real as these flames.

"This one must have been Hugo's," Kārlis remarked, remembering the day it was made. "I was beat for this," he admitted, "almost to death - the night we stole the accelerant from my father's workshop." His hands went to his ribs and kidneys. "I remember at the time being so ashamed." Kārlis sat, leaning against the dead oak to watch the fire dance. "Now I think it may have been the highpoint of my life. We did something, my friends and me, the Nonchalants. I tried to resist. I did try."

Dry wood crackled.

"You'll see, muzais puisits, you find out who you are when life tests you."

Johnny wasn't listening, instead looking behind every rock. "I knew there was buried treasure. I knew it!" The optimism made Kārlis smile. "So like my father, you are."

Kārlis started to sing an old daina, and to his surprise Johnny knew the words, which cheered his spirit. "In the end, mind you, it was our folk songs that won freedom, not Molotov cocktails. Two million brave, song-singing Latvians, Estonians and Lithuanians formed a human chain, held hands across the three Baltic countries and demanded independence. Now there's a statistic."

"I remember we watched it on TV," Johnny said, throwing sticks on the fire.

"Papu loved the old songs."

"Look," Johnny said, pointing with his stick. "The trees are in a neat circle. We're surrounded."

"Yah. So it is." Kārlis said, rising and turning. Around him, small established oak trees grew in a nearly perfect circle. "That's how it works in the woods. This noble one dropped acorns all its life. The sprouts on the very edge got enough sunlight to grow. Then even after the parent dies and decomposes, it keeps nourishing those around the base."

Standing in the center of the fairy ring, Kārlis felt blasted by an unseen force. "If my old Tante Agate were here, she'd chant some confounding proverb that explained this geomancy." Not that he went in for that hooey, but at the moment he couldn't deny the tingling bond of connectedness. Breathing the earthy pine air, his mind's eye saw the symmetry of the branches above and the roots below him, and he a vital link in an ancient web. The urge to uphold the spiritual ties unbroken was relentless.

"I feel like doing something big," Johnny yelled from the prow of his tree-ship.

Kārlis felt the same. "It's taken me all this time to learn it, *muzais puisits*. It's not about who gets to possess the land. It's the land that has me. I am more akin to this oak than to any nation."

Forest alchemy surged through the soil, through roots, passed through the soles of his Nikes and powered his legs. Suddenly they left the ground and, to the boy's whoop, Kārlis was in the air, not as a circling vulture, but a man leaping over a bonfire.

The Linden Tree & the Legionnaire series is inspired by the paintings and accounts of
Kārlis Smiltens (1921 – 2017).

At seventeen, Kārlis Smiltens was called up by the Red Army and underwent the qualifying medical exam. The Germans arrived before he was deployed. Smiltens never evaded military service. The fictitious Kārlis Pērkons, however, was sent to the Red Army training camp in Litene and, as some Latvian soldiers were fortunate to do, escaped the treacherous office massacre into the forest.

Latvian Legionnaire Corporal Kārlis Smiltens donated over two hundred drawings and paintings to the Latvian War Museum in Riga.

K. Smiltens, 2000.

Diana Mathur, MBA cum homeschooling mother, has been privileged to travel to Latvia to research primary sources, collaborate closely with the de facto War Artist of the Latvian Legion, reclaim a summerhouse confiscated by Soviet-era communists, dig up treasure hidden in Latvian soil for fifty years, and travel the trans-Siberian railroad to what's left of the gulag archipelago on the trail of Stain-era deportees. The Mathurs live in California.

Paldies
Thank you

Esteemed Readers

Barbara Peterson, Editor
Georgia Saroj, Graphic Art, Cartography & Illustration

Family Mathur
especially Kris, Anna, Georgia, and Walter,
who insisted on digging for the treasure

The Irwins
Gretchen, Madeline and Penelope

Kim Zanti

Katherine Friedman
and our discriminating Critique Group

Mark Hein, Editor

Leonarda Kesteris and Pauls Kesteris

Arijs and the late Anta Krievins

Clare and the irregulars at
Café Mimosa

Astra Moore and the So Cal Latvian Community

James Mathers
Rodeo Grounds Poet Laureate

Acknowledgement

The following resources are acknowledged: *Latvian Religion, An Outline*, Jānis Dārdedzis, Baltic Crossroads, Los Angeles, 1996, Museum of the Occupation of Latvia, *Latvia in World War II Catalogue-Guidebook of the Latvian Military Museum* by Valdis Kuzmins, *The Forgotten War, Latvian Resistance During the Russian and German Occupations* by Janis Straume, *Baltic Amber* by Inara Mantenieks, *Latvian Legion* by Arthur Silgailis, *Memoires of a Partisan* by Y. Sigaltchik, *In the Partisan Detachment* by Shmuel Margolin, *Laima Veckalne's Story: A Tale of Forgotten Soviet Crimes* by Edgar B. Anderson, *Latvia: Year of Horror* by Baigais Gads, *Latvia in the Wars of the 20th Century* by Visvaldis Mangulis, *Hitler versus Stalin* by Professor John & Ljubica Erickson, www.cyberussr.com by Hugo S. Cunningham, *Occupation of Latvia by Nazi Germany, Forest Brothers* and *Baltic Way* by Wikipedia, *2X2 Divisions* by Frank Gordon from www.centropa.org, *Latvian Legion at Lake* ILMENA from www.lacplesis.com, Welcome to Latvia-Folk Songs from the Latvian Institute, www.li.lv, *These Names Accuse—Nominal List of Latvians Deported to Soviet Russia* by The Latvian Foundation, and *The Baltic Observer* since 1996 known as *The Baltic Times*.

Diligent effort has been made to acknowledge sources correctly. Any errors or unintentional omissions will be corrected in future editions of this book.

GLOSSARY

1991 On Christmas Day, Mikhail Gorbachev, the General Secretary of the Communist Party, resigned. The Soviet Union ceased to exist. President George H. W. Bush announced that the United States recognized Latvia, Estonia, and Lithuania as independent nations.

ak tu kungs! (AWK-te KOONKS) Oh my Lord! Give me patience!

alus ari ira sula! Beer is juice too! Latvian palindrome

apakšbikses (UP-iksh-BIK-shes) Underpants

Auschwitz opened in 1940 as a detention center for political prisoners in southern Poland, became the largest of the Nazi concentration and death camps

Baltics Countries surrounding the Baltic Sea: Lithuania, Latvia, Estonia (also Finland)

besom A tied-twig sauna bath switch for whipping, stimulating and exfoliating the skin

Bier Schtube A *bier stube* is a hall or pub that specializes in beer, German. In the story, Bier Schtube is a proper noun and purposely misspelled to clue readers to its pronounciation.

blitzkrieg A military tactic concentrating forces to attain overwhelming local superiority. Lightning war, German

Bolshevik Russian political party that embraced Lenin's Communist thesis

Budēļi A masked, house-to-house, animal-honoring, musical folkloric procession enjoyed from St. Martin's Day through Shrove Tuesday

Cheka Another name for the NKVD

Corner House NKVD headquarters in Riga. In 1940, 700 "Undesirables" at a time were secretively incarcerated in this fashionable art nouveau building.

Стой, или вы будете расстреляны! Stop, or you will be shot!, Russian

Проклятье Curse, an imprecation that great harm or evil may befall someone, Russian

cilvēk (SIL-vak) Human being, dude, Latvian

dacha (DAH-kuh) Country house or villa, Russian

daina (DIE-en-uh) Traditional form of uniquely Latvian music or poetry

Daugava (DOW-guh-vuh) Latvia's longest river, running through Riga to the Baltic Sea

Dievs, svētī Latviju! National anthem of Latvia, God bless Latvia

fascism An ideology or regime led by a dictator having complete power, forcibly suppressing opposition and criticism, regimenting all industry and commerce, aggressively nationalistic and often racist

Gestapo *Geheimstaatspolizei*, German, Nazi secret police

Gulag An acronym for Russian *Glavnoe Upravlenie ispravitel'no-trudovykh LAGerei* (Main Administration of Corrective Labor Camps), that operated the Stalin-era system of prison camps for political prisoners.

guten tag good day, German

Internationale Anthem of the communist movement

kakis (KAT-kis), Latvian for cat and the name of Biruta's cat

kāpost galva (KAP-ust GAUL-vuh) Stands for vulgar, teenaged slang. Use your imagination.

Ķekatas Season of winter solstice/mummer/masker celebration

kulak (kOO-lak) A peasant wealthy enough to own a farm and hire labor. Millions were arrested, exiled, or killed under Stalin's forced collectivization, Russian

lab dien Good day, Latvian

lassen sofort leave immediately, German

lats (LOTS) Latvian currency

Lāčplēsis (LOCKS-pleesh) Mythical giant Bear-Slayer acclaimed in the epic poem by Andrejs Pumpurs, who based the hero on Latvian folklore.

Lili Marlene Marlene Dietrich's hit soldier's song of WWII. *"Vor der Kaserne, Vor dem großen Tor…"* *"Outside the barracks, By the corner light. I'll always stand and wait for you at night …"*

loudzu (LEWDZ-u) Please, and You're Welcome

Luftwaffe German Air Force

Malleus Maleficarum *(The Hammer of the Witches)* A blood-soaked 1486 guidebook to aid Inquisitors in the identification, prosecution, and dispatching of Witches, especially poets, midwives, and widow landowners, Latin

Midsummer Summer solstice, revered and raucous Latvian holiday

muzais puisits (MUZ-ice PWEE-seets) Little boy

NKVD Abbreviation for Narodnyi Komissariat Vnutrennikh Del, Народный комиссариат внутренних дел, The People's Commissariat for Internal Affairs, i.e. the Communist secret police, later known as the KGB

Name's Day The day of the year to celebrate a particular name and its bearers

the Nonchalants Seven friends in mortal danger for coming of age

paldies (paul-DEE-es) Thank you

pie joda (PEE-eh YO-duh) To the devil

pirts A traditional wood-fired sauna with steam

The Pērkonses: It's only a matter of time, but being optimists, they always hope for one more day.

Red Army Army of the Soviet Union, Russia, the Communists

Riga (REE-guh) Capital of Latvia

rupjmaize Traditional dark, rye bread, a staple of the Latvian diet

The **Servant Attacks with saw and Axe The Lumber, Stack and Cord** A mnemonic device for the vertebral column: Cervical (Atlas, Axis) Thoracic, Lumbar, Sacral, Caudal. Inventor unknown.

stalag a German prison camp

Stuka German dive bombers, Junkers

sveiks (SVAYkes) Hello and See you later

tzitzit specially knotted ritual fringes or tassels worn by observant Jews (Hebrew)

vārda dienas Happy Name's Day (Latvian)

VEF Valsts Elektrotehniskā Fabrika (State Electrotechnical Factory), a manufacturer of electrical and electronic products in Riga, founded in 1919.

Wehrmacht The unified armed forces of Nazi Germany from 1935 – 1946.

Coming next in The Linden Tree & the Legionnaire historical saga:

Made in the USA
Las Vegas, NV
30 September 2023

78359481R00312